This is one of the best first read an authentic thriller that begins in Italy, and just as believable in Washington, DC. Her well-drawn characters feel like real people. The last 75 pages kept me so engrossed I couldn't put it down to eat my evening meal.

—Cecil Murphey

Suspense at its finest! I kept turning pages, looking over my shoulder, and forgetting to breathe.

—DiAnn Mills
DiAnnMills.com

Dr. Katherine Hayes, author of *A Fifth of the Story,* not only draws you into a fifth of the story but the entire story itself. This is an action movie in book form, with pace, drama, and characters we're accustomed to viewing on Netflix. Katherine skillfully weaves a story arc that the reader can't help but turn each page, relishing each nuance that builds suspense. On a visceral level you'll appreciate the protagonists' character and values, rooting him on to complete his mission despite a daunting array of obstacles. Viewed from the top, as this fictional tale unfolds, one reaches the conclusion that story's premise may not be too far from reality. I highly recommend this book for those who don't mind missing out on sleep.

—Pete Cruz
Author of *No Tears for Dad*
www.petecruz.com

Sometimes we read stories. Other times, we live them. Katherine's captivating knowledge, writing, and plot grab us and refuse to let go. Dive into the adventurous and exhilarating world of a CIA operative, Brock O'Reilly, who wrestles with social issues, friendship, costly love, and a worthy mission. But cancel your appointments because you'll not want to exit Brock's world until you must.

—Rodney Combs, Ph.D.
rodneycombs.com
Journey Better

A Fifth of the Story is a heart-pumping, hang-on-for-dear-life novel. The intricately woven tale will engage your mind and senses so that you might feel like you've narrowly escaped death.

—Sarah Wind
Author of *From Recliner to Revival*

They left a war overseas and came home to a war like no other. Federal agents face a crisis of conscience between ethics and emotion, love and loyalty to the brotherhood versus performing their duty. A probing story of bonds and betrayal, cultural conflict and corruption, a glimpse into the inner workings of federal agencies and the toll on those sworn to protect. Racist plots, crime rings, gun battles, bombs, politics, faith, and intrigue converge to create unrelenting heart-stopping action from the opening scene to the last line.

—Rachael M. Colby, Award-winning writer
www.TattooItOnYourHeart.com

A FIFTH
OF THE
STORY

DR. KATHERINE HUTCHINSON-HAYES

HARAMBEEPRESS

A Fifth of the Story

End Game Press books may be purchased in bulk at special discounts for sales promotion, corporate gifts, ministry, fund-raising, or educational purposes. Special editions can also be created to specifications. For details, contact Special Sales Dept., End Game Press, P.O. Box 206, Nesbit, MS 38651 or info@endgamepress.com.

Visit our website at www.endgamepress.com.

Library of Congress Control Number: 2023950852
ISBN: 9781637971284
eBook ISBN: 9781637971963

Cover by Dan Pitts
Interior Design by Typewriter Creative Co.

Printed in the United States of America
10 9 8 7 6 5 4 3 2 1

DEDICATION

First and foremost, I want to thank God for His grace and mercy that have sustained me throughout this journey. Without His love and guidance, I wouldn't be where I am today.

To my loving husband, children, grandson, siblings, uncles, aunts, cousins, and extended family, thank you for being my rock and for supporting me every step of the way. Your love and encouragement mean the world to me.

To my father and mother, thank you for instilling in me the gift of God and storytelling. Your wisdom and guidance have been invaluable to me, and I am forever grateful.

To my little big brother Andrew, who went to heaven first, I know you're cheering me on from there with our parents. Thank you for always believing in me.

To my mother-in-law, college besties, military besties, church family, author community, Edwina Perkins, and Cecil Murphey, thank you for believing in me and for your unwavering support. Your faith in me has been a constant source of inspiration.

To the FBI, CIA, DIA, and police officers who assisted me in crafting a believable story—thank you for your expertise and guidance.

This book is dedicated to all of you with love and gratitude.

CHAPTER 1

How much for the goat?" Brock pointed to an animal whose ribs jutted through its filthy coat. A fly landed on Brock's eyelid, forcing it shut with its bulging weight. He smacked himself, missing the target that lazily flew away. The fly buzzed nearby to a freshly butchered camel's head, then upward, joining a cloud of flies feasting on fish strung by their tails on a clothesline.

Mohammed threw his head back and laughed. His stomach jiggled through his white *bubu,* a traditional Malian gown. "You don't want no goat, man."

"No?" Brock scanned the jagged rock path between the crowd of jumbled buildings behind where the vendor sat. Several Islamic schoolboys ran toward the town center. In the distance, a sign for where he'd slept the last few nights at the La Colombe Hotel glistened in the African sun. He'd spent evenings there as the hotel's singular guest. The adjoining restaurant was a popular eatery during the day, but when the sun set, everyone deserted. Even the manager went home come nightfall.

Brock walked to a rack of knock-off sunglasses displayed on nails tacked through a piece of zinc. He donned a pair and checked his reflection in the full-length mirror perched against the camel's head. It had been more than six months since he'd been taking the canthaxanthin (food-color) pills. But seeing his tall, muscular, bearded image always took him by surprise. This darker version of himself made his green eyes smolder. Dressed in a head-wrap with jet-black curls peeking through and a mud-cloth dashiki, he really did resemble the accredited Egyptian archeologist his colleagues at the excavation site believed he was.

"You want info," Mohammed said. "Right, boss?"

"Right."

"Men you seek." He used his head to point. "Second building to the left, third floor."

"Which apartment?"

"Follow smell."

"What smell?"

"You'll know." Mohammed's mouth opened in an uneven grin displaying betel-colored teeth. "The cost of *that* goat is $400, Boss," he said, brown spittle spraying into his goatee.

"That's a pretty expensive meal."

He shrugged. "Last meal costs more."

Brock folded a wad of bills into Mohammed's meaty palm. "Is there anything else you'd like to tell me?" They wouldn't meet again, something Mohammed already knew.

Mohammed fanned himself, looking directly into Brock's eyes. "No, Boss."

Brock knew this time he was lying.

He picked his way through the bustling marketplace, keeping his head low and his pace even until he got to the second building. Once inside the dank entryway, Brock kept his new sunglasses on but pulled the head-wrap off and reached for the gun strapped to his ankle.

Moving cautiously up the steps to the third floor, Brock came to a landing. He peeked around the corner, checking both sides of the hall before turning left. As he made his way down the tiled hall, a family tumbled from one of the rusted doors. A woman wrapped in a black hijab held the hands of two small children. In true Muslim fashion, she kept her eyes trained on the floor while her husband locked their apartment.

Brock put his head-wrap back on. He bent over, pretending to tie his sandal, and tucked his gun back in its holster.

Dust in the hallway slipped past his allergy medicine and he sneezed.

The father spun around and peered at Brock.

Oh, crap. Bad enough he was paler than most people in these parts. But thanks to the UNESCO archaeological project in the region, the Mali locals saw strangers as looking for drugs, girls, or Allah.

The father smiled politely and bowed. *"Yarhamuka Allah"*—May God have mercy on you.

Brock prayed his Arabic recall would spring into action. He got up and returned the bow. *"Barak Allahu Fik"*—God bless you.

The father indicated drugs were to the left, girls to the right, and the mosque was located below.

Brock switched to French. *"Je suis perdu où est la mosquèe?"* he said, explaining he was lost and needed directions to the mosque.

"Oui." The father volunteered to show him the way, so Brock followed the family out of the building to the mosque. The family then left to shop at the market.

Satisfied he was alone again, Brock retraced his steps.

A voice whispered in his ear, "O'Reilly, we got your six covered."

"I'm tracking." Brock sniffed the air. The burnt skunky smell of marijuana took him further down the hall toward the boom of French rap music.

Brock crept the rest of the way, stopping every few feet to check the area for movement.

"Confirmed nine targets at location," the voice said.

"Still tracking." He reached the end of the hallway. The music from the apartment shook the walls, causing pieces of peeling paint to flitter in the air like brown confetti.

"I'm on location," Brock whispered. He had crouched outside the door and now stood to adjust his bulletproof vest.

An ice-cold piece of metal pressed upon his skull.

Instinctively, Brock lifted his hands in surrender. He turned to face the person at the other end of the barrel—the father from earlier. *Where's my backup? Crap.* Beads of sweat slithered down the sides of Brock's face.

"Allahu Akbar"—God is most great. The father's dark skin glistened in the shadows as he released the safety on his automatic weapon.

"Mashallah"—God has willed it. Brock snapped a sidekick into the father's chest.

The father staggered backward, holding tightly to the gun.

Brock wrenched the gun from his hands and swung the barrel in a wide arc against the side of the man's head.

The father staggered sideways as a maroon-colored gush of blood streamed from his scalp. Then he went for Brock's neck.

The automatic thudded against the tile floor.

Brock kicked it away, snatching his own gun from the holster. His fingers curled around the Glock .22 and squeezed the trigger.

The explosion reverberated through the hall. The father's eyes fluttered open in shock. Blood spilled through a gaping hole in his chest as he slid against the wall to the floor.

"Unidentified combatant down," Brock said, adrenaline coursing through his body. With his eyes on the door, he slung the man's weapon across his shoulder, curled his fingers around his gun, and braced himself.

"We got it from here," a voice whispered in Brock's ear.

Seconds later, two agents, Shuggs and Pang, ran ahead, demolishing the door.

Brock reached up and switched out his earpiece for temporary earplugs. Ensuring his earplugs were in place before the anticipated whoosh of a flash grenade that glided past him.

The blast pierced through the dingy dwelling, disorienting the occupants. Bursts of light and shrapnel thundered inside, causing a small tsunami. The kitchen's plumbing exploded, hurling a wave of water down the hall, bringing with it the contents of the cabinets. Silverware bobbed like misguided missiles in the murky water.

Brock replaced the earplugs with his earpiece, thankful that he hadn't lost his connection when the crackle of static came through.

Six muscled, armed men stumbled through a maze of overturned furniture and half-eaten meals. Blinded by the bomb, with their hands raised, they cried out, *"J'ai besoin d'aide Allah! Sa'idnee Allah!"*—pleas for help from God in French and Arabic. One of the dazed insurgents tried unsuccessfully to force his dislodged eye back into an oozing, hollow socket.

Brock and his companions took down each of the men with clean kill shots—close-range bullets to the head.

"Three targets heavily armed in back room, right corner," a voice said to Brock. "Proceed with caution."

Signaling the agents to follow him, Brock sloshed through ankle-deep water in the dark hall.

The group moved in tactical formation past the mutilated bodies toward the last bedroom.

Brock stepped carefully over a twitching, detached arm with three missing fingers. The metallic stench of gunpowder made his breath come in labored, hard and fast. His heartbeat hammered like a paper drum while a stifling silence settled over the apartment. Brock's fingers coiled around his Glock's trigger. Using his foot, he pried open the bedroom door.

Someone behind the door cursed in French and fired, ripping it off its hinges.

The group of agents took cover behind a large bookcase overflowing with gaming equipment.

Motioning for the others to back him, Brock lowered his body into a growing river of water. He peeked around the door jamb, pumping bullets into a wiry man who popped from behind a barrier of cocaine bricks.

The other agents unleashed another set of rounds into a tall, hulking man who appeared behind a wall of explosives piled onto a mattress. They retreated to reload their weapons.

Brock crawled on his stomach and fired at a third person, a woman who had a rocket launcher aimed at the group from behind a dresser.

An explosion reverberated from within the bedroom toward the agents, blowing out a chunk of wall, narrowly missing Brock. Stunned and bleeding from a busted lip, Brock stood shakily, feeling like someone had belted him in the chest. Pang yelled out a warning.

This warning came as the agent rushed toward a woman with a machine gun pointed at Brock. Shuggs threw a second flash grenade into the bedroom and sprang back into the hall. Shockwaves rocked the apartment in a thunderous roar while Brock and the men knelt, waiting for the remaining sparks to fizzle out.

The sounds from the bedroom faded.

Echoes of sirens clanged in the faraway distance, drowned out by screams of women and children from the marketplace below.

Brock shook his head, and his stomach filled with acid. He checked his watch. They were in a race against time, so the risk of civilian casualties would be low.

"All targets down," the voice said.

Wiping the sweat from his hands, Brock peered around the door's column. Motionless bodies soaked in growing pools of blood told him all he needed to know. Brock gave the okay sign to the other agents.

"Document confirmation of wanted targets," the voice said. "Building perimeter is secured. Vacate in ten."

"Affirmative," Brock said.

The other agents split up. Following protocol, they rushed throughout the apartment collecting everything of value to the agency.

Circuiting the room, Brock readied his agency phone to capture the required images of the three people who'd helped Boko Haram militants terrorize the city for the last year.

Brock crouched on his heels next to the two bodies. They resembled each other. Handsome. Brothers in their early twenties. Both stared open-eyed at the clacking ceiling fan above, limbs posed in unnatural positions. After taking their pictures, he walked to the third body and crouched again.

A dead girl sat erect on the cracked tile floor with her back against the wall, a gun hanging loosely from her hand. Female, about sixteen, with acne covering her forehead, eyes shut as if sleeping. He snapped her picture and got up.

Brock walked to the door and looked back before leaving the space stained with the coppery taste of violent death. Something out of the corner of his eye caught his attention. A wave of a tiny palm quivered from beneath a delicate, embroidered blanket he hadn't noticed before.

Shuggs touched him on the arm and motioned for him to leave.

Brock nodded and released a tense breath.

The bundle trembled and then went still. *Oh, God, no.* He was too small, too innocent to be in a filthy place packed with drugs, deadly Islamic terrorists, and more explosives than Brock had seen in months.

Brock ran back into the room, kneeled, and snapped the last picture.

Held tight by a dead teenage mother was an infant covered in blood. The baby stared lifelessly right through Brock as if seeing a secret deep in his soul before departing a brief life.

For the first time since the mission began, a tremor of sadness, of deep regret, gripped him. Brock tapped the hot barrel of his gun against his temple. *What did I do?*

"Retreat now," a voice crackled in his ear. "Time's up."

CHAPTER 2

Did you hear me?" a high-pitched woman's voice said. "It's your turn to report on this disaster we have on our hands."

A lean, redheaded man to Brock's left nudged him.

"Jet lag," Pang said.

Brock shook himself. "Sorry." He rubbed his eyes, studying his team members seated around an oblong conference table in a stark, windowless office. Glancing at his watch, he made the mental adjustment. It'd been forty-eight hours since his flight from Mali to Washington, DC, and they were now in an obscure CIA-owned warehouse outside of Virginia. "Fact of the matter is, I haven't been sleeping well these days."

Pang stifled a yawn. "These long debriefings don't help either."

A smattering of laughter rang out in the room.

Their supervisor, the Directorate of Intelligence Dr. Elizabeth Harper, said, "Understandable, but before I get you pillows, let's finish our meeting."

Shuggs leaned his huge frame over toward Brock and lowered his deep voice. "She's speaking to item eight on the agenda. The analysts have already given their spiel."

"I'm here to report," Brock used his pen to locate the line item, "on our AFRICOM mission in Mali, Africa. My team and I worked in a paramilitary operation alongside analysts and human intelligence agents, who were able to gather a significant amount of data regarding AQIM's relationship to al-Qaeda Central and their involvement in Mali with Boko Haram."

"Continue, Agent Brock O'Reilly," Dr. Harper said, an unusually icy edge in her voice.

Oh, crap, I'm in trouble. She's using my full name. "We effectively eliminated immediate threats to our national security." Brock cleared his throat. "Our analysts, as well as counterintelligence, determined that Boko Haram is an al-Qaeda offshoot."

"In other words," Dr. Harper questioned, "the mission was *successful?*"

Pretending to look through his brief, Brock racked his brain. *What does she mean?* "Yes, ma'am, you know as much as we do." Brock locked eyes with Shuggs and Pang. "We were able to neutralize all targets without significant loss of civilian life."

Dr. Harper walked to a screen in the front of her spacious office. Using a remote, she connected her computer, and several gruesome images emerged. "These pictures were leaked. Human Intelligence in Mali discovered that the info was hacked. Had we not gotten this back from al-Qaeda, pictures of brutally murdered Africans would have been plastered in a humanitarian magazine this morning. The chip is now back in our possession. But there are now activists who are accusing us of lacking compassion for black lives."

Brock swallowed hard, taking in the new data and seeing the faces of each person he had taken down—including the women *and* children. *If only she knew I grew up in predominantly black neighborhoods. But if I open my mouth now, I'll sound like a hypocrite. The kind that says their best friend is black when they get caught saying something bigoted.*

"To say your mission was successful," Dr. Harper lifted an eyebrow, "is only partially correct." She propped herself against her sleek desk and stared at Brock.

The veterans busied themselves taking sips of coffee. Some scribbled notes.

Dr. Harper adjusted the expensive navy pantsuit on her tall frame and paced the room. She walked past each of the seven men in the meeting before she began speaking again. "What you seemed to have left out," she leaned down, "is that you did not have clearance to kill half of the other people—the innocent women and children."

"That's a lie!" Pang said. "We saved more lives than we took."

"We always do," Brock said, knowing it made no difference.

"After this meeting, I have to report an after-action brief, and I have to justify—" Dr. Harper's voice exploded, "why my people gunned down three children under the age of five and two girls under the age of sixteen!" She peered at Brock. "To whom do I report?"

Crap. I need more coffee and a Xanax. "The NSC." Brock tried to keep his voice even. "The National Security Council," he said, examining his empty mug.

"Exactly, and the NSC reports to the Intelligence Oversight Board." Dr. Harper examined her veined hands, turning her wedding ring around so the fat diamond faced the front. "They ensure certain things are carried out," she said. "What things would those be, Agent O'Reilly?"

"Making sure that everything is ethical and legal," Brock said, his voice escalating. "But where are you going with this?"

Shuggs gently laid a hand on Brock's shoulder.

Lowering his voice, Brock continued. "You asked us to do our jobs, and all three of us did what you commanded."

"We killed those targets," Pang said. "Just like we were told to do. And if anyone says anything different, it's bull."

Dr. Harper forced a tight smile. "Seems like we have been down this road before." She walked back to the front of the room, pointing to each picture with a manicured nail.

Brock's stomach tightened.

"We must review the legality of what happened in Mali, so we do not end up on the front page of every American newspaper as government-sanctioned baby killers." She paused and surveyed the faces of the seven men. "And that we are *not* viewed as imperialists who are in the business of killing innocent women and children in Africa."

"Doc, c'mon, these people don't fight fair," Shuggs said. "Innocent women and children are commonly used as pawns in places like this."

"We had no way of knowing the first assailant's wife and children were strapped with multiple explosives," Pang said. "They had to be taken down to avoid their killing hundreds of noncombatants in the market."

"None of us knew about the infant in the target's house either," Shuggs said.

"Nice speech, Matthew Shuggs and Andrew Pang, but this is not the first time the three of you have been involved in something similar, is it?" Dr. Harper stood with her back to the group, staring at the pictures on the whiteboard.

Brock clenched his fists, reeling from the calculated words his boss shot at them like bullets. He closed his aching eyes and felt himself pull the trigger on the child he'd killed in Afghanistan two years earlier. He smelled the hot, slick blood covering his face when the boy's tiny chest exploded.

Everything had changed that day. It didn't matter that the child, coerced by insurgents, had meant to murder them all. *I'm a killer—that's how the rest of the world sees me.*

Shuggs cursed under his breath and threw his pen across the table.

Pang banged his water bottle and got up from the table.

"I suppose Agent Andrew Pang has left the building?" Dr. Harper asked, still gazing at the pictures. Sighing, she pivoted and turned off the recorder.

"Now that was one heck of a cheap shot." Shuggs met Dr. Harper's stare until she finally looked away. "Pang's wife took his kids and left him over that last scandal. We know what happened, but does it do any good? None of us—and I mean ever—intentionally killed innocent people."

"The truth doesn't matter to the outside world," Brock said, his voice thick with resentment.

"Not once has it been distorted by the media." Dr. Harper glanced across the room at a framed photo of the team taken before their first assignment together ten years ago. "I have decided to dismantle and reassign this entire team."

"Oh, my God," someone gasped. Even the most disciplined within the team began grumbling. Chatter in all directions. The air in the room was more chaotic than a crack house on the first of the month.

"It's settled, guys." Brock stood. "We're professionals and know that once the boss makes an announcement like this, the deal is done. We also know this isn't goodbye. It's see you later. Besides, the real meeting," he winked, "will continue tonight at Rusti's. I'll shoot you a text."

When he sat down, Brock received a sprinkling of applause from his colleagues. He looked up to see his boss, a steel wall of reserve, waiting for silence.

"Thank you for that, O'Reilly," Dr. Harper said unsmilingly. "The analysts will have a scheduled meeting with the directorate of CIA staffing today at 15:00 regarding their options. I will be in attendance. You may go now. I need to meet privately with the paramilitary team."

A hush fell over the room as it slowly cleared. One by one, each of the departing four analysts shook hands with O'Reilly and Shuggs before leaving.

Pang stormed back into the room with his fists balled. "What's going on?"

"Yeah, what happens to us now?" Brock asked matter-of-factly.

"After everything we've done for our country." Pang shook his head.

Dr. Harper pushed back a stray hair from her graying bun. "Gentlemen, please look these offers over. This is an overview of an investigation of local law enforcement agencies." She handed them each a paper with an unmistakable insignia engraved on the letterhead. "It is my strong recommendation that each of you be temporarily reassigned to the FBI, pending your clearances meeting approval."

In silence, the men took a few minutes to read through the offers presented to each of them.

"Wait a second, Doc," Shuggs said. "Do we even have a say in any of this?"

"If you agree to the terms and decide to take a lateral movement into the bureau," Dr. Harper gestured toward a red-stamped envelope next to her labeled *Confidential,* "the agency will not pursue legal action against any of you."

"What a load of bull!" Pang said. "We're the ones that should be suing. I almost lost an arm this time."

"I don't understand." Brock carefully measured his words. "Legal action? That's a slap in the face. Like Pang said, we had some close calls this mission. Fact of the matter is, we have our rights just like anyone else does. And our successes have far outweighed our mistakes." He pushed the offer away. "And this. This is a demotion."

"An offer from the FBI is hardly that."

"Oh, right," Shuggs said.

"This is not punishment," Dr. Harper said.

"Then what is it?" Pang asked, pushing away from the table. "Because it sure ain't a promotion."

Dr. Harper sipped her water. "This is for your benefit. I am buying each of you the precious gift of time. You are my best team. But the smoke must clear before I even attempt to bring you back on board."

"I didn't set my career up to do street hustles," Pang said. "Like some overpaid beat cop."

"So this is what fluency in French gets me," Brock said with a shrug. "A gig with the bureau looking for skinheads."

"Yes, Brock, I know. I also know you have a strong knack for picking up languages. I have your record right here." Dr. Harper tapped a stack of files beside her. "But we want to move past this stigma of us versus them. The CIA and the FBI are both reputable intelligence communities."

"Doc, c'mon," Shuggs said. "Investigating white supremacy in corrections *and* the police force sounds like a nightmare that we'll never wake from."

"This is bull. There's no way we're also selling our souls to the FBI," Pang said.

"I shall ignore that last statement." Dr. Harper swirled the cubes in her glass, making a tinkling sound.

Shuggs laid a hand on Pang's shoulder. "Doc, we've already lost a lot. We shouldn't have to lose our pride too."

"It's unbelievable that we could fit in with the likes of skinheads and angry idiots," Brock said. "I don't see how we fit into *their* world to do *that* sort of work."

"I'd like the weekend to think about this." Pang grabbed his briefcase, stuffing the offer inside. "I feel as if my hands are tied," he said. "But I'd like to pretend I have the freedom to say yes or no."

"I think he's right, Doc," Shuggs said. "We'd like to think about the offer and get back to you on Monday."

"You have until," she examined her watch, "tomorrow morning at 09:00."

Shuggs muttered a string of curses while he walked to the door toward Pang, then looked over his shoulder and let out a breath. "Should we wait for you, O'Reilly?"

"Nah. I'll catch up with you guys tonight for sure," Brock said with a reassuring smile and watched his friends leave the room.

When the door closed, Dr. Harper stood with her arms crossed. Her attention focused on the display of the dead still projected against the wall. "I realize *you* come as a package deal."

"Not necessarily."

She arched an eyebrow. "The leak here was an intelligence failure, and we all take responsibility for it." Dr. Harper turned to Brock. "It will take time to establish what is taking place."

"I suspect similar problems happen at the bureau."

"Of course, but you did not hear that from me."

"I understand."

"You and I both know the CIA and the FBI just coexist. We do not work together. Neither do we monitor nor spy on each other. Ever. You must remember that once you work for them, you are loyal to only them. But they need someone like you to go into deep cover to root *these* people out. Once all of this happens, there will be a place for you here. I promise."

"The fact of the matter is, you can't make that same promise," Brock frowned, "to the entire team, can you?"

Dr. Harper shook her head. "I cannot. But that stays off the record."

Brock nodded, knowing there was no such thing. "Sure."

"*Everything* in the intelligence field you do well; I taught you," she said. "Each of you has talent—a requirement to be hired with the agency. But that's not what sets you apart from all the others." She picked up the offer Brock had pushed away, nudged it back toward him, and pointed to the signature line. "What sets you apart, Brock, is that like me, in order to excel, you must have a higher cause." Dr. Harper reached into her breast pocket, pulled out her prized ballpoint pen, and put it in the middle of the table. "You will fit into *their* world perfectly."

CHAPTER 3

Brock drove through the damp night to Rusti's. His phone vibrated again. Another text. His friends wondering where he was. He'd taken longer to get out of the office than planned. There had been the private meeting with Dr. Harper, paperwork, assessing every detail of the last mission.

What could I have done to avoid this disaster? Brock shook his head. If they fought the decision to leave the CIA, his boss made it clear that she would leverage an investigation against them. They could fight all they wanted, but a probe would almost guarantee the death of their careers. *Dr. Harper is covering herself and the image of the agency.* The offer for them to transfer to the FBI may've been an arrangement with some hierarchy in the intelligence world as a favor owed. Or perhaps, presenting the opportunity to transfer was a rare attempt at kindness on her part. Regardless, if they wanted to continue working within their field, they'd have to leave the agency. At least for now.

While he maneuvered through traffic, thunder boomed around him. A bolt of lightning struck nearby. The distinct clap of gunfire. Brock gripped the steering wheel, his senses muffled by the fog of his thoughts and a distant memory.

That same distinct sound came again. Closer. A lot closer. Brock tore open his glove box, grabbed his Glock, and kept it in his right hand as he drove cautiously. He peered through his window, searching the night. A swirl of red, white, and blue lights lit the interior of Brock's car while a line of police vehicles raced past him.

Brock found himself transported back five years to when the Iraqi sky in a tiny village had burst into scarlet plumes of fire. An ISIS leader they'd been trailing for weeks had been smoked out of a tiny, nondescript complex. The agency had been unsuccessful in using the UAVs (weapon-carrying unmanned aerial vehicles) to carry out the targeted killing. They brought Brock's team in to complete the job. Stationed in a nearby building, Brock had lain on his stomach with his night vision goggles on and his laser trained on the target. Foolishly, he temporarily turned the voice in his ear low so he could concentrate on his shot. Intent on his singular mission, he missed the insurgent's all-but-silent approach.

The man jumped on him. Glittering knife in hand, he went for Brock's throat and sliced into his collar bone. Brock blocked the assassin's next stab but slipped and staggered to the ground. Lost the grip on his gun. He fought to stay conscious and was reaching for his weapon when a kick to his skull stunned him. Brock rolled away. Lights flashed. He couldn't tell the difference between the explosions in his head and the ones on the ground.

The assassin aimed Brock's gun toward him. Brock closed his eyes. Waited. When death didn't come, he popped open his eyes. Pang had crept up behind Brock's attacker and snapped his neck. Brock watched the man's lifeless body slump at his feet like a crumpled brown bag.

Pang ripped the assassin's turban from his head, used it to swathe Brock's wound, and created a sling to stabilize his shattered clavicle. He propped Brock up long enough for him to regain complete consciousness. Then Pang took lethal action.

Pang's swift actions ensured the completion of a successful mission without a single casualty to the team.

Dr. Harper and her superiors scrutinized the mission. The recovery of six children's mangled bodies from the targeted site resulted in complaints to the UN and the US embassy. HUMINT (Human Intelligence) had warned the team of the areas in the building holding minors. Brock never heard the warning because he had turned his sound down. Pang didn't get a warning about the children either. His earpiece had become dislodged in the scuffle with Brock's attacker.

During the investigation, Shuggs lied. He reported he'd turned down the sound in all of their earpieces. He had been in charge of their equipment, and no one questioned his statement. Shuggs took responsibility for the communication breach, resulting in a scathing admonishment in his file.

Brock swallowed, remembering his friend's selfless actions. Shuggs had spared Pang the embarrassment of a reprimand and Brock's removal from being team lead.

Brock realized he was about to run a red light. He hit the brakes and came to a screeching halt in front of a large group. They carried signs, wore masks, jumped up and down, and jeered as if they were in a combat zone.

One of them stopped in front of Brock's car and yelled something that he didn't catch. There was a flash of headlights behind him. Brock jerked his head around. *What the heck's going on?* Over his shoulder, police lights glared through his rear window. He pulled over, tucked his gun under his thigh, and waited. Tires screeched. The officers sped past his car, through the red light, and narrowly missed the pedestrians.

Brock pulled away from the curb and began his drive again. He drove carefully, making sure to avoid the groups of mostly African American people accumulating in the city. Brock was almost at Rusti's when he peered down a side street. Shadowy figures set fire to two demolished police vehicles on a road leading to the local precinct.

He parked in front of the bar and started laughing. Wild, good, familiar—the fusion of emotions surged within him. Brock felt as if he were back in the Middle East on a mission, feasting on adrenaline and about to duck grenades and engage the Taliban. *It's all about the fight, the risk.* And this felt the same. He was stateside about to enter an American bar to hang out with friends on a Friday night. Yet nothing had really changed. He was still at war, still in a fight, just in a different location.

He walked to the bar and opened the worn door. Brock's eyes adjusted to the warm, yellow haze, and he stepped inside a place that was the embodiment of good times and amity. Standing in the weathered, wood-paneled entrance, Brock felt he'd entered the living room of a good friend.

From the peals of laughter coming from a small private dining room in the back of the cramped, rustic bar, the "meeting" had started without him. He headed toward the smell of hot wings and the deep rumble of Shuggs's unmistakable voice.

"It's about time." Shuggs grinned. He rose and slapped Brock on the back. "Glad you made it, buddy. The guys kept asking about you. Thought I was going to have to suit up and go find you myself."

Brock playfully punched Shuggs in the gut. "I'm glad to finally be here, big guy. Hope you're okay meeting in a bar."

"C'mon, you know I stopped smoking and worrying about Cindy, my ex-wife."

Brock looked at the empty bottles by Shuggs's beefy forearm. "I was referring to your—"

Shuggs held up a hand. "I've got a handle on the drinking. Last year was a major setback. But I'm good now."

"Yeah, I want to be sure you're alright. If you need a ride, I'll drive."

"I'm fine, bro," Shuggs said. "Truth is, I was planning to meet Khan here tonight."

"Really?" Brock ran a hand across his jaw. "That's news to me."

"Lots you don't know."

"It appears that way." Brock nodded, then walked around to greet the rest of the men in the group. The rest of the team was there along with a few more analysts from other departments. After making his rounds, he returned to his two friends.

Pang handed a cold brew to Brock and raised his head an inch in a small salutation. "I got you, man," he said and made room for him at the far end of the crowded table.

Brock sat down on the solid wood chair and looked around. "Nice show tonight."

"Good call in suggesting we all get together," he said, his face slightly flushed. Shuggs waved a greasy chicken wing. "The guys really needed this after that doozy of a day we all had."

"Seems like we all never really got a chance to process any of what happened back there in Mali." Brock sighed and reached for a wing. "Then we come home expecting a thank-you, only to get a Dear John letter."

"It's all mind-blowing," Pang said.

"Anyway, how'd it go after we left?" Shuggs asked with his mouth still full. "You sign at the bottom line yet?"

"Did she offer the golden boy a special deal?" Pang took a long pull from his bottle.

"Something about what happened today just doesn't sit well with me." Brock stared at his friends. "I stayed behind to talk to Liz because, as the lead on this last mission, I felt responsible."

"No need to feel that way," Shuggs said. "We're all in it together."

"It's true, man. We're a team." Pang used his bottle to point to

Brock. "So did you make your decision already?"

Brock shook his head. "Of course not. I wanted to speak with you guys first." He took a swig of his beer.

"I'm glad you waited to speak with us." Shuggs winked. "Did Liz tell you the analysts were going to be reassigned?"

"This isn't classified information," Brock said. "I stuck around the agency to do some paperwork. I was there after the analysts had their meeting. I heard they've been placed within the agency with comparable positions."

"Unlike us," Pang said. "They'll still be CIA."

"Good for them." Brock rested his elbows on the table. "I'm guessing they have no idea we're being strong-armed into transferring to the outside."

"What'd you think we should say to the guys when they ask us what we're going to do?" Shuggs asked.

"We make a decision," Brock said. "Then we present a united front to these guys. We keep it cut and dried like we usually do. Keep it professional."

"I just can't believe we've been put in this position." Pang ordered another drink.

"It's unfortunate, but let's be honest," Brock said with a shrug. "We don't have options at this point."

"Especially with the threat of an investigation if we decide to stay," Shuggs said.

"These bastards from the top are just covering their own behinds." Brock frowned. "It's total bull, and we all know it. But then again, what choice do we have?"

When neither man responded, Brock leaned forward. "Wait," he said. "Maybe this isn't so bad—depending on how you look at it. Pang, you're constantly on international missions with us away from your boys. When you're stateside, you're usually hemmed up in family court."

"Things are about to change." Pang cleared his throat. "But you're right."

"Shuggs, you've got the twins in private school, and you're in the middle of yet another divorce. And me ..." Brock took a breath, "my father, the only real family I've got, had a heart attack recently. He's going to need me now, more than ever before, with Mom in an advanced state of dementia."

The men drank in silence until Shuggs spoke up. "Level with me." He gestured toward Brock and Pang. "Why would they break us up and then pawn us off to the FBI?"

"I keep asking myself the same thing. When I'm away fighting, I know who the enemy is," Pang said. "It's easy to see hostiles when hot sand is blowing in my face. But the enemy here is just blowing hot air, and now ... now they ain't as easy to figure out."

"Maybe. Maybe no," Brock said.

Shuggs toyed with his drink. "C'mon, we all know that catching the perpetrators of white supremacy right now will be like trying to catch spiders in their own webs."

"We won't know anything for sure until we're working our actual assignments." Brock sat back and rubbed the scar above his left eyebrow. "We'll get a feel for what we're up against once we're done with the nine weeks of training and start as FBI special agents."

"But we'll be separated and working in underfunded counterterrorism units," Pang said.

"It doesn't change anything." Brock took a deep breath, realizing for the first time since beginning his decade-long career in intelligence that he'd be without them. "Maybe this is where our journey as friends truly begins." He cleared his throat. "After all, we're still brothers, right?"

Pang moved the bottle away from his mouth. "We're still brothers."

Shuggs's brow furrowed. "Always," he said. "Always."

"Good." Brock exhaled slowly. "Because there's this one thing that still bothers me about those pictures of the dead kids in Mali," Brock said. "I keep going over the entire incident, and it doesn't add up. If we were the ones who took the pictures, and they never once left our possession ..." He rubbed his forehead. "How'd they get leaked?"

CHAPTER 4

A young waitress wearing too much makeup and perfume refilled their water glasses plus picked up their plates filled with bones. "Your bill is up front. My manager wants to close an hour early tonight on account of all the protests," she said, flashing a nervous smile, before leaving the private dining room for the men to resume their conversation.

Pang waited for the door to close to the dining room. He glanced over at the analysts deep in sidebar conversations of their own and sighed. "This situation is total bull, and if I didn't know any better," his face reddened, "I'd think you were blaming one of us."

"Yeah, what the heck, bro?" Shuggs rolled his sizable neck and leaned toward Brock. "This is where we are now?"

"Man, I'm just trying to see what the heck is going on." Brock looked at both his friends, trying to read their masked expressions.

"We know how this business works." Pang drained his bottle. "We were hacked by insurgents with an interceptor." He smirked. "Probably stolen from some MI weekend warrior who doesn't know his butthole from a bullet hole."

"That's impossible." Brock shook his head. "Everything in our equipment is encrypted."

Shuggs's eyes narrowed. "C'mon bro, what exactly are you saying?"

Brock rubbed the scar above his left eyebrow, then looked up with a questioning glare. "Do one of you *know* something I don't?"

The men's silence was met by the sudden echo of gunfire sparking instant terror inside the barroom.

Glass cracked. Wood splintered. Outside of the small private room they were in, patrons began to scream.

The bullets ricocheted closer. And closer.

Pang and Shuggs jumped up, grabbed their service weapons, and positioned themselves near the opening of the partition. Like Brock, they'd been prepared to put themselves in harm's way.

Out of the corner of his eye, Brock saw some of the other men run for cover.

Bullets rained down, piercing through the wall, separating them from the bar. A pitcher of beer exploded.

One of the analysts inside the dining room collapsed soundlessly beneath the table. Shards of glass stuck through one of his closed eyes.

Brock motioned for his friends to be quiet. He was seated facing the windowed partition, and he knew he didn't have time to move further without attracting the attention of the shooter. In the short distance before him, he saw a man firing at people who were crawling, cowered in corners, under tables, running.

A man's voice gave muffled orders. Another voice answered. Men's voices.

There's more than one shooter. Two, maybe three. Brock couldn't tell.

"You find him yet? Uncle's instructions were clear." One of the voices was by the bar.

"Don't think so. There's still the bathroom and the room the dude told us about. It's in the back."

Then a man strode toward the private room with his gun angled.

Brock ducked, grabbing his gun from his ankle holster. He shoved a nearby analyst, who'd sat frozen with a beer still in his hand, face-down to the floor.

A blast blew out one of the three windows. A second blast took out another window, showering a wave of glass into the room once again.

With his finger on the trigger, he felt a switch flip on inside his brain. The buzz of the alcohol dissipated. A surge of adrenaline coursed through Brock's body. His heart thundered, sporadic and wild, mirroring the clatter of gunfire.

"Get down, stay down!" Brock shouted and hurled himself under the table. He crouched, not daring to wipe the beads of moisture stinging his eyes.

Brock's fingers tightened around his gun, slick with sweat. He watched while a man—face tattooed, black—stormed into the private dining room clutching an assault rifle.

Shuggs signaled toward Brock, then drilled two shots into the back of the man's head. The rifle clattered to the ground.

Brock ran forward, kicked the gun from the man's reach, and kept his weapon pointed at the still body.

The man's dead black eyes were wide; blood pooled around his head.

Their waitress, covered in blood, stumbled into the room. Her shattered arm dangled from her shoulder, attached only by a few shredded tendons. "There are others," she said, coughing blood before collapsing onto Pang.

Two shots blew out the third window in the room.

Shuggs pointed behind Pang. "Look out!"

Screams echoed through the room.

Pang spun around, the waitress in one arm, weapon in the other.

A burly black man towered before them. He unleashed a torrent of bullets, hitting Pang in the torso, and killing the half-dead woman in his arms. He stepped over their bodies and marched toward Shuggs, then stopped in his tracks, turned away from him, and rushed Brock.

In the chaos, several people bolted from the room.

Not wanting to kill innocent people, Brock flung himself behind a table. Using the table as a shield, Brock jumped up and threw the table at the shooter. He trained his gun on the staggering man. He then pumped two shots into his wide chest.

The man fell to his knees and dropped his weapon. Rivulets of blood spread like a red blanket on the hardwood floor. His eyes were open. He turned to Shuggs with a bewildered, pleading look as he tried to speak.

But Shuggs pointed his gun at the man, pumping another bullet into his forehead.

Finally, the sounds of gunfire ceased. Somewhere in the bar, someone wept. The faint smell of burned flesh wafted through the air.

"What in the world is happening?" Brock asked, trying to catch his breath.

"I got no idea," Shuggs said. "Maybe one of the protests went wrong? Somebody out for revenge? A terrorist?" He wiped his glistening head and looked around the room. "Nowadays, who knows?"

Brock gripped Shuggs's arm. "We got to check Pang."

Both men raced to the pile of bodies and pulled Pang from beneath the waitress and the burly gunman.

Pang's motionless body was drenched in blood. His head lolled to the side, revealing his pallid face and bluish lips.

Brock grabbed his wrist, feeling for a pulse. *Please don't take him like this.*

Shuggs applied pressure to the oozing wounds that peppered Pang's chest.

He shook his head. "Oh, God," Brock whispered. He checked again, not wanting to acknowledge what the facts were telling him.

Shuggs banged on the side of an overturned table. "Check him another time," he said and pulled his phone out to call 911.

Brock knelt to administer mouth-to-mouth. He frantically pumped his crisscrossed palms against Pang's bloodied chest. Checked his pulse again. And again.

Shuggs shoved Brock aside. He began administering CPR himself.

Brock got to his feet and brushed shattered glass from his bloodied knees. *My God, what's going on? Terrorism? Lone wolves?* He cradled his throbbing head momentarily.

Sirens wailed in the background. But the only other sounds in the room were the jazz piano pumped from the speaker system and the crunch of glass as Shuggs knelt over his friend's limp body.

"Don't give up." Brock surveyed the desecrated room. All but two of the analysts from another department had escaped to safety. The others, including the four men on his team, were clearly dead.

Shuggs sat back on his haunches. "I don't want to stop, but ..."

"Just don't give up," Brock wondered if he was really saying the words to himself.

He knelt again and pumped Pang's chest. Shuggs checked Pang's pulse and shook his head.

"No," was all Brock managed to say.

Staring at his trembling hands, now soaked with Pang's blood, Shuggs took a deep breath.

Right outside the bar, sirens screamed. Tires screeched against the curb. Hard boot steps ran toward them. A cop's radio crackled to life beside the door. "Several down. Looking for survivors and the perps now."

Shuggs hung his head. "Pang's gone."

CHAPTER 5

When the police officers swarmed the bar, Shuggs and Brock already had their CIA credentials out in their raised hands.

"Step away from the bodies!" someone yelled through a broken window.

The first string of NYPD officers to enter the disheveled dining room swiftly kicked away the men's weapons.

Guns were trained on Shuggs and Brock while an officer ran their IDs and contacted the agency.

Once their IDs were verified, they were released by a short, stocky officer. "We're sorry about that, fellas. It's protocol. Just can never be too careful these days. I'm the chief detective. You'll be dealing with me for now." He pointed to the outside with his pen. "This area is flooded with hungry reporters. Some resort to tricky tactics to get a story."

Brock's gaze moved first to the detective's broad face, then to the crime scene tape. The red and white banners created an inner perimeter, blocking the entrance to the dining room.

"Remember, it ain't pretty when it's personal." Shuggs had positioned himself between Brock and the bodies, a protective measure. He laid his hand on Brock's shoulder.

Nodding, Brock allowed his friend to play father figure. He exhaled as he looked down. Six bodies. He started with Pang, fixing his attention on his friend. Heat spread across his chest, sending shockwaves throughout the rest of Brock's body. Long limbs splayed awry, Pang's red-haired head rolled to one side. Blood congealed around his trunk. Eyes partially closed.

Brock knelt at his friend's side and called Pang's name until his esophagus felt bloody and raw. He slapped away the hands of the chief and Shuggs when they tried to pull him to his ft

"Leave me the heck alone," Brock heard himself sɛ sounding primal, deadly.

The chief and Shuggs backed off.

He felt for a pulse but couldn't find one. Called Pang's name ʰ er. Again. And again. Brock hung his head. Took a gulp of air. Wiᴛʜ trembling fingers, he attempted to close Pang's dull eyes. But they slid back to their half-opened state. His throat tightened, remembering how Pang had put himself in harm's way. He'd died with a stranger in his arms that he'd been trying to protect. Took bullets meant for all of them. A sudden wave of bile-filled guilt washed over Brock. *Why him and not me?*

Brock sighed heavily, feeling the cool press of the flooring beneath his hands, and pushed himself into a standing position. He wiped his face on his sleeve, while he concentrated on not throwing up. Rubbing his aching temples, he stared at the last man they'd killed. Clad in dark clothes and an expensive watch, he belonged on the cover of *Sports Illustrated,* not shot dead on the floor of a bar.

He scrutinized the face of the first man they'd killed, but there wasn't much left to identify.

Brock zeroed in on the waitress's name tag, which he hadn't paid much attention to when he ordered. Polly. Now her pretty face resembled a hunk of bloody, uncooked meat.

The last four of the dead were middle-aged analysts. Single gunshot wounds that were not survivable. *Single GSWs to the head.* Their limbs jutted in impossible angles. Brock had worked with those analysts for years. They were more than bodies. They had names, kids, wives, and cozy homes they'd never see again.

"Might be too early to call it, but we got an idea about what happened," the chief said.

"We'd like to know what took place," Shuggs said.

"Got a few questions first." The chief licked his fleshy lips. "You mind?"

Shuggs shook his head.

"Go ahead." Brock stared at Pang again. He contemplated doing mouth-to-mouth resuscitation. But it'd be no use. He shook his head and pried himself from his thoughts. He tried to concentrate on the chief's questions. But his mind kept slipping back to what he could've done differently to save his friend's life. *I should've reached for my gun immediately, covered for my friend.*

"Do you have reason to believe you were targeted?" the chief asked.

"I doubt it. C'mon, we all just got back from a long-term mission overseas," Shuggs said. *"Our* enemies are far away."

Brock answered robot-like, "No."

The chief glanced at his notes on a small clipboard. "Looks as if those gunmen were rioters who highjacked a peaceful protest and targeted whites."

"I don't understand what's happening." Brock rubbed his right temple. "Fact of the matter is, we've only been in town for two days."

"We're used to seeing attacks like this in less civilized countries," Shuggs said. "Not here."

"You think the perps got a tip that agency folks frequented this place?" the chief asked.

"Our people came here regularly. But we made it obvious we were corporate programmers. It wasn't a lie," Brock said. "It was our official cover stateside."

"But why *this* bar?" The chief chewed the end of his pen. "None of the others in the area were attacked."

The throb of a memory came to Brock—thick Bronx accents belonging to men's voices, sent by an uncle. They'd been looking for someone. But who? "That's not what happened tonight." His voice was a whisper.

"Excuse me?" The chief squinted at Brock. "Did you want to say something?"

"I'm still trying to process things myself." Brock stared at the paramedics who'd just walked into the room and unfolded six body bags. He felt his legs begin to give out.

"C'mon, Chief, we just lost our best friend and four of our closest colleagues." Shuggs met the chief's beady eyes. "Give us a sec. We'll be right outside the dining room if you need us."

The chief waved them off and walked over to talk to the medical examiner.

Shuggs beckoned for Brock to follow him. They moved past people dusting for prints, taking samples and photos. Leaving the dining room, they stepped into a narrow hallway leading back to the main barroom.

"I'm sorry I spaced out in there, man." Brock struggled to breathe. "I started thinking about how I should've done more to save Pang. He was a hothead, but he was really the best of us. Never took a shortcut. Brave to a fault."

"He always tried to protect everyone." Shuggs stopped himself from choking up. "All he really wanted to do was help make this world a better place. That's why he took everything so hard."

Brock nodded in agreement and closed his eyes briefly to try to keep the room from spinning. When he opened his eyes, he caught Shuggs staring at him with an odd look on his face.

"They'd better get a solve on this." Brock lowered his voice. "I overheard the killers speaking before Pang got shot. I think there's more to this."

"What'd you hear those three men say?" Shuggs leaned over and placed his hand on Brock's arm.

"It's like they knew where to look."

"Really?"

"Yeah. Heard one of them say an uncle sent them." Brock glanced over his shoulder.

The chief came to the door, beckoning to them from the hallway, his face devoid of color. "You may want to step back inside ..."

"Everything alright, Chief?" Shuggs asked. "Me and my buddy will be back inside the room in a few."

The medical examiner pushed past the chief and ran into the barroom. "We got a heartbeat on one of the men!"

CHAPTER 6

The next morning, Brock was released from observation at the hospital where the victims of the bar shooting had been treated. After he signed the discharge paperwork, he received a call from Dr. Harper.

"I have granted permission for both you and Shuggs to visit Pang. He is in the ICU under the name John Smith. His cardiologist, Dr. Shaw, will update you. But later today, I need to speak with you privately," Dr. Harper said. "I will meet you in the hospital's chapel this afternoon."

After the call, he stared at the phone in his hand. He cursed. Wanted to scream. Brock hadn't gotten in a single word. And now she was gone, without so much as an inquiry as to how *he* was doing. He rubbed his temples, and it struck him that his soon-to-be former boss was reptilian. She could be temporarily warmed by circumstances, but, for the most part, she thrived in the cold.

Brock contacted Shuggs, who was in a nearby room, and arranged for them to meet by the elevator on their floor.

"Bullets can't keep a good man down," Brock said when he saw Shuggs leaning against the wall by the elevator with two steaming cups of coffee in his hands.

Shuggs handed Brock one of the coffees. "You've always been the cheerleader on our team."

The two men quietly sipped their brew while they rode the elevator up to the Cardiac Intensive Care Unit. They got off on that floor and walked to a set of double doors, monitored by a camera with instructions to ring the buzzer on the wall. After ringing, they identified themselves and gave the alias of the patient they were visiting. The doors opened to a semicircle of ten rooms monitored by five nurses' stations. A nurse from the nearest station greeted them and checked their IDs, clearing them to visit *John Smith's* room.

"You may see him." She nodded toward the third room. "We have an orderly who'll escort you. But you've got a maximum of ten minutes to visit," the nurse said. An orderly led them to the room and provided disposable scrubs and face masks before leaving.

A plainclothes detective beside Pang's room scanned their IDs, reminded them of the time limit, took his seat outside the door, and raised his newspaper.

Brock pulled the thin protective covering over his clothes. "You think he's going to make it?"

"Hard to believe Pang made it this far." Shuggs frowned before putting on his mask.

"Think of how many times we've dodged bullets overseas, only to be attacked stateside."

"Life is as unfair as it gets."

Brock took a sip of his coffee. "I plan to catch whoever did this."

"C'mon, that's not your call," Shuggs said.

"Like I said," Brock put on his mask, opened the door to Pang's room, and stepped inside, "I'm catching the perps."

A tall African American woman stood by Pang's bed, typing into a computer set on a high-rolling desk. She looked up and greeted them with a wide, white smile. "Good morning. I'm Dr. Shaw," she said in a lilting Caribbean accent. "I've been expecting you." She donned glasses and peered at her screen. "Mr. O'Reilly and Mr. Shuggs. Correct?"

Both men nodded but their eyes were on Pang, unrecognizable except for the tufts of red hair plastered to his motionless head.

Brock's breath caught in his throat at the sight of his friend's bruised, swollen body lying still on an air bed pulsing with a life all its own. "Oh, God," Brock uttered. *I'm so sorry.* Buried beneath a mass of tubes and wires, a regular IV drip was running into one arm, while a bag of blood went into Pang's other arm. From his esophagus, a hollow tube protruded, attached to a respirator. A thin tube was in his nose, and another had been inserted in his chest. Compression sleeves filled with air that puffed and sagged like lungs encapsulated Pang's long legs.

"With the way he looks, I can't believe our boy survived," Shuggs said.

Brock stared at Pang's monitor. "Yeah, it's a matter of unmitigated, straight luck."

Dr. Shaw motioned them away from Pang's bed to come stand beside her in the farthest corner of the room. "Even in unconsciousness, the last sense to leave is hearing. Be selective about what you say in his presence," she said in a lowered voice.

"Does it really make a difference?" Shuggs asked. "He seems out of it to me."

"Yes. What we say around an unconscious patient does matter. Research proves our words, whether positive or negative, have a dramatic effect on a patient's well-being. So please be very careful." She tucked her dreads behind an ear.

"What's the prognosis?" Brock asked.

"When bullets don't puncture major organs, the chances of survival are good," Dr. Shaw said.

"I don't see how it's possible." Shuggs stared at the gleaming hospital floor, a solemn look on his face. "C'mon, the man took five bullets to the chest."

"If a gunshot victim's heart is still beating on arrival at the hospital, there is a 95 percent chance of survival." Dr. Shaw pointed to Pang. "Still, it's like roulette. Anyone who survives a gunshot attack the way your friend did," she said, "is quite fortunate."

He tried to listen, but, all the while, Brock couldn't take his eyes off his friend. There were so many tubes going into Pang's body, that Brock was unable to keep track of what each was for.

Shuggs held his jaw. "What's with all the tubes?"

"The nasogastric tube in his nose is to remove air, fluid, and blood from the abdomen," Dr. Shaw said. "The one in his chest is a drain to remove fluid build-up around the lungs and heart. An endotracheal tube in the patient's throat is attached to a respirator enabling him to breathe."

Why did this happen? What could I have done to save my friend? There were other questions plaguing Brock, but he was afraid of the answers.

The doctor seemed to read Brock's mind. She turned to him and touched his shoulder lightly. "Let me know if you have any questions, Mr. O'Reilly," Dr. Shaw said, her eyes warm, the color of expensive brandy. "From what I've heard, you've been through a lot together." She held out a business card.

"Thanks for everything." Brock took the card. "When will we know if Pang will make it?"

"We won't know for several days," Dr. Shaw said. "It could be weeks before he stabilizes enough for us to know anything."

Shuggs walked over to Pang's side and examined the beeping contraption monitoring his vitals.

"Can we be updated as soon as something changes?" Brock asked.

"His wife is listed on his living will. I expect to speak with her tomorrow when she gets into town. You may follow up with her to get more extensive details."

"You mean Pang's *ex-wife*," Brock said.

The cardiac surgeon checked her computer screen. "Even if they're divorced, it doesn't affect the legal authority she has impacting his medical directives."

"Like hell it doesn't." Shuggs spun around. "There's no way we're letting *that* woman make any decisions on our friend's behalf."

"It's not your call to make." Her tone matched Shuggs's authority without the brashness.

Shuggs turned his back to the doctor and resumed staring at Pang's monitor.

"Please remember it's a privilege we've extended to your agency to allow both of you here." Dr. Shaw walked toward the door.

"Thanks for all you've done for our friend," Brock said. "We're rattled. It's been a rough couple of days."

Nodding, Dr. Shaw gave Shuggs a sidelong glance and left.

"What was that about?" Brock asked Shuggs. "The doctor seemed nice enough. She's just doing her job. What's with the attitude?"

"Did you know *that* woman was still listed as his emergency contact?" Shuggs paced before Pang's bed.

"I had no idea," Brock said. "But it's really none of our business."

"How could he still trust his ex-wife with life and death decisions?"

"Pang doesn't have much family except his two little boys and a few cousins. Maybe he felt he could trust Patti."

"Trust her when she took those kids from him and handed him divorce papers after one of our toughest missions?" Shuggs stared off at the ceiling. "He should've come to us. We could've been listed on his medical directives."

"Are you nuts?" Brock walked over to face Shuggs. "We travel together on missions. More than likely, if something happened to Pang, we'd have been right there with him."

A low moan. From Pang. His chest spasmed, eyelids fluttered. One of the machine's alarms echoed in the small space.

The door to the intensive room popped open. A nurse rushed in and checked the machines. She grabbed her phone and announced a code blue.

"What's a code blue?" Shuggs asked.

"I'm sorry," the nurse said, ignoring his question. "We need this room cleared of visitors."

Dr. Shaw entered, accompanied by two other nurses with a crash cart. "We need you to go to the waiting room immediately." Dr. Shaw's eyes were focused on Pang's labored breathing.

CHAPTER 7

Brock and Shuggs sat in the stuffy, silent waiting room for an entire hour. A white digital clock hanging above a magazine rack ticked off the minutes.

Shuggs broke the silence. "You alright over there, bro?"

"Yeah, I'm okay."

"You look flushed."

Brock gulped down the rest of his tepid coffee. "It's hot in here."

"C'mon, you got to be kidding me. I'm freezing." Shuggs ran a hand over his bald head. "It's chilly in here."

"Nah, this heat is getting to me."

"You're sweating."

Guilt bubbled inside Brock, lighting a fire of pure acid. He jumped up, ran out of the waiting room, and found a bathroom on the right in an alcove. He stumbled into a stall and regurgitated the coffee. Sweat and stomach cramps came in waves. He felt the room sway and had difficulty breathing.

He checked his watch. Five minutes had passed since he ran into the men's room. Then ten. He worried about Pang. Alone. In the sterile ICU fighting for his life. But he had to get down to the chapel to meet Dr. Harper.

After rinsing his face and mouth with bitter hospital soap, Brock left the bathroom. He texted Shuggs and told him he needed time to clear his head. Shuggs texted back that he'd let him know when the doctor came to update them.

Sharp pains stabbed his abdomen. But Brock forced himself to walk upright when he opened the door to the hospital's chapel.

Dr. Harper was already there, glossy salt-and-pepper bun, legs crossed, red bottom shoes on her feet, in a chic blue dress, and designer overcoat neatly folded behind her seat. Her exotic perfume dominated the room.

She smiled enough to show the top row of her capped teeth. Dr. Harper tapped the bench next to her.

Brock sat down as sweat poured down his face and his back.

"The chief detective on the case believes that this was a hate crime," she said. "That it was motivated by radicals with their own agenda."

An overpowering heat that destroyed all logic threatened to overcome Brock, especially when he thought of Pang. He turned to Dr. Harper. "Those are lies."

She arched a perfectly tweezed eyebrow. "Why would you say that?"

"I overheard the men talking before they found us," Brock said. "They were specifically looking for someone. I don't believe for a second this had anything to do with the protests."

Dr. Harper pulled a notebook from her briefcase and licked her forefinger before writing with a pen. "You're saying this wasn't about race or the protests?"

"The perpetrators behind the attack would like for us to believe it was." Brock shook his head. "But the attack had nothing to do with either thing."

Dr. Harper stared at Brock. "A specific target?"

"Yeah."

"Did they ever mention a name?"

Brock shook his head. "They injured people, but the only ones killed were agency folks."

"What about the server?"

"She was collateral damage," Brock said. "I think they shot up the rest of the bar to make it look like a random attack. They were trained killers hitting soft targets. They could've taken out every patron if they really wanted to."

Dr. Harper pushed her lipsticked-red lips into a smile. "You will indeed make an excellent fit for the bureau."

A compliment from Liz? Brock glanced at her. "Thanks, but I'd prefer to stay at the agency."

"I expect you to transfer to the FBI." She continued to write. "Where you will see your assignment through until its completion."

"I'm confused."

"Why?"

"I'm convinced we were targets," Brock said. "I expected some sort of clarification from you about what happened at the bar." Brock locked eyes with Dr. Harper.

Dr. Harper nodded, her business-like signature. "If I could share more with you, I would. But you are on the right track. Keep asking the right questions. I have told you as much as I can."

"Can you tell me anything about my next assignment?"

"Your assignment is highly classified," Dr. Harper said. "A matter that may or may not impact other intelligence agencies. As you move forward, trust no one."

Pondering her words, Brock rubbed his jaw. Finally, he nodded. "Trust no one?"

She patted her bun. "That is all I can say for now."

He wondered at how things had changed so much in a matter of a few days. "I wish I had more info. I feel like I'm going into a war zone with blindfolds."

"What I have shared is more than I should have told you."

"It doesn't seem like you've shared much."

"I realize you feel somewhat helpless, but I am helping you more than you know. Also, I will brief the chief detective on the case about what you shared with me."

"The chief seems to have his mind already made up," Brock said. "It's an easy solve for him to peg the incident on racist, unruly riot-ers. Case closed."

"Still, it is vital for him to have the information." Dr. Harper closed her notebook and packed it into her briefcase. "Do you know why I chose to meet here?"

Looking around at the soft flicker of battery-operated candles, Brock shrugged. "For privacy?"

She shook her head. "When my husband battled cancer last year, he wanted us to spend time in this chapel between chemo treatments. At first, I resisted. I am not a religious person." Dr. Harper twisted her wedding ring. "Eventually, I relented. Most of the time we never spoke. I knew he was suffering, and I quietly sat by his side, using the time to catch up on my cross-stitching. The night before he died, he said something I want to share because, like him, you are at a cross-roads. Would that be satisfactory?"

"Sure. That'd be fine," Brock said.

"He said our lives are stories unfolding through five different lenses. He then turned over one of my cross-stitch patterns and pointed out the ugliness and confusion of the threads. He explained that they represented the circumstances and difficulties of our stories through which four sets of people see and define us through. These people include self, close friends and family, acquaintances, and fact-checkers. Yet the only critical part is God's perspective. My husband turned over my cross-stitch to reveal a beautiful garden and referred to it as a life that is God's handiwork." Dr. Harper tilted her head. "Do you follow?"

"Yeah." Brock stared at his boss, remembering her husband's long illness. He took a deep breath. "I'm not religious either, but I like the notion of life being a story."

"What I am about to say is going to sound completely out of character for me and a bit deep." She took a deep breath. "But I think I need to share this because of the circumstances we are facing, and I do believe it will help you ..."

"Please, go ahead," Brock said.

She nodded. "My husband thought that when living a life pleasing to God, God sees the complete picture and creates something beautiful from it. He believed that was the only part of the story that counted," Dr. Harper said. "That is the *fifth part of the story*. Nothing else mattered to him. I am not telling you what to believe or that my husband's way of thinking is what you should think. But I do know that it is now up to you to decide what matters in *your* story."

Brock bit his lip. "Yeah, I have a lot to process and think about."

"Yes, you do," Dr. Harper said. "It would serve you well to remember the agency's unspoken core belief—that our choices have the ability to impact others."

Brock decided to change the subject. "Speaking of others, did you know Patti was still listed on Pang's medical directives?"

Dr. Harper seemed relieved to switch directions. "Of course. Patricia will be here tomorrow."

"Hopefully, she'll allow us to get updates on our friend."

"That is strictly up to her."

"Spoken like a true attorney."

"Which you know I am," Dr. Harper said with a dry laugh. "This is all going to work out." She got up, collected a briefcase, and neatly folded her coat over her arm. "I promise."

Brock's phone buzzed.

He looked at the screen and caught his breath.

"What is it?" Dr. Harper asked.

"A text from Shuggs. It's about Pang." He hurried to the chapel's exit.

Dr. Harper kept pace with Brock. "What does the text say?"

"Come back now. Things don't look good," Brock said, looking over his shoulder.

"No, no. He will be fine." She shook her head in her typical, I-know-best manner and followed Brock.

CHAPTER 8

When Brock returned to Pang's room with Dr. Harper, a plain-clothes detective jumped up from his seat and blocked their path. "I'm sorry. This room is off-limits."

Dr. Harper flashed her CIA badge. "We need immediate entry."

The detective nodded and stepped back. Dr. Harper pushed past him, dragging Brock behind her. She went through the door into Pang's room, then spun on her foot. "On second thought, wait here."

Brock ignored her and continued into the room.

Dr. Harper's next words were drowned out by the frenzied voices of the medical staff.

Vibrant spatters of color across Pang's sheets stopped Brock in his tracks. He and Dr. Harper stumbled into each other like dominoes before falling.

An out-of-breath Shuggs ran into the room. "This is why I called you to come back," he said. "Pang's bleeding out. But we can't be in here. We have to return to the waiting room. I have something to tell you."

A howling cry came from the doorway.

Their eyes veered to the statuesque woman crowding the room with her sorrow.

Dr. Harper gripped Brock's arm. "Patricia Pang? I thought you were coming tomorrow."

"I'm a day early," Patti said, her hands trembling as badly as her voice. "But really I feel like I'm too late."

With that, she began sobbing.

Dr. Harper walked over and took Patti in her arms. "I know this is painful, but you will get through it, no matter what happens. Besides, you are never alone."

Who is Dr. Harper right now? With widened eyes, Brock stared at Shuggs.

Finally, the crying subsided.

"We should go to the visitor's lounge, where we will have a private area to talk. The doctors need this space." Dr. Harper held Patti's elbow, guiding her through the door and down the hall.

Brock and Shuggs followed.

Once inside the lounge, Patti collapsed into a seat, her head in her hands.

Dr. Harper sat beside Patti and put a hand on her back. "Do you need help with anything?"

Patti nodded. "I have to speak with Dr. Shaw; there's a bunch of paperwork to be signed." She spoke through fingers spread over her face. "I've been getting most of my updates from her."

Taking a notepad from a briefcase, Dr. Harper licked her forefinger. "I will find the cardiologist. What else can we do?"

"I'll need to return to the hotel later to check on my boys. They're only three and four." Patti dabbed her eyes. "My mother flew here with me, but those kids have been upset ever since finding out their daddy got hurt. I had my mother drop me off and left the rental with her. In my rush to get up here, I left my bag in the car, so I'll need a ride."

"Of course." Dr. Harper looked at Brock and Shuggs. "One of you needs to assist Patricia."

Shuggs studied the ceiling fan.

Brock shifted in his seat. "Yeah, I can help out."

"Good. It is settled." Dr. Harper smiled approvingly. "Patricia, I have your number and will text you so you have my information should you need anything more."

"Thank you," Patti said. "It's nice to be among old friends. I wasn't sure how everyone would react." Her voice cracked. "I'm worried about Pang, but this support is a relief."

Brock watched Patti's attempt at composure and tried not to give into the gnawing fear in his stomach. *I'm worried too, Patti.*

"C'mon, we're all grown-ups here," Shuggs said.

Patti's wet hazel eyes turned to the gruff voice. "I know, but ..." A handful of bronze curls fell onto her face.

Staring at Patti, Brock wanted to brush the hair, and the past, out of her eyes.

Dr. Harper cleared her throat. "I will go in search of Dr. Shaw. Shuggs, walk with me, please."

Shuggs raised an eyebrow at his boss and stood. "Sure. I'd love to take a walk."

Chewing the inside of his cheek, Brock watched them exit the lounge. "Everyone reacts differently to tragedy," he said, turning to Patti. "Shuggs is just a big, protective teddy bear. You remember how he is, right?"

Patti frowned. "I remember." She tucked a stray curl behind an ear. "It's really good to see you, Brock." Patti leaned across the empty chair between them and patted his hand. "I'm sorry it took this to bring us together again. Despite the divorce, my family and I still adore you."

"How're the boys?"

"Growing like crazy."

"Your mom?"

"She still has a crush on you." Patti playfully punched Brock's arm. "Probably why she came with me."

He laughed. "I'm no competition for your dad. Senator Lipsett isn't worried," Brock said.

"Is your mom doing any better?"

Brock shook his head. "I think she's worse. Now she thinks I'm her dead brother."

"That's a shame," Patti said. "She's such a sweet woman. How's your dad?"

"Considering the fact that he had a heart attack several months ago, he's doing well. Still running. Still doing some financial consulting and taking care of Mom."

"He must've been sick with worry after this last incident, huh?"

"Yeah, but he's so ornery he tries to pretend it doesn't bother him."

Patti sighed and sank back into her seat. "We all have our methods of handling our fears."

"Like Dr. Harper said, Pang's going to be okay."

"He's a fighter." Patti's voice was soft. "That's for certain."

"Yeah, he is."

"You do know why I'm here?"

"To check on Pang." Brock glanced at Patti. "Have your boys see their dad."

Patti shook her head. "The last communication I had with Dr. Shaw wasn't very good. She said I needed to prepare myself and the children for ..."

"For what?"

"Pang developed blood clots. They've traveled to his lungs." Patti gasped. "His ... heart."

"But I thought he was bleeding out."

Patti nodded. "He is."

"He has blood clots, *and* he's bleeding out?" Brock asked.

Tears streamed down Patti's face. "Which is why I'm needed to sign all this paperwork," she said. "And possibly to say—goodbye."

CHAPTER 9

Patti followed Brock's gaze to a newcomer who had entered the ICU visitor's lounge to purchase something from a vending machine.

Brock tensed and reached for his weapon. After assessing the distracted stranger, he sat back.

A nurse entered the lounge and stopped when the man turned around. "Sir, come quick. Your daughter is awake."

Leaving his money stuck in the vending machine, the man sped down the hall behind the nurse.

Patti groaned. "Some things don't change with time." Sliding down in her chair, she ruffled her curls. "You had me wary of that poor father with a sick child."

Brock got up, removed the bill from the machine, and pocketed it. *I'll return the money to the nurse's station later.* "I suppose caution comes with the job."

"I get it." She tugged at a curl, looking lost in thought. "Pang constantly scared me with his edginess, especially after returning from a mission."

Wishing he could tell her more, Brock adjusted his expression to a neutral one as he recalled an alarming incident with Pang months prior. Brock believed his friend hadn't meant to harm the informant who'd double-crossed their team.

But Pang's temper had exploded when he discovered they'd been betrayed. When Brock and Shuggs joined Pang in the interrogation room, it was too late. They'd arrived in time for the perp to breathe his last. No other movement. No other sound. After Shuggs had pulled Pang's hands off the man's broken neck, Pang kept explaining that he'd just wanted to make the man talk. For a split second, Brock had felt pity for the backstabbing informant, who'd lost his short life in the filthy backroom of a desert shanty. But it would've eventually come down to someone dying. *At least it wasn't one of us.*

Brock sat down beside Patti and leaned forward. "Were you afraid of him?"

"Not at all."

"Was it the long deployments?" Brock asked. "I know they busted up every decent relationship I ever had."

"Don't insult my intelligence." Patti pointed to Brock. "I know you're aware of Pang's indiscretions."

A bead of sweat formed on his brow. Brock took his time answering. "It was never about you."

"Really? What was it about then? Shuggs's bad influence?" Patti threw her hands up. "Enlighten me."

"They were about *his* feelings of inadequacy." Brock rubbed his jaw. "Still ... you didn't deserve how he behaved."

"Please. Don't." Patti sighed. "Don't do that."

"What?"

"Paint me as a pathetic victim. I'm stronger than that."

"Point taken."

Patti peered at Brock from behind a wall of wispy bangs.

"Pang lives with constant regret about that chapter of his life," Brock said. "He knows he was a better man when he was with you."

Patti blew a lock of hair from her face and stared at Brock until he shifted in his seat. "I don't care about any of what you're saying. You've known me long enough to understand the only thing I care about is today, not yesterday or tomorrow," she said.

"Okay."

"And another thing." Patti took a breath. "If you're fishing for pieces of bitterness or resentment, you won't find any."

"That's not what I—"

"You can stop," she said. "You don't have to spin some commercial for how great Pang is every time you see me. I know *who* my ex is. And you want to know something?"

"Yeah, sure."

Patti's face softened with a smile that showed off her deep-set dimples. "I still love that idiot."

Brock averted his eyes, trying not to show his surprise. "Enough to take him back?"

She exhaled slowly. "I already have."

"I had no idea."

"You're one of the first to know," Patti said.

"What're you saying?" Brock asked.

"For the longest time, I've wanted to tell Pang to come back home."

"But you didn't?" Brock gently touched her shoulder. "Why?"

"I was worried."

"About what?"

"We'd talked about getting back together. Each time I started to agree to reconcile, I stopped. He's so hotheaded ..." Tears formed in the corners of her eyes. "I was worried for Pang's safety, for how he'd react to what's been going on."

"What's going on?"

Patti wrung her hands in silence.

"Talk to me," Brock said.

"Someone's been harassing me." She wiped her eyes. "And my boys."

"Like how?"

"Threats," Patti said the word as if it had cut her tongue open.

"What kind of threats?"

"Violent. Hateful. Racially motivated," she said.

"Are there any specific details that stand out?"

"Had to be from someone who knows Pang and I were together."

"Did someone rough you up?" Brock stared at his balled fists, trying to resign himself to logic instead of anger. "Were these threats in person or—"

"I've been getting letters. They say if I'm ever with a white man again, I'm dead," Patti's voice caught. "And the lives of my children will also end."

Brock frowned. "Why didn't you go to the authorities?"

"Don't you think I thought of that?" Patti slapped her thigh. "Give me some credit. I haven't been a teacher my *entire* career."

"Yeah, you're former agency," Brock said, rubbing his temples. "You must've had your reasons for not involving the police. Were you working on any solid leads?"

She nodded. "I tried to get a lead on the threats, but I've got nothing. Whoever's doing it is professional. No fingerprints, hair, residue, zero."

"Have you figured out a possible motive?"

"With racism, the motive *is* hate." Patti's voice cracked. "With love, there is *no* color."

"Might be time to involve the big dogs. This could be serious."

"This *is* serious. The perps know me. My sons. Where I live."

"That's not uncommon—"

"They know about the baby ..."

Brock swallowed. "What *baby?*"

Patti cleared her throat. "I'm pregnant again."

"You're pregnant with Pang's child?"

She pushed a curl behind her ear. "Yes."

"Okay. Maybe he told someone."

"I haven't told anyone," Patti said. "Not even my mom."

"Wait, Pang doesn't know about the baby?"

"No," Patti whispered. "He knows nothing."

CHAPTER 10

Brock reached over and gently placed Patti's hand in his. Her hand was supple, fingers long and slender, nails French manicured. "I'm always going to be here for you and your family. Always. I promise."

"Thank you." Patti leaned closer until her head rested on Brock's shoulder. "But if Andrew dies, I'm literally going to kill him."

Their tear-filled giggles lifted a thickness weighing on the air in the room.

After the laughter faded, they sat hand in hand with their separate thoughts in the shared silence.

Brock and Patti had settled back into the familiar place of well-worn friendship, shrinking the space between them.

Fragments of memories rushed to Brock's mind, receding with identical speed. But one memory lingered. "Remember when Pang passed out right before he walked into the delivery room with your first kid?"

"How could I forget? You had to prop Andrew up during the entire birth. If it wasn't for you, he would've missed the entire thing."

"I think he was relieved you had the second kid right before we made it back from the field."

Patti shook her head. "What about when he brought the boys to your house and forgot to put diapers on them?" She elbowed Brock. "Do you remember what you said?"

"No."

"You said our kids were your birth control because you were never having children."

"I probably said that because they ruined my new couch," Brock said. "It must've taken an entire month for me to get the smell out of my place."

Brock laughed with Patti again, noticing for the first time the slight bulge rounding out her otherwise trim body. "If you don't mind me asking, how far along are you?"

"I don't mind." She closed her eyes as if trying to focus. "Going on four months."

"Don't worry," he said, patting her hand. "Don't worry about anything. We're all in this together."

She turned and looked at Brock. "Does this mean you'll agree to be the godfather for *this* baby as well?"

"Yeah, but I'm going to do a much better job this time."

"No matter what?"

"No matter what," Brock said. "And my actions won't depend on what happens between you and Pang. Or if something happens to ..."

Patti studied Brock's reddened face for a moment. "It's a dangerous thing to make a promise to a woman."

"I know." He sighed. "Believe me, I know."

Just then, there was a noise in the hallway.

Patti turned her attention to the open door, where Dr. Harper and Shuggs had just entered. "Where is she?"

Dr. Harper and Shuggs exchanged glances.

"Were you guys able to find the doctor or not?" Patti sat up. "I need to talk to her."

"We did locate her, but she is unable to meet with anyone right now."

"C'mon, Doc," Shuggs said. "Just tell her."

"Tell me what?" Patti let go of Brock's hand and stood with her arms folded across her chest. "Liz, what is it you're not telling me?"

"You know, you ought to get your rest tonight, Patricia," Dr. Harper said. "Tomorrow is going to be a very long day and—"

Patti stamped her foot. "Just stop with the shenanigans. Tell me the truth. Now!"

Dr. Harper and Shuggs fell silent.

"Very well," Patti said, walking to the door. "I'll find the doctor myself and get the answers I need."

"You cannot," Dr. Harper said.

"Why?"

"Because Dr. Shaw is in surgery." Dr. Harper reached out toward Patti and caught her arm. "She is operating on Pang as we speak.

According to the charge nurse, the surgery will last several hours."

"It'll be morning before they'll know anything," Shuggs said.

"I don't care. I'm staying put," Patti said.

"It's okay." Brock stood. "I'll stay with her as long as she wants to wait."

Dr. Harper's mouth formed a thin line. "We have all been asked to vacate the hospital until further notice."

"That's insane," Patti said, shaking her head. "I'm not going anywhere."

"I can understand how you may feel, dear," Dr. Harper nodded, "but we have been asked by the agency to leave."

"Why?" Brock asked.

"Apparently, they are quite concerned about Pang's safety. Which is understandable. No one is allowed here until given the proper clearance. It should be straightened out soon, though, I assure you," Dr. Harper said. "This sort of thing can happen. You all should know that."

"So now someone above you is involved?" Brock asked.

"Yes, that would be correct."

Fresh tears streamed down Patti's face. "I don't understand."

"Something had to have happened for the agency to up security this way." Brock stared at Dr. Harper and Shuggs.

Shuggs sighed. "Well, that's about the gist of it."

"There was a security breach?" Patti asked. "Here at this hospital?"

Dr. Harper nodded.

"Oh, Lord." Patti's face paled. "Did someone hurt Andrew? Is that what happened?"

Brock swallowed down the lump that had jumped into his throat. *Please tell me that's not what happened.*

"Patricia, I thought this information would have been better off shared by a medical professional." Dr. Harper lowered her voice. "However, I was just briefed by the agency regarding Andrew Pang's labs."

Patti stared blankly at Dr. Harper. "What does that mean?"

"According to the labs they drew right after he began bleeding out, there is an unnatural chemical present in his bloodstream. The levels are very high. There is no mistake; someone injected him with a deadly dose."

Patti slumped over and gasped. "Poison," she muttered before collapsing onto Brock. "It was poison."

CHAPTER 11

Brock glanced at the entrance to the ICU visitor's lounge as the door swung open. A secret service agent stood facing the group. "I'm sorry for the inconvenience, but we need each of you to vacate the premises. This entire floor is in the process of being closed and secured."

The room was deadly silent when Dr. Harper spoke. "Sir, we too are agents and are aware of the situation."

"Besides, we're in the process of leaving." Shuggs went to the exit and stood outside the door.

The secret service agent tensed when Dr. Harper walked toward him. She mumbled something to him and handed him her card.

Brock shook his head. *If someone is planning on intimidating Dr. Harper and attacking Pang now, they might as well give up.*

Patti sobbed and ran out of the visitor's lounge.

Moments later, Brock found her leaning against the wall by the elevators, her head cradled in her hands as she cried silently.

Dr. Harper and Shuggs had followed behind. When they saw Patti's state, they waved their goodbyes and quietly made their exit.

Brock stood beside Patti until her body stopped shaking.

She looked up. "Sometimes I hate the agency," Patti whispered.

"Yeah, I know how you feel."

Patti shook her head. "No, you really don't. You didn't give up your career to make your marriage work, only to have to suffer through the worst of what the job does to families."

"I suppose you're right," Brock said. "I never thought of it that way."

"I knew what I had to do." She dabbed her wet face. "But I didn't know it would cost me everything."

Brock nodded. No matter what the government had done or taken from him, he knew he was still fortunate. And he hadn't lost everything. Not in the way the circumstances threatened his friend's life.

Patti rubbed her stomach. "It's like I can't trust anyone, ever."

"You're not alone in any of this."

She eyed the secret service agent who was making his way toward them. "We'd better get going. I have to get back to the hotel anyway." Patti sighed. "Right now, I need my boys as much as they need me."

"Sure. I'm ready to take you."

While they made their descent in the elevator to the parking garage, a plan formed in Brock's head. He'd go through with the transfer to the FBI, but now he knew there was no going back on what he'd promised earlier. He'd find Pang's attacker. No matter the cost.

Once in the car, Brock and Patti drove to her hotel in silence.

After parking, he hopped out and opened the door for Patti, insisting that he escort her to her room.

When they reached Patti's suite, she turned to him. "Tell me, Brock, why did you want to work for the agency?"

Brock rocked back on his heels and cursed.

"It's okay," she said, watching his flushed face. "Go ahead and be candid. No need to watch your mouth with me. I started out like you did."

"For me, it's not about the money. Don't get me wrong, the pay is excellent. But I'm the only son to simple people who settled for a life of passivity," Brock said. "They fought for our family to climb out of poverty so they would be able to lead a quiet life in the suburbs."

"That's not a bad thing."

"I wanted more."

"Then it's about the excitement for you?" Patti asked.

"It's more than that." Brock scratched his head. "I wanted to make America better. I still do."

"Can you accomplish such a feat if you're constantly *out* of the country?"

"We fight the enemy on their territory," Brock said. "That way we don't have to fight them on ours."

"You really believe that what you do makes a difference?"

"Yeah, I do." Brock nodded, but his thoughts drifted to the images of the bodies of women and children he'd killed. Pain crippled him, which he hid by cupping his fingers around his jaw.

"Let's cut to the chase, Brock," Patti said, an ashen look blanketing her face. "You put your life on the line fighting for the freedom of Americans, right?"

"That's right."

"Yet you return home where Americans fight and kill each other over issues of basic freedoms."

"Yeah, it does seem crazy."

"Don't you see the irony in what it is you fight for?"

"Sometimes," Brock said.

She folded her arms. "You ever get tired of the hypocrisy?"

"I try not to think of it that way," Brock said.

"How is it you can do that?"

"I do my job to the best of my ability and live one day at a time. I keep hoping that by doing my part, I make a difference."

"Is that enough to live for?" Patti's voice was curt. "Don't you want more from life?"

"What do you mean?"

"You spend your time dodging bullets overseas only to have to dodge them in your own country."

Brock couldn't blame Patti for the way she reacted. All she knew was that people had been killed. People she knew and had once worked with. The father of her children had barely survived an attack on US soil. Her reaction was natural. And he'd faced worse.

"No matter what, the government will never," her eyes narrowed, "recognize your service the way they should."

"Listen, Patti, I get it. You're upset."

"You have no idea."

"A lot has happened in a short time," Brock said. "You're tired, stressed, and let's not forget—pregnant. Let me help you."

"You can't." Patti opened her suite. "Good night, Brock," she said before closing the door.

CHAPTER 12

Walking through the hotel's shadowy halls, Brock thought back to the day when Pang had first announced his engagement to Patti, an attractive, young African American woman from a prominent family of lawyers. Deployed outside of Palestine, their stakeout was a burned building that'd once been a resort. The area and mission were more chaotic than normal. While driving the few miles across town to his own hotel, Brock wondered why Pang had kept his relationship private when there were so few secrets between the three of them. Yet Pang's secrecy made sense to him when he mulled the matter over. They'd been trained to be deceptive toward the enemy to protect their identities and national security.

Prompted by the chaos, Pang had stood on a crumbling balcony in the Palestinian resort and declared to a deserted street where the life had been bombed out, "She said yes! Thank God, she said yes to a crazy man and a crazy life!"

At the time, Brock and Shuggs didn't know what Pang was talking about. But a month later, when they'd returned from Palestine, he was married.

When Brock arrived at his hotel, he settled in for what was left of the night. But he couldn't sleep. Something troubled him about the secret service showing up at Pang's hospital earlier that day. Whatever was going on had gotten attention from someone upstairs. And they were taking it seriously.

The whole day—the meeting with Dr. Harper, talking with Patti, the Secret Service, and Pang's poisoning—now coalesced for Brock into one single nightmare.

He succeeded in making Patti feel comforted, but he also knew she felt a connection to him that encouraged her to trust him. He sensed she relied on him to keep her secrets safe and determine who'd attacked Pang.

Brock thought about contacting Dr. Harper to ask her if she knew any other details than what they'd learned. But he decided against it. She'd be sleeping by now since it was after 10:00 p.m. And if the agency was going through the effort of involving the Secret Service, then someone would be briefing them soon enough.

Brock began to doze off into a fitful sleep when someone knocked on his door. Instinctively, he reached for the automatic on the nightstand and stumbled to the door, willing himself alert. "Yeah, who is it?"

"Open up, bro. It's me, Shuggs."

Brock rubbed the sleep from his eyes and let his friend inside the dark room. "Did you come to tuck me in?"

"No," Shuggs said, running his fingers across his bald head. "Not tonight." He managed a weak smile.

"What's up? Can't sleep, huh?"

Shuggs shook his head, took a seat at the desk, and turned on a lamp. "How the heck could this happen?"

"I keep wondering the same thing," Brock said. "I feel terrible. Can't believe there was another attack against one of our own right under our noses."

"This wasn't our fault, bro." Shuggs slapped the desk. "This was a security failure."

"Yeah, but I can't help feeling responsible."

"You couldn't have done a thing to prevent what happened to Pang. If someone is that intent on taking him out, maybe we should be asking ourselves why."

"What the heck are you talking about?"

"It's about time we start looking out for ourselves," Shuggs said.

Brock chewed the inside of his cheek, studying his friend's face. Sorrow was what he detected behind Shuggs's sunken blue eyes, and a look of weariness lined his weathered forehead. Brock swore loudly and sat down in an overstuffed armchair. "Are you questioning Pang's integrity?"

"No, but—"

"If you are, you'd better have a darn good reason."

"The agency received intelligence that demonstrated someone infiltrated our databases. We get home, and we're attacked stateside.

Then Pang was poisoned," Shuggs said. "Following so far?"

Brock chewed his lip. "I guess."

"Our intelligence suggests that this particular breach was an inside job."

"We don't know that for sure."

"Maybe it's time to find out."

"How would we do that?"

"Did Patti say anything to you?"

"Say anything about what?"

"Anything suspicious," Shuggs said. "Something that would help us figure things out."

"She's concerned about her family's safety." Brock shifted in his seat. "Of course, she's worried about Pang." His throat tightened, thinking about one of the best friends he'd ever had. One who was fighting against the odds to live.

"Is that what she said?"

"Yeah, in so many words."

"I know you both have a good relationship," Shuggs said. "She seems like she trusts you more than any of us."

"Yeah. I guess."

"How about her involvement with anyone that may've struck you as strange?" Shuggs asked. "Did she share anything like that with you?"

Brock frowned. He didn't reply for a second. Surely, he couldn't have heard Shuggs right. "I don't know anything about that."

"C'mon, don't get all defensive on me." Shuggs reached out and clapped Brock on the shoulder. "I'm looking out for us."

"You're saying—"

Shuggs dug through his pant pocket and pulled from it a small package. "Go ahead, open it. Despite whatever happened between Patti and Pang, I'm like you. I think she's a good woman. She used to be one heck of an agent. That's why I was confused when I saw this."

"What's this?"

Shuggs shoved the package into Brock's hands. "See for yourself. I'm not sure what to make of it. I was hoping you had some answers that could clear this up."

Brock slumped back against the armchair at the sight of the first picture. The photo was of Patti wrapped in an embrace with a black man who was clearly *not* Pang. There were several photos of Patti with the same man, obviously taken on different days. The last pho-to captured Patti in a meeting with a group of African Americans huddled around a table. "Okay. What're these photos supposed to be telling me?"

"I don't know." He shrugged. "You got any ideas?"

"Not really."

"Do you think," Shuggs leaned toward Brock, "this could be reveal-ing another side of Patti?"

"How do they do that?

"There's a credible timestamp for each of them." Shuggs drummed his thick fingers on the desk. "They're six months old. Which means whatever she was up to was fairly recent."

"The pictures probably mean nothing. Besides, even if she's in a relationship, you do realize that Patti and Pang have been divorced for two years?"

Shuggs grunted, then leaned over and pointed at the last picture. "See there, Patti's in a private meeting with her *friend* and known radicalized extremists. They're black militants."

"How would you know?" Brock had to admit he was shocked, but he'd been trained to maintain a poker face, no matter the situation.

"I ran the facial biometrics for each person through our secure sys-tem." Shuggs took a breath. "Several are on the homeland terrorist watch list."

CHAPTER 13

Brock struggled to keep his voice calm and neutral. "Tell me. What's going on here?" He shook his head. "This isn't healthy."

"What the heck do you mean?" Shuggs asked.

"Even if any of what you're telling me turned out to be true, why were we running surveillance on one of our own?"

"I didn't spy on anyone." Shuggs pushed himself away from the desk. "I already told you. I received the information from one of the analysts the night we were attacked."

"All of the analysts we worked with are now dead."

Shuggs nodded. "That's the problem. We can't get any further information. Everyone who would've been willing to help shed light on what was going on is gone. Seems like we're screwed."

"Yeah, but there's always more than one way to solve a problem. Who was the analyst?"

Shuggs looked away briefly. "Khan."

"The older guy sitting next to me that night at Rusti's?"

Shuggs nodded his head.

"You remember anything Khan said?" Brock asked.

"He said the data collection was part of a broader investigation. Had something to do with an international security breach. Planned to speak with us after everyone else left."

"Anything seem off about his behavior that you picked up on?"

"Seemed jittery and on edge." Shuggs ran a hand over his head. "Kind of like he wanted to tell me something real important but didn't know how. Thought he was on edge because of the meeting earlier that morning. But when the shooting started at Rusti's, Khan was so nervous, he froze."

"So you have no idea how Khan got those pictures? There has to be a good reason for them to be in his possession."

Shuggs pulled his chair close and tapped the top of the shiny desk like an inexperienced pianist. "No, just that it was part of an internal investigation. Maybe the CIA had their eye on Patti."

"Why would the CIA be watching her?"

"Because of her possible entanglement with a militant."

"If that's true, I wonder why we weren't involved."

"Got the feeling Khan stumbled across some info."

"Then Khan discovering the pictures was a mistake?" Brock asked.

"Could be," Shuggs said. "I don't know."

Brock got up and paced the room. "I wonder why Dr. Harper never mentioned any of this."

"Never?"

"Never," Brock said.

"That's strange. Seems a little shady if you ask me."

"Did Khan discuss whether Dr. Harper knew about the pictures?" Brock asked.

"Never got that far," Shuggs said, his voice gruff. "Khan intended to give me more details at Rusti's, okay? That's all I know." He folded his arms across his chest.

"Okay. I'm just trying to make sense of things."

"Got the feeling Khan was more nervous than a long-tailed cat in a room full of rocking chairs. I tried to put the squeeze on him, but he refused to give up any other details. Seemed like he wanted to keep things secretive."

"You think that's why he wanted to meet without the other analysts?"

"That's what I thought."

"With so few leads, I don't know how we come up with a plan." Brock rubbed his jaw. "Although, anything's possible. We'd have to figure out who knows about these pictures and what type of investigation Patti's involved in."

"Can't let this info get out until we know more. I'm an old country boy who still believes what my redneck daddy used to tell me, 'There're kinds of people who're lower than a snake's belly in a wagon rut.' Know what I mean?"

Brock smiled. "It amazes me how easily you can shift to redneck language. I'm not sure I'm following you."

"Patti *seems* sweet," Shuggs said. "Be careful with her type."

"What's that supposed to mean?"

"Remember, Patti's got the agency in her blood. People like that don't play by your rules."

For a moment, Patti's innocent face floated in front of Brock. Dressed fashionably. Smiling. Kind. "I'm sure Patti's a lot of things, but she cares about Pang."

"She's *charming* alright," Shuggs said. "You have to remember that Patti's a trained manipulator."

"Okay ..." Brock said, leaning closer to his friend. "I think we'd better speak to Dr. Harper."

"If I were you, I'd be skeptical of Doc. We both know she's stuck up higher than a light pole."

"Yeah, but maybe she's the one who ordered the investigation."

"C'mon, I doubt that." Shuggs pointed to Brock. "She'd have told her golden boy something by now."

"Where does this leave Pang?" Something flashed in Shuggs's eyes. Brock couldn't put his finger on it.

"Pang's one of our best friends. A real tough guy. Issue is, he's a pushover when it comes to certain people."

Brock lifted an eyebrow. "Like Patti?"

"C'mon, bro, don't deny the evidence." Shuggs gestured to the pictures Brock scattered across the desk. "This is our area of expertise. We're the ones people count on to collect the data and connect the dots."

"I'm not sure what the pictures mean. But I've known Patti for years, and I like her. I can't say I blame her for divorcing Pang."

"Bro, she could've handled things differently. He deserved better."

"Yeah, and we both know he's no Boy Scout," Brock said. "Also, things aren't always as they appear. Sometimes the intelligence we get is strung together to tell a story it shouldn't."

"I guess. Sure." Shuggs nodded. "But I've done my homework. Maybe it's time for you to do yours. It's what we signed up for when we became agents. I know we're employed by this lousy government, but we've got to be better than them."

"I know what I signed up for, and I was in Pang's shoes once before," Brock said. "So were you."

"Your point is?"

"My point is," Brock sighed. "We've been second-guessed by our own before. Can't allow some flaming idiot from up top to divide us."

Shuggs rubbed his head, his posture changing slightly, and morphed into a slump against the desk. "It's like you said, Brock. Details tell a story. It's up to each of us to figure out whether it's fact or fiction."

Stillness hung suspended in the dim room like an invisible weight. "Man, I appreciate you sharing all of this with me," Brock said, rubbing his eyes.

"That's what we do, right?" Shuggs said.

"Right. And down the line, this has got to mean something in figuring out who's after us, huh?"

"I don't know. I'm just delivering the info."

"It's a lot to digest."

"C'mon, bro, I understand. Anyway, we're both dog-tired, and it's late. I've also given you tons to think about." Shuggs stood up and stifled a yawn. "We'd better get some rest and chew on this more tomorrow." His scuffed Oakley boots scraped the carpet as he walked to the door.

Brock bolted his hotel door, a habit he'd picked up through his time in the field. *Can never be too careful.* He flicked off the lights and collapsed into bed. Exhaustion hit him full force. He shut his eyes and tried to go back to sleep. But rest evaded him. Wild thoughts ran crazy through his restless mind.

He sat up and stared out at the dark room, trying to make sense of the latest dilemma. Conflict abroad was one thing, but conflict in your own backyard was another beast. Brock had fought in dozens of conflicts that'd never made the papers. During his time in the field, he'd seen comrades die quietly for their country on several continents. He'd broken bones, bled, and almost died in more missions than he cared to remember.

Between Brock, Pang, and Shuggs, they'd sent more enemies to an early grave than any other team in agency history. But that history was slowly ebbing away into the darkness he looked through. And now things were boiling down to solving the mystery of who could be trusted at home.

Brock threw off the covers and turned the lights back on. He paced the room, trying to organize his rambling thoughts. He knew without a doubt, Pang was in danger, and he probably was too.

A memory sputtered across his mind. He traced the jagged scar over his left eyebrow that made him look like he questioned everything.

The scar was an ugly reminder that maybe he'd been destined to be a killer even as a child. And the problem with killers is someone was usually out to return the favor.

CHAPTER 14

Brock fell into a fitful sleep. Visions of Pang sitting beside him in a Humvee faded in and out. Brock dreamed of riding through the night, escaping bombs and bullets. In his dream, he ran through the Nile River, his pale feet digging into the black mud, the tide rising.

After a mostly sleepless night, Brock decided he couldn't sit around. He needed to fix things his way—or he'd get fixed. And he didn't want to live through that again.

He was used to making snap judgments that caused someone to live or die. He'd tangled with death in an intimate way that was difficult to shake. He understood a man's body odor changed when panic struck. Fear smelled like the gamey tang of sweat. He'd been there when grown men peed themselves in the final throes of death and cried for their mothers.

Brock's mind kept returning to the leaked photos.

That's when he remembered the pictures Shuggs had shown him the night before. He walked to the desk and hovered over the images. The pictures were exactly how he'd left them. Scattered like displaced pieces of a jigsaw puzzle. He examined them one by one. His thoughts again ran crazy. *What in the world are you up to, Patti?* Finally, he stuffed the photos back into the package and decided that this was personal.

Eventually, after what seemed like hours, the answer came to him as he retraced the scar above his eyebrow. Whether Andrew Pang lived or died, Brock knew he was going to bring his attackers to justice. And if Patti was involved, she'd have hell to pay.

Brock examined his watch and decided 8:00 a.m. was late enough to call Patti.

"I was just about to ring you," Patti said over the racket of her sons romping in the background. "You sleep okay?"

"Didn't sleep worth two cents last night. You?"

"I spent the night fighting for the covers with the boys and listening to my mother's snoring, so what do you think?" Patti laughed, then stopped mid-laugh with what sounded like a snort. "What if he dies? What do I tell my boys?" She lowered her voice.

"That's not going to happen," Brock said. "He's a fighter."

"Death is going to come for all of us at some time." Patti's voice cracked. "Maybe this is ... Pang's time."

Brock leaned away from the thought, wanting to admit he struggled with the same fears. "I feel like he's going to pull through."

"You believe that?" Patti's voice was soft, childlike.

"We have to believe, truly believe."

"In what?"

"Believe Pang's going to make it."

"Oh, I thought you were going to say something about God."

"Why? Is that what you think?" Brock asked. "That *God* can save Pang?"

"You know I've always been a church girl."

Brock wondered how much church was left in Patti. Not much, judging from the pictures he'd seen. He shook off the thought and turned on the small coffee maker in the room. "So you believe God is in heaven looking out for you?"

"I don't know what to think right now."

Lying in bed all night, dreaming and reliving his fears, Brock was relieved once he awoke. But Patti seemed swallowed whole by her daytime nightmare.

"If you've always believed, then why stop now?"

"It's hard to focus on what you haven't yet seen."

Brock paused to consider her words while he poured himself a cup of coffee. "Isn't that what faith is for?"

"Have you been going to church?"

"Not at all. Why?"

"Because you're reminding me of what I believe in."

"You never took no for an answer," Brock said. "You had faith."

"Sounds like the old me."

"Who're you now?" He sipped the tepid brew and searched the counter for sugar.

"I'm a cynic."

Brock pushed on. "You've changed in some ways. But you're no cynic."

"Then who am I?"

He gave up trying to drink the watery coffee and drained it in the sink. "I was thinking you could tell me over a good cup of strong, hot coffee. I'd like to ask you about something."

"Have you heard anything about Pang?"

"Not about his health," Brock said. "But I have info I'd like to discuss with you. It could be a lead."

"Pick me up in thirty minutes. I'll be waiting outside."

After Brock got out of the shower, dressed, and walked into the parking lot, he noticed two things. His driver's side door was ajar and there was a note stuck between his windshield wipers. *I know I locked the car.* He looked around at the deserted lot and checked for movement. Brock walked around the vehicle, checking for anything else amiss. Finally, he pulled the paper from the window and got in the car. He read the note, which was really a photocopied picture of Pang lying asleep in his hospital room, then he started the engine.

Brock called Shuggs and then Dr. Harper, but both calls went straight to voicemail. He left messages telling them what had happened, making a mental note to contact the agency after his meeting with Patti.

Afterward, he drove to Patti's hotel on Tingey Street. He saw her as soon as he turned the corner. She wore a scarlet scarf over a yellow jacket and stood beside the light post outside the Thompson Hotel.

Patti got in the car. "I need caffeine and carbs," she said breathlessly.

"Where to?"

"Let's try Milk & Honey in Smith Commons. They have the best berries and cream French toast."

After a short drive, Brock and Patti walked into a modest brick building where they were greeted warmly by a heavy '70's vibe and Motown music. The aroma of real butter, spices, and coffee brewing met them while they took their seats.

They made small talk over a spread of crab hash, shrimp and grits, French toast, and a pot of chicory coffee.

"The boys and your mom okay?" Brock asked. He made his voice calm, trusting. Best to make a suspect, even if they're a friend, comfortable, then go on the attack.

"I ordered them room service." Patti smiled and sat back. "My mother has a whole day planned for them. She's taking them to a children's museum and then to a park by the Navy Yard."

He returned the smile. "I look forward to seeing them."

"I believe that's in the works. Mom heard you were in town and already has supper planned." Patti winked. "Our hotel has a decent restaurant."

"That sounds great." Brock pushed his plate away and drained his mug.

Patti tucked a stray curl behind her ear. "What did you want to talk about?"

"People have been giving me pictures lately." Brock slid the package of photos to Patti.

He sat back with his arms crossed while her face flushed red.

"Who gave these to you?"

"That's confidential."

"You have to believe me when I tell you this." Patti's eyes were ringed with dark circles. "This is not what it looks like."

"What do you mean?"

"First off, I don't know who'd give you these photos and what their exact motives were, but I—"

He held his hand up. "Don't do that."

"What?"

"Deflect."

She shook her head. "I'm not. I want to understand the context of how you got those pictures. You can understand that, can't you?"

"Yeah. But that's not the question. The question is why were you with these *particular* people?"

Patti squeezed her eyes shut and covered her mouth with her hand.

Brock waited. *She's going to get me to empathize with her. Turn on the female charm. Maybe she'll cry some tears.*

"I want to tell you," she said, wiping her face. Patti took a gulp of coffee. "But I can't."

Brock nodded. *Now it's time to attack. Layer the fear with a strike she doesn't expect.* He plucked the photo of Pang he'd retrieved that morning from his pocket and slapped it on the table. "You know anything about this?"

She opened her eyes and gasped when she saw Pang's picture

between greasy plates of leftovers. "No! Where did you get that?"

"Found it on my windshield this morning. Someone broke into my car. I assume they were looking for something, *and* they wanted to send me a message."

"What message?"

Brock tapped his chest, then Pang's picture. "That they have access to us."

"It's a threat." She closed her eyes momentarily as if to process. "You need to report it to the agency."

"I'm handling it," he said. "But let's not forget the other pictures."

"I didn't—"

"What're you into, Patti?"

"I don't understand—"

"You seeing someone else while trying to patch things up with your ex?"

"No." Her eyes opened wide.

"No? Then who're these clowns you're meeting with?"

"I assure you I'm on the up and up." Patti's hand trembled when she put her mug down.

"Explain."

She shook her head and stood, causing silverware to clatter to the floor. "I can't say. Not yet."

Brock glanced at the diners, who were trying not to gawk at them. *I need to console her. Show her I'm on her side.* "Sit down and let's talk about it," Brock said, his voice steady and calm. "Figure things out."

"We're past that." She leaned forward, so close Brock could see her pores. "You have *no* clue what you're up against."

"Tell me."

Patti looked down at her hands. "Earlier this morning, you reminded me of something."

"What?"

"I realized that no matter what happens, God's still in control."

"Is he?"

"Yes." Patti pulled on her jacket, took out several bills, and threw them on the table.

"Was God with you when you were dating an extremist?"

"You know what?" Patti raised her shaking hand and pointed at Brock. "You can kiss my third point of ..." Taking a deep breath, she sighed. "I'm not going to let your ignorance make me stumble in my

Christian walk." She turned to walk away.

Appeal to her emotions. Show her we have history. "Wait. Don't leave like this. We're friends. Please," Brock said, changing his tone and strategy. "I apologize."

Patti turned back to Brock but didn't sit. "I believe in God. Even if Pang dies." She sighed. "Or if he lives. One is better, but either is okay because I have faith we'll meet again. In heaven."

Brock nodded. He stood and walked around the table to Patti. Her grief and pain pulled at him and brought him to where she was. His eyes combed her face, her jittery stance, and her growing stomach. He searched for clues, and what he couldn't see unsettled him. "Do you have an explanation for these pictures?"

"Yes, I do," Patti said, her voice a jagged edge. "But now's not the time."

CHAPTER 15

What do you mean by that?" Brock asked.

"I'd like to go now." Patti pursed her lips and looked at the hardwood floor.

"When you say, 'Now's not the time,' what do you—"

"If you can't take me, I'll walk."

The waiter approached. "Everything okay? Need anything else?"

"Everything's fine," Brock said. "We just need the check."

Writing quickly on the guest check, the waiter gave Brock and Patti a once-over, then set the bill between them before walking over to the next table.

"Don't be ridiculous," Brock said. "I'll take you back to the hotel." He picked up Patti's money and handed the bills to her.

Crossing her arms, Patti refused the money. "I pay my own way. I always do." She spoke with a strained smile on her face as if joking.

I know she's not joking.

They rode back in silence.

Patti closed her eyes, kneading her forehead.

Brock stopped at a red light before turning the corner to the hotel. "Sorry," he started.

"I don't appreciate the way you treated me." Patti opened her eyes and faced him. "We're better than that. I thought we were friends. *Good friends.*"

He met her gaze briefly before pulling off after the light turned green. "We are good friends."

"Then why'd you do that?"

Stall for time to feel her out. Play dumb. "Do what?"

"You made me feel like I was a criminal being interrogated." Her head dropped to her chest. "I hate that feeling."

"I know how you must feel—"

"You have absolutely no idea how I feel. Agents ... you each have your special set of tactics, correct?" Patti asked. "You were using yours." She shook her head slowly. "It's my fault, really, for believing we could pick up the pieces of our past and glue them back together again."

"I wasn't using a special set—"

Patti let out a sharp laugh. "People manipulate. They lie. Especially people like you. To get what you want."

Don't react. She'll look for a way to turn my emotions against me. If I can't stay calm, I must say nothing.

"That's your specialty, Agent O'Reilly, right?" Patti said. "You use and manipulate others until you're finished with them. Then you *dispose* of them like you've done many times before."

He pulled up in front of the hotel and turned toward Patti. "Oh, come on," Brock said. "Stop."

"It wouldn't have hurt for you to have given me a little bit of grace." Her face twisted in a repulsed expression. "Considering everything I've been through and everything we've been through together."

"What do you expect me to think after getting intel like this on my best friend's girl?"

"We both know that accurate intel *always* depends on the source and the motive."

"I think you're missing the point."

"How?"

Brock cleared his throat. "Does it even matter who took the pictures?"

"The mistake you're making is focusing on the wrong questions."

"So what're the right questions?"

"You need to figure it out."

Don't fall for the spider webbing. "I focus on solutions."

Patti smirked like she didn't believe him. "You focus on what's best for you. Isn't that what you've done in the past?"

Keep her talking. He scowled, feigning confusion. "What?"

"Tell me something," Patti said. "In the infamous words of Dr. Phil, 'How's that working for you?' "

Don't take the bait. Go back to identifying with her.

A shout echoed somewhere outside the hotel. Brock whipped around toward the sound.

Patti's mother, a slightly plumper, shorter version of her daughter, ran to the passenger's side of the car, gripping the hands of her two small grandsons.

"Hey, baby!" Mrs. Lipsett yelled. "Get out of that car and give your other momma a great big hug."

Patti tried to smile when she nudged Brock, her face paler than the mocha brown it usually was. "You'd better go before she drags you out of the car."

No sooner had Brock parked and reached the sidewalk than he was engulfed in a hug, wrapped in six arms. Two pairs of arms encircled his legs and one pair held his neck so tight he could smell Mrs. Lipsett's ample spray of Dior perfume.

"You have no idea how much my husband and I prayed for you boys to return home safely." Tears welled up in Mrs. Lipsett's heavily black-lined eyes. "I even had my deaconess board praying for each of you by name. And when Pang was shot—" She clutched her large chest. "I hit my knees and cried out to the Father. Praise Jesus! Pang's hanging on by a thread, but he's still alive. And thank goodness you're healthy and looking as fine as ever."

Brock kissed the older lady on her papery cheek. "Thank you for thinking of us. It means a lot. You're looking just as young and love-ly as usual, ma'am." He then scooped up the boys. They giggled, squirming their way back down to the sidewalk and running to hide behind their grandmother.

When Patti got out of the car, the boys ran to her outstretched arms. "Brock is in a rush to get somewhere. We're going to have to let him get going."

"That's fine, sweetheart, we understand." Mrs. Lipsett beamed at Brock so hard that lipstick stuck to her front teeth. "We'll see you for a lovely private dinner at the rooftop restaurant at 6:00 p.m. this evening," she said. "When Patti mentioned getting together, I booked our reservations first thing this morning. I was even able to hire one of their personal sushi chefs. It'll be delightful."

"He's got other plans, Mom." Patti rocked from one foot to the oth-er. "Brock won't be able to make it."

"I will not take no for an answer," Mrs. Lipsett frowned and ran a hand through her curly salt-and-pepper hair. "I pulled a lot of strings in a short time. I did the impossible. Don't worry," she said. "I plan to have cocktails and dinner with you and the boys. Then I'll let the two of you have your time. I realize you have catching up to do, and the boys need to get to bed on schedule." She nodded and rubbed her palms together as if the matter was settled.

"Oh, no. There must be some kind of misunderstanding." Brock smiled at Mrs. Lipsett and reached to tickle the boys. "I fully intend to join your family for dinner tonight. I've cleared my schedule. I wouldn't miss our time together for anything."

Mrs. Lipsett clapped her hands. "Wonderful. Then it's settled, Brock, darling. I can't wait to play catchup and reminisce about old times. I want to hear all about your wonderful parents and why you're not married yet. We have so much to talk about." She turned to her daughter. "Don't we, sweetheart?"

Patti gave a nervous laugh. "Uh-huh."

"We do have a lot to talk about," Brock said and stared at Patti. "And I can hardly—wait."

CHAPTER 16

Brock was beginning the drive back to his hotel when his phone rang.

"Hey, bro, I slept in, but I just heard your message," Shuggs said. "You okay?"

"Yeah, how about you? Everything alright?"

"I'm fine."

"Good."

"Where're you?"

"Had errands to run." Brock made the turn onto his hotel's street. "I'm almost back."

"Meet me in the parking lot. I'll update you."

He hung up and drove into the lot minutes later, where Shuggs was leaning against his car.

Brock rolled down his window. "So?"

"Where's the picture of Pang?"

Brock reached into his jacket and searched for the folded paper but couldn't find it. He quickly rummaged through the car, but still no picture. *Did Patti take it?* "I don't know what happened to it."

Shuggs frowned. "Mind if I ride with you, bro?"

"Ride where?"

"The boss lady wants to see us in her office. Pronto."

Brock nodded and opened the lock. "She contacted you?"

Raising an eyebrow, Shuggs got into the car. "Bro, she came by the hotel looking for us."

"I don't understand. I called her this morning but never heard back."

"She got your call." Shuggs popped a few pieces of nicotine gum in his mouth. "That's why she stopped by. Said she'd prefer to talk to us together. In person."

"Are you going to tell me why?"

"I don't know," he said, shrugging. "My guess is we're in trouble."

"For?"

"No idea." Shuggs fiddled with the radio controls until he found a news station. "It'll probably be Dr. Harper's parting gift to us before we're gone for good."

"I can't imagine what we'd be blamed for."

"C'mon, that's how she ropes us in," Shuggs said.

"What?"

"You know how she does." He shook his head. "She'll soften you up, then—bam! The woman will flip on you faster than the devil."

"Dr. Harper's not so terrible. Cut her some slack. She's been through a lot herself."

"C'mon, are you kidding me? We're leaving the agency because of her."

"It's not like she doesn't care," Brock said. "Besides, she pulled strings for us to get jobs at the bureau."

"I still don't trust her."

"Why?"

"The woman is more calculating than an accountant. There was probably something in it for her when she worked a deal with the FBI for us," Shuggs said. "Dr. Harper lives life like a chess champion."

"That's too bad." Brock's frown vanished, replaced by a smile. "I was beginning to think you thought she had a heart."

Brock and Shuggs shared a laugh. They continued to make small talk over the hum of the news broadcaster while they drove to 2430 East Street NW. Dr. Harper's office at the Washington, DC, CIA headquarters was the only one the public knew of.

The men cleared security and headed to the receptionist area. Then they were sent to a conference room where they'd been scheduled to meet. When Dr. Harper walked in, her face was all business. "Let me get this straight, Brock. This morning you were given a picture of Pang, which was taken of him in his hospital room and your car was vandalized?"

Brock knew from her tone something was off. "Yeah, something like that."

She leaned forward, her hands clasped. "Tell me. What happened?"

"There was this picture, which was really a photocopy of a picture,

79

folded and placed between my wipers—"

Dr. Harper extended her hand. "I would like to see this photocopied picture."

Heat flooded Brock's neck. In all his years of collecting intel, this had almost never happened to him. *If I had a mirror, I bet I'd see that my ears are hot pink.* "I can't find it at the moment, but I'll continue to look. I'm sure it'll turn up."

She stared at him and took a seat. "Are there any further details you would like to contribute?"

He shifted in his chair. "Yeah, I noticed my car had been opened after I'd locked it the night before."

"I see." Dr. Harper took off her glasses and rubbed her eyes. "And was there anything missing from the vehicle or anything suspicious to report?"

"I checked my car thoroughly, and it appeared intact," Brock said. "But my guess is between the twisted photo and the break-in, the perp did this to send me a message and to—"

"Enough speculation," she said. "You see, here is the other issue. The one related to Pang's attempted murder by poisoning. We need to figure out who did it."

"Yeah, see, I've been wondering about that myself. If there's round-the-clock security, then how'd someone get into Pang's room without anyone noticing?" Brock asked.

Dr. Harper twisted her wedding ring. "I've been checking my sources, and the only listed visitors were the three of us."

The atmosphere in the room was suddenly charged.

"What about Patti?" Shuggs leaned back in his chair.

"She never made it onto the list." Dr. Harper rolled up her sleeves. "As you may recall, Patricia arrived *after* Pang was poisoned. She did not come close to the victim. Therefore, Patricia is not listed on the visitors screening list."

"What else did your sources say?" Shuggs asked.

"They confirmed someone effectively hacked our secure system."

"I thought they'd already figured that out," Brock said.

"It *was* a speculation," she turned and stared at Brock, "and now it *is* confirmed."

Shuggs leaned forward. "Do they know who?"

"Again, the answer is no. But there are reasons to believe whoever it is, is affiliated with a hate group."

What in the world? Brock clenched his teeth, the thought sickening him. "So they're extremists?"

Dr. Harper nodded. "Indeed. They are. The issue is we need to separate both of you from the possible list of suspects. It does not look good that each time Pang has been attacked, you have both been present."

Shuggs pushed away from the table. "C'mon, this is finger-pointing."

"How is this finger-pointing?" Dr. Harper said. "They are *observations,* facts, things the agency has legitimate concerns about. As should we."

"We're the people who've put our lives on the line," Shuggs spoke gruffly. "I'm getting sick of this crap."

Dr. Harper tilted her head, considering Shuggs's outburst. "Listen to me." The red line of her mouth disappeared. "Each of you has reputable bureau jobs lined up. But between the barroom attack and Pang's poisoning, the agency's oversight committee has been raising red flags. It would be best if you heed counsel."

"Is that the reason you wanted to meet with us?" Brock asked. "To figure out what we need to—"

"C'mon, bro, can't you see what's really going on here?" Shuggs drummed the table. "Instead of someone investigating the hospital staff, we're the suspects."

Brock turned to Dr. Harper. "Is this true?"

"As far as the agency is concerned, everyone, *including* hospital personnel, is considered a suspect."

"With all due respect, it feels like we're the ones in trouble," Shuggs said.

"Do you believe *you* are in trouble?"

"Yes. Yes, I do."

"Why is that?"

"Because after he," Shuggs pointed to Brock, "finds his car tampered with and a suspicious picture on the windshield, we're now being treated like the entire incident was somehow our fault."

"What makes you think that?" Dr. Harper said, arching her meticulously groomed brows. "And how did you make that jump in your logic?"

Shuggs shoved more nicotine gum into his mouth and wagged his finger. "I got a hunch."

"I am advising you both to remember that, as of this moment, I am *still* your supervisor. It continues to be my responsibility to make decisions benefiting our country, the agency, *and you.*"

Shuggs sighed. "Sure, but—"

She held up her ballpoint pen like a miniature sword. "There are instances when you may believe I am not acting on your behalf. But you fail to understand we are a small part of a large vision with great purpose. We are under the same scrutiny to which we subject others."

"Are we under scrutiny?" Brock said.

"There is an oversight committee who will have questions for you tomorrow." Her eyes narrowed. "Avoid disclosing anything you do not have proof of—less is more."

"Exactly what would you like for us to say?" Shuggs asked as he picked up a pen from a container on the table and used it to gesture. "Please, tell us."

She straightened and pulled in her custom pinstriped jacket, her eyes sharp. "It is a fact that what lawyers and intelligence agents do, when we must, is lie about our careers for the benefit of *our* country. For most of my life, I have stood by the philosophy that the lies we tell to protect the truth are simply a path to the greater good." Dr. Harper took a sip of water from her lead crystal tumbler and sat back. "That is my counsel to you."

Brock wiped his forehead after hearing his work described in that way. It wasn't entirely untrue.

Shuggs folded his arms. "It's the same song and dance even up until the very moment we're about to leave the agency."

"That is offensive and reprehensible," Dr. Harper said. "I absolutely refute that."

"I'm just speaking my mind. Man, I feel like that whenever there's a loose end," he threw his pen on the table, "then somehow, you use us to tie everything up into a neat bow. How convenient."

She shook her head. "What you are saying is untrue and unfounded."

"I hope so." Shuggs frowned. "Because if the agency really believes that about us, shame on them."

"It is unfortunate you feel that way, but shame is for the guilty," she said.

Brock locked eyes with Dr. Harper. He felt something flicker between them—the flame of a vow, a fire of hope for justice, for Pang.

CHAPTER 17

Both of you know I am not one to circumvent a matter." Dr. Harper tilted her head. "Is that not correct?"

"Yeah, sure," Brock said.

Shuggs folded his arms in front of his chest. "True."

"My apologies in advance for being only slightly off-subject as we wrap up this meeting." Dr. Harper drained her glass and checked her watch. "Help me answer a hypothetical question."

Shuggs glared at the ceiling.

"Sure," Brock said.

"Do you believe we will have a time in America when racism is nonexistent?" she asked.

Brock swallowed. "Ma'am, that's a loaded question." The term *racism* didn't come close to describing the terrors of growing up where he did, how he did. Her words triggered the flash of a childhood memory buried in a closet of his mind. One he pushed back until it was so far away that on most days, he could pretend it didn't exist ... until now.

Dr. Harper ran her hand across the edge of her linen collar and spoke without waiting for another answer. "I think the real issue is power. Too many people believe they have something to lose if *everyone* is considered equal."

"You really believe that?" Shuggs asked.

"Absolutely. I do," she said and stood, snapping her briefcase shut.

Dr. Harper's secretary, a harried, tightly wound woman, barged in. Juggling a fresh tumbler of water and a stack of paperwork, she marched toward her boss. "The gentlemen for your lunch meeting are here."

"Let them know I shall be there momentarily." Dr. Harper slipped the papers into her briefcase, dismissed her secretary with a nod, and turned back to Brock and Shuggs. "Remember to plan on being called in sometime tomorrow morning as the review board wants to speak with you. But you know how they are. They like the element of surprise."

Brock and Shuggs drove back to their hotel. The chatter from the radio providing white noise against the backdrop of silence.

After parking in the hotel's lot, Brock turned toward Shuggs. "Everything okay?"

"Just thinking."

"What'd you think about Dr. Harper's closing remarks today?"

"Which part?"

"The part about racism."

He shrugged. "Wouldn't matter if you shipped all the racists to their own separate planets." Shuggs unbuckled his seatbelt. "There'd still be racism."

"With my background, I think it's safe to say that people really are that hateful."

"We are."

"Yeah, we have our biases," Brock said. "Even when we think we're open-minded." He looked at his hands. "I'm not perfect either. I still have issues I struggle with and need to work through."

"C'mon, bro, you'd be a fool to think biases don't come from all sides and colors."

"Sure, but I think racism is about something else other than exercising hatred toward others."

"Like what?" Shuggs said, looking unconvinced.

"I believe it's about who has power—" Out of the corner of his eye, Brock saw an elderly African American man walk toward his car and knock on the passenger side.

"Can you fellows spare a little change?" His raspy voice rattled through the closed window.

Shuggs froze, grimacing the minute he saw the man.

Brock waved him over to the driver's side. After rolling his window down, he handed him a few singles money.

The man pocketed the money. "God bless you, young man," he said, filling the car with the rank odor of sweat and the city streets before shuffling off toward the hotel's dumpsters.

"See there." Shuggs pointed to the elderly man sifting through piles of garbage. "He's a perfect example of why racism *isn't* about power," he said.

"How's that?"

"He's probably going to use your money to buy booze or drugs."

Brock looked across the lot. The man talked to himself before he bit into a half-eaten sandwich, then guzzled the rest of a discarded soda.

"Maybe life just cut him a raw deal," Brock said as he rubbed his jaw. "Recently, I read that three in ten adults have no emergency savings. Fact is, a lot of us are only one paycheck from being homeless."

"I ain't buying it." Shuggs shook his head. "We all got the power to change, to do and become whatever it is we put our minds to. See, it's like my redneck daddy used to say, 'You can't get no lard if you don't boil the hog.' "

"Some people don't have a hog," Brock said.

Shuggs wagged his finger. "People need to use their power to improve, not take handouts. Now my daddy was tight as a tick and grew up broke as a stick horse. But he worked to provide well for his family. See now, that's what counts."

"Yeah, but it's not only about power. It's also about who has access to it." Brock took a deep breath. "Who knows how much that man was knocked down by life's circumstances?"

"We all have to take our licks from life. It's easy to make a bunch of excuses. I don't care what color you are; it's about toughening up and building the life you want."

"I'm *not* talking about people who make excuses and don't try. I'm referring to those with genuine setbacks and hardships," Brock said, his mind traveling back to the diverse neighborhoods his parents chose to raise him in. "No denying that sometimes women, the disabled veterans, and minorities have their own set of challenges in schools, the workplace, and the marketplace. Even the healthcare system has its barriers." He looked out the window to where the homeless man stood at a distance but close enough to see he was between a grove of trees and a set of dumpsters. Brock gestured to the homeless man, who appeared to be arguing with a nearby tree between bites of his scrounged-up meal. "He may've needed mental health support or treatment for another illness and didn't have resources or the insurance to—"

"C'mon, are you kidding me?"

"No. I'm not." Brock shifted in his seat, feeling red fingers of heat crawl up both sides of his face. His jaw tightened, thinking of Patti and her sons. "The fact of the matter is, not everyone has equal access to power."

"Bro, we got too much in common to disagree about things like this," Shuggs said. "We're both from the same side of the fence, *and* we're friends."

"So?"

"We got nothing to argue about."

"Is that supposed to blind us to injustice?" Brock asked.

"How can you ask me that when you see what's in front of you?" He jerked his head toward the beggar. "We get what's coming to us, what we work for and deserve. You and I understand that because we're the same."

"But should our sameness make us apathetic to people who're different?"

"I don't know why we can't see eye to eye on this." Shuggs's eyes darkened. "I'm just pointing out that we're on the same team."

"Okay," Brock said, frowning.

"You believe we're on the same team?" He raised a brow. "Right, bro? Speak the truth."

Brock shrugged.

Shuggs put his hand on the door's handle and shoved open the passenger's side. "You lost me, man. Besides, I'm not in the mood for an argument with *you* of all people."

"Sure," Brock said, suddenly feeling exhausted. "We can talk later."

"It isn't something I feel like debating," Shuggs said. "Okay, bro?"

"Yeah, okay." Brock nodded.

"I'll catch up to you in the morning." Shuggs exited the car and made his way to the hotel's entrance.

Brock leaned forward, hunched over the steering wheel, catching a glimpse of the beggar arguing with two officers who'd just arrived. One of the officers cuffed the elderly man and tossed him into a patrol car. Brock's gaze met the beggar's when the officers pulled up beside his car to exit the lot.

The older man's face cracked open in a childlike smile, then he was gone.

Brock's thoughts punched through his mind knowing the officers would drive the homeless man to the county lockup.

CHAPTER 18

T he fresh autumn air felt good on Brock's skin as he walked to his hotel room. He kicked up a pile of red and orange leaves and inhaled deeply, staring at the tree the beggar had been talking to just minutes ago. There was always a smell on the streets in Washington, no matter the time of year or the weather. Brock had come to associate the gritty, metal stench with a freshly lit match. A sign the city teetered on the verge of going up in smoke.

"Afternoon, Mr. O'Reilly."

Brock looked up. Two men walked toward him from the hotel's back entrance. His first impulse was to say something flippant, like, "No, the name's Batman." But he knew the higher-level types from the agency wouldn't find him funny. "Who's asking?" he said instead.

A pale, sickly-looking man, who looked like he was a six-foot twelve-year-old (already showing signs of obesity) with glasses thicker than a windshield, stuck his hand out. "Agent Berkley."

The agent's partner resembled a hip Santa Claus with tanned leathery skin. An uneven tuft of white hair sprouted from the crown of his head, blending with his sideburns and wisp of a beard. "My name is Dexter. Agent Dexter," he said, offering his hairy hand.

His name might be Dexter, but it'll be Santa Claus in my mind from now on. Brock looked over his shoulder and checked the empty lot, spilling the rest of his coffee on the pavement. "Just cut to the chase," he said in between cussing under his breath. "What do you want?"

Santa Claus gave Brock a look that told him he'd better check his tone.

"Look. I'm sorry." Brock glanced at his watch. "It's already been a long day, and it's only 2:00 p.m. I didn't expect you to be here."

"Really?" Agent Berkley adjusted his glasses.

"The fact of the matter is," Brock said, "Dr. Harper insinuated that we'd probably meet with you tomorrow."

Santa flashed his badge and a smile that was far from warm. "We're all agency folks here. We understand how to be flexible. Right, son?"

"Sure," Brock said, trying not to flinch in reaction to the agent's patronizing tone.

"Would you mind if we joined you in your room for a quick sit-down?" Berkley asked.

"No." Brock shook his head and took out his hotel key. He knew the agent's question was a formality. His hotel room was rented by the agency and considered fair game as a plausible meeting space.

When Brock opened the lock and pushed open the door, the first thing he felt was the waft of cold air. The window was opened about five inches, and the curtains were pulled wide apart, not closed as he'd left them. His eyes scanned the bed. It was unevenly jammed against the wall, with the covers dumped on the floor. His suitcase had been moved from one side of the room to the other. Whoever had broken into his room wanted him to know they definitely weren't housekeeping.

"Everything good, son?" Santa asked.

Brock stared at the agent's faces, carefully monitoring their reactions. He wasn't used to dealing with NCTC (National Counterterrorism Center) personnel. They were another component of DNI (Office of the Director of National Intelligence). These guys often reported directly to the Oval Office. Everything he said and did from this point on was gasoline or water on the fire of suspicion. "No, this place is a disaster," Brock said. "And I didn't leave it that way."

"Don't worry." Berkley eyeballed the mess. "We just need a few minutes of your time."

"What I'm telling you is I didn't create this mess," Brock said. "Someone broke in."

"That's a problem. We're going to have to relocate you and your partner." Santa frowned. "Clearly, the other team wants you to know they're watching you."

Berkley began walking around the room taking pictures. "After we're done here, we'll have our folks come and dust for prints. Give this place a shakedown for clues." He pushed a few buttons on his phone. "I've alerted our offices. Within the hour, someone from our office will contact you with details of the alternate location where you'll be staying for the next few nights. Security is on their way here to shadow you until further notice."

A rush of relief flooded through Brock's body. "Thanks."

"Mind if we sit down?" Santa asked, already making himself comfortable in the desk chair.

"Make yourselves at home." Brock pulled up the hotel's two armchairs so he and the other agent could sit down.

The three men positioned themselves into a semicircle, with Brock facing the desk. That's when he saw the small photograph of him and his parents taken when he'd first entered the agency, the photo he traveled with everywhere. Only his face had been ripped from the picture.

"Do you know where Agent Shuggs is at this time?" Berkley asked.

What. The. Heck. Brock racked his brain. *Who would've tampered with that photo? For what reason? And who moved it?*

"Son?"

Brock's head snapped around to look at Santa.

"Agent Shuggs. Know where he is?"

An odor stopped him from speaking. He choked, realizing after a few seconds that the smell of panic was coming from his own armpits. "Yeah, he's probably in his room down the hall." Brock gestured toward the general direction of Shuggs's room. "Just dropped him off a little while ago."

"No. We went to his room first," Berkley said. "He's not there and he's not answering his phone."

"Then I don't know where he is." Brock's chest constricted, wondering where Shuggs could be.

Berkley wrote something on a notepad. "No problem."

Brock cleared his throat. He pointed out the altered photo. "My picture wasn't like that when I left this morning. I left it on the nightstand where I always keep it."

The agents stared at the picture in silence.

Santa fished a pair of gloves from his pocket and plucked the framed photo from the desk. He put on a pair of glasses and examined it closely. "These people, who are they?"

"It's a photo of me with my parents. My face has been ripped out."

"I can see that." Santa arched a bushy white brow. "What do you suppose this means?"

Brock shrugged. "I was hoping you'd help me shed some light on what's going on."

"This is most definitely a message to you, Brock." Santa looked around the room. "What are they trying to say?"

"Looks like someone's trying to scare me."

Berkley took off his glasses and wiped them against his shirt. "Figuring out a message has everything to do with the messenger." He put his glasses back on. "Any idea who'd be after you?"

"My guess is it's a radicalized left-wing group," Brock said. "Maybe inspired by racial tensions."

"Why would you say that?" asked Berkley. "Those are serious allegations."

"The reason I'm saying this is because of the riots and protests that were taking place in the area when the shooting took place. The shooters were all black, and the victims were all white."

Santa stroked his beard. "Understood. I'm sorry this has happened to you. I imagine this must be troubling, especially since you lost colleagues. And now one of them is gravely injured."

Brock nodded. "What's the agency doing in regard to Pang's attack?"

"Ah, yes. At present, we have an aggressive investigation put together." Santa clasped his hands. "We have also increased security measures."

"Any leads?" Brock asked.

"There are a few things that have come up. But what we have are a lot of loose ends that don't seem to be adding up," Santa said. "Right now, we're working with the Joint Terrorism Task Force to figure things out."

"We'll have our people retrieve all the info we can from your hotel's security footage," Berkley said. "Now moving on." He opened a folder and showed it to Brock. "I know you know this man. My apologies for the redundancy."

Brock took a breath. "Yeah, of course. That's Agent Andrew Pang."

"Can you give us any details *not* already on the police report from the night he was shot?" Berkley wrote without looking up.

CHAPTER 19

Brock stared at the frayed bedspread lying crumpled on the hotel floor resembling a small body. He shuddered, remembering the infant in Mali and how he had discovered her folded like a dark secret in her mother's arms. He'd watched the child struggle to take her final breath.

She hadn't been the first. He had murdered other children. Innocent children. He'd ruined entire families, destroying their lives by taking their most vulnerable from them. Even if it was accidental, it was part of his job, his identity—killing to keep the peace. *I should've known something like this would've happened. Maybe this is karma. Payback from the universe for my many mistakes.*

Berkley coughed. "If you can't think of anything else to add to the report, it's fine. We can move on."

Brock rubbed his throbbing temples. "I'm sorry. I was thinking about something that happened on my last assignment." He cleared his throat. "The police report documents everything accurately," he said. "However, I swear, I heard three different shooters talking. They each had distinctive accents. All different. Yet only two shooters were found."

"Yes. And they were both killed." Berkley wrote. "We will follow up on that lead. That's vital information to have that there could be a possible suspect at large."

"Whoever it is could also be targeting Pang's family," Brock said.

"Is that so?" Santa leaned forward. "How do you know this?"

"Patricia. She told me."

"Tell me, how well do you know his wife?"

"Ex-wife." Brock lifted his head. "I know her well."

"As a friend?" Santa asked.

"Yeah. Nothing more."

Berkley nibbled the end of his pen. "Why were you late to a meeting you coordinated the night Pang was shot?"

"I had a meeting with Dr. Harper," Brock said evenly.

"Why do you have a prescription for heparin, son?"

Brock stared at the older agent. His heart was in his throat. *How'd they get that information?* "I no longer use it." Now he knew what they were doing. He and his team had done it numerous times. Establish a baseline of emotional responses through random questioning with a person of interest. Catch a perp off guard. Make them feel comfortable. Go back to making them feel discomfort, shock them. Compare behavior. He was an expert at the drill.

"But you used to?"

"Yeah. I had a clot in my lung last year. It was because I'd been caught in a severe dust storm while on assignment in the Middle East."

"You developed ..." Berkley squinted at his notes, "chronic coccidioidomycosis. What's commonly known as valley fever, correct?"

"Correct." Brock's mouth went dry. He wished he had some of the spilled coffee to wash down the bitterness in his mouth.

"You do realize Pang was poisoned *after* he was in the ICU?" Santa asked.

"Yeah. I was there that night."

Santa crossed his legs. "Did you know Pang was injected with a deadly dose of heparin?"

Brock opened his mouth, but Santa shook his head to stop him.

"It's a rhetorical question. We know Dr. Harper verified you never touched him or gave him anything. The real question is, why'd someone want Pang dead?"

Brock studied the stoic faces of the two agents before answering. "Your guess is as good as mine," he said. "Pang is my best friend, so I want the perp caught just as badly as you do. An enemy of Pang's is an enemy of mine."

Forming a steeple with his fingers, Santa sat back. He tapped Brock's headless photo. "It appears the perp is acting out toward you in a deeply emotional fashion."

"Which I don't understand," Brock said. "Sure, I've got a few jaded ex-girlfriends, but all my real enemies are overseas. For the life of me, I can't think of anyone here who has it in for me enough to threaten me in this way."

"Ah, yes. Indeed, but whenever we have a criminal acting on emotions, they're almost always wildcards," Santa said.

"A wildcard?" Brock asked.

Santa nodded. "A wildcard is someone who doesn't act on principles. Emotionally driven criminal behavior is unpredictable," Santa said. "This type is often violent."

"Don't underestimate this person." Berkley chewed the tip of his pen. "They're probably highly intelligent, likeable, and charismatic."

Brock frowned. "Would that rule out these attacks being racially motivated?"

"No. We believe you're probably right about this person's motivation. But you'll soon agree this is all complicated when presented with the facts." Santa shook his head. "It very well could be in the area of a hate crime. Which kind of hate crime?" He held his hands up. "We don't know for sure."

"The perp could've orchestrated the attack from afar," Berkley said. "He or she may even have some sort of emotional attachment to people in the agency."

"Yes, perhaps an outed agent fed up with the system wanting revenge for some perceived wrong?" Santa asked.

"I can't think of anyone in the agency who'd do this," Brock said. "We're a close community." He threw his hands up. "Heck, I've worked with the last crew for almost ten years. I'm a godfather to two of their kids, I've been a groomsman four times, and I've even been to one of their parent's funerals."

Berkley looked up from his notes. "Other profiles similar to this one show that a significant proportion of hate crimes are committed by perpetrators *known* to the victim."

"Then what's this person's profile looking like to you guys?" Brock asked.

"Let's look at what the data says first," Berkley said.

Brock raised a brow. "Yeah, sure. As long as you can help me get a clear picture of what kind of person we're looking for."

"A number of research studies show crimes motivated by hate aren't always motivated by a single type of prejudice but can be influenced by a combination of various prejudices," he said, peering over the top of his bifocals. "They can also be a product of their social environment, especially if the perp's characteristics allow them to leverage an advantage over others. They may feel a sense of latitude when victimizing others." Berkley glanced at Santa. "You want to add anything, Dexter?"

Santa nodded. "This kind of perp," he used his fingers to tick off his points, "they want to experience sheer excitement, they're defensive of their territory, they're retaliating for a perceived attack against their group, and/or they're on a mission to eradicate difference. You see, son, whoever this happens to be is influenced by their perception that certain groups pose a threat to them."

"I can't think of a single soul like that," Brock shook his head, "especially one who'd want to harm any of us."

"Most, if not all, hate crimes are linked by *perceptions* of threat," Santa said. "These threats can be linked to economic stability, access to resources, a sense of safety in society, and/or values and social norms."

"But who the heck here in the US would consider me to be a threat?" Brock asked. "This person could be someone with a vendetta from an overseas mission. They could be using other angles as a cover."

Santa leaned back and stroked his beard. He looked directly at Brock. "I get paid to see what others don't." He gestured to Brock. "So do you. Maybe it's time for you to look around and see what could be hiding in plain sight."

CHAPTER 20

W e have files with us on the two shooters." Berkley spoke in his careful monotone.

Brock turned to Berkley. "The ones killed at Rusti's the night of the attack?"

Berkley nodded.

He raised a brow. "That so?"

"Yes. They're quite extensive," Berkley said.

"Anything helpful in them?"

"I believe so."

"Go ahead, shoot," Brock said, leaning forward.

Berkley opened a thick binder. "Both men were raised in separate foster homes in different parts of New York City."

"They were never adopted?"

"No. After leaving foster care, they spent a good amount of time in and out of city and upstate detention centers." He looked up. "It gets a little more interesting after they joined a local boxing club in the Bronx, which is how they met." Berkley licked his upper lip. "The owner of the boxing club also owns an exclusive gentleman's club in the upper east side of Manhattan where they worked security. They played cards on Wednesdays with the mayor's bodyguards and—"

"Sure, I get it. They were black men from the rotten apple. They had screwed-up lives, probably victims of an imperfect and often crappy system," Brock said, contemplating the information. "Even so, it seems odd for two bouncers to travel across state lines, go rogue, and randomly shoot up a bar."

"Sometimes people act out of passion for a cause they believe in. In their case, they may've been angered by a specific incident or a turn of events," Santa said. "They could've purposely targeted a crowd that was predominantly white."

"Let's say these crazies were triggered and the shooting was racially motivated. It doesn't seem to fit the men's MO," Brock said.

Santa clasped his hands behind his head. "Perhaps there's more to their modus operandi than what we're seeing."

"Like what?"

He shrugged. "We're getting off track," Santa said to Brock. "We don't truly know what the exact motivation was for this shooting. We know the shooters had a reason for the attack. They had a criminal history and were once members of a gang. They *murdered* CIA agents. Those are the facts."

"Yeah, you're right." Brock gestured to Berkley. "What else do you think I need to know?"

"They worked off the books for both the boxing club and the strip club. They provided security, protecting the boxers during and after fights. At the strip joint, they protected the girls from aggressive customers."

"What about their criminal history?" Brock pointed to the binder. "What'd they do time for?"

"Both had rap sheets for armed robbery, carjacking, and illegal gun possession. Judging from the paper trail, it appears they had powerful connections." Berkley looked over his glasses. "Someone with money and plenty of influence. If they didn't, they would've been serving long prison sentences."

"Who'd they work for?" Brock asked. "Seems like we need to be talking to him."

"They worked for a man who goes by the name Uncle Buck." Berkley glanced at his notes. "The agency is continuing to investigate him. For now, we know his legal name is Tucker Buckler. He's African American, middle-aged. Owns a house with a white picket fence on Long Island. Golfs with the mayor on Saturdays. Attends Allen AME in Queens on Sundays. Married to a former beauty contestant. Has three kids. It's speculated he's laundering money through his businesses. But no one's ever been able to prove it. He's got excellent lawyers and accountants. Not to mention, we suspect he has friends in high places."

"What do you make of that?" Brock turned to Santa.

Santa lifted his chin a notch. "What do *you* make of it?"

"With this new information, I'm not sure what to believe." Brock bit his lip. "Is any of this adding up to you?"

"Not yet. But there's more," Santa said, pointing to the pile of papers on Berkley's lap. "We can connect Uncle Buck to the two dead men. He's been a father figure as well as their employer. That part makes sense. But we need to figure out how to connect the perps to the victims of their killing spree."

Brock nodded. "I still can't come up with a convincing motivation for them to carry out this attack."

"That's the wall we keep coming up against. These men were affiliated with a gang through their prison stints. But they didn't belong to an extremist group or adhere to any religion." Berkley looked down at his notes. "Which could contradict the theory that this was racially motivated."

"Tell me more about their gang involvement," Brock said.

"They belonged to a sect of the Bloods while in prison," Santa said. "But when inmates serve time at Rikers Island, they almost have to join a gang in order to survive. Their height, muscular builds, and intelligence helped them move up quickly in the gang's ranks. They worked as pseudo commanders while serving time at Rikers. Once they got out and began working for Uncle Buck, it appears their gang activity went underground. But we're sure they maintained ties as the Bloods' motto is 'Blood in, Blood out.' "

"What does that mean?"

"Once you join," Santa said. "You're in for life."

Brock stared at the ceiling. "Any intel on other people in their circle?"

"We're still in the process of gathering more data," Berkley said. "So far, we haven't found girlfriends, children, or spouses. We've about given up on grilling any of their old gang associates. The Bloods are tight-lipped. Snitching gets them killed. But one of the perps had two brothers."

"We know anything about them?" Brock asked.

"The younger of the two died several months ago. Shot to death."

"Shot by whom?"

"It's a cold case," Berkley said.

"What do the records say?"

"Records don't list a known suspect or conviction for the murder. The police report surmises the killing was possibly gang related." Berkley shook his head. "We haven't been able to locate the other brother. Sources say he disappeared after the bar attack. But he too worked at both clubs."

"These guys, have they ever come up on the FBI's radar?"

"No, they haven't," Santa said.

"What about Uncle Buck?"

Santa shook his head.

Berkley held up his forefinger. *"They* haven't, but an organization they've done business with a few times is on the FBI watch list."

"Business? What kind?"

"The perps provided security services for a suspicious organization named TWA. Could be they didn't realize they were working for TWA because they were recruited by a third party."

"You have a description of that organization?" Brock asked.

"It's a nonprofit providing educational resources." Berkley peered at a paper. "The education is dedicated to the heritage, identity, and future of people of European descent in the United States and around the world."

"In less polite language," Santa said, scowling, "TWA is a white power group."

"What do the letters stand for?"

Santa shrugged. "We don't know that TWA stands for anything in particular. According to the organization, it bears no significance and—"

"They're probably lying." Berkley stroked his chin. "Everything is significant in groups like that. We're still digging to figure out what TWA *really* means."

"Very true," Santa said, stroking his beard. "We do know that TWA is an educational nonprofit and is legally on the books as a 501(c)(3). Everything from that point on is vague. The perps provided security for TWA a few times and were paid in cash. However, most, if not all, of TWA's funding is through cryptocurrency, which doesn't transmit personally identifying information. This prohibits us from seeing who supports them."

"Why's TWA on the FBI's watch list?" Brock asked.

"It's an alt-right organization, which isn't illegal." Santa frowned. "But they're being watched because of their alliances with violent hate groups. The FBI suspects TWA is funneling money to these fringe factions. What also concerns us is that TWA has been able to raise millions of dollars through crowdfunding, speaking engagements, paraphernalia, and literature. Because of their 501 statuses, they don't have to pay federal taxes, and donors can take deductions on their personal taxes."

Berkley sniffed as if he'd smelled something foul. "In other words, the provision of a tax-exempt status carries an *implied* governmental approval of the organization's activities."

Santa looked down at the desk and ran his hands against the knotty wood. "Lately, with the racial tensions, protests, and whistleblowers, the feds have come under fire for giving financial privileges to groups that espouse a belief system now seen as fundamentally anti-American."

"Okay, now I'm beginning to understand." Brock nodded. "But how's Uncle Buck in the middle of everything?"

"From the paper trail it appears TWA went through another source to get Uncle Buck to hire the perps," Santa said. "That way, there would be no trail to TWA if they used the men for illicit activities."

"Why would Uncle Buck work with an organization like TWA if he's black?"

"According to our sources, the only color Uncle Buck really cares about is green." Santa folded his arms. "Again, it's possible that even if he knew it was TWA, he didn't realize what they were about."

"It still makes no sense. The perps were black men who'd been former gang members and ex-cons," Brock said. "TWA is a white supremacy organization." He shook his head. "The two don't mix. Why would TWA go out of their way to hire these guys when they could've gotten other white supremacists to do the job?"

"We're looking at an incomplete picture right now. Things will eventually fit together in a way we probably never imagined." Santa stood up and adjusted his Burberry overcoat, gesturing to Berkley that it was time to leave. "Once we get all the facts and connect them to what's happened ..." He smiled. "And we will, we'll figure this all out."

After Berkley and Dexter left his hotel room, Brock packed up his belongings and awaited further instructions. Then he sat motionless, listening to the pelting rain and staring at his butchered family photo. The roar of a vacuum in the next room jarred him from his musings, and he remembered Shuggs.

When he couldn't reach him by phone, Brock jogged down the hall to Shuggs's room. No one answered. But what appeared to be a bloody handprint stained the door. "Shuggs! Are you okay?" He banged on the door repeatedly, his heart racing. "It's me, Brock. Open up!"

The maid, who'd been vacuuming a few rooms down, stuck her head out into the hall. "Can I help you, mister?"

"Yeah, I'm a federal agent." Brock reached into his pocket and produced his badge. "I need this door opened. Now!"

The woman dropped her vacuum and ran to open the door for Brock. She backed away when Brock pulled out his service weapon.

He turned to her before going into the room. "You need to clear this area," Brock said, his voice low. "There might be trouble."

When he entered the dark room, the air was tainted with stale, burned-out cigarettes and bleach. Brock drew his service weapon and searched through the hotel room, but there was no sign of foul play or of his friend. The blue lights of a blinking computer screen caught his eye. Brock bent over and stared at the monitor. His hands moved swiftly across the keyboard, tapping the keys to read what popped up. It appeared that Shuggs had begun writing an email but never finished. In the body of the email were the words "Abort mission." The subject line of the abandoned draft read "TWA."

This is weird. His fingers dug into both sides of his head. He tried to focus his thoughts while the rush of endorphins kicked in. *I've got to call Dr. Harper.* Brock dialed her line, but his call went to voicemail. He repeatedly called before finally leaving a message. Brock tried Shuggs's phone a few times, but he got no answer. He then took pictures of the room and handprint, which he sent to Dr. Harper. Brock pulled Shuggs's door closed and hurried down the hall, wiping beads of sweat that'd formed on his brow.

By the time Brock returned to his room, he was soaked with perspiration. His clothing clung to his body like wet wrinkled skin. He decided to pack his car while he waited for the security team and grabbed his bag, knocking something off the desk. Brock's shoulders stiffened when he picked up the overturned frame and stared at his headless photo. *I do feel like I'm losing my head.*

A sudden sting crippled his grip on the cracked frame. In agony, Brock dropped the picture onto the desk. Opening his clenched fist revealed pieces of glass embedded in his hand. Brock squeezed the fragments from his fingers and sucked the bloody wounds. He cleaned the cuts and wrapped them with bandages he kept in his toiletry bag. This he could handle because he could *see* the problem. But the past few hours had left him in a blinding storm of uncertainty. He'd been grilled by senior agents who had more information than he did but were plagued with questions of their own. His coworkers were dead. Men he'd considered friends. Pang, his best friend, a man who was the closest he'd ever come to having a brother, still fought death's punishing stranglehold. And now his other close friend, Shuggs, was missing.

CHAPTER 21

A knock on the door jolted Brock from his thoughts. "Agent O'Reilly, I'm your security detail here to provide assistance to your next location," a deep voice with a slight Hispanic accent said.

Brock checked the peephole. Seeing the badge, he opened the door with a steady hand on his Glock.

A giant of a man towered before him. His thick hair was pulled back neatly into a ponytail. His muscles protruded through his padded leather jacket like he'd been chiseled from a hunk of black granite. He wore danger like a cloak and had a brilliant white smile. He stuck out his hand. "Collin Gentry, sir. Pleased to be working with you."

Brock shook the man's massive, outstretched hand and stepped back into the room. "Be out in just a minute."

"Take your time." Gentry nodded and reclined against the wall beside Brock's room. His massive frame cast a wide shadow on the hallway floor. "I'll be right here waiting for you."

Brock went to the bathroom and splashed frigid water on his face. He ran a hand through his damp hair, giving the room a quick once-over for anything he may've missed packing. He'd already closed the drapes, blocking the afternoon's late sunlight. It might as well have been midnight.

He picked up his duffel bag, slung his briefcase over his shoulder, and headed to the door. Before exiting the hotel room, he reached into his jeans and took his cell out of his pocket. Brock tried reaching Shuggs, then Dr. Harper. Still no answer. He checked his messages. Nothing. *There must be a logical explanation for Shuggs's disappearance.* His chest tightened, trying to ease from his mind the image of Pang lying in the ICU and the bloody handprint on Shuggs's door. The images ignited his latent rage. He took a breath. *I'll get to the bottom of this. No matter what, I'll find out who attacked us and harmed my friends. I will avenge them. That's what I do.*

With his hand on the doorknob, Brock's phone vibrated, pulling him back to the present. He didn't recognize the number on the caller ID. That had to mean it was someone from the agency.

"O'Reilly, are you safe?" A familiar monotone voice asked.

"Yeah, is that you, Ber—"

"Don't say anything. Just listen." Berkley spoke quickly. "There's a man outside your door known as Snake. He's an armed and extremely dangerous member of a black militia. Snake's impersonating Agent Gentry. Stand your ground and don't go anywhere with him. Await backup."

"Is that someone from the agency calling?" the man outside Brock's door asked.

"No, it's a telemarketer," Brock lied.

"Everything else okay in there, sir? I was told you'd be ready to leave." Snake's voice thundered through the door.

Brock had worked up an instant sweat, but he willed himself to stay calm. "Yeah, man, I'm so sorry. I had some bad clams last night, and I'm paying the price for it. Bear with me. I got one more run to the bathroom, and I'll be right out."

"No worries, sir," Snake said, relief in his tone. "I'm not going nowhere."

"Thanks. I can't wait to get out of here." Brock closed his eyes for a second. *Think. What should I do?* He swallowed and opened his eyes to pale-yellow light bathing the area below the curtains. *Yes, it'd have to be through the window.* His room was only on the second floor. Brock dropped his duffel bag and secured his briefcase firmly across his body. Running to the bathroom, Brock made as much noise as he could.

Each time he flushed the toilet, he tiptoed to the window and eased the sill up enough for his body to get through the opening. Looking down, he calculated a drop of about twenty-five feet. Thankfully, there were tall bushes surrounding the building, which he knew would soften his landing. With luck, he'd be able to clear the window, land in the bushes, and creep through the lot to his car.

Brock was wedging his body through the window when the sound of gunfire from the hallway hyped him up to make the jump. He shoved off using his right leg to thrust himself off the floor and over the ledge just as the hotel room's door crashed open. Brock felt the tendons in his legs tighten and pull as he plummeted to the ground. A black rush of pain tore through his body as he landed on his hands and knees.

The jump hadn't been bad, but the previous cuts on his now bruised hand opened back up wider than before. Both legs of his jeans were torn open at the knee. Blood was flowing from his raw hands and scraped legs while he limped toward his car in a tortured run. Blasts of gunfire at his back made him stumble forward. He fell onto the hood of another car and rolled behind it for cover. Peering through the car's back window, Brock tried to catch his breath while Snake angled his assault rifle in Brock's direction.

Brock kept his eyes trained on Snake as he retrieved his Glock from his ankle strap. Snake used the scope on his gun to scour the parking lot for his victim.

Crouching, Brock leaned against the car and tried rebandaging his gushing wound. He closed his eyes when Snake let off a round of shots, blowing out the tires of the car next to him.

Brock checked for his car. It was still intact a few feet away. His limbs began to ache from his jump, but he had to get to safety. He got onto his stomach, his breathing sidling up a level with each movement, and army-crawled to the passenger's side of his vehicle. Brock gently pried the car's door open and slid his bruised body inside. He had just gotten the key in the ignition when a blast took out the glass on the passenger's side. Brock threw the briefcase in the back seat and peaked up through a bottom corner of the windshield.

Snake had his gun trained on him.

Brock ducked and contorted his body, bending across the console and into the driver's seat. He kept his body hunkered down.

Another wave of gunfire took out the driver's side rear window.

Stretching his muscles to the max, Brock aimed his gun at Snake and returned fire through the broken passenger's side window. He then put the car in reverse and his foot on the gas. He drove the car backward away from the torrent of fire blasting from the window.

A stray bullet ripped through a parked van in Brock's path, and it exploded in a burst of flames.

Brock maneuvered quickly, narrowly missing waves of fiery gases blowing pieces of the decimated vehicle all over the lot. He kept his body tight and low, managing to reverse onto the main road to the sound of tires screeching.

Motorists in the oncoming traffic scrambled to avoid his swerving car as Brock skidded through the intersection and raced through a red light.

The rush hour traffic had begun in the city. After a few minutes, a cluster of cars soon surrounded Brock. He exhaled when his cell phone rang. It was Berkley again.

"The hotel is now secured, and Snake has fled. The *real* Agent Gentry is on location to help you to safety. Are you okay?"

"Yeah, I'm peachy," Brock said.

"Where are you?"

"I couldn't wait. I'm on the move."

"Are you hurt?"

Brock wiped the bloody steering wheel with his shirt. "No, I'm good."

"Meet us at the safe house in twenty minutes."

"What safe house?" Brock asked.

"You'll figure it out," Berkley said.

Brock felt a growing sense of dread. Berkley and Dexter had never discussed a safe house with him. Just then, his cell phone rang. "Yeah, who's this?"

"Return to the restaurant you were at this morning and ask for table ten," a stranger's voice said before the line went dead.

What the heck is happening? Who'd been following him? Brock's cell rang again. He slammed on his brakes, nearly hitting the taxi in front of him when he saw the number on the caller ID.

"Where're you, Shuggs?"

Shuggs cleared his throat. "I'm at the hospital, bro. Can you help me? I need a ride back to the hotel."

"Yeah, of course," Brock said breathlessly. "My God, did Snake get you?"

"Who?"

"Never mind," Brock said. "Are you at County?"

"No, come to the medical center."

"Where Pang is?"

"Yes, I'm at the ER." Shuggs's voice sounded weak. "I'm waiting to be discharged."

Brock nodded and made a sudden U-turn. "I'm on my way."

CHAPTER 22

Brock pulled up to the medical center, wondering if he needed to admit himself to the ER. A thin puddle of blood had trickled onto his lap from beneath the bandage over the gaping wound on his hand. The floor beneath his feet squished and crackled. Sweat, blood, and glass had accumulated on the mat from the blown windows and injuries sustained from his second-story jump.

He dialed Shuggs. "I'm out front."

When Shuggs opened the car door, he froze and stared at the splintered glass. "I thought I had it bad," he said, brushing off his seat and getting into the car. "What in the world happened to you today?"

"You've seen me look worse." Brock pulled away from the curb. He headed to the hotel, giving his friend a sideways glance. "You look like crap yourself. What happened and where've you been for the last few hours?"

"Bro, it's complicated." Shuggs stretched his neck muscles. "First, tell me why you look like hell warmed over."

"You missed the special agents assigned to interview us. They showed up at the hotel right after I dropped you off."

Shuggs opened his cell phone and checked the screen. "Okay, so those must've been the calls I missed. I thought they were supposed to do that tomorrow at Dr. Harper's office."

"You know how they like to operate. Show up when you least expect it," Brock said. "Anyway, they were looking for you and ended up speaking with me in my room. Problem is, my room had been ransacked."

"They take anything?"

"Nothing was missing. But whoever broke in ripped my face out of that photograph I take with me everywhere."

"That's strange," Shuggs said. "Probably trying to send you a message."

"Yeah, that's exactly what I think." Brock frowned. "The special agents who met with me assigned security detail with an escort to another location. After they left, I went to your room and found a bloody handprint on your door and no one inside."

"Bro, I'm sorry. I was so upset about a personal situation that I punched a hole in the bathroom wall and busted up my hand." Shuggs held up his bandaged hand. "Grabbed an Uber to the ER to get some stitches."

"Why didn't you tell me?" Brock asked. "I could've driven you."

"I was embarrassed. Didn't know how to tell you what a mess of things I'd made," Shuggs said. "But go ahead and finish telling me what happened to you."

"I was about to leave with whom I *thought* was my security escort." Brock breathed deeply. "Then I get a call from a special agent warning me that an imposter came to pick me up and to fend him off until backup arrived."

"No freaking way."

Brock wiped a bead of sweat from his brow. "I stalled the guy and escaped through the window just as he broke down the door and started firing at me."

Shuggs looked around at the inside of the vehicle. "He sure did a number on the car. Seems like a close call."

"They told me his name is Snake," Brock said.

"He's got to be long gone by now."

"Yeah, they told me Snake already fled the scene. Besides, they sent people from the agency to escort me to another hotel. You'll need to be moved too. But for now, I've got to meet with the special agents again. They're waiting for me to fill them in about Snake."

"I'll pack up and return their calls," Shuggs said. "See what they want me to do."

"What's going on with you?" Brock rubbed his throbbing temples. "What personal situation has you punching holes in walls?"

Shuggs closed his eyes for a moment. "Bro, I've been living a nightmare."

Brock turned to Shuggs. "Are you okay, man?"

"No. I'm not okay."

"What's up?"

He rolled his shoulders back. "I'm being blackmailed," Shuggs said.

"Blackmailed? By who?"

Shuggs stuffed a piece of nicotine gum into his mouth. "My ex."

"Which one?"

"The last one."

"So your ex-wife, Cindy, the twins' mother, is blackmailing you."

Shuggs nodded. "She's using stuff she knows to bribe me," he said and sighed. "Threatened to take away my visitation rights. Turn my girls against me."

"How would she be able to do that?"

"Cindy knows things."

"Like what?" Brock asked.

"Personal things."

"I'm listening."

Shuggs avoided Brock's steady gaze and cradled his head. "Cindy knows I've been running my own intel on Patti—"

"Patricia Pang?"

Shuggs nodded.

"Okay, let's figure this out." Brock ran a hand across his jaw, his mind racing. "You could take the stance that you were a concerned friend," he said. "Tell her you had suspicions and wanted to check out a few hunches. Maybe say you were working with OSINT (Open Source Intelligence). Nothing wrong with that."

Shuggs shook his head. "It isn't that simple, bro. When I went out of town, I allowed her to go to my house to pick up the twins' ski equipment. She snooped around, found my recordings, pictures. You name it. Knows I used agency equipment to collect data on an American citizen without clearance. That's a clear violation. You know that."

Brock took a few moments to process what he'd heard. This meant Cindy was aware of the threat Patti posed. She knew of Patti's possible involvement with black extremists. *But what would she do with that info? She and Patti were still good friends.* The hair on the back of his neck prickled. "Have you told anyone?"

"No. You know me, bro. I ain't afraid of much." He hung his head. "But not only could Cindy sink my career to keep hers afloat," Shuggs said. "She'll take my kids away. Make them hate me. I can't let that happen. Those girls are my everything."

Brock swallowed. He knew from bitter experience that even good people did the unthinkable when they were hurting. Shuggs and Cindy had been through a lot in their marriage, but he never knew her to be the blackmailing type. "What does she want? Money?"

Shuggs slowly shook his head.

"Then what?"

"She wants the story."

"I don't understand."

"Cindy's been struggling as a reporter, especially now that she's aging out. Younger aspiring reporters are lining up ready to take her job. She'd hoped to make anchor by now." Shuggs ran a hand over his sweaty scalp.

Brock's eyes widened as he began to understand where Shuggs was going. "So she wants to use the story to propel her career?"

"Yes. She's such a selfish bi—"

"You said no, right?" Brock's pulse quickened, thinking of how this leak would affect them. "Please tell me you said no."

"I told her I wouldn't do that," Shuggs said, his voice filled with rage. "I begged her to drop it."

"But?"

"You have to understand I was desperate, bro. I ... I ... asked someone to try to talk sense to her."

Gripping the steering wheel, Brock turned into the hotel's lot, which was now crawling with police. "What do you mean?"

"I hired a 'black' agent to reason with her."

"When you say 'black,' do you mean illegal or the agent's color?"

"The guy happens to be African American," Shuggs said. "But I meant illegal. Someone off the grid that the agency keeps on reserve when they don't want any loose ends."

Brock shook his head. "We both know those type of 'black' agents kill. They *don't* talk."

"That's what I paid him to do," Shuggs said. "Just talk."

Brock parked at the farther point from the hotel but kept the engine idling. "You paid an illegal agent to *talk* to your ex-wife?"

"I had no other choice." He looked at his hands. "I was painted into a corner."

"Where's Cindy now?"

"I don't know."

"My God," Brock grimaced. "He didn't kill her, did he?"

"You know how those guys are." Shuggs stared off into space. "I'm praying to God that she's just frightened."

"Did whatever this guy do to her make her upset enough to disappear?" Brock asked.

"The girls haven't been able to find her. She hasn't been to work in two days."

"You're going to have to tell Dr. Harper."

"Can't do that. Not yet." Shuggs threw his hands up. "I'm praying Cindy comes home. That way, I can reason with her. Maybe I'll ask her to take me back, make things work. If that doesn't pan out, I'll offer her the house, money, anything to put this behind us." He unbuckled his seatbelt and opened the car door, his face ashen.

"What's your next move?" Brock asked.

"I must find Cindy," Shuggs said. "And then I have to convince her to kill the story."

CHAPTER 23

Brock waited until his friend disappeared into the hotel's lobby. He instinctively put a hand on his Glock and scanned the lot for anything or anyone suspicious. Despite the presence of law enforcement, the eerie image of Snake leaning from the hotel window pumping bullets haunted him. Attempting to get a handle on the situation, he ran a hand over his clammy face. He glanced at his watch and sighed. Pulling out of the hotel's lot, he then headed to Milk & Honey in Smith Commons.

Weaving through traffic, Brock tried to ignore the pulsating pain from his wounds. He checked his bandaged hand and cussed. Seeping blood had soaked through another layer of gauze, staining it a muddy red. Another wave of pain ran up his legs. He thought about stopping at a nearby drugstore for painkillers but dismissed the idea. *Got to meet these agents while I can. Figure out who's leaking intel and who's trying to kill us.*

Brock reached the restaurant and looked for parking while he pondered the mess Shuggs had gotten himself into. His mind jumped from the mess to the prospect of adjusting to a new job in a different intelligence agency.

He found a parking spot and then riffled through the dash compartment until he found a pair of gloves. *This should do the trick. I can't go out into a public place with my hand like this.* Brock winced as he gingerly pushed his swollen, bloody hand into the glove. He got out of his car and limped to the restaurant. Each step became more excruciating than the last. He kept his eyes down and his peripheral vision sharp, watching every person who walked by. Brock entered the rally point and looked around but couldn't get a visual on Berkley or Dexter.

While waiting for the hostess to seat the patrons ahead of him, Brock wondered if he could've prevented any of the recent nightmarish events. Like a TV rerun, he continued to replay the deaths of his fellow agents, and an abysmal chasm opened within him. *Maybe I'm responsible.*

"Any particular table for you today?" the hostess asked.

"I'd like to be seated at table ten if possible."

"Right this way." She led Brock to a dark corner booth separated by a wide glass partition he hadn't noticed earlier. She handed him a menu before walking back to her station.

Brock picked up the menu and instantly decided he needed caffeine—lots of it.

"Sir, are you dining by yourself, or are you expecting company?" his waiter asked.

He looked up. "I'm expecting two friends," Brock said. "But I'll take a triple expresso while I wait."

No sooner had the waiter hurried off than Berkley walked into the restaurant.

Brock waved him over to the table.

"Good timing," Berkley said breathlessly and handed Brock a nondescript backpack. "This is for you."

"Thanks. I think?" Brock hauled the heavy bag onto the seat next to him. Before long, the front pocket of the bag began vibrating. He opened the pocket, retrieved the vibrating phone, and answered it. "Yeah?"

"You can hang up. It's just me making sure you're connected," Berkley said. "Go ahead and check the inside pocket."

Brock searched the pocket and found a ticket to JFK for the next day. He was flying under an alias. He nodded to Berkley. "Got it."

"Also, inside the backpack is a wallet complete with an ID card with your new name and enough cash to get to New York. Pay your portion of today's bill with the cash provided."

"Wait a second, where's Santa's lookalike?"

A high-pitched laugh rang through the restaurant. "I suppose you mean my partner, Agent Dexter. He'll be here in a few. The guy's a total foodie and stopped to chat it up with people he knows in the kitchen," Berkley said. "I wouldn't be surprised if he went ahead and ordered for us."

Brock looked up while he was being served his expresso. Santa had walked from the kitchen and was headed toward their table. "Speaking of the devil," Brock said.

"Might I recommend item number eight?" Santa winked and sat across the table.

Brock checked the menu. "Thanks. I think I'll go with your recommendation."

"I'll get the North Pole special too," Berkley said, chuckling.

"Excellent choices." Santa tapped his menu. "Because I already ordered for us."

Turning to Brock, Berkley threw his hands in the air. "See, I told you."

Brock laughed. "Yeah, you did warn me."

"Figured I'd help you out." Santa squinted at Brock. "Heard after we left, you had a hell of a day."

"Looks like Snake did a real number on you." Berkley leaned forward and slid a small paper bag over to Brock. "Inside, you've got a wound kit and medication. You'll need to get that hand taken care of, but for now, this will tide you over. Blood's seeping out your glove." He pointed to the tiny splatter of blood on the table by Brock's silverware. "As for the meds, better take it right now. You need to take the edge off the pain."

"Thanks." Brock opened the bag, took two pills, and washed them down with a mouthful of the potent brew. He tackled cleaning and bandaging his hand discreetly on his lap. Then disinfected the stained table with the package of disinfecting wipes inside the kit.

Their waiter arrived and served their food. "Three North Pole specials. Sausage, cheese, and egg crepes with maple bacon waffles."

The men ate in silence until Berkley held a forkful of food in midair. He cleared his throat and pushed his glasses back. "Did Snake say anything suspicious?" he asked and chewed his last mouthful of crepe.

Brock swallowed the rest of the waffle in his mouth. "Nothing at all. No."

"He's an expert. Used to work for the agency. Knows the ins and outs," Santa said while brushing crumbs off the table.

"Any idea why he's after me?" Brock asked. "And how in the heck did he know where I was?"

"This situation is evolving. We believe this may be an inside job," Berkley said.

"Makes sense. I suppose that's why we're meeting like this."

"Exactly right." Santa pointed to Brock. "We're taking extra precautions because there're lots of oddities with this case."

"Which concerns us." Berkley leaned forward. "These last few events have been especially inconsistent and deadly."

"Yeah, I was almost taken out earlier today," Brock said, feeling his stomach knot. "I want that bastard Snake taken down."

"He's not the mastermind. But he's highly effective at executing orders." Santa folded his hands together on the table.

"Have any idea who's the shot-caller?"

"We don't know." Berkley shook his head. "But we're working on—"

Brock held his hand up. "I want authorization to take Snake down." *When I find out who the shot-caller is, his butt is mine too.*

"Someone's already assigned to bring him in alive," Santa said flatly.

"Who?"

"Collin Gentry. The guy Snake was impersonating. He's tracking Snake," Berkley said.

"Interestingly enough, Snake's being protected," Santa said.

"Why?" Brock asked.

"Snake's a piece of work. Brilliant. He's a black Hispanic." Santa squared his shoulders. "Speaks three languages. Linked to black extremists. And the feds want him alive."

"Basically, he's been working the system," Berkley said.

Brock frowned. "How?"

"Snake was once a valuable government asset who went rogue," Berkley said. "The guy has no loyalty. Anyone who pays the most is who he answers to."

Brock sipped his expresso, no longer tasting it. "It doesn't seem to make sense."

"We need to be patient." Santa sighed. "Use our training and logic."

Brock shrugged. "I guess you're right."

Berkley took off his fogged glasses and wiped them on his shirt. "Did you ever find Agent Shuggs?" His eyes met Brock's.

"Yeah, he ... Shuggs was at the hospital." Brock rubbed the back of his neck, wondering why he suddenly felt guarded. "He had a freak accident and needed stitches. Shuggs ... you see, he's under lots of pressure personally and with the job," Brock said quickly, rubbing his chin. "I'm sure you can relate."

"Absolutely. Problem is, we still haven't been able to speak with Shuggs." Santa ran a thumb around the edge of his napkin. "We've been playing phone tag with him. A lot."

"We'll be sure to catch up with him at Dr. Harper's office tomorrow," Berkley said, nodding.

"Should I be there?" Brock asked.

"No, you don't need to be in attendance." Santa stroked his beard. "We need you to head to New York. The bureau needs your skill set for a sensitive matter."

Brock raised a brow. "Do I need anything else before I leave?"

"You'll find everything you need in the backpack, including where you'll stay tonight. Your supplies include additional prescription-strength painkillers and antibiotics." Berkley folded his beefy arms across his midsection. "Use the new phone for contacting us *and for nothing else*. No matter what happens, trust no one."

"I've heard that before," Brock said, recalling Dr. Harper's warning from not long ago.

Berkley chuckled, pushing his empty plate aside. "Uh-oh, I suppose I sound like Dr. Harper, don't I?"

"Yeah, you do." Brock forced a tight smile. He undid the top button of his jeans and shifted in his seat, trying to find a comfortable position. Something about the repeated warning made him feel empty despite being full. *I'd better remember that. No matter what happens, trust no one.*

CHAPTER 24

When Brock finished his lunch meeting with the senior agents, it was five in the afternoon. He grabbed a clean outfit from his bag in the car, tidied himself up, and changed in the restaurant bathroom after the men left. The men had gone to brief Dr. Harper, leaving Brock with only an hour to kill before his dinner date with Patti and her mother. He couldn't think about eating anytime soon. But Mrs. Lipsett was a persuasive woman. If she asked him, Brock supposed he'd scarf down an elephant.

Brock planned to check into his hotel after supper with the women at the Thompson Hotel's Rooftop Restaurant since his new location was beside the airport. He decided to head to the Thompson, park his car, and hang out nearby at the Navy Yard. He slowly walked a short distance down the busy Navy Riverwalk. Tangerine ripples lapped the shore of the riverfront, reflecting the sunset washing over the sky.

He thought of Pang lying helpless in the ICU, unaware of another day's end. Clenching his fists, Brock prayed his friend would survive. He wasn't certain when he'd visit Pang again, and it tore him up inside that he couldn't say a proper goodbye. Berkley and Dexter's steely determination to find the enemy comforted him. Despite his reservations about the new job, the prospect of locating the barroom killer stirred something inside him.

Brock breathed in the heavy air, wishing he had time to make the two-hour trip to his condo in the Chesapeake Bay to recharge. In times like these, he pined for his spacious house on the beach—his one luxury in life. Brock rejected returning to his home, knowing it was in the capable hands of his caretaker, a fifty-year-old woman he'd met in Guatemala five years ago. He'd helped rescue her from a ruthless drug cartel. Now she and her fourteen-year-old daughter lived with him. In return for room and board, they took care of meals, laundry, and cleaning when he was there. They also cared for his dog and the place when he wasn't there, which was often. He inhaled another mouthful of cool, wet air. The intake of oxygen felt good. It was the jolt he needed while he walked to the Thompson Hotel.

An inner alarm—something—caused Brock to sense he was being followed. He looked over his shoulder, his stomach tightening. Behind him, a dark, muscle-bound man hovered by a tree. *I think this guy's been behind me the entire time. Whenever I stop, so does he.* The man was also disturbingly familiar. But before Brock could place his face, the man turned around, vanishing into the crowd and the shadows of dusk.

Brock stood in front of the hotel with a possible stalker behind him. He felt trapped. *Should I try to find the guy? See what he's up to. Could my mind be playing tricks on me?* A sharp pain in his knees reminded him that he'd jumped from a second-story building earlier that day and was due for another round of painkillers. He retraced his steps through a throng of pedestrians to find the mysterious stranger. Just then, he heard a woman's shrill voice call his name.

"Brock! Brock O'Reilly! Don't think I don't see you," Mrs. Lipsett shouted.

Brock turned around and hurried to her.

"Ma'am?"

She had a hand on each curvy hip. "What on earth are you doing, baby?"

"I'm ... I'm sorry, I thought I saw someone I know."

Mrs. Lipsett wagged a finger at him and pulled out her cell phone. "Patti, you can bring the boys up to the rooftop now. I found him."

He glanced at his watch. "I'm not late."

She stared at him with a strange expression on her face and reached for his arm. "We were worried. You know, after everything that's happened at the hospital today."

"Wait, what?" Brock asked. "What happened?"

Mrs. Lipsett wrapped her arm around Brock's waist like a long-lost lover, guiding him through the bustling lobby toward the elevators. "Listen to me, baby. Your friend Andrew is in trouble. Terrible trouble. And if you want to know the truth, I believe that daughter of mine is in harm's way too. She's just good at pretending everything's peachy, but I know better."

"I'm confused right now, ma'am," Brock said. "I don't understand."

Mrs. Lipsett pressed the call button for the elevator. "You will soon."

They rode in the packed elevator to the seventh floor, at which point Mrs. Lipsett motioned to Brock to get off.

"I thought the restaurant was on the roof," Brock said.

"It is," she whispered. "We have to make a pit stop."

Brock walked down a long corridor as Mrs. Lipsett led the way.

She stopped in front of a suite, reached into her bra, and produced a room key. Mrs. Lipsett sighed and opened the door. "Please get in here before Patti comes looking for us. I need to share something private with you."

"Okay."

"Sit on the couch." She pointed to an overstuffed chenille antique and hurried down a marble hallway. "I'll be back in two shakes of a lamb's tail."

Brock sank into the soft cushions and could've fallen asleep on the spot if it wasn't for the fact that Mrs. Lipsett would not have approved and he had jitters from the painkiller. He sat straight, rubbing a dull ache in his knees, taking in the vast room, from the matching chenille draperies to the dazzling chandeliers. The suite even boasted a white baby grand piano. Three colossal halls led to various rooms. He whistled. "Senator Lipsett is doing well."

"What's that, sugar?" Mrs. Lipsett asked, appearing from one of the rooms with a shoulder bag.

Brock waved, gesturing to the surroundings. "Nice suite."

She flashed a quick smile. "That's my husband. He's always treating me like a queen." Mrs. Lipsett tugged on her ear. "Now for the bad news."

"What is it?"

"I hope you don't mind me sharing this." She sat down beside Brock. "But your friend Patti is pregnant. And excuse my old-fashioned frustration, but I'm furious about it because she and Pang are divorced," she said, pursing her lips. "I don't want my grandbabies brought into this world under cursed circumstances. A child needs the spiritual covering of holy matrimony."

"She's a smart girl, Mrs. Lipsett."

"Yes. But she thinks I'm a fool." She shifted in her seat. "And that

I'm not onto her and the things she's up to. A mother *knows* her child."

"What else are you worried about?" Brock glanced at his watch. "And what happened at the hospital today?"

Mrs. Lipsett wiped her eyes. "Honey, Andrew went into respiratory failure today."

Brock's throat went dry. "Why wasn't I contacted?"

"Because foul play is suspected. *Again.*"

"What?"

She looked at him, her eyes wide. "Don't get me wrong. No one suspects you, of course." Her hands flew to her chest. "Oh, my. This is coming out all wrong."

Brock folded his arms against his torso.

Mrs. Lipsett reached into the bag. "Here's a copy of the police report. I wanted you to have one. I know you'll probably be privy to all this at some point. But I feel like you'll be able to figure things out, so I wanted you to have it now."

She pulled out another paper and handed it to him. "This is his medical prognosis. I got the doctor to print out an extra copy for me. Told her my daughter lost the one she gave her and needed it for insurance purposes."

Brock scanned the papers. "Says here an African American orderly is suspected of intentionally cutting off Andrew Pang's oxygen supply this morning." His throat constricted, and he found it difficult to breathe himself.

"Keep reading the report, and you'll see that they almost killed that defenseless man." Mrs. Lipsett pursed her lips. "Right under the nose of security."

CHAPTER 25

T he room spun out of focus while Brock processed the words he read on the report. Bronze candelabras blurred into the floor-to-ceiling curtains, and the chandeliers became flickering orbs of fire. He rubbed his eyes. "Am I reading this right? Someone cut off Pang's oxygen *while* he was in the ICU?"

Mrs. Lipsett stared at the medical records in Brock's hand as if they were alive. "Yes, that's what happened." The muscles in her face twitched. "And as a result, Pang suffered from hypoxemic respiratory failure."

"What is that?"

"It's when your respiratory system cannot remove enough carbon dioxide from the blood, causing it to build up in your body. The condition can also develop when your respiratory system can't take in enough oxygen, leading to dangerously low oxygen levels in your blood."

His chest contracted, and he found it difficult to take a breath. "How'd this happen?"

She shook her head. "No one knows for sure."

"Anyone speak with you about how he'll be kept safe from here on in?"

"Andrew's going to be moved to an undisclosed hospital. Only next of kin knows."

"Was the agency informed?"

"Yes, Dr. Harper knows." Mrs. Lipsett laced her fingers through a delicate string of pearls adorning her neck.

"Anyone else?"

"Dr. Harper and these lovely men." She looked up at the ceiling. "Mr. Berkley and Mr. Dexter. They're the ones who contacted us."

"What about the orderly? Is he locked up?"

"No. He's dead."

"How?"

"Suicide." She arched a brow. "Supposedly."

"Thanks for trusting me with this information, ma'am." At that moment, Brock felt torn. *Why hadn't they told me about Pang?*

She patted his shoulder and got up from the couch. "Sugar, you're the kind of man I can count on."

Brock got up and turned to face Mrs. Lipsett, her kind eyes looking for the best in him. "I won't let you down."

He wanted to prod her further about the special agents but decided against it. After years of seeing the line erode between right and wrong, he believed in sticking by the book.

She stretched out her hand. "I'll be needing those documents back."

"Oh, yeah." Brock returned the papers to Mrs. Lipsett.

Mrs. Lipsett peeked in a large mirror above the couch and ran a hand through her curls. "We'd better get going to join Patti and my grandbabies upstairs," she said, meticulously folding the papers and pushing them into the bag.

"Okay," he said.

Mrs. Lipsett cradled the bag in her arms, rocking it like it was an infant. "Is there something you'd like to tell me?"

Where would I begin? He ran a hand across his face. "Let's just say I've had a difficult day."

"I get it," she said. "You look like you want to get something off your chest."

"I think you should know ... that ...."

She looked at him. Her head tilted to one side. "Yes?"

"To be honest, I ...."

"Go on," she said, her kind, papery face damp and tired. The wrinkles etched around her mouth and eyes told the story of a woman who wasn't afraid to put up a fight.

Brock rubbed his sore hand. "I'm concerned about the safety of—"

"Baby, hold that thought." Mrs. Lipsett clutched the shoulder bag to her chest and turned around.

"Yeah, okay." He leaned back on the wall, watching her hurry down the hall to one of the rooms.

Mrs. Lipsett click-clacked from the room across the veined marble to the door. "I'm sorry, but I could not forget to put the bag back. I don't need my daughter upset with me for meddling in her affairs. We can chat on the way upstairs. Patti's already texted me twice."

He longed to tell her he'd escaped death by a narrow margin that afternoon and may've been followed to her hotel. But her faded brown eyes struggled to suppress the fear she hid with an outward show of strength. So he elected to conceal his news.

"I wanted to say," Brock hurried behind her to the elevators, "I know you're worried about Patti, about Pang, the kids."

She punched the call button on the elevator. "Yes, sugar. Of course, I am."

"I promise I won't let anything happen to any of them," Brock said.

"That's sweet." Dabbing her eyes, she got into the elevator. "Do I have your word, baby?"

"You do."

They were quiet for several seconds as the elevator rose, the circumstances of their lives like bricks on their shoulders.

"I'm glad you're back," she said, her eyes shining.

Brock raised a brow. "Really?"

"After the divorce, I saw less and less of you." She twirled a loose curl between her fingers before tucking it into place. "It bothered me."

"Me too."

"When my daughter and Andrew divorced, it broke my heart. I hated to see two people who loved each other decide to give up fighting for their marriage."

"Yeah, when they split, they split all of us apart," Brock said. "I know there were issues between them, and then there—"

She held her hand up. "Nowadays, people know how to fight against who they hate but give up on the fight for love. Why do you suppose that is?"

Brock searched his mind for the correct answer. "Maybe ... maybe people are more afraid of each other than ever before."

"So you believe it takes courage to love, *despite* our fears?"

"There's no courage without fear," Brock said.

"How about you, sugar? Do you know what it is to fight courageously?" Mrs. Lipsett leaned close to Brock. "To fight for love?"

His mind flickered back to the fights he'd been through in his life, in the mission field for his country, his friends, his parents. "Yeah, I do," Brock said, clearing his throat.

The elevator dinged, alerting them they'd reached the rooftop. Mrs. Lipsett stared at Brock for a few seconds, then straightened up and walked through the open door.

Brock followed close behind.

Mrs. Lipsett arrived at the brass doors of Anchovy Social, the rooftop bar and restaurant. She pointed through the massive glass windows to a table situated by a waterfront view. Patti and the boys peered through the glass, watching the activity below.

"Don't let Patti scare you off. She needs you, but she's stubborn and too afraid to admit it. Besides the pregnancy, I think she's keeping something else from me." Putting one hand on the door, Mrs. Lipsett turned to him. "And it's killing her," she said, then opened the door and walked through.

CHAPTER 26

B rock walked through the door behind Mrs. Lipsett. The smell of garlic and baking bread, along with the sounds of jazz piano, greeted them.

Patti and her boys were oblivious to their arrival as they talked, pointing at boats and pedestrians on the Riverwalk. Through the glass windows, the sun had almost completed her descent, coloring the sky with flaky layers of burgundy and ginger. Beneath, the river shimmered in waves of rose gold.

He took a deep breath, feeling wired from the mix of painkillers and adrenaline coursing through his blood. Brock was careful to plaster a smile on his face, even though his mind was in free fall with worry for Patti.

"Now remember what I said. Don't be afraid." Mrs. Lipsett spoke over her shoulder, her voice low.

Patti spun around and folded her arms. "What're you two whispering about?"

"Stay out of grown folks' business." Mrs. Lipsett waved her daughter off, then bent over to scoop up her giggling grandsons.

Brock kept his smile frozen in place. "Good seeing you again so soon."

"Same here." Patti glared at Brock like she wanted to knock him straight through the glass.

"Grandma, we're hungry," Patti's older son said, tugging on her nose.

The younger son chimed in. "I'm starving, Grandma. I need a lot of French fries." His chubby fingers pinched her cheeks.

Mrs. Lipsett laughed. "I'd better go see where the staff is before these boys *die* of starvation." She marched off in the direction of the kitchen with the boys in tow.

Brock leaned forward as several yachts sailed by. "This is some view."

"Yes, it is. Happens to be one of my parents' favorite spots when they visit the area." Patti's voice was cool and polite.

He took in the modern bar, dining room, and outdoor seating area. "I'm surprised it's vacant at this time of day."

Patti shook her head. "You didn't know?"

"Know what?"

"Mother reserved the entire rooftop for dinner."

"Just for the five of us?" he asked.

"Yes." Patti nodded. "I told you my mother has a sweet spot for you. Always has."

"I guess she does," Brock said, taking in the view.

Mrs. Lipsett came trotting back from the kitchen, her grandsons running ahead. A man and woman dressed in aprons trailed behind her.

"I was fortunate to have secured one of the town's best chefs." Mrs. Lipsett clapped her hands together. "The waitstaff will take care of my grandbabies and me out on the terrace. That way, you both can have some privacy. Brock, honey, I'll stop back to say goodbye." She touched his back before hurrying to the outdoor dining area.

Just as Brock and Patti sat down at a corner booth, Brock's cell phone vibrated. He pulled it from his pocket, glanced at the caller ID, and frowned.

"Where are you?" Dr. Harper asked when he answered.

He took note of her urgent tone. *Something's wrong.* "Why?"

"O'Reilly, I do not have time for idle chatter."

"I'm with Patti." Brock cleared his throat. "Patricia Pang?"

Brock showed Patti the caller ID. She nodded and sat back.

"Let me rephrase the question," Dr. Harper said. "What is your location?"

"The Thompson Hotel," Brock said quickly.

"On Tingey Street in the Navy Yard?"

"Yeah, that's it."

"What room?"

"I'm in the rooftop restaurant."

"Is it crowded?"

"No. It's five of us. Patti and her family."

"How many staff members?"

Brock's thoughts raced. "What's going on?"

"How many?" Dr. Harper asked, her voice sharp.

Brock surveyed the people around. "Let me see ... looks to be three, no, make that two, waitstaff."

"Describe them. Give as much detail as possible."

"There's a white female, probably mid to late twenties. Tall, medium build, brown hair and eyes. The other is a white male, a little over six feet tall, athletic build, long blond hair, blue eyes."

"Anyone else?"

"Yeah. I believe there's a chef working the kitchen."

"Get up and check."

"Okay."

"Wait," she said. "Are you armed?"

"Of course." He bent to adjust his ankle holster.

"Good. O'Reilly, go to the kitchen and see who else might be there. Then check the entire floor. Security cameras picked up biometric images of Snake in the vicinity of your location. We do not know how we missed him before. Our only conclusion is someone is jamming that frequency spectrum in your area."

"I'm headed there now," he said. "Hold the line."

A bead of sweat broke out on Brock's forehead. He got up and muted the phone, managing to give Patti an apologetic smile.

"Is it about Pang?" There was a tremble in Patti's voice. "Everything okay?"

"Don't worry." Brock patted her rounded shoulder. "It's not about Pang. It's a work thing. But I've got to take this call privately."

"That's fine. I'll be out on the terrace with the family until you get back."

"Yeah, okay," Brock said before he unmuted his phone and headed toward the kitchen.

"I am sending Agent Collin Gentry to assist you," Dr. Harper said. "I have undercover securing the hotel, setting up eyes and ears in the area. I will stay on the phone until I know the rooftop is secure. Then I will call back when I know more."

Brock passed the waiters who were returning from a run to the kitchen. They moved past him, carrying trays laden with food and drinks on the way to the terrace.

He slipped his gun from its holster, continued to the revolving doors of the kitchen, and peeked through the round glass window. Things appeared normal in the compact, stainless space. There was one chef with his head lowered, preparing sushi.

"So far, so good." Brock exhaled. "Everything's all clear. The chef's busy at work."

"That is a relief. And O'Reilly?"

"Yeah?"

"No need for us to alarm Pang's family at this juncture." Dr. Harper's tone suggested he'd do otherwise. "They have been through enough."

"Okay."

"We have taken extra safety measures due to the significance of the perpetrator's threatening actions. Additionally, the family will have security for the remainder of their stay, beginning tonight."

"That's probably a good idea," Brock said before he hung up.

He scanned the terrace where Patti and her family seemed to be enjoying dinner while the staff doted on them. Their laughter rang through the glass, nudging a smile from him. He headed away to secure the rest of the floor.

Brock glanced at his watch, noting the time. Soon, when supper was over, he needed to get to his hotel and settle for the evening before his morning flight. He felt a sense of relief knowing Patti and her family would now have security in his absence.

With his survey of the venue almost complete, Brock pulled out his cell to contact Dr. Harper. But his gaze was drawn down the corridor leading to the restrooms. From the men's room came the echo of running water.

Maybe it's just a leak. He edged down the hall, his gun drawn. Moving closer he saw a growing puddle had formed outside the bathroom door.

That's when the first shot exploded like thunder, triggering screams of instant panic outside on the terrace.

CHAPTER 27

The bullets behind him stopped when Brock reached the men's bathroom. His feet sloshed through ice-cold water that seeped steadily through the gaping door. He twisted around, lost his balance, and crashed into the adjacent wall. Brock bent over and steadied himself momentarily with one hand on the wall and the other on his knee.

Out of the corner of his eye, he saw what appeared to be a naked man with his legs at an odd angle, protruding from beneath a privacy stall. *What the heck?* Brock had a split second to react. He yelled at the man. Getting no response, Brock opened the stall's door. A man's head was stuffed in the toilet while the water ran, causing it to overflow. Brock pulled the man's body up from the toilet and dragged him into the sink area where there was more room. After checking for a pulse and finding none, Brock left the body in the bathroom and ran out into the hall. *Whoever he is, he's clearly beyond my help right now.*

Brock sprinted down the hall in the opposite direction. Not even the most powerful painkillers could mask the fiery bursts of pain radiating down his thighs and the insistent throbbing in his head. Ignoring his agony, Brock kept up a rapid pace toward Patti's family.

A second thunderous clap of gunfire hit the terrace. Brock rounded the corner. A panel of glass in the restaurant shattered, splintering across the dining room. He covered his eyes, unable to see clearly through the spray of flying glass.

Brock almost collided with the waitstaff, who were running back inside the dining room. The man and woman were hit with a flurry of bullets from behind before they made it to the door.

Diving to the ground, Brock shielded himself behind a pillar while he caught his breath. Seconds later, he peeked around the wall. The bodies of the waitstaff were sprawled in what appeared to be a life-less, bloody tangle. Brock scanned the area beyond the dead bodies. No clear line of sight to the smoky terrace. Cursing, Brock pulled out his cell and tried calling for help. Unable to get a signal out to emergency services or to the agency, he stashed his phone in his pocket.

Brock breathed deeply and listened. A lull in the shooting, an eerie silence, the rapid boom of his own heartbeat. *Time to move.*

Shakily, Brock struggled to his feet and pulled his shirt up to cover his nose and mouth from the smoke. Despite the pulsating pain, he ran in the direction he'd last heard shooting and screaming.

His feet slipped over a mound of broken glass. Brock skidded to the entrance of the terrace and stopped.

Patti had used her body as a human shield for her two small sons and her mother. They were all crammed under a table.

A bullet ricocheted off the side of the building from inside the restaurant.

"Brock, behind you!" Patti screamed.

He dove under another table, recognizing the distinct snap of high-velocity rounds.

A tree in a massive planter nearby exploded in every direction. The branches flew up into the air before crashing to the ground and spreading soil, shattered limbs, and leaves around the cowering group.

Engaging his weapon, Brock rolled onto his stomach and aimed at an approaching man. Snake, dressed like a chef.

Brock fired into the man's broad chest.

Snake fell back against a bar stool. He glanced down at a growing splotch of red on the center of his white uniform and quickly retreated behind a nearby pillar.

In the distance, police sirens and bewildered shouts from people below saturated the chilly salted air.

Brock kept the gun steady. Pointed.

Seconds later, bullets erupted from Snake's gun. Two light posts exploded, and the chairs close by were pelted, new holes strewn throughout the material.

Patti's sons screamed. Their high-pitched cries pierced the air.

Brock jumped up to face Snake.

Patti's younger son ran from under the table and into the line of fire.

Mrs. Lipsett quickly crawled out after him. "Baby, get back here!" She leapt to her feet and snatched her grandson by the shirt.

There was the crack of a semiautomatic as a sniper's gun from the other direction lit up the terrace.

A bullet grazed the side of Brock's hand. Grimacing in pain, he lost his grip on his weapon.

Mrs. Lipsett screamed, held onto her grandson, and dropped to her knees. Blood streamed down her arm, her eyes glazing over in anguish. Her grandson wiggled safely from under her and scrambled to his mother, who was already applying pressure to her mother's flesh wound.

"Everybody get down! Stay down!" Brock wiped his bleeding hand on his jeans. He reached for his weapon, cussing when he saw a large crack in the lock plate. His gun was useless. His heart pounded harder. Faster. He turned to Snake, who had a slick, twisted grin painted on his face.

From across the room, Snake waved away the smoke, shielded his eyes, and raised his gun.

Brock threw a chair at Snake.

Snake dodged, lifted his gun, and aimed at Brock's head.

Brock threw another chair at Snake, then raced toward a fire extinguisher on the corner of the terrace.

Snake stumbled backward.

Brock caught the motion in his peripheral vision and turned around.

Snake clutched his wide chest, gun clattering to the ground.

Brock ran to Snake. Kicked the gun from his reach. He grabbed the weapon and trained it on the vicious killer.

The assassin stared at Brock with cold black eyes, choking out sporadic breaths. The red stain engulfed his torso.

Brock edged closer. He tightened his grip on the gun, slick with blood dripping from his hand.

Snake dropped to his knees, both his hands wrapped about his bluish throat. He gasped for air. Writhing. Foaming from the mouth. His body went completely limp.

CHAPTER 28

The sniper's bullets stopped. The smoke began to clear.

Below the hotel's terrace, sirens screamed over the frantic cries of people in the Navy Yard.

Patti's two sons, huddled between her and their grandmother, started to whimper.

"Brock," Patti said. "Don't take any chances with that guy. Make sure he's really dead."

Brock stared out past the terrace into the night for anything suspicious, then back to the man on the floor. "Yeah, you're right."

Brock prodded Snake with his foot, his gun ready.

Snake's body flopped like a rag doll.

Gripping the gun, Brock waited a few moments. The faded scar over his left eyebrow pulsed the way it did whenever he was stressed. His scar traced back to the first person he'd ever killed—a young boy. Then again, he'd been a child himself. Brock shook his head. *Got to remain focused.* Brock nudged the assassin again, this time with more force.

Snake's head lolled to one side, arms sagging as if they didn't belong to his body. His limbs moved as if a puppeteer had suddenly cut the strings.

Keeping the gun trained on Snake, Brock stooped and checked for a pulse. Finding none, he used the weapon to push aside the top of the chef uniform, exposing the man's bare chest.

Pulling out his phone, he snapped pictures of the gunshot wound on the man's upper right breast above the sternum. He noted the bullet hole appeared skin-deep, superficial. There was an exit wound and no gunpowder stippling. Brock chewed his lip. *That shot shouldn't have killed him.*

He got to his feet and studied the killer's bluish face.

Snake's dead black eyes were slightly open and staring back at him. Lifelessly, they reflected the brightly lit chandelier above. A thin line of white spittle trickled from the man's mouth.

Brock grimaced, pushing the childhood memory back into the darkness. He surveyed the scene, resisting the urge to revisit the past any longer.

He breathed deeply, noting the restaurant reeked of gunpowder, sushi, and strong rum. Shadows like ghosts swayed in the room's elegant periphery.

Broken glass, overturned tables, and chairs decorated the upscale eatery.

Light emanated from the multitiered fixture dangling over Snake and the moonlight streaming through the cracked panes of glass.

Brock paused to call for help. Still no signal. He shook his head, feeling his communication failure was part of the attack. For a few seconds, Brock couldn't help himself. His mind flittered to September 11, 2001. A day when foreign intel through al-Qaeda managed to manipulate the airwaves and airspace to carry out a heinous attack against Americans. As a high school JROTC (Junior Reserve Officer Training Corps) student, he'd sworn he'd never let anything like that happen on his watch if he were ever able to join the agency. Yet here he was, very much a part of the agency and battling another unseen enemy. Trying to figure out what was going on.

A helicopter buzzed overhead. Dirt, broken tree branches, and leaves blew across the terrace.

"Brock?"

He turned. Gun cocked. Ready.

"Can you check what's going on out there?" Patti motioned to him from her position outside on the terrace overlooking the riverfront.

"Yeah, I got us covered." Brock walked toward her, his feet crunching broken glass.

He crouched, looking down at the Navy Yard through the slats. "The place is surrounded by cops," Brock said, his voice soft. "Sniper's lying low. Thank God." He turned and looked back at Patti. His eyes met hers.

He used the gun to gesture. "I think things are stable now with all the police present. But just to be safe, we need to get everyone inside."

Patti stood. "Do you think we should stay put or leave?"

"I say we wait here until help comes," Brock said, checking his phone. "I'm surprised no one's contacted us yet. Might be some sort of security breach. That'd be my guess."

"Okay." Patti hoisted one child on her hip and held the hand of the other.

Brock came to her aid by taking Mrs. Lipsett's shaking hand and guiding her inside the restaurant.

"I'll stay posted in the hall by the elevators and stairwell," Brock said. "Stay away from doors or windows."

Patti nodded. "I'm on it," she said, situating her crew in a secluded section of the restaurant.

Brock jogged to the shadowy hallway to await backup.

At that moment, his phone came to life. It vibrated each time a message went through. He had multiple missed calls.

One by one, top operatives, police officers, and agents began making contact.

The first message was from Shuggs. He informed Brock that he was in the vicinity of the Thompson Hotel helping with intel support.

Brock also received a communication from Dr. Harper directing them to stay put until help arrived.

Brock knew that Dr. Harper would make sure no one ever stopped until the job was done and each of her people was accounted for. Even if she had to use other intelligence entities to assist with the mission.

It didn't matter that the agency didn't always have boots on the ground in the US. Still, it did mean they'd call in the big guns, SO-COM (Special Operations Command), the organization that ran all of America's special operations.

He tried calling Dr. Harper again. She picked up on the first ring.

"Are Patricia Pang, her children, and her mother safe?" she asked.

"They are."

"Excellent."

"What's the plan for getting us all out of here?"

"We would have reached you by now if the traffic network had not been hacked, as well as the hotel's security panel."

"The perps hacked the city's and hotel's camera network?" Brock ran a hand across his jaw.

"We are now in the process of overriding both systems."

"With the analysts dead, our best bet is Shuggs. From his training as a digital forensics engineer, there's no one better equipped to counter cyberattacks."

"I concur," Dr. Harper said. "He is currently working on it."

"Okay," Brock said, nodding his head. If Shuggs was involved, it was a plan he trusted.

An office phone rang in her background. "Hold the line." A muffled, rushed conversation transpired before Dr. Harper returned. "O'Reilly?"

"Yeah, I'm here."

"I am sorry. There has been an update."

"What's up?"

"We have confirmed that there is a live bomb planted on the rooftop."

"Here?" Brock asked, the scar above his eye throbbing. "At the Thompson Hotel?"

Dr. Harper cleared her throat. "Yes. I am afraid so."

CHAPTER 29

Brock glanced over his shoulder into the dining room where Patti and her family sat huddled in a booth. "Exactly where's the bomb?"

"According to our data, the bomb is located in the stairwell of the rooftop."

"Any other info?" he asked.

"Not at the moment."

"Crap," Brock muttered, pacing the hallway. His stomach lurched, contemplating how easily a handful of people with twisted agendas could tear the country apart. *These days, it wouldn't take much with all the division between Americans.*

"What?"

"I didn't mention this earlier," he lowered his voice and pressed the phone to his ear. "Snake followed us up here, murdered two servers, and also injured Mrs. Lipsett. It's clear he was hired to—"

"Wait, I thought you said everyone was fine."

"We are. But Mrs. Lipsett did sustain a nonlethal bullet wound before I took Snake down."

Dr. Harper cleared her throat. "Are you sure she is fine?"

"Yeah."

"How did that happen?"

He shook his head. "I don't know.

"Let me assure you," she said, "we had our people watching."

"Snake disguised himself as staff."

"What kind of staff?"

"Dressed up like he was a chef," Brock said. "Snake was even in the kitchen cooking."

"Since the security cameras were hacked, our people must have missed that detail. Without IDing him, they would have been unable to stop him."

"Someone might have tried to stop him. I found a naked stiff in the bathroom earlier. I'm almost positive it was Snake who offed him."

"The deceased man is not one of ours. All of our people have been accounted for. In fact, several of them are helping Shuggs to get access to some of the area's cameras.

"We can't wait for help to come," Brock said, checking his watch.

"Do not be ridiculous," Dr. Harper said.

"We've already been up here for over two hours under attack from a sniper, Snake, and God only knows who else."

"There is no way out of—"

"Got to get everyone to the ground to safety. I have a bad feeling about staying up here." A shiver ran through Brock's body just thinking about the Washington, DC, sniper who'd shut the state down for weeks with a gun, a jalopy, and a brainwashed eighteen-year-old stepson.

"The elevators are down, and you are eleven stories up."

"There are ways around—"

"Look, O'Reilly. We absolutely must protect Mrs. Lipsett at all costs."

"Yeah, I know," Brock said. "She's a *politician's* wife."

"That she is." Dr. Harper sighed. "The entire group is equally as important. But every news station and two-bit paper would have a field day with the agency if she were to perish. Especially since her husband is a likely Democratic candidate for the next election."

Brock arched a brow. "For president?"

"Yes."

He ran a hand across his jaw. "We'll take the stairs."

Patti's older son scurried over and pulled on Brock's pant leg. "Mommy said you need to take me to the bathroom."

Brock looked up as Patti motioned to him from inside the restaurant. He nodded and grabbed hold of the child's small hand. "I'll just have to play it by ear."

"What do you mean by that?" Dr. Harper asked.

"When Pang gets better, he'll need a family to come home to." Brock looked down at the child as he walked him to the bathroom. "I'm making sure that happens."

"You are no longer on international soil, fighting and eliminating insurgents."

Brock grimaced at the reminder of how he'd spent most of his career. "I would prefer if you'd give me the green light to proceed."

"Please do not panic and act rashly to bring any more media attention to this matter."

"You handle the media," Brock said. "I'll handle protecting everyone under my watch." *I'm on my own now.*

"We have our best people working on effective solutions."

"I understand, and I have faith in Shuggs. The man can crack any encryption cipher. In the meantime, I'll keep things together."

"As much trust as I have in *your* ability," Dr. Harper said, "it is the bomb I am concerned about."

"I've dealt with situations like this before."

"Understood. But I still need you to hold your position until further instruction."

Brock swore silently. "Yeah, okay."

"Hold on," Dr. Harper said. "Something urgent just came in."

Brock stared at the phone screen while he waited, fighting the brewing anger inside. Those he'd trusted to have his back had already failed him. They'd allowed the attackers to slip through their fingers and waltz right through security to kill him and those he cared about deeply.

Dr. Harper came back on the line through a buzz of static. "O'Reilly, take … immediate cover … wait for further instructions. We have intel … more attackers are in close proximity to your location. Do not engage. They are … extremely dead—"

"They're what? Hello?" Brock shook his head, staring at the blank screen. He felt a cloud of distress overcome him as he turned and studied the innocent face of his best friend's son staring up at him. He repeatedly tried reconnecting the call but couldn't get through.

"We're here." The boy pointed to the bathroom door with the picture of a man on it.

Brock pocketed his phone. Opening the heavy door for the child, he suddenly remembered the body he'd discovered earlier inside the men's bathroom and abruptly shut it. "You know what, son? I totally forgot there's a big mess inside this bathroom."

The child began jumping up and down. "But I got to go."

"We're going to use the other bathroom."

"That's gross. It's for girls."

"I know, but it's okay. Just this once." Brock tugged the child's hand and steered him across the hall to the women's bathroom. They entered the restroom and Brock stumbled over something on the floor before regaining his footing and flicking on the lights.

The boy ran and hid behind Brock's leg. "No!"

Brock's head snapped around, his hand on his gun. *What the heck is going on?*

With wide eyes, the child pointed to the floor.

Brock looked down. A man and a woman, badly beaten, lay bound together.

"They're dead!" the child screamed.

CHAPTER 30

Brock instinctively reached for the crying boy, pulling him into his arms. He glanced back at the pair of bruised, disrobed bodies and swallowed.

The child stiffened against Brock's chest. "I'm scared."

"Everything's going to be fine." Brock pivoted, shielding him from the bodies on the floor.

"But the dead people are staring at me."

"Close your eyes," Brock said softly. "Don't look."

The child squeezed his eyes shut. "I want my mommy." Tears escaped from the corners of his eyes and slid down his nut-brown cheeks.

"Don't you have to use the bathroom?" Brock asked, hoping to distract him.

The boy nuzzled his head into Brock's neck. "No."

Judging from the flow of warm liquid trickling down his arm and chest, Brock realized the child had already relieved himself. "Let's clean you up, son."

Brock walked to the sink and propped the crying child up on the edge. He began the job of tidying the both of them as best he could with bathroom soap and paper towels.

After a few minutes, the child tapped Brock's arm. "Uncle Brock?"

Brock arched a brow. "Yeah?" The child hadn't referred to him as uncle since they'd reunited, and the term of endearment made him forget he was covered in the boy's urine.

The child pointed to the bodies. "Did the bad man kill them?"

Brock looked down into the boy's questioning eyes. "Yeah. I believe so, son." He grabbed a wad of towels and attempted to dry off. Brock glanced over his shoulder and began to put the puzzle pieces together.

More than likely, the victims in both bathrooms were probably staff members, slaughtered for their uniforms and identities. Brock assumed they'd been accosted by Snake and his deadly team. The servers he'd watched get killed fleeing the sniper were probably loose ends being tied up by whoever had orchestrated the attack.

"Uncle Brock?"

Brock shook himself from his thoughts. "What's up, little man?"

"Please don't tell Mommy ..." He hung his head. "About my accident. Okay?"

"Okay." Brock patted the child's back and pulled him from the sink's edge. "Let's get out of here and go see Mommy."

The child wrapped his tiny arms around Brock's neck. "I'm glad the bad man is gone. He can't come back to our house and make Mommy cry anymore."

The hairs on the back of Brock's neck rose while he walked to the exit and out into the hall. "The bad man came to your home?"

The child wiped his nose on his sleeve and nodded.

Brock made a mental note. *Each time I think I've figured out Patti, she surprises me. If she kept her relationship with Snake from me, then what else could she be hiding?*

A few moments later, Brock rounded the corner and walked past the elevators. He could see Patti and her family. Suddenly, he heard a noise in the stairwell. He dodged behind a wall as the door to the stairwell creaked open. Brock covered the child's mouth and motioned for him to be quiet. Time seemed frozen as he stood still, not daring to breathe, the echo of his heartbeat drumming in his ears.

The stairwell door creaked shut.

Hushed voices traveled the hall heading toward Patti and the other two.

Brock put the child down and combed the area for a hiding place. An oversized garbage container sat close by. *Perfect.* He knelt next to the child. "There're some more bad men Uncle Brock has to get. But don't worry, if you follow my directions, everything will work out." He pointed to the container. "I need you to hide in here and not come out until I come back for you."

"Like hide and seek, Uncle Brock?"

"Yeah, just like that," Brock said and carefully tucked the child into the container, then closed the lid. He reached for his gun and caught up to the men, training his weapon on their backs as they crept down the hall.

The men were whispering in broken English as they walked, holding their guns at a strange angle in front of them like amateurs. Listening to the men, Brock figured it was a type of Caribbean patois.

He inched toward the two men until he had a clear shot, then fired, hitting the back of their knees.

The smaller man dropped his weapon on his way to the floor, clutching his leg in agony.

Brock kicked the man's Beretta aside, quickly angling his weapon at the larger man, who'd crashed into the wall and was aiming his gun at Brock with shaking hands.

"Bad idea," Brock said, shooting the big man twice in the skull.

Brock turned back to the smaller man who was writhing in pain. Blood seeped into the thick carpet. He aimed his gun at the man's open mouth.

"Don't kill me. I'm begging you. I've got kids."

"Yeah, somehow the enemy always has kids." Brock raised the weapon, knowing he had no intention of pulling the trigger. Not yet.

The small man moaned through clenched teeth. "Please. I don't want to die. Not here."

Brock stood over the bleeding man. "We don't have time for games. You're bleeding out, and there's a bomb that needs disassembling. If I'm going to spare your life, you have to help me."

"Yes, yes, anything."

"Who sent you?"

He shook his head. "I don't know."

Brock sighed, propped his foot on the man's gunshot wound, and leaned over, exerting pressure. "That answer is definitely *not* working for me. You've got one more chance to make me happy before you end up like your friend."

The small man turned his head and vomited. "I ... really ... don't ... know."

Frowning, Brock stood back, took aim, and shot through the man's other kneecap. He wondered if he'd gone too far as the man's body convulsed in shock. His eyes rolled back and closed. *Crap. I need this perp alive.*

"Hey, buddy. Wake up," Brock said. "If you want to live for your kids or whatever, you've got to give me a name. I need something."

The man's eyes fluttered open. "I swear it. I don't know. I ... just work for ... people. I do jobs when they need it."

"What kind of jobs?"

"We shut people up ..." His eyes glazed over. "We handle people who talk too much. Or know too much."

"Who were you coming to shut up?"

The man's eyes rolled into the back of his head. His breathing came in ragged spurts.

Using his foot, Brock nudged the man in his chest. "Hey, buddy! Stay awake, or you die here in this hotel hallway."

The man's bloodshot eyes popped open. "Um ... Patricia."

He shook his head. "Not good enough," Brock said. "I need a last name."

The injured man attempted to speak but vomited onto his chest. He wiped his face and gasped. "It's ... ah, ... Pang."

Brock resisted the urge to finish the man off right then. Instead, he took a breath. "Why would someone want to come after her?"

The man moaned and reached for his shattered knees. His hands came back dripping with blood. "Oh, God ..."

"Yeah, I do suggest God in your life from this point on." Brock knelt down and pressed the gun against the man's temple. "But like I said, I need answers. My patience is done."

"Um, ... some cocky business suit ... contacted me. He, he ... said she, she ... was messing ... with his ... money."

"How was she doing that?" Brock asked, pressing the gun harder into the man's temple.

The man curled into a ball. "He ... found out ... she was ... undercover."

"Undercover what?"

The man opened his mouth, but nothing came out. His face turned purple from the effort. "Government ... secret squirrel ... stuff," he said and then passed out.

CHAPTER 31

Brock's heart sank. He feared the perp would die on him without giving up information he desperately needed. He had to concentrate on what had to be done. *Find the shot-caller. Get Patti and her family to safety.*

"Hey, buddy, wake up. We're not finished here." Brock slapped the man's face repeatedly.

The injured man didn't respond.

Staring down at the unconscious man, Brock fought the onslaught of his thoughts racing through his head. Could Patti still be on the job? As an undercover? Did Dr. Harper know of this? If she knew, why did she withhold the info from him?

Brock sighed and stooped to rifle through the men's pockets.

He started with the dead man. Brock pulled a pack of cheap cigars from his back pocket. In the jacket he found additional ammunition, a wallet, and a cell phone. "Now we're talking." Brock stuffed the extra ammo into his own pockets and opened the wallet, finding an ID belonging to a Jamal Brown. Brock grabbed Jamal by his dreadlocks. He held the dead man's face up to the screen to gain access to his phone, then scrolled through the memory.

Several pictures taken at a strip club with various strippers popped up. He took note of pictures of Jamal in the ring boxing. Fighting in what Brock assumed was a boxing gym. Brock went through a bunch of nondescript text messages and phone records. He reached a message from someone in the dead man's phone called Uncle Buck.

His thoughts turned to the man whom the special agents had told him about, Tucker Buckler, affectionately called Uncle Buck, who'd mentored the killers from the barroom attack.

Jamal's phone rang. Brock peered at the caller ID, and a shot of adrenaline flooded his brain. A stroke of luck in the middle of a crap-shoot.

Maybe I should ignore it. Let voicemail pick up.

Instead, Brock answered the call.

The voice on the other end sounded like a radio disc jockey. He spoke over gospel music playing loudly in the background. His voice boomed from the phone with confidence. "Jamal? Everything go according to plan, son?" Uncle Buck asked.

Brock decided to wing it. *Maybe he won't realize I'm not Jamal.* He kept his reply low, curt. "Yeah."

"Superb. Send me the pictures of your *jobsite,* and I'll transfer the money into your account immediately. Time to clean up this mess we were tricked into getting involved with."

Brock answered again. "Yeah."

"Very well. Now that those loose ends have been tied up, the last thing I'll need for you to do is to eliminate Snake. The one who set us up."

Brock was about to use his one-liner again when the line clicked dead.

Slowly Brock began to formulate the blueprint of a plan.

He had a name. He had a connection. Uncle Buck had unwittingly confessed to confirming and ordering a hit. Brock looked through the dead man's contacts and found Uncle Buck also had an address, a condo in the upper east side of the Big Apple a long way from his cozy family home in the suburbs of Long Island.

Brock balled his fists and was tempted to head straight to New York City and put a bullet through the man's skull. But that impulse would serve no use other than to placate his anger and thirst for revenge.

Brock forced himself to inhale and exhale several times. He screen-shot Uncle Buck's info, then sent it to himself, the special agents, and Dr. Harper. *Need to stay focused.* He had a mission to lead Patti and her family to safety. After, he'd be sure to stop by and pay Uncle Buck a well-deserved visit. Brock made a solemn promise to himself that it'd be the last visit the man would ever get. From anyone.

While he thought about his next move, Brock began searching the unconscious man. Who, according to his ID, was Jorge Watts. Something fell out from Jorge's jacket. Two rumpled pictures.

Brock flattened out the photos.

"What the heck?" he muttered.

The first photo was of the brothers who'd died carrying out the barroom attack. They posed beside two men with striking resemblances to them. *Probably more siblings.* Marked on each face was a small red check mark.

He picked up the next photo, examining it closely. Vivid memories punched him in the gut. Him and Pang posing at the agency in Dr. Harper's upscale conference room four years ago. Before their lives took twisted turns. The photo captured happier times. They'd been celebrating a promotion, colleagues waiting at Rusti's to continue the party. Since then, they'd progressively aged with the baggage of death, loss, and deceit.

But where was Shuggs? And then Brock recalled Shuggs had taken the picture. Like a proud father, he'd stood in the shadows allowing the spotlight to shine on them, showing no sign of envy, only support. *What a guy.*

"Hurting ... bad," Jorge said, clutching one of his bloody, shattered knees.

Tasting metal, the coppery smell of death clogged Brock's nose and throat. He looked down at the growing pool of black blood beneath Jorge's body and flinched. *"Don't ever let empathy for the perps cloud your judgment"*—Dr. Harper's advice rang through Brock's mind.

In his world, a world of apparitions and chameleons, there would be no time for empathy toward the enemy. It was time to collect a debt.

"Who sent you here, Jorge? Who, exactly?"

The man's eyes blinked at the mention of his name.

"Why the heck do you have a picture of men with check marks on their faces? Were you contracted to kill the surviving brothers?"

Jorge tried to say something but coughed instead.

"What about the photo of me and my friend in your wallet?"

"Given to ... us. Nothing ... personal ... contract work."

"That answer isn't very good, Jorge. In fact, it's downright unacceptable." Shaking his head, Brock slammed his foot down on the torn knee Jorge had just grabbed.

Jorge shrieked in torment, his eyes rolling back into his head once more.

"Let's try this again," Brock said. "How was Patti messing with the shot-caller's money?"

Jorge gasped for breath. "His ... businesses," he said, his voice cracking.

Brock kept his foot on top of Jorge's leg. "What kind of businesses?"

Grimacing, Jorge coughed up red mucus. "Strip club."

"I promised to spare your life if you gave me info. It's just not enough." Brock removed his foot from the man's knee and raised his gun. "I told you I needed a name."

Jorge turned his head to the side and vomited. When he looked up, Brock stood directly over him.

Brock released the safety. "Time's up, buddy."

Jorge's eyes widened. "Tuck ... Tucker ... Buckler."

Lowering the gun, Brock leaned over Jorge. "As in Uncle Buck?" He arched a brow. "Is that who ordered these hits?"

Jorge nodded slowly and closed his eyes.

CHAPTER 32

Black anger engulfed Brock's heart. Too many people he cared about were dead. Or damned close to it. His mind flashed to the photo of Pang lying in the ICU that had been left on his windshield, then to the photo he'd just discovered on Jorge.

The Three Stooges, he, Pang, and Shuggs liked to call themselves. They were friends. Inseparable. Through wars and peacetime. Woven together by death, laughter, and loyalty. A band of brothers.

He rolled his tense shoulders back and studied Jorge's listless face before pocketing the photo of him and Pang. People like Jorge would never experience friendship like he did. Never. They didn't know what it was to put their selfish lives on the line for others.

Cursing, Brock reengaged the gun's safety, shoved the gun into his ankle holster, and bent closer to the man's still body. Jorge's walnut skin had turned an ashen color, resembling drying papier-mâché.

Brock placed his warm hand on Jorge's cold wrist, checked for a pulse, and found a faint but steady beat. *Good. Need more answers.*

"Wake up." Brock shook Jorge by the shoulders. "Stay with me."

The gunman twitched.

"You got some explaining to do."

Jorge's eyes flittered open for a few seconds before sliding shut again.

"We're running out of time."

"Hurts. Bad."

"You need my help, right?"

Jorge blinked.

"First. Help me," Brock said. "Got it?"

Jorge muttered something, his voice strained, his breathing shallow.

Brock squatted next to the man, realizing Jorge had soiled himself. "Did Tucker Buckler work with or for *anyone* else?" He spoke fast, trying not to let the putrid stench into his nostrils and mouth.

Nodding, Jorge pointed at something behind Brock, then his arm flopped to the ground.

Brock breathed through his mouth quickly as he scanned the vacant hallway, then focused on Jorge. "What're you trying to tell me?"

The injured man struggled to speak. "He ... was hired ... by Snake." Jorge tried sitting, suppressing a gag, before lying back down. A thin line of bloody phlegm leaked from a corner of his cracked lips as he mumbled unintelligibly.

"Is that who Buck was working with?"

Jorge nodded.

Resisting the urge to kick Jorge in the ribs, Brock clenched his fists, willing himself to speak calmly. "Was Snake working with anyone else?"

"Y—Yes ..."

"I need a name. Only then will I help you."

"He went ... by ... Ghost ..."

"Who the heck is that?"

Suddenly a rattle echoed through the hall.

Brock jerked his head toward the sound. "Hello?"

For a moment, he wondered if the child had crawled out from the safety of the garbage can.

He glanced down at Jorge.

Jorge's bloodshot eyes fixed on the shadows, his breathing labored.

Brock squinted, peering back into the dim darkness.

The dark moved, a massive growing shadow against the slender hallway walls. Toward him.

Brock swiftly reached for his gun.

There's no way that's a kid.

He aimed at the silhouette. "Freeze or you're dead!"

"Uncle Brock, I'm scared." His godson's weak voice floated down the hall.

The shadow froze.

"Stay put, little man," Brock said hoarsely. The air had left his lungs. "No matter what, stay put. Stay down."

"I'll try," the child said, his voice low.

Brock braced himself against the wall and took a deep breath.

Moisture gathered under his arms and ran down his back. Sweat stinging his eyes, he sprinted to the stationary shadow.

A bolt of orange sparks blinded Brock. Thunder exploded past his ringing ears and down through the end of the corridor.

Instinctively, Brock dropped low to the ground. Dampness slid between his palms and the gun's handle as he tried to get his bearings.

A man screamed. It was Jorge's voice but high-pitched, coiled tight, laced with agony. "Can't ... bre—" he wheezed.

"My God ..." Gripping the gun, Brock crouched and swiveled in the direction of Jorge's pained voice. Squinting, Brock stared at the spot where Jorge lay, but the man was a distorted blur.

He turned back around and moved through the sulfur-thick air to where he'd last seen the shadow. "Drop your weapon, or I'm shooting!"

Beneath the soft glow of an etched glass sconce, the thick arms of a man waved in surrender.

If things had been different, he would have allowed the attacker to live until he could get information out of him. But under these circumstances, the stakes were higher.

This time he chose the only other option.

Plastering himself to the wall, Brock released the safety and zeroed in on the shadow's head for the kill shot.

I'm not risking a child's life. Not this time. Not ever again.

"No, no! It's me!" The familiar baritone voice shot through the air.

Brock stiffened for a second before regaining his composure. "What?" He wiped his eyes with one hand, gripping the gun with the other. His ears still rung. *Maybe my mind's playing tricks on me.*

"Don't shoot!" The shadow leaned forward, tossing his weapon to the floor with a clatter.

Brock's mouth went dry like he'd swallowed dust. He inched closer, attempting to make out the figure before him. He had to be sure. *No more mistakes.* "Shuggs? That you, man?"

A pale, bald head bobbed, shining in the shadowy light. "Guilty as charged."

Brock sighed. Took a step toward Shuggs.

"That you, O'Reilly?"

"Yeah, Shuggs. You did it." Brock wiped away beads of perspiration from his face, lowered his gun, and exhaled.

"Did what, bro?"

A surge of pride washed over Brock as he walked to Shuggs. But as Shuggs's face came into better focus, his reddened eyes glowering in the light were clouded with adrenaline and rage. The skin circling his eyes was a purplish black. Brock had never seen an expression like that on his good-humored friend.

Brock cleared his throat.

"You made it," he said, watching while Shuggs stooped to retrieve his gun. "Thank God."

CHAPTER 33

Shuggs straightened, ran a hand across his glistening head, and propped himself against the wall.

"You alright?" Brock asked, scanning the eerily quiet area.

Shuggs pulled a pack of cigarettes from his back pocket. "Sure. Sorry if I scared you," he said, juggling his gun and a lighter.

Brock shrugged, wondering when his friend had taken up smoking again while he watched Shuggs light up. Once Shuggs started, he tended to chain-smoke. It'd been a long time since Brock had seen his friend shaken enough to smoke openly.

There'd been the time the twins' mother had served Shuggs's divorce papers. Brock recalled, with a knot in his stomach, that Shuggs had begun binge drinking. Then stopped. Then started. Since then, when Shuggs was troubled, he smoked. That usually led to bingeing.

Shuggs hadn't been drinking for at least a year after a close call with the CIA's internal investigation department. Brock had covered for Shuggs's sloppy paperwork and missed meetings. Though he'd drawn the line when Shuggs arrived for a mission inebriated. Brock had given his friend an ultimatum. For a time, it seemed to work.

He'd reasoned that Shuggs deserved the chances he'd been denied as a kid. Early in their CIA careers, Shuggs had confided in him that he'd never gotten over his father's abuse and suicide.

Brock suspected Shuggs still battled his addictive demons. But if he did, he had kept it hidden well and hadn't allowed it to affect his work again.

"There's a lot at stake right now." Brock sighed. "And I'd never be able to live with myself if I hurt any of you."

Walking to Brock's side, Shuggs patted his friend on the shoulder. "C'mon, man, you didn't do anything wrong," he said. "Things happened so fast."

"Yeah, that was crazy."

"We've seen worse."

"True."

"Glad we survived, unlike that perp who attacked you." Shuggs picked up his gun and shoved the service weapon into his shoulder holster.

"You mean him?" Brock jabbed his finger behind him to where he'd left Jorge.

"Yes."

"I had him subdued."

"He seemed dangerous."

Brock walked the few steps back to where Jorge had once been. Most of Jorge's head was missing.

He turned to his friend. "I needed him alive," Brock said.

"For what?"

"To tell me more about who sent him—and why."

"He'd probably lie anyway."

"Found out one thing."

"What's that?"

"Uncle Buck's connected to this mess."

"As in Tucker Buckler, the black guy the special agents talked about?"

"Yeah, that's the man."

"Okay. Now what?"

"Now we've got to get Pang's family out of here."

Shuggs snatched a cigarette he'd tucked behind his ear, used the old one to light it, and took a pull. "That isn't going to be easy."

Brock sniffed the air and frowned at the sour smell of alcohol between them. *Shuggs is struggling. Again.* And that was terrible news.

"Since you got up here," Brock said carefully, "I assume you've figured a way out, right?"

"Wrong."

"How'd you manage to get past the bomb?" Brock stared at the elevator doors and then at the exit to the stairwell, hoping the law would come bursting through one of them. "You don't have backup?"

"No."

"An intel guide?"

"None of that, bro." Shuggs shook his head, and a surge of

confidence filled his booming voice. "Fact is, I snuck in here alone."

Brock arched a brow. "What?"

"Bro, I did everything I could to help by hacking into the city's network. But I lost my patience dealing with the red tape it takes to eliminate the perps. So I took matters into my own hands."

"No one knows you're here?"

"No one."

"Not even Dr. Harper?"

"C'mon, she's the last person I'd tell."

"She's still—"

Shuggs held his hand up, flicking ashes onto the carpet. "Doc's a suit. She'd find every reason for me to sit around waiting for the other suits to hash things out. All while my best friend's fighting for his life."

"What're you talking about? Dr. Harper's still our boss."

"Not for long."

"Did you at least clear anything with Berkley and Dexter?"

After taking a long drag from his cigarette, Shuggs disappeared behind a bluish cloud of smoke. "I wouldn't cross the street to spit on them if they were on fire, so I sure as heck wouldn't ask their permission to save my friends."

"Then what's your plan?"

"To save the lives of those who matter to me." Shuggs inhaled. "Beyond that, I ain't got no plan."

"But we need to figure out how—"

"You hear that?" Shuggs dropped his cigarette and stomped the butt.

"Hear what?"

"Crying."

"My godson!" Brock took off running with Shuggs at his heels. "I hid him in the garbage can."

The men reached the container at about the same time.

Brock lifted away the heavy lid.

A whimper ricocheted through the tin interior.

Bending over, Brock peered into the can.

The child's huge, brown eyes stared back at Brock, his pupils dilated with fear. "You came back."

"Yeah, told you I would," Brock whispered, pulling the boy into his arms. "You did really good, son."

"Thought you died."

Brock pressed the child's quivering body to his chest. "No. Not to-day."

CHAPTER 34

Brock's hands were steady. He firmly held the trembling child to him. The boy's ragged breathing and racing heart proved to Brock how the child felt.

No doubt this kid will have nightmares for a long time. He knew this all too well from his own encounters with childhood mistakes and misfortune.

Lifting his head, the child pointed to Shuggs. "Who's that scary man with the red eyes?"

"He's your daddy's friend," Brock said. "You remember Uncle Shuggs? Don't you, son?"

Squeezing his tiny hands tight around Brock's neck, the boy peeked at Shuggs and shook his head. "I don't know him," he whispered.

"Sure, you do. He was even there when you—"

"Uncle Brock," the child said, tears welling in his eyes. "I need my mommy. Now."

Brock smoothed a layer of sweaty curls out of his godson's eyes. "We're going to go back to where your mommy is."

"You promise?"

"Yeah, I promise."

"Is the kid alright?" Shuggs asked.

His heartbeat quickening, Brock stared at his godson's contorted face.

"Looks like he's spooked," Brock said, his voice low. "It's to be expected."

"Poor kid."

"Unfortunately, he's seen too much today."

"Man, I know what that's like."

"We'd better get him back to his mom."

"Then we can figure things out. Right?"

"Yeah. Just follow me."

"Okay. Where to?"

"The main dining room. That's where Patti's hunkered down with her mother and other son." Brock moved swiftly down the hallway with Shuggs behind him.

When the boy laid his head in the crook of his neck, an abrupt rush of emotions seized Brock. It'd been ages since someone held onto him, ages since he'd held someone he loved.

The feeling brought Brock back to his early years.

A memory sped through his mind of the bullying, a bloodied knife he'd stolen from his dad, his mom's tearful embrace, an unresponsive boy his age. A boy who'd never open his eyes again.

But he didn't have time to handle his tormented past. Not while on the deadly rooftop of the Thompson Hotel. *I've got to come up with a plan to evacuate Patti and her family to safety.*

Despite what his choices as a child had robbed from him, Brock had avowed to protect the innocent. At all costs. By any means necessary.

He'd failed miserably. Children had died under his watch.

It was now time to make good on his promise to himself.

In his world, the people he did life with were closer than any relative. They were his real family. Today he would keep his family safe.

He had to.

And then he noticed it. An air-handler vent a few feet away from him in the ceiling. It would likely connect to vents on the floors below. To others, it probably meant very little. But for Brock, it was the beginning of a plan. A way out.

"See that?"

Shuggs looked around. "No."

Brock motioned upward with his chin. "Right there."

"What're you trying to show me?"

"The vent."

"What about it?"

"We can climb through there and reach the main air shaft. Then crawl to another floor below."

"No way," Shuggs said, blowing smoke in front of him.

"Why not? I've done it before."

"C'mon, it's too narrow."

Brock stared at the vent. "I have a hunch it's big enough."

"Doubt it. Besides, we'd have to bust the caging around it."

"Yeah, but the inner vent is wide."

"Wide enough for each of us to fit?"

"Yeah."

Shuggs shook his head. "Ceiling's too high."

Brock inched forward and stood directly under the vent. "I'm guessing this ceiling isn't more than twelve feet high."

Shuggs walked over and peered at the ceiling. "Give or take."

"We'll search for a ladder." Block shifted the child to his other hip.

"Doubt we'll find anything like that around here."

"It's worth a try."

"Maybe," Shuggs said.

"Not like we got a lot of choices."

"You got a point."

Brock turned, continued down the hall to the dining room, and searched for a utility closet until he saw one.

At the same time, Shuggs shuffled forward. "I'm on it, bro."

When Brock reached the closet, Shuggs had already entered the doorway, resurfacing with a stepladder. "Found one."

"Good. Let me get the others."

"Now?"

"Yeah. Remember?"

"Remember what?"

Brock rubbed the child's back. "The little guy needs his mom."

"Shouldn't we try to reach the vent first?"

"No. I think from this point forward we need to stay together."

Shuggs glanced in the direction of the stairwell. "Time's not on our side, bro."

"I know."

"Be smart. Don't act off of your emotions."

"I'm not," Brock said. "No need to worry. We have a plan."

"I'll wait down by the air-handler."

"We'll be right back." Brock rushed toward the dining room.

"Don't forget," Shuggs said, his voice trailing behind Brock. "There's a ticking bomb nearby."

CHAPTER 35

A chill ran down Brock's spine hearing Shuggs's voice ricochet in the hall. His friend's reminder about the bomb was a stark reality check. They were in a race against time to get to safety. He shook the negative thought from his head. *No. I will get them to safety. Even if it kills me.*

The child groaned softly.

Brock stumbled and braced himself, feeling like the boy's body had doubled in weight.

Wondering if the bundle in his arms understood the danger they were in, Brock peered down at the boy. "You okay, little man?"

It appeared the child had fallen asleep.

He adjusted the child's weight back onto his other hip. Brock glanced at the lights lining the hall, the majority of them broken in battle.

Brock felt his blood pressure rise as he jogged down the corridor into darkness.

His cell phone rang.

Brock tried to catch his breath and answered as soon as he'd sucked enough air into his burning lungs. "Yeah?"

"O'Reilly, are you alright?"

"Dr. Harper?" He leaned against the wall and hugged the child to him.

"Yes. Are you in a safe location?"

Brock stopped and squinted at the shadows in front of him. "For now." He could only faintly make out the entry to the restaurant. *Thank God. I'm only a few feet from the doors.*

"Where?"

"I'm looking for Patti and her family—"

"Exactly where are you?"

"Directly in front of the restaurant."

"Are you alone?"

"I'm with one of Patti's sons."

"Good. You are safe."

"I'm *not* safe. There's a bomb a few feet away from me."

"Yes. We are working on a solution to defuse the bomb."

"How much time do we have?"

"We gather you have about sixty minutes before it detonates."

"Besides the bomb, things up here have been changing at warp speed."

"We have experienced changes down here too."

"Like what?"

"Do not be alarmed," Dr. Harper said quickly. "But we are having difficulty locating Shuggs."

Brock bit his lip. "Okay."

"I understand he is desperate to ensure your safety. However, we want to prevent any further disaster by rash actions."

His mind began to race, recalling Shuggs's admittance of going rogue. *This is exactly what Shuggs feared.*

"I understand." Brock wiped a bead of sweat from his damp face.

"If Shuggs manages to get to you before we do, I need you to inform me."

Brock took a deep breath. He deliberated whether he should disclose that Shuggs had come to rescue him. But he reasoned that while he didn't condone what Shuggs had done, he wouldn't betray his friend's trust. Not now. Not when so much more was at stake.

"O'Reilly? Are you still there?"

He shifted his weight from one foot to another and patted the child on his shoulder. "Yeah, I'm here. I'm just trying to process everything." He looked behind him. "I still have to figure a way out of here."

"Your instructions were to wait for help," she said. "Correct?"

"Understood."

"Then please adhere to protocol."

"A lot has happened since we last spoke."

"What happened?"

The child wiggled in Brock's arms.

Brock patted the restless boy's back, lulling him back to sleep.

"O'Reilly?"

"Yeah?"

"What else has happened?"

"I found more dead bodies." His voice was low.

"Did you ID them?"

"No. But they're probably staff."

"I see. Anything else?"

Brock put his hand on the door of the dining facility and pressed his face against the glass, praying for a glimpse of the family. "I had to take down two perps who were up here looking for Patti. And, um, ..." He stalled while contemplating whether to tell Dr. Harper about Shuggs.

"Please continue," she said.

The more Brock thought about it, the more convinced he was that disclosing the fact that Shuggs had broken ranks with the intel team to rescue him wouldn't sit well with Dr. Harper.

"That's it."

"I apologize for giving you so much flack during this stressful time."

"I get it. We're all anxious."

"Seems like you are doing an excellent job protecting Pang's family."

Brock edged closer to the door. "My job won't be done until they're safe." He took a couple of steps into the restaurant.

Dr. Harper was quiet for a few moments. "I assume you have not had any other contact with Shuggs since you have been trapped."

"Not really."

"Is that a yes? Or a no?"

"No. Not exactly."

"Remember, if he contacts you, you must contact me immediately."

"Why?" Brock shook his head. "He's on our side."

"We are concerned about Shuggs's frame of mind."

Brock took a gulp of air. He caught movement out of the corner of his eye. A small shadow. *Might be the other kid.* "I understand. Fully."

"No. I do not believe you do."

He gazed at a corner of the room. *There they are. Under the table.* Brock sighed. "What about the situation *don't* I understand?"

But Dr. Harper had already hung up.

CHAPTER 36

Brock shoved the phone into his pocket, glanced at the sleeping boy drooling on his shoulder, and cursed under his breath.

It's times like these I wish I were operating like I was overseas. Things were different in the States. There were legal procedures. Protocol. Politics. Paparazzi. It didn't matter that the entire hotel was a booby trap rigged to blow.

Brock edged his way to the overturned table in the farthest corner of the restaurant. *My mind is made up.* No way would he wait for the entire intel community to arrive and consult with FBI lawyers moving like robots through their spreadsheets and strategies.

He'd seen it happen too many times to count. Times when law enforcement followed the rules like they were cake recipes. They waited. They gave the enemy the upper hand. Resulting in lots of innocent dead people.

With him, there would be no waiting. No hesitating. No negotiating with thugs. As long as he was packing and on the right side of the dirt, he'd do his part to keep his people safe. Alive.

He inched forward, securing the boy with his open palm, and bent over, checking beneath the table.

Three pairs of widened eyes stared back at him.

"It's me, Brock. It's safe to come on out."

"No," Patti said, her face ashen.

Her younger son clung to her neck. "Want to stay with you, Mommy," the boy whispered in her ear.

"Patti, you know you can trust me. We need to get out of here."

Patti shook her head. "It's not you I'm worried about."

Turning to Mrs. Lipsett, Brock extended a hand. "Let's get you out of here, ma'am."

Mrs. Lipsett stared blankly at Brock. She looked as if she'd aged twenty years in the last twenty minutes.

"My mom is in shock," Patti said, her face drawn. "She's completely shut down."

Brock gestured at the exit. "The good thing is, I've figured a way out of here."

"I say we wait for help."

"We're sitting ducks waiting here."

"I'm not leaving."

"You have to. There's no other way."

"Whoever carried out this attack ..." Patti sank further back under the table beside her mother. "They're looking to eliminate me," a tear slid down her face, "and my family."

"No. They're after everyone. Probably terrorists."

She shook her head. "They know each of us by name. Even my boys. My mother."

"How do you know that?"

"I heard it on the radio."

Brock glanced around. "What radio?"

"Over there," Patti said, her finger shaking, pointing to where Snake lay on the floor in a pool of congealing blood.

"Okay," Brock said, walking over to the body. "This is progress. Now we have a radio."

"How's that going to help?"

He reached down and picked up the handset. "We have a direct line to the perps."

"But that radio doesn't work anymore."

"It might."

Studying the radio, Brock crouched, balancing the boy on his shoulder.

"I've already tried using it," Patti said. "It's no use."

Brock turned the equipment over in his hands. "This type of radio operates on biometrics," he said and pressed one of the buttons on the radio against Snake's limp hand.

Within seconds, the radio crackled to life.

"Hello?" Brock spoke into the radio repeatedly.

But he was met with static from the other end.

Brock closed his eyes briefly. They needed to move. He had no idea what kind of time was left on the explosive several feet away from them.

And then the radio buzzed with a booming voice on the other end. "Snake? You there, man?"

"Yeah," Brock said quickly.

"You don't have much time to evacuate. We've been holding off on detonating the bomb because of you. Get downstairs now."

Brock frowned. "How?"

"Are you kidding me right now?"

"No."

The man on the other end rattled off several colorful obscenities. "Use the exact route on the map we gave you."

"Yeah." Brock clicked the mute button before pocketing the radio.

"The map's probably on him," Patti said.

"I'm going to need some help locating it."

Patti pushed her whimpering son into her mother's arms and ran over to Brock and her other son, her arms outstretched.

"Thanks." Brock carefully placed the sleeping boy in Patti's open arms.

He knelt beside Snake and went through every blood-soaked pocket he could find but couldn't locate a map.

"Try his shoes," Patti said. "Maybe you'll find it there."

He wiped his bloody hands on his jeans, then pulled off each boot and shook them. Nothing.

"Check for a pocket or a zipper in his shoes."

Brock dabbed his sopping forehead and grabbed a boot again. His fingers grazed a small Velcro strap on the outside.

Patti paced, patting her son on the back. "Yes, check under the strap."

He pulled back the strap, noticing a small pocket lodged underneath.

A light flashed in Patti's eyes. "Yes, I bet you that's it."

Reaching into the pocket, Brock fingered a slip of paper and pulled it out.

"Is it the map?"

He nodded. "Jackpot."

CHAPTER 37

Brock absently rubbed his temple while he studied the scrap of paper.

Patti stood beside him, peeking over his shoulder. "What does the map say?"

"Wait a sec," Brock said, trying to make sense of the handwritten diagram.

"Something wrong?"

"I'm not seeing how this is a map."

"Let me see it."

Brock held the paper up so Patti could have a clear view.

Her brow wrinkled. "What's with the numbers?"

"Could be a code of some sort."

"I agree." Patti nodded. "But we need the key."

"It's not like I can radio the perp and ask for it."

"I think it's worth a try."

"No, absolutely not," Brock said. "They'll catch on that I'm not Snake."

"Maybe Snake has the key somewhere."

"Could be, but I've gone through every pocket."

"Are you sure?"

"Yeah." Brock scratched his thickening chin stubble and stared at Snake's lifeless frame. He knew how men like him worked. Efficiently. Smart.

It gave him an idea. He knelt over Snake's body and checked the man's wrist for a watch.

Brock removed the watch and tapped the small screen. "I've got the game plan."

"The codes are on the watch?"

He nodded. "These guys planned a way out," Brock said. "The codes line up with the vent system, tracking a pathway to avoid making a wrong turn."

Patti shook her head. "Thought I was thorough when I searched him. Can't believe I missed—"

"Yeah, but according to this," he said, comparing the paper with the codes on the watch, "Shuggs is working on removing the seal from the wrong vent, *and* we're almost out of time."

"Crap. What do we do?"

"Follow the criminal's directions."

"Okay." Patti moved her son to her other hip. "Let's do it."

"What about your mom?"

Patti held her son out to Brock. "I got an idea."

Brock rocked his godson while Patti dashed to the nearby bar in the restaurant. She returned with a shot glass full of brown liquid.

"What the heck is that?"

"Brandy," Patti said, kneeling beside her mother. "Grandma used to give it to her for her nerves."

While Patti gently coaxed the alcohol into her mother's trembling mouth, Brock glanced at his watch. It was 11:00 p.m., and having read the details on the map, he had exactly forty-five minutes to escape to safety. If he screwed up, he knew they'd all be dead. But if he were cautious, nothing would go wrong.

Mrs. Lipsett's labored breathing came in gasps while she gripped the legs of a toppled stool. Straining, she rose slowly from beneath the table.

Patti stayed close, steadying her mother's shaky stance.

A loud crack split the air when one of the heels on Mrs. Lipsett's pumps broke. She moaned weakly, grasping the edge of the table's base.

Brock rushed to Mrs. Lipsett's other side, grabbing hold of her elbow.

The older woman wobbled unsteadily and kicked off her shoes after leaning her full weight onto Brock. "Thanks for coming back for us, baby," she said, breathing heavily and patting his arm.

"Hold onto me, ma'am. I got you."

Patti picked up her half-asleep son.

Brock led the way to the exit and into the hall.

Patti trailed behind him.

Brock turned around, signaling to Patti that they needed to hurry. Getting an injured senior, along with her daughter and two small children, to safety seemed impossible under the circumstances. Ordinarily, on dangerous missions he had a protective detail. *Can't recall a time when Pang and Shuggs weren't by my side during times like these. Got to figure out a way to overcome the challenges.*

"Stay here," Brock said to the women once they reached the area leading to the rally point.

"I want to come with you," Junior, the older child, cried, clinging to Brock's leg.

"No, you stay here." Brock picked the child up and placed him beside his mom and brother.

But Junior scrambled back to him and held on tighter. The more Brock tried to untangle himself from the child, the more he wailed.

"When he gets like that, he's not going to stop," Patti said. "Besides, he's bringing attention to us. Just take him with you, Brock."

"I'll take Junior with me, but I have to go back for Shuggs. He's working on the wrong vent."

Patti dashed to her mother's side and propped her against the wall. "Hurry."

With his godson over his shoulder, Brock crept through the dim hall that led to where Shuggs was supposed to meet him while being careful to check for any hidden attackers. The most difficult obstacle was the lack of light. Brock compensated, using his free hand to lean on the wall. Finding nothing extraordinary, Brock continued his trek.

A loud clanging noise greeted Brock before he saw sparks flying from the ceiling next to the vent. On a ladder, a looming figure stood working to remove the casing around the opening.

The figure spun around with part of the casing dangling from one hand and a pocketknife in the other. The sudden motion caused a spray of glowing embers to fly into the air. "It's about time." Shuggs stepped down from the ladder they'd found in the utility closet.

"Found a map on Snake." Brock shifted the boy onto his opposite shoulder. "The vent is *definitely* our ticket out of here."

"I know. That's why I was working on it to—"

"Don't bother. I chose the wrong entry point. The right vent is the one by the elevators," Brock said, a river of sweat running between his shoulder blades.

Shadows painted Shuggs's eyes jet-black. "How'd you know?"

"From the map." Brock checked his watch. "But we *must* go now. We're almost out of time."

Shuggs hastily closed the ladder and hoisted it over his shoulder. "Lead the way, bro."

Brock pivoted, closing the last few yards to Patti and her family.

The ladder slapped against Shuggs's thigh as he sped behind.

Brock held the boy tight, moving swiftly through the tunnel of darkness.

The bomb would detonate in thirty minutes.

His feet beat the floor in time to his racing heart rate.

CHAPTER 38

n the hotel's dark hallway, the air was dry. Still. Tomblike. The only sounds were two pairs of heavy footsteps on the carpet and the rhythmic thump of the ladder against Shuggs's legs.

While he ran, Brock thought through the plan of escape he'd discovered on the map. *There's no way that I'm just going to sit on my hands and wait to be rescued while these perps decide our fate.*

His stride elongated, and he breathed rapidly through flared nostrils.

Only seconds away from Patti and her family.

Just before Brock made his final turn around the last corridor, the child on his shoulder tensed.

"There's a monster chasing us!"

"He's our friend." Brock patted the child's back. "Remember?"

The boy's eyes widened. "No, he's not!"

"Calm down, little man." Sweat poured into Brock's eyes from his forehead. Using his free hand, he wiped it away with his forearm.

The child wailed and wormed from Brock's grasp, almost slipping onto the floor.

"Kid's about to fall!" Shuggs warned.

Before the child could hit the ground, Brock seized his godson by the shirt. "Got him!"

Pounding footfalls struck the ground like a broken drum. Another pair of feet had merged with the cadence of running on the carpet. A rumble came from the opposite corner.

"Wait," Brock whispered. He slowed his pace.

"What?"

"I heard something."

Just then, women's screams cracked the air wide.

Dr. Katherine Hutchinson-Hayes

"What in the world?"

Brock slipped his free hand under his damp shirt, reaching until he felt the gun.

In this area, it was nearly pitch-black. But an image was illuminated by a slight crack below a nearby bathroom door. A man. In the shadows.

Shuggs poked him in the back. "I think I seen someone. Over there." He pointed.

Brock looked up, blinked, and again wiped sweat from his brow.

He couldn't see the face of the man yet, but he didn't need to. He knew who it was. The waiter's distinctive height and enormous build. His blond mane.

No. It's impossible. I saw the man die alongside the waitress.

Brock went numb, not feeling his legs, holding the child with one arm.

The dead waiter from the restaurant earlier. Alive.

In a blood-soaked shirt and long blond hair in a ponytail weighed down by sweat, he staggered toward them.

"Watch out!" Shuggs shouted and ran in front of Brock. "Take cover, bro!"

Patti turned the corner by the restaurant and ran up from behind the waiter. She about-faced before him, not backing down.

The waiter's mouth fell open.

"You pulled a gun on us!" She lunged and climbed him like a tree. Her hands went around the man's throat. Her legs wrapped around his body.

The waiter contorted, grabbing wildly at Patti. Her eyes were glazed when she drove a knife into the side of his neck.

Shuggs chucked the ladder off to one side and advanced toward the waiter and Patti.

Brock crouched behind a trash can, clung to the crying child, and engaged his weapon. "Hush, little man," Brock said.

The waiter's body jerked and twisted. The rope-like veins in his neck protruded.

At that moment, Shuggs came to Patti's side with his gun aimed at the waiter's head.

Patti still had her hand on the slick weapon, her legs wrapped around his torso.

"Move, Patti! Move, now!" Shuggs shouted.

169

She sprung down, backing into the shadows where her small son and injured mother waited for her return.

Shuggs pumped several bullets into the waiter's convulsing body. The killer gurgled through gritted teeth, choking on a mouthful of blood.

Brock checked his watch and wanted to scream. They'd used up most of their time. "Let's go. We've got fifteen minutes." He got to his feet and threw his godson over his shoulder.

"Straight ahead. To the hall by the elevators," Shuggs said, grabbing the ladder and running ahead of the group.

They followed behind him down a hall that curved around into an open area with dim bluish lighting.

By the time the group arrived under the air-handler, Shuggs had already stationed the ladder and completely unlocked the hatch.

He removed the casing and stepped down. "You lead," Shuggs said to Brock. "I'll be last."

"Put the kids between the adults." Brock placed his screaming godson in Shuggs's arms and scaled the ladder.

Getting to the top rung, he motioned for Shuggs to hand him the children. Brock checked his watch. Ten minutes and thirty seconds before the bomb detonated.

The tunnel was dank and poorly lit. It curved back and forth through the dark.

Ignoring the pain of his bloodied legs, Brock led the group that trailed close behind. They crawled through the icy metal tube of the cylinder hardly big enough for a child, much less a man.

They scooted on their hands and knees. Single file.

The shaft they crawled through emptied downward into a square concrete tunnel.

There were four different directions they could take.

Relying on his memory of the map, Brock closed his eyes and recalled the directions on a watch he could no longer see. Then he looked down the steep incline and remembered he'd have to make a left, even if it plunged them into complete darkness.

There would be no time for alternate routes.

No turning back—just straight to the correct destination.

There was no room for a single mistake.

Brock licked his cracked lips, tasting the ripe, familiar acidic taste—adrenaline.

It was then he heard the distinct click.
The sound reverberated through the tunnel.
They were out of time.

CHAPTER 39

With the echo of the bomb's click still humming in his ear, Brock crawled downward through the spiraling tunnel. Sucked in oxygen. Sped. Doing everything he could to put space between the group and imminent danger.

Silently, he prayed for the others to keep up with his steady pace. Gulping patches of dust, his dry mouth gaped with each jerky movement.

At times, Brock struggled to push his body through the narrowing ventilation system, especially when it sloped.

Around the first turn, Brock bumped his head on duct sealant. "Watch your heads," he yelled. Quickly recovering, he crept lower.

Sharp sheet metal lacerated his palms. He balled his fists. Not having time to pull his sleeves over his hands, he pushed his body further. To safety. It felt as if someone had dumped a bucket of razors in the vent, and Brock's hands and knees had found each of them.

Dust clogging his throat, Brock hacked up phlegm from his lungs. Gravity pulled him toward a row of nails. As they gleamed like a row of shark's teeth in the shadows, he desperately tried avoiding them. He wiggled to the other side, but with the vent narrowing, there was nowhere to escape.

Sharp spikes gashed his elbow. "Watch out! Nails on your left!" he shouted. "Keep low."

From behind, Brock's younger godson whimpered, his cries reverberating through the tunnel's walls.

"Uncle … I … I'm … scared," the older child said, coughing. "I can't see. Help me!"

Ignoring an impulse to reach back and help the child, Brock's stomach lurched. "You can do it, little man. I know you can."

"Keep moving," Patti said. "Mommy's right behind you."

"So am I." Mrs. Lipsett's fragile voice pierced the dust-laden air.

Brock squinted into the murky shadows through watery eyes. He crawled swiftly into the tunneled darkness on raw knees, sore hands, and a rush of momentum coursing through his body.

Veering off to the left, like the map instructed, Brock wanted nothing more than for his people to get to safety. "Follow close, gang. Keep going. No matter what."

"I'm holding up the rear!" Shuggs's voice thundered. "We got this, bro!"

"Yeah, we do," Brock said. "Don't give up." *The only problem is surviving.* Before the inevitable boom.

At that moment, he sensed a void. A suction. Felt his hot face redden. Gusts of sudden heat on his back.

Then the emptiness of air, before the bomb detonated like a mixture of static from an old analog radio and a mosquito buzzing in his ear.

Don't want to scare them, but we've got to hustle. "Faster! Go ... faster ... fast as you can!" Brock hurled the words over his shoulder.

That was when it felt as if someone had turned up the volume in the tunnel. It started off as a low hum, quickly magnifying the children's cries. Coughs. Knees scraping metal. Hands hitting tin walls. Keys jingling.

A door separating them from Hades ripped open. Darkness overwhelmed any light the tight space held. The blast shook them as though an angry hand of a giant had grabbed the tunnel.

Brock glanced back, temporarily blinded, when he saw a tiny red ball of flame racing toward him. "Don't look back! Go!" he screamed. *The fireball is still far enough away for us to outrun it. But not by much.*

Brock raced forward unseeing, a hissing sound in his ears so loud it drowned out the group's screams and sealed him in complete silence.

Something blunt snagged his pants. Brock flinched but kept moving, even when the nail speared his thigh. His quads ached, but the adrenaline was pumping away the pain while his hands and knees continued to crawl over piles of uneven debris.

Brock traveled as fast as he could. Constantly fighting the urge to stop and look back. Forcing the pain from his mind.

Scuttling through the dark. Blind. Deaf. Choking on the stale thick soot collecting around him, Brock hoped everyone was still behind him. But he couldn't tell for certain.

Suddenly, his head connected with a wall, temporarily dazing him. Using his hands like a blind man, he could tell that he'd approached the end of the tunnel. *Here's where the path gives way to the air-handler two floors beneath the rooftop.*

Still blinded, his nails scrambled along the steel wall, searching for the interior casing. His forefinger caught behind a hinge and wedged there.

No matter how hard he pulled, his finger stayed stuck. His heart pounded.

There's no other way. Closing his eyes tight, Brock shoved his other fist into his mouth and tore his wedged finger free, leaving his fingernail behind. A blend of fire and ice shot from his nail bed up through his entire arm.

He didn't have to see the wound to know it was bleeding profusely, and he had nothing to wrap it with. Brock put pressure on the finger, tore off a piece of his shirt to dress the cut, and kept working.

After a few seconds of wrenching the casing away from the base, Brock loosened it. He twisted his body around in the small space so his feet rested above the vent.

Raising both legs, Brock let them down with all the force he could muster.

The first kick didn't budge the casing. Neither did the next.

He tried more times than he could count. His legs trembled and gave out. Still, the casing remained intact.

Bent like a pretzel, Brock sat in the tunnel. Stunned.

Staring out at the dark, knees gathered up near his chest. Trapped. *Unbelievable.* Brock pushed away the guilt that was choking him worse than the smoke. *Can't save myself, much less Pang's family.*

Brock squinted, searching the tunnel. *Where are the others? Could they have maybe taken another way?* He prayed Shuggs would bring up the rear. Meet him with the family at the rendezvous. *Heck, they're probably dead for all I know.*

Immediately, Brock pushed the thought away. Now wasn't the time for negative thinking. Now was the time for finishing what he'd started. Execution of the plan.

CHAPTER 40

Taking a deep breath, Brock willed himself to use every bit of reserve he had left.

He raised his shaking legs, intending to strike the vent one last time.

With his feet in midair, something caught his eye below, out-of-focus but there.

Brock eased his legs down slowly and twisted his body around to get onto his stomach. Controlling his labored breathing, he peered through the grill.

Blinking away the haze of white spots still obstructing his vision, Brock strained to see through the mesh partition. He made out one, then two blurs walking beneath him.

Forms emerged. Cloudy images dressed in what appeared to be tactical gear. The closer Brock pushed his face to the grating, the clearer the images became.

From where he perched, about twenty feet in the air with limited visibility, it was difficult to tell what type of uniforms they wore. *Who are they?*

One of the men briefly pointed to the ceiling. For a second, Brock held his breath and froze in place. *Heck, if I can't tell which side of the law they're on, I can't disclose my position.*

Brock figured he was hidden away from view, but he was still in a vulnerable spot and had probably made a racket trying to get out of the vent.

Brock slid backward on his stomach as quietly as he could manage, easing his bruised torso from the screen.

He moved back far enough so that his entire body was away from the vent's opening. But close enough to be able to hear through the mesh.

At first, he couldn't hear or see much. Sounds were muffled. Everything looked blurred.

Seconds later, the ringing in Brock's ears subsided. Voices floated up to him through the grill. Men's voices that sounded as if they spoke through a whirling fan.

Not perfect, but it's an improvement. Brock pressed his swollen face to the steel floor of the tunnel as close to the screen as he could get. He peeked over the edge.

It appeared the vent let out into a spacious conference room. Surveying the room with its variety of equipment, Brock could see the area was being used as a small-scale staging area.

Then Brock saw one person. A heavily armed man outfitted police paramilitary style. The armed man took a swig from a flask and handed it to another man. The other man drank, pocketed the flask, and took a deep pull from what appeared to be a cigarette.

Once the aroma reached Brock's nostrils, he couldn't hold his breath anymore.

He got a whiff and knew it was no ordinary smoke. Weed. Skunk. Marijuana. He'd recognize that smell anywhere.

What're these men doing standing here on the job, drinking and getting high in the midst of all this? Had the force really gotten that lax since the last time he'd left the States?

Rubbing his irritated eyes, Brock looked closer.

It was strange.

The men looked exactly like SWAT police officers to Brock. But even while hovering many feet above them, something seemed wrong about their demeanor.

It wasn't just the men's obvious deviant behavior. Brock had been around long enough to know that even the *most* elite and respected people were capable of villainy and deceitfulness.

The way the officers carried their guns bothered him. A lot.

SWAT officers acted as paramilitary units that tackled situations beyond the capability of conventional police forces. SWAT was called whenever an incident presented a major risk to law enforcement officers or the public. While all SWAT officers are deemed experts with in-depth training, most play a highly specialized role within the team.

Yet these men had high-caliber machine guns slung over their shoulders like women's cheap pocketbooks.

Brock wanted to jump down, beat the crap out of the men, and fix the assailants for good. He shook his head in disgust. If it was one thing he hated, it was posers.

One of the men's radios crackled to life.

Brock still carried Snake's radio. Earlier, he had turned the volume up slightly, then down again almost all the way, but it hummed against his hip. Reaching over, Brock flipped the radio's switch to the mute position again.

In the meantime, the smaller poser reached for his radio.

The bigger poser instantly reached for his gun.

Brock grabbed his weapon, training it on the man holding the radio.

"Come in, Razor 6," the small poser said.

"That you, Spook 6?" the radio blared.

"Yes, sir."

"Who's with you?"

"Spook 5, sir."

"We need you both at the rally point."

Spook 6 looked at his watch. "But we haven't found Buck's men or the spiders yet. We were told the first order of business was to eliminate them, sir."

"We find Buck's people, Pang's family, and O'Reilly," Spook 5 said, using his gun to accentuate his words. "We terminate on sight."

"Who gave you those instructions?" Razor 6 asked.

"The General," Spook 6 said.

"Then proceed."

"The only problem is there're children involved, sir."

"And?"

Spook 6 cleared his throat. "I didn't think we'd be instructed to eliminate kids is all, sir.

"The General is fully aware of the two boys with the group."

"I ... I understand, sir."

"You have permission to carry out your mission."

"Copy that, sir."

"But listen to me carefully, Spook 6."

"Yes, sir, what is it?"

"Do not under any circumstances underestimate the capabilities of this group."

"It shouldn't be too hard, sir. With kids *and* a senior citizen with them, they're mostly soft targets—"

"Shut up! You don't know what you're talking about. One of the spiders is a skilled classified associate of the agency. She's got lots of interesting tricks up her sleeves. Defuse her by eliminating the children first. Then her mother."

"What about the guy, sir?" Spook 6 asked.

Spook 5 nodded. "Yes. We need as much info about Brock O'Reilly as possible."

"He is the most concerning," Razor 6 said.

"Why, sir?"

"He's one of the deadliest agents the intelligence field has ever encountered. Do not engage him. Do not speak to him. Or let him get into your head. Just eliminate him."

CHAPTER 41

Brock lay on his stomach in the musty air-handler doing his best not to sneeze. He listened to the opposition discuss his fate and decided that retracing his steps would be their best chance of survival.

Thoughts of his friend Patti and her family flashed in his mind, and he prayed. *God, help me find a way out of this for us. No more cheap liquor, cheap women, and five-dollar cuss words. I promise I'll go to church.* He felt awful that he called on God only in dire situations. *When will I learn?*

He waited until he could be certain the men had cleared the area. After they left, he contorted his battered body around to face the opposite direction. Beginning the crawl to find his crew and another way out.

A few feet into his journey, Brock's phone buzzed to life. He twisted and fumbled, retrieving the phone on the third ring. "Yeah?"

"O'Reilly, I am glad you are safe," Dr. Harper said.

"I'm not safe."

"But after the bomb detonated, you answered the—"

"I'm in trouble," Brock said, trying to control his voice. He wanted to scream into the phone but knew the noise would carry through the handler.

"Where are you?"

"In an air vent."

"Can you be more specific?"

Brock's head throbbed. *Screw it. I might just yell.*

Footsteps pounded the ground below him, and he pressed the phone to his chest until the steps passed.

"O'Reilly, are you still there?"

"Listen for a minute, Doc, please," Brock whispered as loudly as he dared, staring through the cracks to see if there was any sign of the enemy below.

"Yes?"

"These people. I think they could be white supremacists."

"You could be right."

"And as crazy as it sounds, I believe they've been working with Uncle Buck's people."

"That does not add up."

"I know. But they're looking for Buck's people and us because they're planning to kill—"

"Wait. They are looking for Buck's men?"

"Yeah, but we've already killed them—"

"You killed Uncle Buck's men?"

"We did."

"Sounds like you are holding your own."

"No, I'm in serious trouble here—"

"Are you hurt?"

"I'm banged up some, but that's not—"

"Were you able to find a safer location than the one you were in before?"

"Well, yeah, but—"

"Be patient. You did survive an explosion," Dr. Harper said. "And from all accounts, the worst is over."

"How so?"

"Apparently, the bomb didn't detonate properly. It could have been far more lethal than it actually was. We have regained security of the building. Also, we have our men on the way up to the rooftop to rescue the group. Get out of the vent and return there."

"Impossible. Terrorists are in the building. They've breached security and are posing as SWAT law enforcement."

"You saw them?"

"I did."

"How many?"

"Two. There was a third man on a radio. Four if you count some guy they're referring to as the *General*."

"Is he the person calling the shots?"

"Yeah."

"I have made a note of the information you provided. However, our intelligence assured me all of the assailants were contained or eliminated."

"Your intel is wrong. Hostiles are alive and actively searching the building. I overheard them planning to kill us."

"We will be on high alert for the remaining terrorists you've described," Harper said. "But returning is still the best course of action."

"The rooftop's too dangerous. Between the bomb and the attackers, we had to make a run for it and got separated. I've been searching for—"

"Let me get this straight. You lost the group in an air vent?"

Brock took a deep breath and let it out through his nostrils. "Yeah."

"I am depending on you to locate and protect them," Dr. Harper said. "Once that happens, how do we find you?"

"We'll be in the air-handler somewhere between the roof and the tenth floor."

"I will redirect the team and get back to you."

"Please hurry," Brock said. "This is life or death here."

The line went dead.

Plastering his sweaty, bloody palms on the tin floor, Brock leaned forward and peered into the shadows.

Ahead there was a dark shape.

Squinting, Brock tried to make out any features. The form of a child, a woman ... anything that might give him a hint as to whether it was a friend or foe.

He moved closer.

The mound didn't move.

Brock's heart was in his throat.

"That you, baby?"

His breathing was heavier at the anticipation of finding Patti's family. Sighing in relief, Brock slid closer. "Mrs. Lipsett?"

"It's me."

He held his hand out, feeling his way to her shoulder. "You okay, ma'am?"

"My head feels fuzzy."

"I'm sorry, ma'am."

"Last thing I remember was a loud bang."

"Where're the others?"

"Don't know." Mrs. Lipsett coughed.

"Have you seen them since the explosion?"

Mrs. Lipsett shook her head.

"Think they're hurt?"

"All I know is that after the blast, I must've passed out."

"So you woke up here alone?"

"Yes. Where's my family? I don't understand why Patti would leave me."

"She would never do that purposely. After the explosion, it was hard to see and easy to get disoriented."

"I hope my grandbabies and my daughter are safe."

"Patti's tough. I'm sure she's fine," Brock said. "All that matters is I get you and the others to safety."

CHAPTER 42

Gunshots rattled beneath the handler like a subway train, each bullet blast rumbled against the walls echoing up to the tunnel.

Brock squeezed Mrs. Lipsett's hand. "You did sustain an injury. How're you holding up with that bullet wound?"

"It looks worse than it is. But it's a flesh wound, so I'm okay." Mrs. Lipsett's voice cracked as she squeezed Brock's hand back. "But I'm more scared than hurt. I'm so scared."

"Don't worry," Brock said. "I'm here."

"What about those people after us?" Her tears began. "They're determined to kill us."

Using the cuff of his shirt's sleeve, Brock wiped Mrs. Lipsett's paper-thin cheek. "With me here, no one's getting to any of you."

"Brock!" A familiar voice echoed indistinctly from the direction the group had started.

Brock strained to see in the shadows. "Patti?"

"Yes. Almost there."

"Where're my babies?" Mrs. Lipsett asked.

"Right behind me," Patti said, coming into view, her boys close behind. "You okay, Mom?"

"I'm fine."

Patti crawled out from the shadows and rubbed her mother's shoulder.

"Uncle Brock," his older godson said. "I cried a lot when we lost you."

"Glad you found me," Brock said.

"Grandma! I want my grandma," the smaller boy cried.

Mrs. Lipsett stretched out and gently caressed her grandson's hair. "I'm right here, sugar." She tried to support herself on her hands but flopped down onto her elbows.

Brock rested his hand on the older woman's back. He peered into the dark behind Patti's family. "Where's Shuggs?"

"He vanished after the explosion," Patti said.

"My God. That's terrible." Her mother took a deep, composing breath. "I hope he's okay."

Where in the world could Shuggs be? Brock hoped they didn't find his body wedged somewhere in the tunnel. "We must turn around," he said.

"Why?" Patti asked.

"Things are compromised in the direction we were supposed to take."

"Where do we go now?" Patti motioned behind her. "Back to the rooftop?"

"No. Too dangerous. We backtrack until we find an exit before we get to the roof. You'll have to lead. We don't have space for me to maneuver past to get out in front," Brock said.

"Where am I going?"

"The map's right here." He tapped the small screen of Snake's watch. "I'll give you the codes and help to direct you from the rear."

"Okay, got it." Patti reached over her mother and took the slip of paper Brock held out to her. "Boys, get behind me. Mr. Brock will protect you. He'll stay behind you."

"I'm scared to go back," the older boy said.

"Me too," his brother wailed.

"I promise to protect you," Brock said. "Now that I'm here, I'll make sure you're safe. Keep following your mom. Like she said, I'll be right behind you."

Watching while the children maneuvered, Brock could see the black shapes their bodies made against the vent's walls.

Brock guided Mrs. Lipsett by the shoulders and helped her twist and turn in the narrow corridor until she faced the opposite direction. Directly in front of him was Mrs. Lipsett, the boys, and Patti.

He then focused on the map while Patti called out the first code she read from the paper. "I see an A-4-1 on the duct overhead that matches the one on the map," she said.

He checked the watch. "That means we need to turn left at the next bend."

Orange smoke snaked through the tunnel, drifting lazily and low to the ground while the air-handler dipped in a steep downward curve.

The next few seconds seemed to happen in slow motion. Brock watched, unable to intervene, while the tunnel's floor suddenly fractured.

"Help, Brock!" Patti screamed as the floor splintered. She teetered on the edge of the rift, shoved forward by the bodies of her children and mother.

"Hang on!" Brock shouted a warning that came too late.

Patti plunged through the hole in the vent, with her sons and mother flailing and falling right behind her.

Brock clutched wildly at the slippery walls. He slid quickly toward the gaping chasm. And then he plummeted ten feet to the floor below in a haze of sheet rock and metal fragments.

Blinded by a cloud of dust, Brock struggled to breathe as the shock of slamming into the ground compressed his chest. Debris rained down in a shower of gray snow. A thunderous echo rolled around the maintenance room they'd fallen into.

Brock felt the world pause, and the ringing in his ears returned. He forced himself to stay alert and not succumb to the irresistible urge to collapse from exhaustion.

Then he saw a flash of white, the flashlight from a phone beaming from Patti's fingers.

"Brock, speak to me. You okay?"

He blinked and pushed the light away. "Yeah. Got the air knocked out of me is all." Brock sat up slowly and cracked his neck. He tried to look around, but his head was still spinning. "What about you and the others?"

"We landed in a pile of fiberglass, so we're okay. Looks like you didn't do too badly either. You landed on a stack of drop cloths."

"I broke my teeth," Patti's younger son said, showing off a bloody grimace.

"Open wide." His mother used her fingers to help open the child's mouth. "Looks like you lost a baby tooth, sweetheart." She pulled a tissue from her pocket, folded it, and put it in the child's mouth.

Brock got to his knees. "How's your mother?"

"I'm alright. I landed on top of a roll of builder's insulation," Mrs. Lipsett said, pointing to her grandson, who sat nearby coughing. "But I'm concerned about Junior. He's begun wheezing."

"Oh, no! He's allergic to just about everything in this maintenance room," Patti said, shining the flash around the room. "Mom, please give Junior his inhaler."

Mrs. Lipsett nodded. "Sure. Where is it?"

"In his pouch. Where it always is."

Junior shook his head, coughing incessantly.

"Come on, Junior. Help Grandma out." Patti rose to her feet and walked to her son. "We have to make sure you take your medication within minutes of being exposed to anything you're allergic to."

"I ... lost ... it," he said, pointing at the busted vent. "Up ... up ... there."

"Just give him the meds from your backup pack, baby," Mrs. Lipsett said.

"It's in the hotel room, Mom. And he won't be able to travel there in his condition."

Rolling his shoulders back, Brock rose shakily to his feet. "I'll get the boy's meds and bring them back here," he said.

In the hallway outside the room, gunfire crackled like lightning in a thunderstorm. Footsteps thudded past the door. Then someone let out a bloodcurdling scream.

CHAPTER 43

Patti silenced the children's whimpers with an index finger and a hiss, letting a show of teeth and her scowl do the talking.

Junior blinked back tears, burying his head in his hands while his younger sibling took to sucking his thumb.

"Maybe the child can get by without that inhaler. At least until after we're rescued," Mrs. Lipsett whispered when the noise in the hallway subsided. "It sounded really dangerous out there. I just don't think it's safe to leave."

Junior coughed and lifted his head. "I ... don't want ... Uncle Brock to ... to ... leave."

"Me too," the smaller child said, his eyes wide.

"Don't worry, boys," Brock said. "I would never do anything to put you in any danger. As long as I'm around, even if I have to leave for a little while, I'll always protect you."

"You promise?" Junior asked.

"I promise." Brock looked at Patti. "What do you think?"

Patti knelt beside her son and carefully examined him. Leaning over, she listened to his chest. "He's in a bad way."

Brock frowned. "How bad?"

She sat up and rocked in place. "The last time he was like this, he ended up in a pediatric critical care unit for an entire week."

Brock sighed and rubbed his jaw. "Then it's settled." He took the hotel key from Patti's outstretched hand. "I'll grab the meds from the hotel room and have the rescue team meet us back here shortly."

"Move fast. It's probably safer to take the stairs," Patti said.

Mrs. Lipsett pulled both children onto her lap. "Whatever you do, don't get caught."

He nodded while sending Dr. Harper a text, letting her know their new location. "Lay low. Keep quiet. You should be safe here until I get back."

"Does the team know where we are?" Patti asked.

"I just texted Dr. Harper an update. She'll know where to find you. I should be back in time. I think your room is just a few floors above the maintenance room." Brock went to the door, opened it slowly, and peered through the crack, making sure the area was clear. He then motioned to Patti to lock the door.

Brock moved slowly through the darkened hallway. The solitary lighting, a dull red sign over the exit to the stairwell several feet down at the end of the hall, cast an eerie glow. But otherwise, the hall was murky, lacking windows or backup lights.

Opening the flashlight option on his phone, Brock ran to the exit. Pushing against the door leading to the stairwell, he moved it an inch at a time, checking his path, before thrusting it open and bounding up the steps.

The illumination bounced on each gleaming concrete step giving him just enough vision to get to the next stair.

In the stairwell a level above, Brock overheard voices. He stopped and stood motionless, straining his ears to hear.

Brock grabbed his gun and pressed himself against the icy cinder block wall, waiting to see if the voices would move away or toward him.

When he took a step back, his foot slipped. He lost his balance and fell forward on the stairs in front of him. With the gun still in his hand, Brock grimaced in pain and held his breath. Rolling onto his stomach, ignoring his throbbing knees, he awaited an attack from above.

But nothing happened.

Pressing his feet against the concrete floor, Brock tried to regain his footing and slid backward. This time he skidded in a slippery substance and stumbled over something. Something bulky and cumbersome. *I hope this isn't what I think it is.*

Carefully tucking his gun in his ankle holster, Brock used the flashlight to assess the location. He cursed under his breath when the light exposed a set of feet in a pool of congealed blood.

A wave of gunfire rattled above him in the distance.

Hurriedly Brock turned off his flashlight and engaged his weapon, flattening his frame against the wall behind him. He waited for the hailstorm of bullets to subside.

Brock listened as blasts of gunfire and voices shattered the air above him.

Suddenly the noise dissipated, and the only sound left hanging in the air was the echo of Brock's heart thundering against his chest.

Turning on his flashlight, Brock found an already cooling victim in a corner of the concrete stairwell floor. He knelt to get a closer look at what appeared to be a very dead average, white, middle-aged male civilian. *Probably undercover.*

Moving fast, Brock searched the body for evidence of his identity. The man's clothing was nondescript—jeans, boots, a sweater, and a jacket. But his wallet and radio told the rest of the story. *I was right. He's a plainclothes detective.*

At that moment, the detective's radio crackled to life. "Don't bother coming up to the roof. It's a mess. Hold your position. Wait for backup. We're hijacked by people pretending to be SWAT. Over."

Screw it!

He began charging forward.

Brock sprinted to the level of Patti's hotel room, realizing he had no plan for what lay ahead of him. He no longer cared. The enemy were purposely targeting law enforcement of all agencies. A line had been drawn for him. There would be no playing by the rules or playing fair. He'd do what he must to protect himself and his family.

He opened the door to the floor.

The hallway was empty.

He headed to Patti's suite, praying he'd be able to find the medication for Junior in time.

Three men dressed as members of SWAT emerged from around the corner, guns nestled on their shoulders. Correctly.

Brock sprinted to them.

And that's when everything went to hell.

CHAPTER 44

From several feet away, suppressed gunfire blasted behind Brock. Stray bullets shattered an overhead chandelier. Handblown glass splintered and rained down.

Brock narrowly dodged the colorful shards flying through the air.

The reverberations shook the walls around him and echoed down the corridor.

The SWAT team in front of Brock raised their weapons and aimed.

You can do this. Brock willed himself further down the hall toward the heavily armed men. He knew even if he had time to reach for his automatic, he wouldn't. He'd rather die than attack one of his own.

Steps before crashing into the men, Brock came to a halt and slid to his knees, hands high above his head. "Agent O'Reilly. Badge is in my breast pocket."

Suddenly, a bullet zipped past his ear and landed in the wall nearby, creating a smoldering, golf ball–sized hole.

One of the men on the SWAT team, a muscle-bound giant, waved him out of the way with the butt of his gun. "Police! Down now!" He spoke with a clipped New York accent.

As he face-dived, Brock's hands, slick with sweat and blood, barely touched the floor before a blaze of bullets fired above his head. He stayed close to the ground while twisting his body to see behind him.

Two men, one short, the other stocky and tall, lumbered down the hall from the opposite direction to face off with the SWAT team closest to Brock.

They wore SWAT paramilitary gear, complete with Magpul Core Patrol gloves, Kevlar helmets, tactical assault vests, and steel-toed boots. They looked exactly like authentic SWAT team members. Except for the way they held their guns. Like cheap women's pocketbooks.

The posers I saw inside the vent. The ones who were planning to kill me.

"Execute shot," the muscle-bound giant said to his two fellow SWAT officers.

Assault rifle gunfire ignited the darkened hall, turning the two posers into dancing, smoldering shadows. Their bodies fell in a bloody heap.

The second the gun battle ended, Brock rolled over and crawled to one side of the hall. He sat with his back pressed against a wall, hands over his head, and eyes glued to the scene in the middle of the hall.

"Just what in the heck is going on?" one of the SWAT team members asked the giant officer.

He shook his head. "Don't know," he said, prodding the fallen men with his boot. "Looks like we got more security breaches."

"Seems like they're all over the place," another officer chimed in.

This ain't good. Brock watched the SWAT team realize they probably knew less than he did about the situation. He looked around desperately, secretly hoping Shuggs or Dr. Harper would pop up and explain everything.

But wishful thinking was a luxury he couldn't afford at this juncture. He cleared his throat in an attempt to indirectly call the attention of the officers without startling them.

Brock swallowed when the giant pointed his gun at him.

"Who the heck are you?" the officer asked.

"Brock O'Reilly, sir."

"You said you're some sort of agent?"

Brock nodded. "Yes, sir."

"Which agency?"

"CIA."

"Why would CIA be here?" he growled.

Brock knew better than to offer an extensive explanation to an adrenaline-charged officer holding a gun. "Long story. Dr. Harper, my boss, can vouch for me."

The officer stood directly in front of Brock, his massive body rigidly postured. "Dr. Harper, you say?" he asked, raising an eyebrow.

"Yeah."

"Show me your ID."

Brock quickly reached for his badge and held it out for the officer.

The giant examined the badge and handed it back to Brock. "Okay, he's clear," he said, gesturing to the two other men with him. He turned back to Brock. "Let's go. We need to get out of here."

Brock got up. "What's the plan?"

"We're responsible for eliminating all threats."

Brock pointed to the lifeless bodies. "Were they the first threats you've encountered?"

"No. While my men and I've been securing the floors assigned to our detail, we've encountered two other similar groups."

"You think there're anymore like this?"

The officer shrugged. "Don't know. Ever since the bomb detonated in the stairwell, our intel has been haphazard and unreliable. We're practically operating blind. Have you been able to reach your people?"

"Off and on," Brock said. "I've had similar issues with communication."

The officer sighed and glanced at his watch. "We need to keep moving. Got one more floor to clear. You have a weapon?"

"Yeah, I do."

"Then get it out. Be ready to use it to defend yourself if we come under enemy fire."

Brock shook his head. "I can't go with you."

"You'll need to stay with us until we can safely bring you to the rally point."

"I have an emergency."

"Are you kidding me right now? This entire mission has been an emergency from—"

"I have to get my godson's asthma medication." Brock took a breath. "He's very sick."

"Where's the kid now?"

"He and my family are hiding in a maintenance room." Brock pointed to the ground. "Right below this floor."

"Where're the meds?"

"In one of the suites on this floor. Down the hall."

Suddenly, a torrent of stifled gunfire sputtered in the hall above them.

The SWAT team immediately engaged their weapons while scanning the area.

Brock held his breath and grabbed his gun from his holster.

"I'm sorry, man. We leave now," the giant officer said, walking backward and gesturing to his team to follow.

"I *have* to get what I came for," Brock said. "But can you take my family to safety?"

"The best I can do is look for them *after* we finish our mission. If you decide to get that medication, you're on your own." A bead of sweat ran down the officer's face as he spun around. "Time's running out."

CHAPTER 45

G unfire from the level above exploded loudly, then began petering out while Brock cautiously ventured down the shadowy corridor. He peeked over his shoulder, noting the SWAT team had already made a swift exit.

Straining his eyes, he focused on moving through the hall undetected. He kept his flashlight turned off to avoid drawing unwanted attention from the wrong people.

The hallway leading to Patti's room was vacant and gloomy. An occasional shaft of light came from beneath the doors, casting a yellowish glow across his path.

Confident he was alone, he sprinted through the shadows to the hotel suite.

Brock opened the door, locked it behind him, and attempted to turn on the lights, but they didn't work. Though his eyes had grown accustomed to the gloom, the darkness inside dizzied him. He stumbled and caught himself. His eyes finally adjusting as he tore through the vast suite in search of Junior's medication.

He combed through the drawers and cabinets in the bathrooms, but he had no luck there. Then he rifled through suitcases, dressers, night tables, and even the mini-fridge. Nothing.

Brock cursed and kicked the wall.

He was certain the inhaler wasn't anywhere in the suite. As he turned to leave, he caught sight of a small safe. Reaching into the cavity of the unlocked safe, his hand gripped the L-shaped plastic inhaler unit. *Bingo.* Brock hastily shoved the medication into his breast pocket and went to the door.

Once he exited the room, he carefully checked each side of the hallway before sprinting toward the stairwell.

Brock remembered the two posers who'd been eliminated by a real SWAT team. Retrieving his phone, he flicked on his flashlight and combed the area for the dead bodies.

Brock's feet hit a puddle. His shoes made a sucking sound before the beam of light found the two corpses. A sulfurous tang hit the back of his throat, his nose catching the iron musk of blood in the air.

He took a step toward the bodies, shining the light across the larger man's blood-spattered torso. He lay sprawled on top of his smaller partner whose one eye stared unseeingly at Brock, the other eye a sunken hollow.

Crouching down, Brock examined the men's pockets for something that would tell him who they were. It was then the smaller man's radio crackled to life.

Simultaneously, the radio he'd lifted from Snake's body hummed against his hip. He strained to hear what was being said while scanning the area, checking to ensure he continued to be alone.

"Calling all TWA soldiers, this is Razor 6. Come in if you can hear me," a familiar voice rasped over the man's radio.

"Yeah," Brock said, praying he was convincing, posing as the small man lying nearby.

"Who's this?"

He sucked in a deep breath and lied. "Spook 6, sir," Brock said.

"Good. Is Spook 5 still with you?"

Brock stared at the corpse lying on top of Spook 6. "He is, sir."

"Forget about Buck's men. General confirmed they've been eliminated."

"Yes, sir."

"We're going to need you to track the spiders."

"Who, sir? Patricia Pang, her family, and the CIA operative with them?" Brock asked.

"Who else would we be looking for? And why the heck are you using real names over comms?"

"Of course, sir. I'm sorry."

"General just confirmed the spiders were in an air-handler."

"How, sir?"

"General has boots on the ground and eyes everywhere. You understand that, don't you?"

"I do."

"The spiders have been traveling from the rooftop inside the vent system. That's why no one's been able to locate them."

"Understood, but how—"

"Will you please shut up and listen?"

"Sure, I—"

"Figure out where they are now," Razor 6 said. "Then terminate the spiders on sight."

Brock swallowed. "Got it."

"We're depending on you to finish this mission before the real bomb detonates. All other soldiers are eliminating opposition forces."

"Real bomb, sir?"

Razor 6 clucked his tongue. "Spook 6, I thought you were a sharp, true patriot, ready for the war."

"What I—"

"We don't have time for this. We've been over the plan hundreds of times. General recruited you directly from the force, so I don't get what the problem is. You have the needed training."

"No problem, sir."

"Then get going."

"Copy that, sir."

"One last thing."

"Yeah?"

"You're a dead man *if* you don't complete this mission," Razor 6 said before clicking off.

Brock let out a ragged breath and took one last look at the corpses. *I'm already dead.* Before turning to sprint toward the stairwell, he turned down the radio and tucked it into his pocket.

That's when he recognized it.

A burning sensation prickled his sweaty scalp, traveling down his spine and into his legs.

Something was off. Something unmistakably wrong. It wasn't just the war zone he'd found himself in the midst of on US soil or the fight to protect himself and the people he loved. It was the sense that what he was looking at wasn't the full picture. He had no idea what the complete story was, but he'd know when he discovered it.

Brock's stomach tightened and rumbled.

But not with a hunger for food.

He hungered for answers.

One question pressed him more than the others. *How would anyone have known we were in the air-handler?*

CHAPTER 46

Brock got to the end of the hallway and slowly opened the door, checking to see if the area was clear.

The dark stairwell was filled with an eerie silence.

Gone was the echo of gunfire or voices shouting. He took a few steps down the stairs, stopped, and listened for signs of the enemy. The only sound was his heart pounding in his chest.

Brock flew down the next flight of stairs until he got to the area where he'd found the body, and he slowed his pace. *What the heck?* The man's body had disappeared. Stooping down, Brock squinted at the clues left behind on the ground. In the corpse's place was a crimson smear and a crumpled pack of cigarettes.

Nothing about this night makes sense or surprises me. He shook his head, continuing to the exit.

Opening the door, Brock eased from behind and slowly ventured into the dead-quiet corridor. He breathed a sigh of relief, knowing he was alone.

Then his second radio hummed against his hip. He turned up the sound.

Staring at the crackling radio, Brock frowned. Coming from it was the voice of Razor 6.

"Can you hear me, Spook 6?" Razor 6 asked.

Brock checked his watch. He'd stopped being tethered to the boundaries of time. Ten minutes had passed since he'd last impersonated Spook 6. To him, it felt like it had been an hour.

"Yes, sir."

"Both you and Spook 5 are unharmed?"

"Affirmative," Brock said swallowing.

Razor 6 said, "I received word that some of our soldiers were attacked while countering the Deep State antifascists."

"No, we're good, sir."

"What's your current position?"

"Like you asked, Spook 5 and I are on the way to locate the spiders."

"Just answer the question," Razor 6 spat.

Brock bit his lip. "I'm headed to check on possible places the spiders could be in the vent, sir."

"Abort that plan."

"Are you sure that—"

"We have accurate intel from General. Turn around."

"We'll turn around," Brock said. "But where are we supposed to—"

"General has boots on the ground and eyes in the air," Razor 6 reiterated. "Go to the main level," his voice rasped.

"Yes, sir. And then what?" Brock broke out into a cold sweat, realizing he was in the exact location Razor 6 was asking him to go. *Do they know about Patti and her family's hiding place?*

"Check each and every room on that floor thoroughly."

"Is there a reason for—"

"The spiders are there."

Brock scratched the stubble on his chin. *Maybe I can delay things. Ask lots of questions.* "I thought they were in the vent."

"General knows they're gone."

"How's that, sir?" Brock asked. "The hotel has a huge system, and the—"

"He put a tracker on one of the kids."

A bead of sweat ran down Brock's face. "Then why don't we have an exact location, sir?"

"Signal's not the best but good enough to calculate general vicinity."

"I understand, sir," Brock said, rubbing his clenched jaw.

"Don't screw this up. It's about the mission of *our* people."

"I won't disappoint you, sir," Brock replied.

"The next time I hear from you, it'd better be news of the spiders' terminations," Razor 6 said and ended the radio call.

Before Brock could process the information from Razor 6, a bullet whizzed through the air past him, landing with a soft thud into the carpeted floor.

He crouched low and grabbed his gun, searching the hall for where the attacker lurked but seeing no one. *Who the heck is shooting?*

Gunfire followed, raining bullets with earsplitting, booming, and thudding sounds speeding through the air like an indoor lightning shower.

Breaking into a sprint, Brock took off and skidded on the scattered bullet shells. Tumbling forward, he broke the fall with his hands, but not before his teeth pierced through his lip.

Tasting blood, Brock jumped up. Glancing upward, he saw the butt of an assault weapon poking out of the ceiling tile. He plastered himself against the wall and wiped at the dark droplets dripping from his mouth.

The gun withdrew.

He ran quickly in the opposite direction of the invisible attack.

Hard boot steps thumped above him.

Looking up, Brock saw nothing. He tried the door of a nearby hotel room, then several others, before finally gaining entry to one and locking the door behind him.

Brock bent over, trying to catch his breath.

The hard boot steps moved down the hall, thumped louder, and came closer.

Brock calculated the maintenance room was about ten rooms away. *Could they have located Patti and her family already?*

Outside the door, screams rang through the hall in waves of sustained terror, but they were soon drowned out by the clatter of more gunfire.

CHAPTER 47

B rock rocked in his squatting position, pushing himself to figure out a solution. His breath snagged in his chest while the hard boot steps hammered toward the door.

Dodging behind a dresser, Brock aimed his weapon at the entryway. Waiting. The echoing footsteps passed by and disappeared down the hall.

Brock stood upright, leaned forward, and retched. He brought up a slimy lump of waffles, stained brown with a double expresso from earlier that day. It plopped onto the lush carpet between his feet. Lifting his throbbing head, he wiped his mouth and listened for any sign that someone had heard him vomiting.

Outside was eerily silent. Completely quiet. Even the sleek monochrome photos hanging on the walls seemed to reflect the hush covering the room.

Brock grabbed a towel from the pristine bathroom and quickly wiped off his clothes, wishing he had time to rinse his bile-filled mouth in the ornate porcelain sink. Glancing at himself in the mirror, he hardly recognized the sweat-soaked reflection staring back.

Breathing deeply, Brock tucked in his shirt, dried his face, and straightened up. *Stay disciplined. Focused. Keep Patti's family safe. Execute the plan.*

He hurried to the door and stared out the peephole. Scanning the hall, Brock focused on a body lying facedown a few feet away and instinctively gripped his gun. He stopped in front of the door for a few seconds and looked again through the peephole. *The hall seems clear.*

Keeping his attention on the body, Brock eased the door open and tiptoed into the hallway, one slow measured step at a time.

Blinking, he cleared the sweat from his eyes, searching for

movement in both directions. He scrutinized the ceiling tiles, checking for any guns poking through. *Good.*

Brock crept in the deep shadows, keeping his body pressed against the wall. He got to the dead man dressed in a SWAT uniform and used his foot to turn him over. Because of the man's missing face and the gray matter oozing from his cracked skull, Brock couldn't identify the body.

Shuddering, his throat tightened. *Control yourself.*

Looking up, Brock checked for signs of the enemy and knelt by the corpse to rifle through his pockets for clues providing further identification. He had just gotten through the first pocket when his spine began to tingle.

He jumped up, gun raised.

Brock couldn't see or hear a thing, *but he knew.* Someone had been watching him. Adrenaline flickered throughout his entire body like an intense electrical charge.

He glanced to the left. To the right. Nobody.

The air carried the faintest aroma of cigarettes.

Out the corner of his eye, he caught a blur of a man darting from one end of the corridor to the other. Brock spun around as fumes rose from a hastily thrown smoke bomb. Behind it stood the silhouette of a man brandishing a gun.

Brock ducked behind the dead body. He gripped his weapon and looked up.

The blur had disappeared.

Who are you? Brock got up and inched forward. *Must've hidden in a suite next to the maintenance room.*

He checked his gun, making sure it was off safety, locked, and loaded. Satisfied, he kept the gun in firing position and rushed down the hallway, staying as close to the wall as possible. *There's no time to hide. Stay in the shadows.*

The maintenance room was still three body lengths away when Brock heard screams.

Picking up his pace, he moved down the corridor. Closer. Another foot. Then another. *Breathe quietly.* He stood in front of the room's entry.

Slow. Hold your breath. Brock studied the opened door, adrenaline coating his brain. He gently pushed the door open wider with his elbow. Moved inside. One careful step at a time.

Inching forward, he moved with the shadows dancing on the wall.

Brock edged ahead, moving behind disorderly stacks of ladders, paint cans, and mops. He searched the room from behind the ladders, studying the area where they'd landed through the vent in the ceiling. No trace of Patti and her family.

Somewhere in the dark, near the room's rear wall, a radio sputtered. Brock stiffened as Razor 6's voice rasped through the room.

He stooped down and looked through the slats of a nearby ladder.

A flashing red light beamed from a far corner of the room, accompanied by the beep of the radio. "General, we relayed your intel to Spook 6. Proceed to your next assignment."

Spook 6's radio hummed against Brock's hip.

"Copy," a man's voice boomed.

Brock bent over to try to get a better look at the man. He lost his balance and tripped over a loose extension cord. A stack of ladders swayed, then came tumbling down in all directions, pushing him onto his back.

Another smoke bomb ignited. The room filled with putrid yellow smoke.

Brock pushed a ladder off his chest, and a blur of a man dashed out the door.

Who was that? He shook his head in disbelief and rubbed his jaw.

"Spook 6, what's your position?"

Fumbling through his pocket, Brock located the radio and turned it up. "We're here, sir," he whispered, tasting sulfur.

"Where is *that?*" Razor 6 spat.

"By the spiders' location."

"The maintenance room?"

"Yeah."

"You got eyes on them?"

"No."

"You check out the closets?"

Brock blew air and didn't answer.

"Spook 6?"

"Not yet, sir."

"Then hurry."

"Doing that now, sir," Brock lied, glancing around the room and searching for a closet. He zeroed in on a door in the opposite corner of the room.

"Call when the spiders are exterminated."

He was already making his way to the closet. He looked over his shoulder, checking for the enemy. "I'll call," Brock said. But the radio had already gone dead.

He put his hand on the knob and turned. He opened the door slowly. His gun angled for a kill shot, Brock stared into the cavernous space, anticipating, focused.

With his free hand, he reached for the switch. No lights came on.

Brock listened for noise. Sensing no movement, he tiptoed further into the closet, reached for his flashlight, and shone it inside. The beam bounced off a rounded wall of the closet that led to a corner space.

Trying not to be heard, somebody around the corner was breathing hard.

Could be Patti's family. Could be the enemy.

Moving forward, Brock cocked his gun and rounded the corner.

His chest constricted, and his mouth went dry at the sight of Patti's family. Silent. Scared. Huddled together.

Junior was sucking air. Pale. Eyes glassy. Chest heaving. The small child waved weakly at him. "Uncle Brock ... you ... came ... back," he gasped, then passed out into his mother's arms.

CHAPTER 48

Trembling, Brock dropped the flashlight he'd been steadily shining on Patti's family. The darkness engulfed them while he groped the floor, trying to locate his phone.

Junior wheezed from his slumped back position on his mother.

His baby brother began crying softly. "Don't ... die."

Patti's fingers dug into the fleshy part of Brock's upper arm. "My kid's in a bad way."

He found his phone, turned on the light feature, and let out a breath he'd been holding. "Hold the light. Please."

"Junior's *got* to have that inhaler," she said. "Right now."

"Give me a second." Brock pushed the phone into her hand.

Ten seconds later, he was still searching his pockets for Junior's medicine. *Don't panic. Focus. Find Junior's medicine.*

"My kid's life is on the line!" Patti yelled. "I could just—"

She didn't finish. Patti lowered her chin and began crying.

Mrs. Lipsett leaned forward and gestured for Brock to move in closer. "Baby, I think you may've dropped that inhaler somewhere. Better go back and get it before my daughter kills you." She spoke in a low voice only he could hear.

The clock in Brock's head showed anywhere from two to three minutes since he'd walked into the maintenance room. Mentally, he backtracked his steps, recalling that he'd fallen and knocked so much stuff down. *Maybe the inhaler fell out of my pocket then.* It was likely.

"Yeah, I think you're right. When I first came into the maintenance room, I must've dropped it when I fell down." Brock threw his hands up. "I promise I'll find it."

"Hurry! You have to hurry!" Patti's hand shook while holding the light, hugging her child to her chest with the other.

"I will." He threw the words over his shoulder. "I promise."

Brock crawled through the narrow space to the exit of the closet in the dark. He'd decided to leave the light with the women since he would return soon.

Just as he stepped out of the closet, footsteps pounded the industrial concrete floor like an uneven heartbeat.

Got to be quick. Don't know who this could be. Brock sped to the nearest wall.

Someone moved unsteadily toward him.

Brock waited for a beat, ducked around the corner, and ran for cover by a stack of ladders.

The footsteps drew closer.

Planting his feet, Brock shot out his hand and gripped a wooden slat. A splinter twisted into his palm. He glanced down to see blood had started to flow from a break in the fragile, thin skin. Brock sucked the wound, returning his focus to the footsteps haunting him.

He listened. There was no movement.

He carefully checked the area all around him.

There was no sign of the enemy.

It pained him to do so, but Brock shifted and moved his sore limbs as quickly as he could muster. He sped to the area where he'd fallen and searched the floor quickly with his hands.

The inhaler lay on the floor next to a paint can.

Reaching instinctively with his dominant hand, Brock snatched the medicine and grimaced. Blood trickled from his injured palm.

He wiped the wound on a pant leg and tucked the inhaler deep into an inside pocket of his jacket. *I'll be damned if anyone perishes on my watch.*

Brock shook his head. It about killed him that he had made a costly blunder that could affect Junior's health.

Patti had been right. He'd been careless. No more mistakes.

Straightening up, Brock scanned the area.

All was clear.

He exhaled and moved toward the closet.

Then Brock's phone buzzed. *I forgot about the other phone.* The one from the special agents, Berkley and Dexter. He frantically searched his clothes to locate it. He wrapped his fingers around the small item hidden away in an inner pocket.

It was a text. "C. S. found dead today."

Remembering Shuggs had told him he'd hired a black agent to frighten his ex-wife, Brock swallowed back a mix of dread and anger. *Have to text them back after I deliver this medicine. I will make sure Junior lives to see another day.*

He waited and listened, hearing nothing except the few deep breaths he took.

Pulling the medicine out of his pocket, Brock hurried into the closet.

Patti waited for him near the entrance. She grabbed the inhaler from his outstretched hand and crawled into the shadows.

Seconds later, the hiss of the inhaler going into the child's lungs bounced against the walls. Junior coughed and cried aloud.

Brock took it as a good sign as he sat back and texted the agents. He had to be clear. Didn't have room for ambiguity. "Is Cindy, the twins' mom, dead? Shuggs's ex?"

Five seconds passed, then Brock's phone buzzed again. Another text from the special agents. "Affirmative."

Photographs of the attractive middle-aged TV anchor popped up on his phone.

After viewing the gruesome pictures, there was no doubt in Brock's mind.

Shuggs's ex-wife, Cindy, had died cruelly.

Brock's stomach tightened, thinking about the dilemma his friend could possibly face. He took one last look at the phone and deleted the messages and pictures as instructed. Brock hid the phone away while worrying about his friend being dealt another unfair hand. All the man ever did was try to protect the people around him that he loved. And the twins. *My God. Poor Shuggs doesn't need this now. None of us do. I can't imagine how Patti will take this news.*

Brock began crawling back to Patti's family.

In the distance, once more, gunfire echoed through the night.

CHAPTER 49

The moment the gunfire started, footsteps pounded down the hallway. If his instincts were correct, they were moving closer. Soon they'd be by the maintenance room.

He shoved the phone into his pocket and reached for his weapon, praying the fight didn't reach the safety of his hiding place. Perhaps whoever was fighting didn't have a clue where he and Patti's family hid. But he wasn't taking any chances.

He believed in fighting defensively if forced into it. Today he'd be on the offensive. *Expect the unexpected. Be ready. The effective way to beat an ambush is to be prepared.*

Inching the door open, he moved slowly until he was certain no one was watching. The moment he was outside the closet, he sensed someone was already there in the maintenance room.

His eyes adjusted to the dark, but he couldn't see anyone. Not yet.

Cocking his head, he listened, but he couldn't hear them. Brock sniffed the air, catching the faint aroma of stale smoke. A chill snaked around his neck and slithered down his spine.

Primitive instinct kicked in. An internal mechanism sounded like a built-in alarm. Someone was nearby. Maybe whoever was out there was watching him.

Hardwired to stand his ground and fight, Brock glanced over his shoulder and kept moving. He refused to be an easy target. *I'm living to see another day. Not going to be a sitting duck. Not getting shot by some perp.*

The shadows hid him while he strained to see or hear the enemy. Brock moved quickly. He scanned the stacks of ladders casting long murky silhouettes on the ground. Looked through a collection of paint cans covering the floor. Inspected a row of chairs. He checked for movement.

Brock saw nothing.

He took a few steps toward the door. The air shifted.

A pair of shoes scraped softly against the tiled floor.

Waves of prickles traveled down Brock's arms.

Spinning around, he scoured every square foot around him.

Still, he saw no one.

Brock reasoned that whoever was out there couldn't have wanted him harmed. If so, he would've already been dead.

"That you, O'Reilly?" a distinctly familiar voice came from a corner of the room.

Chewing on his bottom lip, Brock peered into the shadows for possible hiding places. "Depends on who's asking."

Shuggs appeared from behind a stack of chairs pushed against a wall. "Where you been, bro?" Blood streamed from his head, but he didn't seem to notice.

Brock lowered his weapon. "Should've known it was you." He sighed.

"Why?"

"You're the only man who can sneak up on me and live."

"Glad I found you. Night's been crazy. Fell through the ceiling from the vent."

"Same thing happened to us."

Shuggs staggered.

Brock reached out and steadied his friend. "You okay?"

"Just a flesh wound," he said.

"What happened?"

"Bullet grazed me."

"Who shot you?

He shrugged. "Hard to tell."

"I know. Seems as if no one is who they claim to be tonight."

"That's true."

Brock pulled off his jacket, removed his shirt, and ripped a sleeve from it.

He wrapped the material firmly around the wound.

"You didn't have to do that," Shuggs said.

"But you're bleeding."

"Probably looks worse than what it is."

"Could be," Brock said. "No harm in being careful."

"Where's everyone?"

"Patti and her family?"

Shuggs nodded.

Brock motioned with his head. "Hiding in the closet."

"Everyone doing alright?"

"They're banged up some, but they're alive."

"That's what counts."

Nodding, Brock put his shirt and coat back on. "You know what's going on in the hallway?"

"No idea." Shuggs stared at the maintenance room door. "Best to lay low until things calm down."

"Yeah. We'd better check on Junior. Make sure the family's okay."

"What happened to Junior?"

"Asthma attack. He should be better. Just gave him his inhaler."

"Good. You figure out where our help is?"

"They should be on the way."

"According to who?"

"The special agents."

"Let's hole up until backup comes."

Brock put his arm around Shuggs's broad shoulders. "Lean on me, man."

A figure appeared from out of the shadows.

Bending, Brock deftly retrieved his gun and aimed.

"Don't shoot." Patti stumbled into a small sphere of light coming from a gaping hole in the ceiling.

"Good Lord." Brock still had his gun trained on her.

"You scared the living daylights out of us," Shuggs said.

Her sallow skin gleamed with sweat. She opened her mouth, but nothing came out.

Brock left Shuggs's side and went to his other friend. "What's wrong?"

She gripped his hand, palms sprouting sweat. Her skin looked two shades lighter than her usual nut-brown complexion. "Come quick. Junior's not breathing."

CHAPTER 50

Before the men could respond, Patti grabbed Brock's arm. Her eyes were wide, looking as if she'd pass out.

She pointed back to the closet and turned around, trying to drag Brock with her. "We have to go!" Patti shouted.

Brock took off, motioning for Shuggs to follow.

He sped past Patti and left Shuggs breathing hard but holding up the rear.

The threesome clumsily moved through the cluttered space, knocking over more paint cans, chairs, and ladders.

There was no sign of anyone. But Brock kept his gun out, hand firmly on the butt. Maintaining the lead, he glanced over his shoulder. "Left." He pointed to the far wall ahead for Shuggs's benefit. "The closet door is there. We'll take it to a crawl space that runs the length of the wall."

He eased the door open, bracing himself for an unexpected attack, and slowly entered.

The closet's entrance was clear. Soon, Patti and Shuggs caught up to Brock.

Looking into the darkened space, Brock crouched low and knelt, crawling the rest of the way to where Patti's family hid.

Junior's small body was lying on his side, directly in front of his grandmother. His younger brother knelt beside him, holding his limp hand.

"He still has a pulse," Mrs. Lipsett said, tears streaming down her face. "It's faint, but it's there."

"Mind if I work on him?" Shuggs's voice boomed through the cramped space, sounding more like a command than a question.

"Please ... please bring my baby back to me," Patti said, her voice cracking.

Brock made room for Shuggs to crawl past him to the sick child.

When Shuggs got to Junior, he bent over with his ear close to the boy's mouth.

Junior gasped and went still. A single line of drool slid from his slack mouth.

"Oh, my God!" Patti cried.

The boy remained still.

"Give me some room," Shuggs barked.

Patti backed away slightly, her fingers close enough to caress her son's legs.

Turning Junior from his side to his back, Shuggs used his fingers to check the child's mouth. "What happened?"

"Asthma attack," Patti said, choking on each word.

Shuggs nodded. He gently pinched Junior's nose shut, tilted his head back, and lifted his chin. Making a complete seal over the child's mouth, he blew in for one second, causing the child's chest to rise.

Leaning back, Shuggs let the air escape from Junior's mouth.

The child's chest deflated.

Shuggs gave one more breath.

Junior's chest expanded.

After delivering two breaths into the child's mouth, Shuggs sat back on his heels.

"Did it work?" Mrs. Lipsett whispered, eyes glued to the child's chest.

Without answering, Shuggs knelt beside the child, placing the heel of his left hand on the center of Junior's chest. He then placed the heel of his right hand on top of his left hand, laced his fingers together, and administered thirty quick compressions about two inches deep.

Junior didn't budge.

"Is ... my baby okay?" Patti asked, wringing her shaking hands. "Please say he's okay!"

Brock hung his head. *Please, God. Don't let this child die. Not on my watch.*

Mopping his damp forehead with the back of his hand, Shuggs bent over the child and again delivered two breaths.

Still, nothing happened.

Patti collapsed against her mother.

Shuggs ripped off his own coat and threw it aside.

Bending over the unconscious boy, Shuggs readjusted Junior's head and neck, giving him two more rescue breaths. He followed up with thirty more chest compressions, each one seeming more intense than the other.

Brock bit his lip. *Hope he doesn't crack the boy's sternum. Then we'll have a worse problem.* He gathered Patti's younger son in his arms and rocked him while he whimpered.

Sweat dripped from Shuggs's face. "Junior! C'mon, I know you're in there. I can feel it."

The child's body trembled.

Holding Junior's sibling tight, Brock prayed silently for a miracle.

Shuggs pressed into the child's torso, administering fast compressions and counting out loud.

As he reached the count of thirty once again, Junior coughed, his tiny body writhing.

Shuggs leaned back onto his haunches, "Breathe, boy!" he shouted, wiping his sopping face with the back of his sleeve.

Turning his head to one side, the child took a giant breath and vomited.

"I want my mommy," Junior said, his voice weak.

Patti pushed past everyone in her way and lifted her son's head onto her lap. "I'm here, baby," she said softly, cleaning his mouth and face with the bottom of her shirt.

Letting out a breath he'd been holding, Brock's body relaxed. It was then he recalled Razor 6's tip about a tracker being planted on one of the children. Brock whispered instructions in Patti's ear. He waited as she took off the boys' shoes, starting with the youngest, and checked for the minute device. It turned up on the insole of Junior's sneaker. Brock took the tracker from her hand and pocketed it.

The child he'd had on his lap pulled away and crawled back to his grandmother's open arms.

He slapped Shuggs on the back. "Thank you, man," Brock said.

"It's nothing. What's that you found?"

"A tracker. Good thing I found it *and* you when I did."

Shuggs shook his head. "No. I found you. Give me the tracker. I'll destroy it."

Brock reached into his pocket and gave Shuggs the tracker. "How can you say you found me when—"

Holding his hand up, Shuggs's gaze shifted to something in the shadows behind Brock.

Brock glanced over his shoulder. "Something wrong?"

Reaching for his gun, Shuggs turned to the group and put a finger to his lips, motioning for silence. "Kill the light. Stay dead-quiet."

"What's up?" Brock whispered into the dark.

"Get your gun," Shuggs said, his voice low. "Someone opened the closet door."

CHAPTER 51

Stretching his neck while keeping his body as rigid as possible, Brock peered out into the inky darkness. The confinement of the closet contributed to the increasing rhythm of his staccato heartbeat and the deafening rush of blood pulsing through his head.

He and Shuggs were shoulder to shoulder, as still as statues.

Brock caught the smell of sweat, fear, and stale cigarette smoke seeping into the thick air between them.

Straining his ears, Brock flattened his back against the sloped wall and held both his breath and gun steady.

Out in the hallway, blasts of gunfire were getting louder.

More shots fired, sounding closer. *Sounds like multiple shooters on both sides.*

Brock kept his eyes focused for any sudden movement up ahead.

Black shadows appeared on the closet's wall.

Calculating in his head, Brock figured the intruder was about twenty feet away from the back of the closet where they hid.

A soft whimper escaped from the smaller boy, and the shadow froze.

Terror crept through Brock's veins. His mouth went dry. He had his people to protect. *No way I'm sitting tight and waiting.*

He glanced back at the shadowy outlines of the people he fiercely loved, realizing if anything happened to them, he'd die too.

Motioning to Shuggs that he wanted to move past him, Brock crouched and crab-walked in the direction of the intruder.

Brock flinched when gunshots rang out, sounding as if they'd ripped through the wall of the maintenance room. But from all appearances, the shots hadn't penetrated the closet. *Don't get distracted.*

His heart twisted remembering the ominous conversation he'd overheard earlier when he was in the vent. *Who are these monsters, and what did they want?* Whoever was out there could be part of the group willing to murder children in cold blood. A new wave of fear struck him, and he had to force his shaky limbs to continue through the narrow space. He gritted his teeth and kept moving.

He spotted the black shadow in front of him, sucked in his breath, and raised his weapon. He aimed for the head of the shadow. One kill shot was all he needed. He pulled the trigger. Nothing. His throat constricted. Realizing his piece had jammed, Brock cursed.

The metallic click of the intruder's gun ricocheted in the small space.

Brock swallowed hard, knowing it was likely that his life would be snuffed out in a dirty janitor's closet. He lunged at the invisible attacker, bracing for a bullet.

Instead, the shadow in front of him grunted at the impact of a bullet that had just whizzed through the air. A second later, the man crumpled at Brock's feet.

"Got him," a familiar voice vibrated from behind.

Brock slapped the perp's gun out of his limp hand, retrieved it, and spun his head around.

Shuggs shined his flashlight in Brock's direction.

The blinding light made his throbbing head hurt more.

"You alright, bro?"

"Yeah," Brock replied weakly.

The attacker groaned. "That you, sir? I came ... to ... help ... you ... Gen ..."

"Eliminate the perp," Shuggs hissed.

Brock froze, staring blankly between Shuggs and the wounded man.

Attempting to sit up, the attacker's glazed eyes appeared to focus on Shuggs. He tried to say something else, but blood dribbled out in place of words.

Hastily, Shuggs adjusted the silencer on his gun, aimed, and shot the attacker point-blank in the temple.

The sensation of fresh, tepid blood on his face made Brock want to puke. He gulped air, steadying his trembling body by pressing himself against the wall.

Using a sleeve of his coat to remove what he could of the man's blood from his face, Brock turned his head, heaved, and threw up. "That man. He seemed to know you," he finally managed to say, wiping a string of bile from his lips.

Shining his light over the length of the corpse, Shuggs dabbed at the blood that'd sprinkled like red freckles on his forehead. He shook his head. "Don't know him."

"Didn't think so," Brock said, tracing the scar above his eyebrow. *Probably some mix-up.*

"We're going to need to move the stiff out of the way."

Brock nodded. "I'll grab his arms."

"I got his legs. You pull, I'll push."

When the men were done carrying the body out of the closet, they scanned the room and found it unoccupied.

The hallway outside was eerily quiet.

Satisfied the intruder had acted alone, they returned to the closet.

"Fact of the matter is, Patti's family has been through enough." Brock put his hand on the knob. "Hope they're doing alright."

"They should be okay," Shuggs said, his voice low. "At least for now."

"Think we should move everyone out?"

"We'll have to. The kid needs immediate medical attention."

"You *did* get him breathing again."

"Problem is, he's completely dehydrated."

"I'll get him water."

"It *won't* matter."

"Why?"

"He needs more meds."

"I found his inhaler," Brock said, opening the door.

The two men began their journey in silence, crawling through the dark closet back to the hiding place. Shuggs's light bounced unsteadily on the floor ahead, picking up a glistening trail of blood. They had no choice but to crawl through the cooling, sticky substance.

"Albuterol's not enough," Shuggs whispered.

Brock squinted, making out the shadowy figures of the family huddled together several feet away. He lowered his voice a notch. "How do you know?"

"Experience. My twins got asthma. That boy needs a nebulizer."

"What's that?"

"Something we don't have."

CHAPTER 52

Brock quietly crawled the rest of the way to the small group. Crouching beside Patti, he caught his breath, trying to shake the uneasiness gnawing at him.

"How's Junior?"

"Better. But he's lethargic and short of breath." Patti traced the dark circles under her son's closed eyes. "I don't like that his lips and fingertips are blue."

Shuggs made his way to a spot a few yards from Brock and collapsed against the wall, his ragged breathing filling the small area.

"That boy's going to need medical attention. Real soon." Shuggs hung his flashlight around his neck using the attached lanyard.

An anxious hush fell over the group. The only light came from Shuggs's flashlight, illuminating the dried blood spatter on his chin, already turning a blackish red. The stench of violent death inundated the air around him.

Moments passed before anyone spoke again.

Mrs. Lipsett had an arm around her younger grandson while he lay with his head on her shoulder. The child's large brown eyes trained on his grandmother's mouth while she hummed him a tuneless song.

Patti held Junior on her lap with one hand. She tucked her free hand into Brock's. "Who came in here?"

"No idea," he said, aware that Patti still wore her wedding band. The ridges of the diamond-crusted jewelry rubbed against an open wound on his palm.

"I'm ... scared ... Mommy," Junior said, gasping.

Pulling her hand away from Brock, Patti wrapped both arms around the child and whispered something in his ear. Then she straightened up and looked at Brock.

"Don't worry," Brock said. "We took care of the bad guy."

Shuggs cleared his throat. "That's right. He won't be bothering us anymore."

"I hope he didn't lead anyone else here to us," Patti said.

"I doubt it."

"Being found by the wrong people is the last thing we need." Patti combed her son's damp curls with her fingers. "I don't see how I can run anymore. Not with a sick child on my hands."

"We checked the entire room," Brock said. "I'm certain he was alone."

Patti rubbed her chin. "Have you heard *anything* from anyone?"

Brock shook his head.

"I thought we'd be extracted by now. My poor husband must be sick with worry." Mrs. Lipsett sighed and pulled her grandson onto her lap. She turned to Brock. "I saw you update someone about where we were hiding. Didn't I?"

"Yeah."

"Can't you contact them again?" Patti asked. "It's been a while."

"Don't think I haven't tried." Brock took out his phone, tapped the screen, and sighed. "I can see that my last message went through. Since then, I've had no signal and no other contact from Dr. Harper." He pocketed the phone, his fingers brushing against the other phone.

A joyless smile stretched across Shuggs's weathered face. "Typical for the suits to tell us to sit and wait for help, then pull a no-show."

"They're trying their best, man." *I need to reach out to the special agents. Earlier, they assured me this phone was for emergencies.* Brock took the other phone from his coat, checked for messages from Berkley or Dexter, and found none.

"Seems like their best is as worthless as gum on a bootheel," Shuggs said.

Brock shot a text to the agents informing them of the child's medical emergency and the group's location.

He turned to face Shuggs. "Fact of the matter is, this is a highly unusual situation," Brock said, his voice low.

"Highly unusual is the nature of the things the agency handles."

"You have to admit we've never faced anything like this," Brock said, "not here in the States."

"When we shoot our way out of this corner, they'll still have plenty to complain about."

"No. This is different. I can feel it."

"How's that, bro?"

"I believe the agency is as confused as we are about this particular attack." Brock rubbed his jaw.

"The government ought to know more than us. Just goes to show."

"Goes to show what?"

"Our country's infrastructure ain't as airtight as we'd like to believe."

"What do you mean?" Brock asked.

"Look how easy it was for a few perps to send some of our highest ranking intelligence offices into a tailspin."

Brock frowned. His friend was right. *But where is he going with his line of thinking?*

Shuggs continued, his voice a gruff whisper. "As we speak, the folks at the White House are probably crapping their pants."

"Why would this particular matter concern anyone in the White House?"

"The Dem's candidate pick for the next presidential election is Senator Lipsett."

Brock glanced at Patti and her mother.

Both women were eyeballing him and Shuggs.

"Clearly your attempts at confidentiality have failed," Patti said.

"That's right, baby, my husband is being groomed to be on the ballot in four years," Mrs. Lipsett said softly. "Things look hopeful."

"I doubt that your husband being a possible candidate for the presidency would justify this type of attack," Brock said. "Besides, how would anyone know for sure he'd be elected. I'm not buying—"

"It's the only thing that makes sense. Please trust me when I tell you—I know," Patti said.

Staring at Patti's flustered demeanor, things began to take shape in Brock's mind. The pieces started fitting together, painting a picture, one that *did* make sense.

"Let me guess, your teaching gig is a front. You've been working deep-cover for the bureau the entire time, infiltrating homeland terrorist groups." Brock stopped and examined Patti's shock, feeling in his gut he was on the right track.

"Makes sense. These left-wing liberals are destroying our country." Shuggs nodded.

Patti held a hand up. "You have no idea what—"

"Fact of the matter is, based on the intel brief for my new job," Brock said, "there's a white supremacy organization targeting promising influencers and politicians as backlash from the Obama era."

"That president created lots of race problems for the US," Shuggs said. "I can see why it happened that way."

Leaning as close to Patti as he could, Brock stared into her eyes. "Now, members of this dangerous group have taken an oath to take back their country. They've also promised their loyal members that they will give their lives to ensure no other African American becomes president. Am I right?"

Patti stared at the floor and took a deep breath. "You know I can't deny or confirm that information."

A tear slid down Mrs. Lipsett's frightened face. "So we were purposely targeted."

"Please stop, Momma. Don't work yourself up." Patti gently laid a hand on her mother's shoulder.

"Were you in deep cover?" Mrs. Lipsett stared at her daughter. "Yes or no."

Patti's mouth became a thin line. "I *cannot* deny or confirm any of this," she said. "Now, let's figure out a way to get us out of here. Junior needs to go to a hospital."

Mrs. Lipsett began sobbing.

Watching the older woman cry made Brock think of his mother. Her thin pale face, hollow green eyes, and white-haired bun flashed across his mind.

Old guilt tugged at his racing heart. He hadn't been able to protect his mother from the shame his childhood criminal act had brought to the family, or to her. She'd never been the same since the other child's death. It'd been his fault. Maybe if he'd been a different person, she wouldn't have slipped into early-onset dementia. And maybe if he were a better agent, a better friend, he would've seen this coming a long time ago.

Brock swallowed the giant lump in his throat. "We need to leave the closet. Immediately."

"I thought we were safe here," Patti said.

"We're not safe." Brock turned to the exit. "You're right. This attack isn't random. It's a statement," he said, crawling back toward the door.

CHAPTER 53

Brock crawled as fast as his aching limbs would allow, recalling Patti's reaction of dread when he'd uncovered her well-kept secret.

Silently, he prayed she and her family would continue to trust him. Follow his lead away from imminent death. Allow him to guide them to safety. He was sure had he decided to wait in the closet for help, they'd have played into the hand of the enemy.

Though certain they'd been set up, he knew he was missing something important. *But what?* No matter how he racked his brain, he still had no idea.

Judging from the rumble of knees on the tile floor, the women and children weren't far behind. Brock exhaled. He filled his lungs with the dank, dusty air clinging to his sweat-soaked face.

Glancing over his shoulder, Brock looked past Patti's family to his friend's head bobbing in and out of the shadows. *I knew I could count on Shuggs to bring up the rear.*

"I got your back, bro," Shuggs said, his yellow teeth flashing.

"Okay, good."

Brock faced forward, never slackening his pace.

"What's the plan when we leave?" Shuggs's voice cut through the darkness.

"Keep everyone close and quiet. Once I leave the closet, I'll scope things out and signal for when it's safe to come out."

"Got it."

Moving over the congealed trail of blood now thick as pudding, Brock's nose wrinkled. His mouth filled with saliva. The scent in the air was that of a meat market combined with a rusted, oxidized car battery.

He forced the bile backward, held his breath, and continued down the dark path to the door ahead of him.

Reaching the closet's door, Brock slowly opened it and peered through the crack. He stalled to scan the room and ensure the enemy hadn't entered.

As Brock started to tiptoe past the corpse to the exit, the dead man's radio sputtered to life.

"Spook 4, we need your position," a familiar voice said over the static crackling through the radio.

Brock knelt down beside Spook 4, pressed the talk button, and remained silent.

"Speak up, Spook 4," the man's voice rasped. "Razor 6 here. We need confirmation you've eliminated the spiders. Also, General has soldiers coming your way in fifteen minutes. Time to wrap our mission."

Brock flipped the off button on the dead man's radio and turned up the radio he'd taken from Snake. He jumped up, ran through the maintenance room, and peeked through a crack in the door jam. He saw no one but knew he needed to hurry before it was too late.

Leaning into the hallway, Brock waited for a beat, allowing his eyes to adjust to the light thrown by the few fixtures that were intact.

His pupils narrowed, bringing the area into focus. He sniffed the air and searched the area for any signs of trouble. There were none. Not yet.

Brock examined the corridor. Eying the farthest end of the hallway to his left, he saw a series of rooms. If his memory of the hotel's exterior served him right, those rooms would have balconies. They were now on the second floor, and the lobby below the first floor meant they were about twenty feet up. Dangerous but close enough to the ground for them to be safely extracted or jump if necessary. Their situation called for desperate measures.

He eased down the hallway, hoping he'd luck out and find a room open. But each door he tried was locked tight.

Cursing, Brock retraced his steps back to the maintenance room. He didn't have many options. Not without backup. Not without Dr. Harper's intel and the guidance of the special agents. He examined his watch. He was operating blind with less than fifteen minutes to spare.

Think fast, Brock.

The first option was to make a run for the nearest exit, guns blazing, and hope for the best. The second was to find a way into a balcony room. Surely, they'd have a better chance of survival then. *I need Shuggs.* His friend was the one person he knew who'd be able to hack into the keycard system in less than a minute.

A buzzing sound rang out, and Brock instantly tensed, preparing his exhausted body to spring into action. He engaged his weapon, then realized the sound had come from his pocket.

"Yeah?"

"O'Reilly, where have you been?" Dr. Harper asked.

Brock cursed silently. "I've been trying to find a safe place to—"

"Never mind. What is your precise location?"

Brock glanced around. "Level two, hallway B. I'm trying to get into one of the rooms on this floor because—"

"It is vital that you take cover until our team finds you."

"We'll be in," he examined the number on the nearby room door, "suite 238 B."

Brock bit his lip. *I pray Shuggs doesn't run into an issue breaking into the room.* It'd never happened before, but with the way things were taking shape, the predictable seemed abnormal.

"The team will extract you and the other soft targets—"

"And Shuggs."

"Is he currently with you?"

"Yeah. Thank God."

"I will call you back shortly with another solution."

Maybe Shuggs had been right about these suits after all.

"No. Please, ma'am," Brock said, a bead of sweat running down his back. "We're in trouble. Someone's out to kill us—"

"Do not do anything rash. We will—"

"You don't understand. We must be extracted now. Junior needs a doctor. It's bad."

"I understand." Dr. Harper sighed. "But we have a problematic situation."

"How can you do this to us?" Brock's jaw tightened. "We need your help now!"

"Help *is* on the way."

Brock was suddenly worn out, the stress depleting every bit of strength from his body.

Get yourself together. You have a job to do.

"When?" he asked, prepping himself to enter the maintenance room.

"Very soon. I promise," Dr. Harper said. "Just not the way you may have expected," she said before the line went dead.

CHAPTER 54

Brock held his gun with one hand and was reaching to open the door with the other when he heard a whisper.

He spun around, scanning the area, looking for danger, but seeing nothing.

Did I imagine that?

Brock glimpsed a slight movement. He flattened himself against the wall, staring into the dark.

Again, someone moved. They were down the hallway, close to the exit, beside a set of vending machines he hadn't paid much attention to before.

Holding his breath, Brock readied his weapon.

The sound appeared to come from the machines, but that would've been impossible. Brock estimated that the voice belonged to someone about twenty feet away.

But where, exactly?

He stayed glued to his position. Chest heaving.

Brock decided running into the maintenance room would endanger Patti's family. Protecting them could cost him his life, but it was a chance he had to take.

Brock was ready to burst into action and charge the person who called from the shadows when a man stepped out from beside the vending machines.

An explosion of testosterone flooded Brock's body in a sudden surge. He held tight, forcing himself to suppress the instinct to kill.

Straining his lungs, he willed himself to wait for the man to make the first move.

"Please! Don't shoot," the male from the shadows said, his hands up.

Squinting, Brock focused on the man's rugged features, realizing as he came into view that he was the leader of the SWAT team he'd met earlier.

"What the heck are you doing?" Brock lowered his voice and gun. "Trying to get yourself killed by friendly fire?"

A portion of the policeman's face was hidden by the shadows and partially illuminated by a red light cast from the vending machines behind him.

"My team—" he said, his voice cracking.

"Are you alright?" Brock took a step.

"We ... were hit." He stumbled, then steadied himself. "I'm the only one ... who ..." The policeman staggered forward, revealing the mangled left side of his head. "I'm the only one who made it out ... alive," he said, blood dripping from his exposed skull. A flap of scalp lay haphazardly above the man's eyebrow, his ear dangling by a single tendril of flesh that reached his chin.

Taking in the injured officer standing in front of him, Brock recoiled and sucked in a breath. "My God. What'd they do to you?"

"Don't know ... it ... it happened so fast. One minute we're sweeping the area ... the next minute ... two of my men are dead. Blown to bits. Right in front of my ... eyes."

"Must've been explosives," Brock said.

The policeman hung his head. "They had families ... kids ... wives ... parents."

Brock gently placed a hand on the man's blood-soaked shoulder. "Sorry about your men. But we have to keep moving. The shooters are still out there."

"They're not ... who you think ... they are."

"I know. They've been posing as law enforcement."

"Not just that ... but they're ... people who we ...thought we could trust."

"Yeah, my people and I are trying to figure out who to trust too." Brock glanced at his watch. "I have to go—"

"Let ... let me come with you."

"I will," Brock held a hand up, "but right now, I've got to get my people and move them to a more secure location."

"There's nothing secure ... eyes are ... everywhere."

"Stay put. I'll be back in thirty seconds," Brock turned to leave, "then you'll come with us."

"I'll wait ... but ... you'll see," the policeman said. "Someone's watching ... our every move."

Brock centered his focus on returning to the closet and getting everyone out safely. He robotically opened the maintenance room door while continuing to process what he'd just seen and heard.

As he entered the room, he racked his brain and walked past the corpse to the closet.

The question remained unanswered—*who was the policeman referring to? Who was behind the vicious attack against the law enforcement agencies of the United States?*

"It's me, Brock. Come on out," he said through the door, checking the area around him.

"It's about time." Shuggs opened the door.

"We need to get moving." Brock checked his watch. "We've got exactly ten minutes to hunker down in one of the rooms."

Jumping to his feet, Shuggs helped Brock usher Patti's family from the closet.

Brock pulled Mrs. Lipsett to her feet. "I know we're hurting and tired, but we have to move quickly."

"Lead the way." Shuggs handed the flashlight to him.

Brock stared at his friend when he reached for the light. Something in the way Shuggs's eyes glistened sent a shudder down his spine.

Reaching to steady Patti as she struggled to walk while carrying her son's dead weight, Brock gestured to Junior. "I'll carry him."

Patti sighed. "Thanks," she said, handing her son to him.

Shaking off the strange feeling in his gut, Brock hurried to the exit with the sleeping child on his shoulder. "Hey, man. I'll need you to use your skills to open a particular suite."

"Sure thing," Shuggs said.

"You hear anything from anyone?" Patti whispered.

"Yeah. Heard from Dr. Harper." Brock got to the door and opened it. "We're going to be rescued shortly."

"Thank God," Mrs. Lipsett said, her voice shaky.

Brock edged his way out into the hallway, peering into the dark shadows. A policeman's coming with us," Brock said, his voice low.

Shuggs came alongside Brock. "Where is he?"

"The man was just here. He must be close. He's hurt bad."

A sound came from the area by the vending machines.

"We've got our hands full," Shuggs said, reaching for his gun. "I say we take care of ours and keep moving."

"Exactly," Patti said. "Besides, we don't know if he is who he says he is."

Brock glanced at her, then looked down the hallway to where another sound came from the vending machines.

"I'll check it out and be right back." Shuggs jogged into the red shadows cast by the machine's glow, coming to an abrupt halt. Using his silencer, he fired a single shot between the vending machines.

The distinct thud of a body hitting the ground echoed through the hall. The policeman fell facedown at Shuggs's feet.

A cold tingle traveled around the base of his neck as Brock watched Shuggs hurry back to the group. "What'd you just do, man? I told you he was an officer."

Shuggs shook his head. "No. You're mistaken. He was definitely the enemy."

CHAPTER 55

B rock's hand trembled in anger as he reached for Mrs. Lipsett's shoulder, turning her away from the twitching body of the officer. Fighting the urge to confront Shuggs, he bit the inside of his cheek, drawing blood. For the first time in their long career together, he struggled with his friend's behavior. Why would he kill a man whom he'd personally vetted? What was happening to his friend? Maybe the stress? Alcohol? Or both? *After being in the field, I know it's hard to readjust.* But now, the unthinkable had happened. Killing one of their own. An innocent man, who was on their side, was gone.

Fighting back the tears, Mrs. Lipsett covered her grandson's face and pulled him closer to her.

"Is the policeman dead?" the boy asked.

"No. He's just sleeping," Patti said softly, reaching into her mother's arms to take her son. "You need to stay quiet until we get somewhere safe. Okay?"

The child nuzzled his mother's neck, stuck a thumb in his mouth, and closed his eyes tight.

Brock glanced over his shoulder. *At least we're safe.*

Shuggs held up the rear, gun cocked.

Patti and her son were sandwiched between them.

Checking his watch, Brock turned around. "We've got eight minutes to get into the suite." He waved, indicating they should follow him. Hurrying down the corridor with Junior on his shoulder, Brock used his free hand to guide Mrs. Lipsett. "We need to stay together and keep moving."

The group traveled through the shadows. The echo of their feet and shallow breathing filled the dead silence ahead.

Brock slowed his pace as he reached the row of suites, recalling he'd chosen room 238 B. "It's right here." He motioned to Shuggs.

Shuggs hurried to the door and knelt down. "I need you to hold up the flashlight so I can see."

Holding the light, Brock scanned the area around them.

Fishing in his pockets, Shuggs produced his phone and a small cord. "I just need to plug it in, power it up, and the lock opens."

"Are you sure it'll work?" Patti asked, her eyes trained on the officer's still body.

"Hope so." Shuggs fiddled with the mechanism on the door. After a few seconds, he sat back on his haunches, his jaw clamped.

"What's wrong?" Brock asked.

Shuggs frowned and pointed to the door's keycard reader. "Most of these locks have a DC power port under the keycard lock. I just plug a microcontroller into the port, and it reads the 32-bit key stored in the memory location. I can't seem to engage the port."

Biting his bottom lip, Brock checked his watch and cursed under his breath. They had less than five minutes.

"Let me try something else." Shuggs punched in a series of numbers on his phone and tried to pry the door open. After several attempts, it still didn't budge.

Brock paced in front of the suite. "Maybe we should try another room."

"I'm not giving up," Shuggs said, his forehead slick with sweat.

Brock checked his watch again. "We've got two minutes," he said.

"Give me a second, bro."

Brock shook his head, his unease increasing with each passing second. "We have to try another—"

The click of the suite's door confirmed Shuggs's skill. "We're in. You should know by now that my method has never failed." He got up and pushed the door open for the group.

Brock ushered the women in first, then followed. Once inside the room, he waited, expecting Shuggs to enter. But Shuggs remained on the other side of the door, a strange expression on his face.

"What're you doing? We're almost out of time. Get in—"

Shuggs's gaze locked on his. "I'm staying out here. Keep safe, bro."

"Your safety's important too."

"I'll patrol outside the room. It's like my daddy used to say when he quoted his favorite Confederate Army general, 'You usually win if you get there first with the most.' I figure at least I can be there first."

"That's ridiculous," Brock said. "The hallways are landmines."

"I need to be sure the *wrong* people don't get in here."

"We're better off together."

Shuggs shook his head, looking unconvinced. "Not necessarily." He glanced down the hallway. "I did my job by getting you into the room," he said before closing the door.

Brock locked up behind him. *Got to shake this feeling.* He rubbed his eyes, sore and gritty from exhaustion. *Think straight.*

"Alright, we need to secure the room." Fixing his eyes on the sliding doors leading to the balcony, he gestured to Patti, who stood nearest to the balcony. "We need to close the curtains. Stay away from the windows and entry points."

"I know you're worried about your friend," Mrs. Lipsett said, easing into an armchair. "But I have a feeling Shuggs knows how to take care of himself."

Patti closed the drapes that opened to the balcony outside. "Me too. The best we can hope for is that he runs into the rescue team."

"Yeah, I suppose you ladies have a point." Brock walked to the bed and lay the sleeping child beside his brother.

He clapped his hands together. "For the sake of safety, we need to keep our movements to a minimum, voices low. If anyone needs to use the bathroom, don't flush."

The women nodded.

Patti sat on the floor beside the bed, her back against the wall, facing the door.

Mrs. Lipsett rubbed her knees from her seated position in the armchair. "Why would these people be targeting women and children?"

"Wish I had the answer," Patti said grimly.

"I plan to find out." Brock looked at the women, a promise in his eyes.

"How?" Mrs. Lipsett asked.

"By figuring out who the shot-caller is and what it is that he wants," he said just as his phone buzzed. Glancing at the caller ID, Brock saw it was Dr. Harper. "Yeah?"

"What is your location?"

"We're in suite 238 B."

"Who is with you?"

"Patti and her family." Brock licked his dry, cracked lips. "Shuggs is patrolling outside."

"Very good."

"Is rescue coming?"

"Yes, but I must warn you. We have been thrown another curve—"

What are you people doing? "I don't understand the hold-up—"

"We secured an emergency warrant for Tucker Buckler based on the data you sent us earlier."

"You mean Uncle Buck? The guy behind the barroom shooting?"

"Yes. He is now in the state's custody."

Brock swallowed. "That's a good thing, isn't it?"

"It is. Unfortunately, we have uncovered something we did not expect."

"Like what?"

"The special agents have sole access to highly classified information. It would be best to get the intelligence brief directly from them."

"Why? It's not like I've got the time to—"

"Once I disconnect, they will contact you. Their findings will help make sense of the situation we are dealing with."

"Okay. But what happens now?" Brock's stomach lurched, feeling sick of reacting to other people's moves. "Soon this area will be crawling with men trying to kill us. It'll be only a matter of time before they find us and—"

"Our men are in transit to you." Dr. Harper let out a long sigh. "In the interim, barricade the main entry. And remember, trust no one."

CHAPTER 56

Brock rubbed his temples and walked to the balcony, peering past the fringe of the thick drapes into the murky courtyard. The otherwise bustling area was empty, cordoned off with brightly colored police caution tape. If officers patrolled the yard below, they weren't anywhere he could see.

Something sinister was going on at the Thompson Hotel. It was more personal, malicious, and bigger than he'd ever encountered. Bigger than Patti and her family. Without a doubt, Brock recognized the attack as a vigilante's payback. Executed with the precision of a master chess player. *But why? What had they done in the twisted mind of the accuser?*

Patti reached up from her seated position on the floor and tugged on Brock's pant leg.

He jumped back. For a fraction of a second, he'd forgotten he wasn't by himself.

"What was that exchange about between you and Dr. Harper?"

Turning toward Patti, his weapon aimed at her, Brock looked down and quickly lowered it. He grimaced with aggravation. He felt shame flush heat over his face.

Patti flinched. "What's gotten into you?"

"I'm sorry." He stared blankly at Patti's open mouth.

"Why would you point a gun at me?"

"Force of habit. You caught me off guard," Brock said and forced a smile.

Mrs. Lipsett called to Brock from the armchair. "Baby, why don't you get yourself something to drink," she pointed to the minibar, "and then wash your face."

Hearing the concern in the older woman's voice soothed Brock. A familiar tone in her words brought him comfort. He nodded, hearing his mother's voice in his head, remembering the last time he'd helped her bake one of her signature apple pies. She'd laughed, pointing out that he'd made a better crust than hers. He could hear the tinkle of her laughter ringing through their sunlit kitchen filled with love, lard, and cinnamon.

The memory cradled him. It rocked him back to a bittersweet placeholder in his life. He thought of her as she had once been. Before. After they'd sat down to eat the pie, he'd been sent outside to play. To try to fit in. Being the only white kid on the block challenged him in ways his prepubescent mind couldn't understand. Against his hopes, it'd happened again. The neighborhood bully targeted him as he always did. Called him names and made fun of his pale skin and sharp features. Others joined. Once the hitting began, the pain in his heart far outweighed the agony of a broken jaw.

That same day, Brock retaliated in an unusual act of defiance. His aggressor fell backward, snapping his eleven-year-old neck on impact. The boy's parents pushed to have Brock tried as an adult for a hate crime. When an investigation discovered the evidence proved the reverse, murder charges were dropped. The bully's mother had paid Brock's mother a tearful visit the day of her son's funeral. She said that for *her* people, injustice *was* the standard, and she and her husband didn't expect the authorities to prosecute a white kid for the death of their black son. Brock recalled that his mother never fully recovered from his actions and the sting of her neighbor's words. Later, the courts determined Brock had responded in self-defense to a habitual bully. It'd been an accident. But the dead don't know that; sometimes, the living don't either.

Bringing himself back to the present, he left his post by the window to walk to the minibar. Brock didn't realize how thirsty he'd been until he guzzled an entire can of soda in what seemed like one long swallow.

Four pairs of eyes stared at Brock.

"I guess I needed that," he said, massaging the back of his neck.

"Don't forget." Mrs. Lipsett waved him to the bathroom. "Your face."

Brock took in her troubled expression. "Do I really look that bad?"

Both women nodded in unison.

"Okay." He shrugged and went into the bathroom.

Brock gaped, scarcely believing the harrowing image reflected in the bathroom's mirror. A pair of piercing, bloodshot, green eyes stared back at him, set in a face covered with abrasions and dirt. His right eye was surrounded by puffy, purplish skin. Blood dried a blackish red plastered his face and jet-black hair.

Brock poured a handful of soap into his hands, scrubbing his face and head the best he could. After patting himself semi-dry, he exhaled. Leisurely. Soundlessly. *That's it, soldier. Get yourself together.*

When Brock returned to the room to rejoin the group, the two boys were awake, sharing a drink. The women were doing the same. The scene felt like he'd just been invited into their family room.

Mrs. Lipsett beamed. "That's more like it," she said, finishing her drink.

"Feeling better?" Patti asked, on her way to the bathroom with her sons.

"Yeah. Now we can do what Dr. Harper asked," Brock said, wearing a weak smile.

"What's that?"

"We stay put."

"So we hide out in this room the entire time?"

"Yeah, until they get the rescue team here."

"Okay. What if the opposition finds us first?"

"If it comes to that," Brock cleared his throat, "we'll have to barricade ourselves in the room until the team arrives."

"Shouldn't we barricade ourselves in anyway?" Patti asked. "I'll help you with that."

"I don't want to chance bringing unnecessary attention to our new hiding place."

"Makes sense."

Brock paced the room while Mrs. Lipsett dozed off, and Patti and the boys used the bathroom. He checked his phone and the peephole. Seeing nothing, he tried to relax.

Brock sat on the edge of the bed and examined his watch, wondering if the enemy had already discovered they'd left the maintenance room.

A fresh wave of anguish shot through his body, sending restless quivers to his leg. An old habit he'd fought for years to tame had returned in an instant. *Maybe the assailants had been intercepted by the rescue team. Was that what happened?*

A moment later, the answer to Brock's question became obvious. Down the hallway, the resonance of an authoritative, booming voice rang out, followed by feet grating against the ground.

Brock strained his ears.

Metallic clicks like low thunder. *Guns.*

Frozen, he stared at Mrs. Lipsett, who had a finger across her ashen lips.

Snake's radio crackled to life on Brock's hip. "Come in, brothers of TWA. Spiders caught in the web. Move now."

The sound of feet echoed, heading in the direction of the suite.

Brock jumped up. Held his breath. *Think. Fast.*

Adrenaline surged through his body as he shoved the nearby dresser and armoire against the door. He pulled the mattresses and box springs off each of the two beds, pushing them onto the furniture, barricading the room as best he could.

Shoes scraped the ground. The metal clicks of weapons came closer.

Brock ran to a dazed-looking Mrs. Lipsett. "Move somewhere safer, ma'am." He pulled her from the chair and hurried her to the bathroom.

Patti threw the door open, grabbed her mother's elbow, and pulled her in.

Brock jerked his chin in the direction of the hallway. "The enemy's here. Lock the door. Don't come out until I tell you."

Outside the room, a man's shout rang out. Nearer.

Brock patted his jacket, pulled everything out of his pockets, counted his remaining bullets, and cursed. He had enough ammunition for a very short gun battle.

Feet thundered against the ground, several feet away.

Instantly Brock's muscles tightened, priming his body to leap into action. He lifted his gun and took aim at the door from behind a heavy wooden TV stand.

CHAPTER 57

The closer the enemy came to the door, the tighter Brock gripped his weapon. *Got a job to do. Protect Patti and her family. Even if it costs me my life.*

What sounded like a man's voice called out.

What the heck? Walking backward, Brock kept his eyes trained on the front door while alternately checking the area by the rear sliding doors. He didn't see anything and went back to his post.

Again, a voice floated to him from behind and louder this time. *Maybe it's the rescue team.* He hurried to the balcony, scanning for help.

A tall, skinny young man waved to him, flanked by what appeared to be two cameramen.

Brock peered into the dark lot below. "Who are you?"

"Local news team," the skinny man said, waving a badge. "And I was—"

Brock started to slide the door closed.

"Please! I want to help. We snuck through the barrier," the reporter said quickly. "We put our lives on the line to get to you."

Watching the hotel room door, Brock spoke over his shoulder. "How're you planning to help?"

"Is it true a senator's wife—a *black* senator's wife—has been kidnapped?"

"You're wasting my time."

"No, like I said." The reporter licked his lips. "We're here to help."

"You're covering a story." Brock used his gun to point at the men. "We're fighting for our lives—"

"You can lower the hostages down to us. We'll catch them."

Brock squinted, calculating the distance to the ground in his head as he had earlier. He sized up the three scrawny men, barely holding up their skinny jeans. "It's too far a drop to risk."

"The lack of police force has been baffling. They underestimated the seriousness of the attack," the reporter said. "We're helping to direct others here to get you the support you need."

The sound of feet was almost at the hotel's door.

"What I need," Brock gestured to the bathroom, "is to safely evacuate kids and women out of here."

"We're working on that." The reporter pointed to one of the cameramen who was speaking into his phone. "We're putting a call out to anyone who can help—"

Brock's cell rang. Glancing at the screen, he answered the special agent's call. "Yeah?"

"Are you alone?" Agent Dexter asked, sounding out of breath.

Backing up to the sliding doors for more privacy, Brock kept his voice to a whisper and his eyes trained on the men below. "The family's in the bathroom. I've got three men outside the balcony claiming to be reporters."

"First, exterminate the *reporters*," Dexter said. "They may look unintimidating, but that's intentional."

Forcing a smile, Brock gave the men the thumbs-up sign. "Then what? I've got an army of hostiles approaching the hotel room. I'm outnumbered and almost out of ammo," he whispered.

"My partner, with the help of Agent Gentry, is working on a distraction."

"Like what?

Suddenly, a smattering of bullets hit the wall by Brock's head. Instinctively he crouched, trying to determine the direction of the attack. *From the lot!*

A curse bubbled up in his throat as Brock threw himself facedown onto the floor, leaving half of his body inside the room.

The next round of bullets from outside the balcony whizzed over Brock's head, exploding a vase on the coffee table inside. *Stay focused.*

Brock swiveled his body around, angling his gun downward. *Save your ammo for kill shots.* He aimed for the cameraman, whose equipment was replaced with a high-caliber rifle. Brock hit him in the neck.

The surviving men returned fire while retreating.

Once Brock had a clear shot, he took down the reporter with a single bullet just above his clavicle. Brock lost track of the surviving cameraman, who'd disappeared into the darkness.

Feet thundered outside the hotel's door, followed by a barrage of bullets.

Brock jumped behind the TV stand and returned fire, calculating and aiming for where he thought the triggermen were standing.

Another wave of gunfire rocked the makeshift barricade of furniture wedged against the entry point.

Checking his ammo, Brock sucked in his breath and fired two of the remaining ten bullets he had in his possession.

A series of deafening thuds plowed into the door, signaling to Brock that the enemy was using a battering ram to break in.

He held his position, lungs burning, a tsunami of angst flowing through his body. *Crap. They'll be in here in minutes.*

A muffled shout further down the hallway echoed like a death rattle.

Brock leaned forward, eyes on the quaking door, hands on his knees, using the breather to think through his options.

The enemy's cry was followed by a flurry of activity outside the door.

He bit his lip, took aim, and waited.

Several cries rang out.

Every option Brock could think of was garbage. Unlike the action flicks, jumping from the balcony could prove deadly, especially for the children.

The reverberation of even more feet shook the bullet-riddled wall.

Brock focused on the source, listening intently.

More boots scraped the ground.

Brock tried to ignore the whimpers of the inconsolable children hiding in the bathroom with the two women, whom Brock loved as much as he did his own mother. He doubted he'd be able to protect them much longer.

A roaring sound flooded the hallway.

What was that noise? Resisting the urge to fire everything he had left at the wall, Brock racked his brain for a way out. Tying a sheet to the balcony was a possibility. But with an onslaught of bullets, a battering ram, and an army of enemies coming through the wall, it'd be impossible. Almost.

CHAPTER 58

At the last second, as Brock prepared to fight, the commotion in the hallway stopped. He maintained his position, his lungs laboring, blood surging through his veins in a swell, commanding every part of his body to rush into combat.

The only sound ringing in Brock's ears were the cries of the two small boys nearby, layered with the muted whispers of their mother attempting to console them.

Brock slowly bent forward, straining to listen to the activity outside the door, fearing a sudden movement would draw unwanted attention. *Could this be some sort of trick?* He didn't put it past the enemy to draw them out of the room by pretending to retreat. But why would they do that now? They had them right where they wanted—trapped, vulnerable, and outmatched.

Checking his watch, Brock timed the silence outside. Two minutes. Five minutes. He filled his lungs with the stuffy recycled air, letting his breath out a little at a time. *Why would they leave when they had the advantage?*

Patti eased the bathroom door open, a red-faced child on each hip. "Did they go?"

"I don't know if they really left."

"Can you check to make sure?"

Brock trained his eyes on the door. "This could be a set-up."

"Maybe they've really gone."

"Why would they do that?" Brock said, frowning. "They have us cornered."

"Something could've happened."

"Like what?"

"A distraction."

Brock checked his watch, remembering Agent Dexter's words, and let out a soundless whistle. "You might be right."

Patti juggled the squirming boys. "Go ahead. I'll be your eyes," she said, handing off the children to her mother.

"We can't be too careful. If you hear or see anything, signal me," Brock said, rubbing his jaw. "Then go back into the bathroom and lock up."

She nodded. "Okay."

Staying as near to the ground as possible, Brock held his gun close and hurried to the exit. Once he got there, he pressed an ear to the adjoining wall, listening for movement in the hallway.

When he glanced back at Patti, she gave him the thumbs-up sign.

Brock pushed aside the furniture to clear a path to the door. He eased upward and peeked through the peephole. The hallway was completely clear of people but filled with swirling plumes of smoke. "Oh, no," he muttered as the overhead sprinkler system opened and sputtered, issuing droplets of water, which then began pouring down in a steady stream.

"What is it?"

He wiped his sopping wet face and kept his eyes on the black clouds pouring into the hallway from both directions. "Smoke. Lots of it."

Patti ran to the door, squeezed beside him, and looked through the peephole. "So that's why they left."

"Yeah, exactly."

"It looks bad. I doubt there's a way out."

"Yeah, it could be. I'll check it out."

"Be careful," she said with a hand on his shoulder.

"Close the door behind me." Brock opened the door, instantly feeling tongues of heat licking his face. Ignoring his internal instincts that were warning him to run in the opposite direction, he pulled the bottom of his shirt over his face to breathe better and crept into the smoke and water toward the nearest exit.

As he got closer, despite the sprinkler system, the heat became unbearable. Smoke stung his eyes, and breathing caused him to choke on the bitter, burning air. Blinking back the water his eyes produced, Brock dabbed his face just as a swarm of sparks exploded across his path, igniting everything in the way, including a massive silk plant.

The plant became an instant inferno, the torrid heat of the flames singeing his eyebrows and stopping him in his tracks.

Brock took a step back from the intense blaze. He coughed incessantly, watching the fake plant sizzle as it burned. Brock estimated that they didn't have much time before the entire floor succumbed to the fire. He crouched low and scurried back to the suite.

Patti swung open the door. "Any luck?"

Brock shook his head and collapsed onto the floor in the suite, sucking in the smokeless air as fast as he could. When he opened his eyes, Patti handed him a glass of water and a wet towel. He wiped his face and eyes and chugged the water.

"I hope Shuggs is okay."

"There's no … sign of him."

"Don't worry." Patti patted his back. "Well, we both know Shuggs knows how to take care of himself. Is it totally hopeless out there?" she asked.

"We … don't have … much time," Brock rasped.

"That bad?"

Brock pointed to the fat fingers of black smoke snaking their way under the door. "Quick! Wet towels—under the door."

Crossing the room in two long strides, Patti gathered an armful of towels, ran them under the faucet, and ran back, stuffing each crevice.

Pulling himself to his feet, Brock steadied his trembling body against a mattress and motioned to Patti. "We … we … all need wet towels around our noses and mouths."

"And then what?"

"We leave."

Patti gave Brock a puzzled look. "I thought it was too—"

The roar of a booming explosion shuddered and groaned outside the door. Despite the towels, smoke seeped into the confined space, setting off the sprinklers in the room.

Brock dragged the mattresses across the door and through the growing puddles, securing them by pushing a dresser behind them. "This is going to hold for only so long. We've got no other choice but to take our chances escaping." He pointed to the sliding doors. "It's the only way."

Patti pulled her jacket over her head, wiped her face, and nodded.

"I promise … you," Brock said, choking back a cough. "I'll do everything to keep your family safe."

"I'll get the boys and my mom," she said, rubbing her thick

midsection.

When Patti's family joined Brock, he'd already stripped the mattresses of their sheets. He began ripping each sheet in half and knotting them.

"What's that supposed to be?" Mrs. Lipsett asked.

His eyes still stung, but Brock held Mrs. Lipsett's steady gaze. "Two makeshift ropes, ma'am."

The older woman pursed her lips. "For what, baby?"

"We're going to have to escape through the balcony," Brock said.

CHAPTER 59

Brock hurried past Mrs. Lipsett and unlocked the sliding doors to the balcony. He knelt, firmly knotting the ends of the sheets to the base of the rails encasing the outdoor space.

Rails that resembled the fence encircling his modest childhood home. Rails that Malcolm, the neighborhood bully, had fallen over after Brock pushed him, causing his neck to break.

He blinked back the image of his nemesis scrolling across the movie screen of his mind. The pictures the lawyers displayed at Brock's brief trial had sent shock waves through the juvenile court. Blood spattered on the concrete like spilled finger paint. Malcom's lips were a cerulean blue. Traces of dried bile stuck to his rubbery brown cheek. The animalistic cries of Brock's mentally disturbed mother ricocheting through the courtroom.

But remember, a tiny voice reminded him, *you were found not guilty.* Set free from the crime of murder.

The screeching sound of the sliding doors tore Brock from his memories.

Mrs. Lipsett was out of breath when she came through the door leading to the balcony.

Brock frowned. "Where's everyone?"

She removed the wet towel from her face. "Patti and the boys had to use the bathroom."

"I'll need you to get them if they're not out here soon," Brock said. "The smoke won't stay back forever. We need to move fast. Before long, even the balcony will be in flames."

"Are you absolutely sure about this?"

"You mean jumping from the balcony?"

Mrs. Lipsett nodded.

"We don't have any other options."

"What I don't understand is," she placed a hand on one hip, "where're the agents meant to protect us?"

"This entire situation has been bizarre." Brock bit his lip. "Our agents have been met with unexpected challenges. But they'll come through."

Mrs. Lipsett folded her arms across her chest. "Speaking of agents, where's Shuggs?"

Brock pulled a piece of fabric through a loop to form a slipknot in one of the ropes. "Probably somewhere fighting off the attackers."

"You're not worried about your friend?"

"Knowing Shuggs, he's safe."

She leaned over the railing and looked down. "What about my daughter?"

Brock glanced at Patti's mother, immediately pained by the look of hopelessness on her twisted mouth. "What do you mean?"

"Remember, she's pregnant." Mrs. Lipsett choked back tears.

"I'll protect her with my life." He added an extra knot to the sheet, making the rope about four feet. "You have my word."

"I hope that's enough." Mrs. Lipsett scooped up her younger grand-son when he crawled past her, following behind his mother and brother, looking like mummies with their heads wrapped in damp towels.

Brock checked his watch. "Crap," he muttered. The screen told him five more minutes had elapsed since they'd discovered the fire.

The hotel's thick concrete walls stifled the sound of the blaze, but the accumulation of smoke entering the room was tough to overlook. Every few seconds, a thicker curl of smoke passed through the wad of towels stuffed under the hotel's door.

"Let me help you." Patti pulled her towel aside and bent to examine Brock's handiwork.

"I've got it. Just close the door and pull up a chair so its back is against these rails," he said while he completed tying the final knot and securing it.

Patti dragged a patio chair across the balcony. "We're ready."

A spike of adrenaline compressed Brock's esophagus causing his baritone voice to rise an octave higher. "I'll make the first trip to help everyone make it safely down."

Patti selected one of the two ropes Brock had made, turning it over in her hands. "What do we do?"

"Have the boys stand one at a time on the chair and guide them over the ledge. One of you has to hold the child against the rail while the other ties a rope around the boy's waist using the slipknot I created," Brock said. "After you secure the rope, lower them. Once the boys are with me, you and your mom will take turns using the same method."

Mrs. Lipsett picked up her grandson and positioned him on the chair. "Do you think this will work?"

Brock nodded and craned his neck to peer into the darkness beyond the courtyard, silently praying the assassin posing as a cameraman was gone.

Grabbing the rail, Brock climbed over, pulled the slipknot over his head and torso, and tied it securely around his waist. He gathered the bulk of the material, wound it around an arm, and then dove backward into the night.

Searing pain shot through his arm. *I need more slack.* The weight of his body on his arm threatened to rip it from the socket as he dangled over the ledge.

Clenching his teeth, Brock reached above his head with his free arm to release the rigid tension in the fabric.

Instantly, Brock plummeted to the ground at an extreme speed. He closed his eyes, forcibly relaxing his muscles like he'd been trained to soften the impact and avoid broken bones. But as quickly as he'd dropped, he stopped. Midair. His body swung below the ledge like a human pendulum.

Opening his eyes, Brock looked down, estimating he was about ten feet from the ground. He undid the slipknot with one hand and held the top of the rope with the other. Once he was untied, he took a deep breath and let go, spiraling downward.

Brock met the rugged, icy earth, knocking the air from his lungs. He lay still for what seemed like an eternity but was only a few seconds.

"Are you okay?" Patti's voice called down to him.

He carefully sat up. "Yeah, I'm fine." Brock checked each of his aching limbs for fractures.

Mrs. Lipsett leaned over the rail. "Baby, we're sending the boys down now."

Brock dug his fingers into the frigid dirt as he struggled to stand to his feet, his eyes drawn to a row of windows lit with the glow of a raging fire.

"Fast! Get the boys down here," Brock said, forgetting about his pain.

CHAPTER 60

Kneading his throbbing temples, Brock saw flashes of an orange, golden light flickering from a row of windows to his right. He swallowed and looked up, beckoning to his godson, who stood twenty feet above on the hotel room's terrace. Gripping the rails with both hands, Junior tottered on the chair pushed up against the balcony's ledge.

Patti and her mother each had a hand on the child's back, whispering affirmations in his ear. Their voices floated through the air as if speaking into a megaphone.

Brock cleared his throat. "Time to be a big boy, Junior," he said. His voice calm, eyes locked onto the boy's pupils.

The child buried his head in his hands. "No. I can't do—"

"Keep looking at me."

"I'm scared—"

"That's okay. Then close your eyes and take the biggest jump you've ever taken."

Junior peeked up at his mother, shaking his head.

Brock clenched and unclenched his jaw. "Come on, son. I know you can do it."

"Yes, baby. We *know* you can do it." Mrs. Lipsett stroked her grandson's cheek.

"You'll get a chance to be a real superhero, just this once," Patti chimed in.

"I ... I ... need ... a cape." Junior's bottom lip poked out.

Brock made a fist and punched his thigh. "What the h—"

"Of course. One cape coming up." Mrs. Lipsett ran to the door. She leaned inside and pulled down the curtain, returning with an armful of material as a ribbon of black smoke escaped from the door and spiraled behind her.

Patti helped her mother tie the curtain into a cape around Junior's neck.

"I want one too," the younger child cried.

"Got you covered." Mrs. Lipsett pulled another curtain panel from the bundle and tied it around the second child's neck.

The smoke intensified, and flames started licking the outside of the windows. He waved his hands. "Time to jump!"

Junior's tired eyes were wide as he peered at the ground far below.

"Just breathe," Brock gave him an encouraging smile and a nod, speaking as if he could hear the child's thoughts, "then fly."

The boy gave him a thumbs-up.

Brock's bruised, sweat-soaked fingers reached up in the air toward Junior. "Now jump. Once you're hanging there, let yourself loose from the slipknot and jump into my arms, and I'll catch you."

"Promise?"

"I would *never* let you fall. Never."

Junior closed his eyes, opened his arms, and sprung from the ledge.

"Good boy!" Patti cried.

The ache in Brock's eardrums reflected how hard his heart was beating when he leaned in and caught the child, ignoring the abrasions that opened back up. The force of the child's weight knocked Brock backward onto his tailbone, but he didn't let go of his godson.

"That was so fun!" Junior giggled. "Can I do it again?"

You're one lucky kid. Brock tried not to groan.

"Not this time, baby." Mrs. Lipsett steadied her younger grandson on the chair.

Patti picked up her son from the chair, balancing him on the ledge while her mother pulled the slipknot over his head and secured it around his waist. "It's your brother's turn."

"We also have to find our friends." Drops of sweat coursed down Brock's back as he sat up, dusted himself off, and checked Junior for injuries.

"And get away from the bad guys." Junior looked up at him. "Right?"

Brock pulled himself up. "Yeah, that's right."

"Let Uncle Brock concentrate, Junior," Patti said. "He has to catch your brother."

Brock moved Junior several feet out of the way and opened his arms wide. "Are you ready to—"

The small child vaulted his body into the air, barely stopping before releasing himself from the slipknot.

Brock panted hard, his lungs gasping for every mouthful of the salty, soggy air. "Got him!"

"Oh, thank God," Mrs. Lipsett clapped her hands.

"You okay?" Patti asked, already positioned on the ledge.

Brock put the child down beside his brother and wiped his bloody palms on his pants. "We're fine." He then turned toward Patti and prepared himself to break her fall.

Patti leaped into the air with the precision of an acrobat, untangled herself from the rope, and landed soundlessly on both feet beside Brock and the boys.

"Wow! Mommy's a superhero!" Junior cried.

Mrs. Lipsett pulled up the loose end of the rope, tied it around her midsection, and began maneuvering herself over the ledge.

Brock heard the faint murmur of voices. It was only then he sensed movement in the nearby shadows. The air shifted just the way it always did when someone else occupied the same space. An icy tingle traveled down his spine. He silently prayed it was the rescue team while mentally tallying the few bullets he had left. As he pulled his gun from its sheath, his hand trembled and he used the opposite arm to steady it. *Stay calm. Keep it together, soldier.*

Brock put a finger to his lips, eyes locked onto an oncoming threat he couldn't yet see.

The boys huddled under their mother's arms. Her hands clamped firmly across their open mouths.

He waved Patti's family to a hiding place behind a tall clump of fountain grass.

Like a department store mannequin, Mrs. Lipsett stood frozen halfway over the balcony's ledge. A single tear leaked from her eye.

Breathe. Concentrate. Focusing his sight, Brock strained his ears. His senses led him on autopilot, pumping pure adrenaline into his body. He reacted as if he'd been instantly transported to the frigid nighttime deserts of Iraq and curbed his rising panic.

Gunfire was sporadic at first, coming from the left side of the building. Then the shots sounded more targeted at them as the noise got closer. Brock estimated a few hundred yards away. *But from where?*

"Look out!" Mrs. Lipsett screamed, pointing to the bushes behind them.

CHAPTER 61

Brock positioned himself behind the thick layers of spongy bark and peeked out into the darkness. His heart kicked into overdrive while searching for the enemy. The soft patter of cool rain pelted his face. Wiping his eyes, Brock leaned into the wet, dim lighting.

Figures cautiously advanced toward them through the shadows along the edge of the hotel grounds.

"Brock," the older woman called to him in a hoarse whisper.

Looking up, his eyes met Mrs. Lipsett's. "Ma'am?"

Patti parted the bushes she and her sons hid behind. "Talking isn't a good—"

"Hush. Just keep my grandbabies safe."

"But, Mom—"

"Stop."

Patti stared at her mother. "What're you planning to—"

Mrs. Lipsett held her hand up, climbed back onto the chair, slipped off the rope, tied the second rope to the end, then leaned toward Brock. "Tie your gun to the rope. Send it up to me." She threw down the tied sheets.

Brock shook his head just as a bullet ripped past him, sinking into the wide trunk of a neighboring oak with a dull thud.

"I can see clearly from up here," Mrs. Lipsett said, her face streaked with rain and tears.

Brock's stomach tightened. "How many?"

"Two."

A bolt of lightning lit the sky with purplish streaks. Brock stretched to grab the rope. He stared across the expanse of greenery, seeing nothing but sheer sheets of rain. Wiping his slippery hands on his damp pants, he secured the gun to the material dangling from the balcony.

Mrs. Lipsett turned over the table and pushed it behind the row of concrete planters lining the balcony. Positioning herself behind the overturned patio set, she pulled up the gun.

"Only eight bullets," he said.

"I'm a decent shot."

Mrs. Lipsett removed her bangles, wedged herself behind the wooden latticed table, and centered herself. Using the seat cushions to prop up her elbows, she flattened the rest of her body against the floor. She slid the gun through an opening in the lattice, engaged the weapon, and pointed at the approaching shadows.

Think, Brock. Think. Gritting his teeth, it took everything Brock had in him to keep still and not instinctively fight for the people he desperately needed to protect. Not knowing if he'd get the chance to do so again killed him inside. *I need a plan.*

A blur of motion emerged in front of him. The outline of two men's bodies, lit by the glow of a low-hanging moon, loomed close, then disappeared.

Squinting, he scanned the obscure darkness.

A few feet away, the shadowy figures reemerged, searching each clump of bushes.

Groping along the watery cold ground he knelt on, Brock sucked in a breath and raked up handfuls of pebbles and dirt. He pulled off his shoe, removed his sock, and filled it with the mixture he'd gathered.

The figures inched closer.

Brock crouched low, knotted the opening of the sock, then shoved his naked foot back into his shoe. He worked the bundle in his sock into a compact baseball size ball, poised with his homemade weapon, and waited. In the heavy, dead, black silence that ensued, dread spread through Brock's chest. Squeezing his eyes shut, he prayed for a miracle. One he knew would be impossible to fulfill with the odds stacked against him and the people he'd tried so hard to defend.

The air shifted, carrying with it the earthy scent of rain mingled with the tang of his sweat.

Just when he couldn't hold his breath a second longer, a sudden noise from above froze Brock to his spot.

Mrs. Lipsett let off two quick rounds.

Peering through the rain, Brock watched in terror as the two men returned gunfire with more than a hundred rounds.

Explosions turned the silence and dark into earsplitting bursts and flashes of white-hot light.

Brock was numb. *This situation could not be worse.*

Children's cries pierced the night air.

The boy's voices swept through Brock like a chill. A part of him wanted to panic and run from the sound of gunshots and of the helpless. *Suck it up, soldier.*

The clouds parted, and the moon radiated scarlet light across the grass. The light spilled onto the figures of the two assassins, cautiously moving nearer.

No matter what, take control. Brock hugged the tree and steadied himself.

He pulled himself up on shaky legs and stumbled forward.

A dark figure aimed at the balcony. Fired. The light fixtures on the terrace exploded, sending flecks of glass into the air, showering the patio.

Mrs. Lipsett returned fire.

Brock squinted, unable to believe what he saw. One of the men had been hit in the leg, sending him to his knees.

The perp's partner pulled his fallen comrade up and slung him behind the oak tree beside Brock, not seeing his motionless figure. Then he unloaded a barrage of bullets on the left side of the large patio table.

In return, Mrs. Lipsett fired twice, carving chunks from the oak nearby and putting a hole into the perp's forehead. The man let out a gasp and slammed facedown onto the ground. His fatal wound colored the rain puddle he lay in like a watered-down burgundy wine.

Brock had just slammed the heavy sock into the hurt man's right temple, killing him instantly, when out of the corner of his eye, Brock caught a sudden movement coming from the hedge.

Patti's two sons ran from the bushes toward the open courtyard.

"Boys, no!" Patti screamed. She crawled from her hiding place and chased behind her two small children.

As his body went into action, Brock went cold, feeling something snap inside.

A dark shadow swiveled around to Patti's family and took aim.

Brock charged from his hiding place and faced off with Patti's attacker. He stared at the man revealed by the moonlight, only steps ahead. The phony cameraman.

The skinny man turned toward Brock, his mouth twisted in a sinister smile as he pointed his weapon at Brock's head. Suddenly, the perp's grin was erased by a blast, leaving him with a seeping, red cavity in his shoulder.

A fresh bolt of electricity coursed through Brock's veins as he ran toward the perp, raised his arm, and swung his makeshift weapon against the man's nose with all his force.

Against the backdrop of a bloodcurdling scream and the baritone roar of thunder, the night sky exploded. Again. And again.

CHAPTER 62

Brock jumped back, instantly bracing himself as the cameraman's flailing body dropped at his feet, narrowly missing him. He raised his handmade weapon, ready to strike another deadly blow.

After staring down into the dead, empty, open eyes, he lowered his arm and bent over. Blood spurted from a wound above the man's right ear, already matting that side of his face. Brock's mind raced, haunting him with his near brush with death. Droplets of sweat ran down his chin, falling onto the dead man's unblinking face.

Using his sweat-soaked, exhausted hands, he peeled the man's fingers away from the gun's hot barrel. Brock pushed himself upright, pocketing the gun, a utility knife, and the remainder of his ammunition.

Swiveling around, he examined the balcony for signs of life. Slowly Mrs. Lipsett pulled herself up and limped to the rail. It was only then that Brock realized how hard his heart was beating. He swallowed. *But where was Patti?*

"Patti?" Mrs. Lipsett shielded her eyes from the drizzle and leaned over the balcony's ledge, her wet dress clinging to her.

"Over here. Behind the oak."

Turning to look behind him, Brock stared at Patti and her boys and released a breath.

"I see you now. You okay?"

Patti nodded.

"My grandbabies?"

She held tight to the hands of her whimpering boys. "We're ... fine, Mom." Patti's eyes welled up with tears. "You?"

Mrs. Lipsett nodded. "And you, Brock? Are you hurt, baby?"

His fingers dug into the bloodied sock, and he looked down at the dead cameraman. "No, ma'am." Brock's jaw tightened. He gripped the center of the compact wad of dirt and pebbles as if clinging to an avalanche of memories.

Those memories brought him back to his childhood home. Back to his yard in Long Island, New York, twenty-one years earlier. It was the beginning of seeing things no one should get used to seeing. He stood over Malcolm, who lay deathly still. His neighbor. His nemesis. Brock remembered how he'd held his hands above his head in silent surrender, an affirmation of guilt, long before the homicide detectives reached the scene. He'd wanted to run, but he hadn't.

Patti roughly shook his shoulder, bringing him back to the present. "Brock!"

"Yeah?" Brock said, trying to focus in on Patti's scrunched-up face.

"Mom's asking for your help getting down." She frantically pointed to the smoky balcony. "The fire's getting worse."

A window exploded, sending sparks and shards of glass through the air. The ebbing rain caused the light show to fizzle before hitting the ground.

He blinked hard, cursing himself for getting into his own head. *I can't let them down.*

Staring into the flames that now licked the right side of the balcony, Brock willed himself into action and ran closer to the fire, directly beneath the ledge. "Mrs. Lipsett, just stick to the plan. Don't look at what's around you."

"Oh, my God." Mrs. Lipsett covered her mouth when another window closer to her exploded.

"Ma'am, tie the rope around your waist like I showed you." He licked his dry lips. "Then climb over and jump."

She shook her head. "I can't."

"Yes, you can!"

"The rope's destroyed." She glanced behind her at the rising smoke and held up the bullet-riddled cloth that disintegrated in her hands. "I—I don't want to die."

"I don't want my grandma to die!" Junior cried, wheezing, sending his younger brother into a crying spell.

Patti knelt, pulling both boys into her arms. "No one's going to die."

"Not on my watch!" Brock shouted, picturing his mother's face and the long list of those he'd hurt or failed to protect.

"What do I do?" Mrs. Lipsett cried, the panic in her voice barely audible over the roar of the fire and the thunder rumbling in the distance.

Think, soldier. What the heck do I do?

Patti's hand clutched his arm so hard that her nails broke into his skin. "Do something!"

"Stay as close to the edge as possible!" Brock yelled, a rush of adrenaline flooding his system as sweat and rain coursed down his face. "Hold tight and lie under the seat cushions until I get back." He spun around and ran toward the dead men.

"What're you doing?" Patti asked, her voice high-pitched with alarm.

"Making new rope." Brock got to the cameraman and began disrobing him.

"How?"

"Give me just a few minutes," he glanced at the balcony. "That's all we need before the fire breaks out. I'll show you."

"Tell me what to do."

"Help me get the other two guys' clothes off too." Brock motioned to the perp by the oak tree he had just killed and the one with the bullet hole in his forehead.

Patti's head turned. "Okay." She had her sons huddle under a nearby tree, then ran to assist Brock by doing what he'd asked her.

In seconds, they had a pile of damp clothing.

"Watch me. We need to work fast." Brock hastily pulled the recently acquired knife from his pocket and got to work shredding the men's clothing into thick strips. He worked the strips into a makeshift rope by twisting a strip at a time away from him, then pulling the twisted strip over toward him and repeating the process.

Patti helped by tying the pieces firmly together, leaving a trail of five inches in between, and wrapping a new strip of fabric around it.

Brock checked his watch. It'd been ten minutes, and the flames had begun engulfing both sides of the balcony. He grabbed the makeshift rope, estimating it at ten feet in length. *Enough to do the trick. Hopefully.*

"Mrs. Lipsett! Come out now!"

The older woman poked her head up from behind the cover of a cushion and struggled to get to her feet. She pushed herself up and clung to the rail.

Brock threw the rope up to her. Mrs. Lipsett caught it on the third attempt.

She shook her head. "It's not long enough—"

"Mom, pull it together!" Patti shouted. "You. Will. Be. Fine!"

The gears in Brock's mind shifted into automatic. "Keep your eyes on me. Do everything I say. No looking at anything else. Understood?"

Mrs. Lipsett tilted her head from side to side and stared at him, a blank look in her eyes.

Brock cursed under his breath. He'd seen that look hundreds of times. *Nothing good ever comes from being in shock. Nothing.*

"You got this. I'm right here to catch you." Brock glanced at the black pillow of smoke behind Mrs. Lipsett and tried to believe his words. "Tie the rope around you!" He held his breath, feeling out of place speaking that way to a woman he respected and loved, but praying his tone would focus her on surviving a fire that would soon engulf her.

The older woman stood frozen, seemingly oblivious to the cries from her family urging her to act.

A freezing wind grazed Brock's face, carrying with it ashes from the crumbling balcony. *Whoever's behind this will pay.* He spat out the taste of fire that'd filled his open mouth, consumed with rage at the prospect of losing another innocent person. "Move now or die!"

CHAPTER 63

Mother. I *know* you can jump to safety," Brock said, lowering his voice. He cleared his throat.

Mrs. Lipsett's eyes had regained focus. She gripped the rail tighter in response, leaning toward him. "I'm so scared."

"Of course you are. I was too. But that's okay. Do it afraid."

"You sure?" Mrs. Lipsett raised her hand to push back a curly lock of salt-and-pepper hair dangling in her eyes.

"Absolutely." Brock cracked a smile. "Tie the rope around your waist, hold the rails and get your legs over, then jump." Brock motioned to Mrs. Lipsett. He kept his voice calm, his eyes locked on hers.

She tucked her sopping wet dress between her thighs as she exited the balcony.

Brock prepared himself to grab hold of Mrs. Lipsett's legs. But as he gauged the distance between them, he realized he couldn't come near to grabbing her legs. Then the rope only held for seconds after her jump.

She swayed in the air momentarily before crashing into Brock's gut hard enough to knock him onto his back, stunning him, and causing him to choke like he was taking his last breath.

He didn't have the energy to pull away from Mrs. Lipsett's body, pinning him to frozen black mud and rotting leaves. On the verge of passing out, he was unable to suck in air fast enough.

Mrs. Lipsett gasped for breath for a few long seconds and, with the help of her daughter, rolled off Brock. "I ... I'm ... sorry, baby."

"Grandma! I think you killed Uncle Brock!" Junior cried.

Junior shook Brock's shoulder. "Are you dead?"

"I'm ... okay. Just ... just give me a ... minute." Focusing on the child, he bit down hard and concentrated on telling his body to breathe normally.

At least a mile away, sirens whirred. Brock closed his eyes and pictured his mother once again, hearing her screams when the police had placed the handcuffs on his eleven-year-old wrists.

"I'm better now." He sat up and pointed to the building. "Besides, we need to move away from the balcony. It's about to collapse." Brock planted his feet and took Junior's small, outstretched hand to help leverage his bruised body off the ground.

Once he steadied himself, he grabbed the hands of the two children and staggered away from the burning structure as fast as his legs could muster.

The group followed Patti as she guided them to a cluster of trees a safe distance away. Seconds after they stopped, the balcony crashed down in a burst of flames.

"We need to get out of here," Brock said.

"Where to?" Patti asked, holding her mother's elbow.

"The Riverwalk looks safe." Mrs. Lipsett pointed shakily to the well-lit area.

He swept his gaze in a full arc through the courtyard and from left to right across the riverside's deserted boardwalk lit by well-spaced streetlights. "It does. But let me check on something first." Brock pulled out his phone and tried unsuccessfully to connect to Dr. Harper and the two agents.

What's wrong, soldier? Cursing under his breath, he strained his ears for signs of the rescue team, hearing the creak of cricket frogs instead. The rain had stopped, but the air was heavy, scented with fish, rotting moss, and the acrid stink of his sweat.

Patti frowned. "What is it?"

"I'm thinking." Walking in a circle on the wet grass, Brock rubbed his jaw, struggling with a nagging feeling that something seemed off. He'd learned to trust that feeling. Just then, his phone buzzed.

He glanced at the caller ID, recognizing Dr. Harper's number.

"O'Reilly, are you with Mrs. Lipsett?"

"I am."

"Is she hurt?"

Brock glanced at the older woman leaning on her daughter. "She'll live."

"I take it you got the family to safety through the balcony."

"Yeah, but how would you've—"

"We knew you would figure it out," Dr. Harper said. "A fire was set to get the assassins away from the suite."

"One of *our* people set the fire?"

"Yes. We were left with no other options but to—"

"Your tactics could've killed us." Brock clenched his fist. "We've also got Patti and her two children to protect."

"Understood. Despite the risks, it presented better odds of survival."

"Where's the rescue team?"

"In place. To meet them, return to the hotel's rear entrance at once. SWAT will meet you in the basement. Then, they will lead you to—"

"Heck, no!" Brock shook his head. "We're not returning to a burning building with gunmen lurking around every—"

"I repeat, the fire was a controlled burn made to appear worse than it was. It only affected the second floor and has already been extinguished."

Looking up, he stared at the Thompson in disbelief. The fire was gone.

"O'Reilly, leave the courtyard—"

"Wait. Why?"

"The gunmen have now taken an offensive position nearby. Move quickly," Dr. Harper said before the line went dead.

Biting his bottom lip, Brock turned to the group. "We need to go back to the hotel—to the rear entrance."

"Have you lost your mind?" Patti asked.

He pointed to the building. "See for yourself."

"There's no way we can go back inside and risk—"

"Look."

Folding her arms, Patti shook her head, refusing to look at the hotel. "You're clearly not thinking straight. There's no way. After escaping that death trap, I'm not subjecting my family to suicide by returning."

Mrs. Lipsett nudged her daughter. "Something's going on over there." She pointed to the Thompson.

Patti swiveled to face the building, taking in what Brock and her mother had observed. With the exception of the smoldering balcony, the fire had dissipated almost entirely. "What the heck?"

"Dr. Harper said it was a controlled burn," Brock said. "They set the fire so we could escape."

Turning to face him, Patti grimaced. "Then why would we return?"

"My daughter's right," Mrs. Lipsett agreed. "It's time to find somewhere safe. Away from those crazy people trying to kill us."

Brock scanned the deserted courtyard, a shiver running down his spine. "I have my orders. This area isn't safe either."

Patti stared at him, concern etched onto her face. "I don't understand—"

Bullets pierced the air, simultaneously shattering the glass streetlamps on the Riverwalk, plummeting the area into darkness.

"Uncle Brock, turn back on the lights!" Junior repeatedly screamed while gasping for breath before his mother ran and gathered him in her arms. He buried his head on her shoulder beside his crying brother, wedged on her other hip.

Mrs. Lipsett clamped a hand over her mouth and stood frozen.

Brock squinted into the night, acid rising in the back of his dry mouth. The courtyard was lit by a smoky glow reflecting the stormy, starless sky overhead.

He put a finger to his lips and waved the family down to the ground. As he watched them take cover, a wave of black rage ignited his body, erasing away his pain and fear.

Crawling through the grass, Brock peered across the street. Once he got to the edge of the property, he held his position, slowly breathed out, and waited for the enemy to make the first move. Pulling out the dead perp's gun, he counted five bullets. *I'll have to make every shot count.*

Whoever the enemy was, they'd been trained well. Driven by an oath to protect the United States from enemies foreign and domestic, he had done the same—stalked men. Countless times he'd taken out hostiles in their homelands before they could execute their sinister plans. Even when the deployments were brutal and endless—when he experienced wounds, exhaustion, and regret—he would willingly do it again if his country needed him.

These opponents were fighting an invisible war that Brock could never respect. He reasoned they had some rationale, probably politics, power, or both. Yet they carried out their acts of terror on innocent people, in *his* country, on American soil. To him, it was the ultimate act of betrayal.

Just then, he saw it. Outlined by a bluish moon against the backdrop of the river, an assault rifle was aimed in their direction.

CHAPTER 64

Staring into the black shadows at the powerful weapon pointed at them by a dark figure, Brock knew they were outgunned. Based on the calculated way the streetlamps had been shot down, the assault rifle had to have been one of many. *What do these guys want?*

Brock fumbled, reaching into his holster. His fingers trembling from the adrenaline of the moment. His life was on the line—and the lives of the people he cared for the most.

Remembering that he had only five bullets remaining, he wiped the sweat from his eyes. He'd gotten himself into a deadly battle he couldn't win. Not without a miracle.

What should I do? Hundreds of possible scenarios popped into his mind, all ending with him failing to protect Patti and her family. Momentarily, he found it impossible to breathe or think. His heart beat wildly in his chest and his mind raced.

Again, he asked himself, *What choices are open to me?* His decisions were set in a trap of hidden dangers and invisible enemies. He closed his eyes briefly, wishing Pang and Shuggs were here.

Together they were invincible, fearing nothing.

Brock frowned, wondering where Shuggs was. "Where are you?" he yelled, his tongue reacting before his brain could catch up. He froze, praying no one had heard him shouting like a madman to himself.

"That you, bro?" a familiar hoarse voice replied.

Brock squinted, finally able to see the shadowy outline of his friend, whose voice came from across the street. "Yeah. Lower your weapon, man. What're you doing over there, anyway?" he asked, letting out a sigh of relief.

"Stay put. It's dangerous as a diabetic in a candy store out here," Shuggs called out. "I'll come to you."

Brock's phone buzzed. He peered at the caller ID and smiled before answering. "Berkley, good news. I just found Shuggs—"

"O'Reilly, this is urgent! The man who breached our intel *is* Shuggs! It's Shuggs! Get to safety!"

Brock blinked, swallowing the lump in his throat, and killed the call. He jerked his head around to stare across the dark street, taking an involuntary step back in shock. A bead of sweat formed on his brow. His arm dropped numbly to his side as he choked out a single warning to Patti. "Run!"

In horror, he watched Shuggs aim his gun while the family dashed across the open field into a kill zone. In military tactics, the family was in the perfect position to be quickly slaughtered by the enemy.

"What the heck?" Slamming to his knees, Brock hurriedly trained his gun on Shuggs until he had a clear shot. He sucked in a breath, fired once, missed, and lay flat.

Shuggs returned fire. "This ain't your fight, bro," he repeatedly said while unloading a series of rounds, hitting the branches off a nearby tree.

Brock rolled away just in time to avoid being crushed by the weight of the tree's heavy limbs.

Using his elbows to steady his aim, Brock fired another single shot, cracking the pavement beside Shuggs but leaving his target uninjured.

Glancing behind him, Brock saw Patti's family scramble around the corner of the hotel and run to the entrance. *Good. They are almost out of the kill zone.*

"You weren't supposed to be here!" This time Shuggs fired several rounds at Brock, ripping up the ground where he lay.

One bullet grazed Brock's upper arm, dazing him. *Have to remain focused.* He dabbed at his bloody shoulder, thinking of Patti's family, of Pang, knowing he'd rather die than have something happen to them. He rubbed his eyes and shook his disturbing thoughts away. *Focus, listen, wait, soldier.*

Brock army-crawled backward. The pain in his shoulder racked his body, reminding him that one of his best friends had just tried to take his life while trying to kill their other best friend's family.

He peered over his throbbing shoulder, estimating he had about another hundred feet to the hotel's rear entrance. Brock willed himself to use his aching shoulder to maneuver his body through the wet grass and mud.

When the searing pain threatened to cause him to black out, Brock stopped to catch his breath. If he stood, he could move faster, but there was a chance of getting shot. *It's a risk I'm going to have to take.*

As Brock struggled, pulling himself to his buckling knees, his radio crackled to life, and the firing suddenly ceased.

"Calling Head Razor," Shuggs shouted. "It's the General."

"Yes, sir. Razor 1. Over."

"Calling Head Spook! General here."

"Come in, General. Spook 1 here. Our soldiers are ready."

"Have all surviving Razors and Spooks rounded up."

"Report to the rally point, General?" Razor 1 asked.

"Yes, time to kill the spiders!" Shuggs shouted.

CHAPTER 65

Watching Shuggs retreat briefly to reload, Brock felt something stir inside his gut. He was close enough to shoot and make the shots count. His pocket buzzed, and his mind kicked into high gear. Keeping his weapon engaged, he reached for his phone, but it tumbled to the ground. He didn't have to pick it up to see the glowing text Dr. Harper had sent him:

"Help is minutes away. Distract Shuggs. Stay alive."

Brock looked up just in time to see Shuggs aiming his gun at him once more. His heart racing, he ducked into a clump of thorny bushes, biting his tongue as the thorns tore into his skin.

How am I going to hold off Shuggs and his army? The endgame was what the suits up top had surmised—the danger was internal. Their intelligence security had been hijacked by someone within the ranks, one of their own. Shuggs.

Brock scanned the deserted courtyard and surrounding area. He shuddered, attempting to ignore the penetrating frost of the wind blowing off the river through his wet clothes.

Checking vehicles, doors, or any other places he hadn't noticed before, Brock frantically searched for a way of escape.

He watched Shuggs travel closer until his shadow darkened the sidewalk in front of him. Shuggs stood several feet away while he spoke into his radio, a gun steady in his hand. *I'll try to appeal to him. Get into his head. See what he's thinking.*

Cursing under his breath, Brock concentrated on trying to make sense of the situation while thinking of an exit strategy before Shuggs's people arrived.

Brock crawled away from the bushes and hid behind the wide expanse of an oak tree. A string of bullets missed him by inches. "For

God's sake, stop! We're friends. Put down the gun. Let's talk. Just you and me."

"*Friends* see things the same way."

"For years, we *have* seen things the same—"

"No. We haven't. You weren't paying attention."

"What're you setting out to prove by being part of a national intelligence security breach and—"

"What're you doing?" Shuggs said. "Trying to get into my head?"

"No, I—"

"Not going to work." He shook his head. "Not today."

Peeking from behind the tree, Brock ducked back into hiding and lowered his body, keeping his eyes trained on Shuggs. "I can't believe ..." He felt his throat tighten and go dry.

"Believe what?" Shuggs asked. "That I have the courage to fight for my country to preserve my way of life?" He peered down the street and walked to the edge of the curb, keeping his gun cocked.

"What in the world are you talking about?"

"I'll admit, at first, I thought you could be one of us, but I was wrong. And I never expected you to come here on your own to chase after the likes of Patti and her family." Shuggs heaved a deep sigh. "You weren't even supposed to be here. You were on your way to a new job in New York. Remember?"

"Are you serious? You're creating a national security nightmare because you don't like our friend's wife."

Shuggs gestured into the air with his gun. "You can't be that dumb, bro. This is about the *movement.*"

"What movement?" Brock asked from his position behind the tree.

"Our people are sending a message to the *true* American patriots and the inferiors who war against us. No one's going to replace us. We're reclaiming our territory by taking no prisoners."

"Why Patti?" Brock asked, glancing behind him at the hotel.

Shuggs pointed the gun. "Just stay your butt by that tree. Don't move. Not until I try talking some sense into your head. You probably have only a handful of bullets left anyway."

"I can't believe we're fighting like this. It's always been the three of us against the world. Never against each other. Doesn't our relationship, our history, account for anything?"

Shaking his head, Shuggs's face hardened, his eyes unblinking.

"I'm begging you, man. Stop this train wreck. It's not too late. I swear I'll vouch for you," Brock said. "I'll tell everyone it was PTSD jacking up your head. You don't—"

"Shut up!" Shuggs raised a fist and cursed. "Listen to me."

Stay focused, soldier. Death isn't an option. "Yeah. I'm listening."

"I really don't want to kill you, bro. You and I both know the only thing standing between you and me is that stupid tree and my kindness. I could've laid you down where you stood a long time ago."

"What's your point?"

"I'll spare your life if you'll get Mrs. Lipsett and bring her back to me."

"I can't do—"

"It's her life or yours."

"You kill any of Pang's people," Brock said, "you'll have to go on and kill me too."

Shuggs walked into a half-circle of moonlight. His lifeless smile never reached his cold eyes. "Don't you get it, bro? Senator Lipsett is the favored pick for the leftist socialists on the Democrat's ticket. We could have another black as president over us."

Brock licked his lips, his mind spinning, looking for angles, something, anything. "You're wrong. Mrs. Lipsett told me her old man's got serious health issues. He's reneging on the entire presidential run."

He shrugged. "I'm still going to need insurance."

"Insurance?"

"In case you're lying." Shuggs lit a cigarette with one hand, holding his gaze and gun on Brock. "I'm using the Lipsett family as an example to illegals, Muslims, gays, blacks, Jews, Hispanics, mixed-breeds, race-traitors, and other miscreants about what happens when they go to war with us."

"Who's *us?*"

Shuggs took a long pull from his cigarette. "Teachers, police officers, CIA, FBI, military servicemen, custodians, lawyers, accountants—people from many walks of life, everywhere in the US, with a unified purpose in preserving *our* conservative way of life. People may call us white supremacists. But we're proud warriors who're tired."

"Everyone with your political leaning doesn't think like you."

"They don't. But they're not true patriots."

"We've served our country together," Brock said. "The three of us put our lives in danger for an entire decade to ensure the freedom of our fellow Americans. We're the real patriots."

Glancing in the direction of a distant rumble sounding like an approaching mob, Shuggs exhaled a cloud of smoke. "No. That's where you're wrong."

Brock stared into the darkness, searching the shadows. *They're coming. They're a good distance away, but they're coming.* He wiped away the trickle of sweat beading on his forehead. "I don't understand—"

"True patriots are tired of multiculturalism, waiting for our votes to count, posting our anger online, protesting behind the scenes, hiding in fear—until now."

CHAPTER 66

Brock's fingers trembled against the grip of the gun. He didn't know if it was the cold or Shuggs's behavior causing his body to shiver. *How did things get this bad without me noticing?*

"Don't be like one of the suicide bombers we dealt with in Afghanistan," Brock said. "Not realizing their mistake until it was too late."

Shuggs cleared his throat. "I'm not following you."

"Remember the guy in the Kabul market?"

"What're you getting at, bro?"

"At Pul-e Khishti Bazaar, there'd been a father just like you. At the last minute, he was trying to get his young son to remove the bomb strapped to his back when—"

"I'll *never* change my mind about dying for the movement."

Brock's jaw tightened, feeling a flash of electric current run down the back of his neck. "What about your girls?"

"What about them?"

"Who'll look after the twins when you're in prison or dead? Have you—"

"Enough!" Shuggs shouted. "I'm not worried. I'll leave this country a better place for my children. And for the record, I've got no intentions of going to prison."

A wave of fear traveled down Brock's arm, numbing his freezing fingers. "What do you mean?"

"What do I mean? C'mon, bro, you know exactly what I'm saying!" Shuggs took a pull from his cigarette. "Besides, I'm going to get nailed for my ex's death. The black agent offed her."

Brock gripped his gun so hard his knuckles cracked. Memories of Shuggs telling him about the illicit agent he'd hired to frighten his ex-wife played in his head, exposing a side of Shuggs he'd tried hard not to see.

"Like I said, I'll protect you. I promise I'll tell the authorities the job got to you. I was there. I know how those missions can mess with your—"

"Are you really going to keep using those tactics on me?"

Brock's mind flooded with clarity, recalling Shuggs's disdain for his ex and the targeted attacks unleashed that day. A deep sense of dread rose within him. There was no Kevlar vest sturdy enough to prevent the deadly wounds of hate. *My God, did I ever truly know Shuggs?*

Brock swallowed hard, forcing courage into his voice. "I have no choice. As your friend, your brother, I won't give up on your human-ity—"

"What's your point?"

"You're giving up on yourself."

"Ain't no going back for me, bro." Shuggs shook his head like he had realized no matter what he did at that point, his life, as he'd known it, was permanently changed.

"Please, man. I'm begging you, call this whole thing off. Think of the consequences, think about your—"

"We're just getting started," Shuggs said.

A burst of white heat from the muzzle flash exploded in the air as Brock pulled back behind the tree. He dodged a burst of rounds, shredded wood chips spraying him.

Cursing, his brain did the mental math. He had exactly three bullets left.

Another round of bullets thudded into the tree above Brock's head.

Suddenly, a muscular figure emerged from the side of the hotel's rear, cautiously edging through the bushes.

Brock froze. From his position behind the tree, his gun cocked, Brock peered at the approaching shadow.

Crouched low, wearing a camo tactical jacket, a weapon in his hands, a man came into focus.

"It's no use," Shuggs said. "You can't outrun bullets. May as well come out and stop hiding."

The man made a shushing gesture to Brock before crawling through the brush out of Shuggs's line of sight.

"You can't blame me for trying to make a run for it," Brock said, his lie slipping with ease from his dry mouth.

"I'll spare your life if you kick your gun over to me. Then come out with your hands up."

"How do I know you won't kill me as soon as I surrender?"

"Because I need you."

"For what?"

"You'll be my insurance."

"How?"

Shuggs tossed his cigarette to the ground, grinding the butt with his heel. "For our last and final mission."

"What mission?"

"You and I are going to take a walk."

"A walk?"

"We're going to get our friend, Mrs. Lipsett."

CHAPTER 67

Brock's heart hammered against his chest while he watched the fog float above the water. It seemed a fitting backdrop to the day's madness. *Where's my help?* Edging from behind the tree, he wondered if Shuggs intended to kill him the second he surrendered. Nothing appeared to be off the table between them anymore.

"Engage the safety. Then come on out real slow," Shuggs said.

What am I getting myself into? Moving into the courtyard, Brock closed his eyes, bracing his body for an onslaught of bullets.

"Throw your gun over to me."

Opening his eyes, Brock gingerly threw his weapon across to Shuggs and held his breath, beating himself up for not having another solution to escaping an impossible situation.

As Shuggs carefully walked from his position toward the gun, Brock scanned the area for the agent he'd seen sneaking into the courtyard, but he'd disappeared.

Sucking in a breath, something nagged Brock deep within. Dr. Harper's warning echoed his premonitions that there'd been an intelligence leak. Haunting facts that Berkley and Dexter had shared with him about the white supremacy group TWA flashed across his mind. The group had recruited black men for the barroom attack. They'd made it appear as a hate crime, black against white, when it'd been the opposite. In truth, it was the neutralization of targeted victims—calculated assassinations.

Brock understood this tactic. When he, Shuggs, and Pang were deployed in enemy territory, they neutralized undesirables. Working together, they'd seen people in the basement of hell at their worst. They'd eliminated whoever the CIA wanted gone, doing the sullied work of the government, operating in the dark. Justifying the assassinations because of the depravity of their victims.

Through destroyed relationships, the alienation of his father, and his mother's mental illness, he'd personally tasted the bitterness of loss. Brock thought of Pang and how close they'd come to losing him. An icy tingle ran through his body, and he couldn't stand to think of never seeing Pang again. *My God, Shuggs meant to kill Pang to cover his tracks.*

The entire situation pointed to one thing—Shuggs had been behind the barroom attack that claimed the lives of the CIA analysts. Their friends. He'd been the mastermind behind multiple atrocities. How could it be anything else? Brock's jaw tightened, mulling over the times Shuggs appeared when heinous things occurred. People who could've ratted him out were conveniently killed. Shuggs had been pulling the strings of the entire TWA operation, using his intel clearance to stay one step ahead from being caught until now.

When Shuggs bent to retrieve his weapon, Brock tasted the salty tang of blood from his chewed lip. A fresh surge of anger charged through him as he realized General, the shot-caller of his current nightmare, *was* Shuggs.

Brock's thoughts turned into words. "You're going to pay!"

Shuggs straightened up, pocketing Brock's weapon. "Back up right now," he ordered, stopping Brock in his tracks with his pointed gun.

Brock thumped his chest. "I swear it, you'll pay!"

"Put your hands up high!" Shuggs shouted, spittle flying into the stubble on his chin. "Where I can see them!"

"I don't get it." Brock raised his arms, trembling with rage. "After all these years, how could you do life with me, with Pang, and then betray us for TWA?"

"No, bro. I see that differently."

"How so?"

"I was loyal to my brothers, The White Adamites."

"You terrified our … families." He choked on his words. "Hunted us alongside those thugs—"

"Enough! I know what's upsetting you," Shuggs cut off Brock with a maniacal smile so tight it appeared as if it would split his skin. "It's the fact that you now know who I *really* am."

"Who you really are?" Brock shook his head. "My God, I loved you like a brother. Why would you—"

"It's like my daddy used to say, 'Sometimes love ain't enough to save everyone.' "

"It dang sure wasn't enough to save your ex-wife from you." Brock's eyes met Shuggs's steady gaze. "She loved you. Would've done anything to make things work."

Shrugging, he nodded. "You got me," Shuggs said. "I was the one who had her eliminated. But she had it coming to her."

"I can see clearly now." Brock's senses switched on. "You're a special kind of evil, killing the mother of your girls."

"Who's to determine what's good or evil?"

"We both know running around trying to kill innocent women and children is evil."

"Ain't it about whose perspective we're looking at?" Shuggs held a hand up. "Besides, you've done your share of killing women *and* children."

"Casualties of our jobs. Unfortunate accidents," Brock said.

"It's all the same thing."

"That was different," Brock swallowed, "and you know it."

"Not all of it, bro."

"I'm not playing your head games—"

"You killed that eleven-year-old black kid with your bare hands. Now ain't that interesting how you kept it a secret all those years?"

A cold shiver ran down Brock's spine as he tried to catch his breath. "Excuse me?"

"You heard me." Shuggs scratched his head, frowning as if trying hard to think back. "If I recall the details as they were told to me, the murder occurred right on your property in your old neighborhood. It figures. Your parents had you living in that black neighborhood. No good would've come from that."

Brock clenched his fists, taking a step forward, forgetting there was a gun pointed at him. "What the heck are you talking about?"

Shuggs smirked, using his free hand to point to himself. "You might be a lot more like me than you think."

"How ... what do you know—"

"Your batty momma." Shuggs gestured with his gun. "She's the one who spilled your dirty little secret when I called there looking for you last Christmas—"

"Shut up!" The horrific emptiness Brock had felt after the accident clawed at him, filling his soul. His childhood neighbor was gone, and so was his mother's mind ... because of him. He traveled back to that dark place with nowhere to hide.

"I remember." Shuggs nodded. "Mrs. O'Reilly was babbling and crying about it like it'd happened yesterday—"

"You don't know a freaking thing!"

"I know a whole lot more about you and your family than you think, buddy."

"You've got it all wrong—"

"Seems to me, I'm the one who finally got it right. I know about who Brock O'Reilly truly is." Shuggs nodded. "I ain't no shrink, but I believe you could've been the one to make your own momma nuttier than a fruitcake."

Brock staggered, opening his mouth to speak, but nothing came out. He was no stranger to death. Images of bodies filled his throbbing head. Women and children. His neighbor.

Sweat dripped from Brock's forehead, his own anger and salt blinding him. *Screw it. Screw trying to survive. I'll die a man. A man who knows his destiny.* He charged Shuggs just as the first shot was fired.

CHAPTER 68

B reathing hard and consumed by fury, Brock was forced to stop just inches short of plowing into Shuggs. The jarring thud of a bone-crushing impact disoriented him. His anger, putrid and boiling over, turned into disbelief.

"You shot me!" Brock screamed, eyes locked in on the gun in Shuggs's outstretched hand. Gasping for breath, he frantically felt his chest for gunshot wounds and the blood he thought would be spurting from it. But his torso was dry.

Staggering backward, Shuggs stumbled, his weapon hanging limp in a shaking hand by his side.

Brock's feverish thoughts tried to make sense of what was happening, taking a second to figure out why he wasn't dead or even close to it.

He stared at Shuggs, seeing him as if the scene before him was being played out in slow motion. "You didn't shoot?"

Shuggs shook his head.

Where's that coming from? A sinking feeling grew in the center of Brock's gut. "Then who was—"

A weapon fired, rocketing slugs in the air.

Brock hit the ground, taking cover in the nearby shrubbery.

Shuggs stood frozen, his gun pointed at the shadows.

Peering through the mist, Brock saw a pair of boots advancing toward them. "Get down!"

At that instant, the clatter of an automatic filled the air.

Crouching low, Brock ran over, reached out, and pushed Shuggs to the ground. Crawling back to his hiding space, Brock peeked through the bushes in time to see the boots retreating.

"Give me back my gun," Brock whispered.

A strange expression distorted Shuggs's face. "I ... can't," he wheezed and struggled to his feet.

Checking to see that the courtyard was empty, Brock stood and edged closer to Shuggs. "Why not?"

Shuggs slumped against a tree. "I ... just can't."

Brock's radio crackled to life at the same time Shuggs's radio did. "General, backup is minutes away. Stay put."

Shuggs spun around.

Cursing, Brock stared into the empty darkness but couldn't see anyone.

Brock turned back around. "You have to return my gun."

Shuggs bent over with both hands on his knees. "I need ... a minute."

Brock's feet splashed through mud puddles as he worked his way to Shuggs's side and snatched his gun back. "I'm running out of time. I have to get out of the courtyard. I'm a sitting duck."

Attempting to straighten up, Shuggs instead vomited.

"You okay?"

"Something's ... wrong," he rasped, clutching his chest and his weapon.

"Were you hit?" Brock asked, offering a supportive hand on Shuggs's back. Instantly, he knew what was wrong.

"Think ... so," Shuggs nodded. "I'm ... hurting bad, bro."

Brock pulled his bloodstained hand away from the seeping gunshot wounds and took a breath. "We need to find cover, get you help."

"How ... bad?

"You're bleeding out."

"I ... can ... make it."

"Okay. But I'm going to need your gun too."

Shuggs shook his head.

Brock stared at Shuggs, meeting his unflinching gaze. "The gun," he said, his hand outstretched.

"Can't do ... that." Shuggs coughed up a wad of bloody phlegm.

"What're you thinking?" Brock looked at Shuggs with a mixture of confusion and disgust. "I can't protect us with three bullets. Give me your gun. You've got more ammunition."

Grunting, Shuggs tried pulling himself up and collapsed. He kept his eyes and gun trained on Brock. "Give me some help, bro," he said, stretching his hand out.

"I'm trying to protect you." Brock reached down and steadied Shuggs on his feet. "And you still want to hold onto a gun you won't be able to shoot?"

"I ... need ... Mrs. Lipsett."

I should've subdued him when he fell. What's wrong with me? Sucking in a deep breath, Brock forced himself to calm down. He contemplated rushing Shuggs and overpowering him, but he held onto his weapon. Trying to take an injured man's gun was a bad idea. *Stay focused, soldier. There's always a way out. You just have to see it.*

Shuggs motioned with his gun. "Move. Lead ... the way," he stammered.

Brock moved ahead, looking over his shoulder at Shuggs, seeing a pair of dead, cold eyes. But Brock could see the pain in them, carefully shielded, camouflaged behind resolve and strength. Despite his knack for managing stress and ignoring trauma, Shuggs couldn't defeat the callousness that'd crept into the windows of his soul.

Stepping out of the darkness, Brock hurried into the open courtyard and to the rear of the hotel. His own eyes blurred, maybe from his multiple injuries, betrayal, or exhaustion, but he blinked away the haze and led Shuggs toward the back door.

As he rounded the corner, he saw another figure appear out of the shadows of the hotel grounds. *Who in the world is this?*

A SWAT officer took a step forward and aimed his gun. "Freeze and show me your hands!"

Brock stood still and held up both hands. For a moment, he figured he was a dead man but then noticed the officer wasn't looking at him. He was staring behind him. *He's after Shuggs.* Every defensive instinct within him awakened. "No!"

"Drop, O'Reilly!" the SWAT officer commanded.

The shock of hearing his name called by a stranger broke him out of his fog. Brock dropped to the ground, his world standing still, glancing behind him at Shuggs, who had his hand on the trigger of his gun.

"I ain't rotting in nobody's jail," Shuggs rasped.

"We can work this out too—"

"No way, no how!" Staggering, Shuggs pointed his weapon.

The thunderous echo of an assault weapon cut Brock's words short.

Shuggs's chest rose and fell in a staccato rhythm. He took a step forward, the gun shaking in his trembling hand.

How's he not dead or at least passed out at this point? He's been shot multiple times. It was then Brock remembered that Shuggs always wore body armor when dealing with hostile and deadly situations. *He's probably been protected the entire time. But even bulletproof vests don't save us from everything. There are chinks in the best armor.*

Another round of fire exploded, lighting up the night.

Shuggs opened his mouth, and something unintelligible came out. His reddened face faded to a pasty white as he soundlessly collapsed to the ground.

CHAPTER 69

L ying facedown, Brock gritted his teeth. Anger boiled inside, thinking of everything he'd been through over the past few hours. It was as if the curtain of night had closed, imprisoning him in darkness. Listening to the sudden flurry of activity around him, he slowly lifted his head, staring at the scene before him in disbelief. *The FBI came through after all.*

A voice from his radio crackled through the air, "General, come in! We're surrounded and outgunned. What should we do?"

Brock searched the spot by his side and glimpsed Shuggs reaching for his radio's transmit button. He'd fallen onto his back, spread-eagle, gasping for air.

"Stop!" The SWAT officer commanded, gun cocked.

Shuggs's hand froze in midair.

"Instruct your men to surrender, or they'll be eliminated. Tell them to give control to the SWAT team!"

Shuggs did as the officer requested. "Soldiers, this is General ..." he paused, his chest heaving.

The officer grabbed the radio. "TWA, surrender now, or you're dead! There's no way out! Confirm request!"

Moments later, the radio came back on. "Declaring surrender."

Lying helpless as the officer stripped him of his radio and weapon, then handcuffed him, Shuggs croaked, "Need help. My chest ..."

While he called for an ambulance, the SWAT officer kept his cold, emotionless eyes and gun trained on Shuggs.

Consumed by shock, Brock lay paralyzed on the freezing, wet earth. He stared at Shuggs but couldn't see where he'd been struck. Blood seeped from Shuggs's body, forming a fast-growing puddle around his midsection.

Seconds later, sirens pierced the air, their high-pitched screams reflecting Brock's inner voice.

As the officer spoke to his team, Brock tried moving again. Shockwaves of agony pulsed through his heart. Shaking uncontrollably, he crawled a few feet toward Shuggs. "Stay strong," he whispered.

"Doing ... best ... I can."

Brock patted Shuggs's shoulder, scanning the bustling scene. "Shouldn't be much longer before the ambulance arrives."

The once-deserted grounds had become an instantaneous buzz of activity, crawling with agents and special forces. They rushed across the lawn of the courtyard and the surrounding area.

Shuggs looked up at Brock. "Need to say ..."

Brock took his outstretched hand. "Go on."

Shuggs stared like he was trying to focus on Brock's face. "Hurting you ... wasn't personal."

Brock flinched, thinking of Pang and his family. "Hurting our friends, their children, that was very personal." *It would be so easy to put my hand over his mouth and suffocate him.*

"Our country needs ... soldiers." Shuggs's watery blue eyes glistened. "Real men ... like you ... and ... me ..."

"To do what?"

"Protect ... our heritage."

I should feel hate for him. "Never." Brock's eyes bore into Shuggs's, feeling instead the deep sadness of loss.

"Maybe ... if you had ... kids, you'd understand." Shuggs coughed up a thin trickle of blood and sighed.

"Nothing's worth risking not being around for them."

"The future ... of America is," he said, nodding weakly.

"My God, Shuggs, I don't know who the heck you are anymore. Your long career packed with highlights, fatherhood, friendships, battles, and victories were undone in a matter of hours." Brock's stomach had constricted in knots. "And for what?"

"For change." Shuggs took a long, labored breath. "Tried giving my girls the best chances ... they could have."

"By killing innocent people and aligning with a hate group?" Brock's jaw tightened.

"My actions ... showed courageous love." Shuggs's brow furrowed. "Showed I'm a protective father."

"That wasn't courage *or* love." Brock inclined his head curtly. "You

282

showed you're a white supremacist."

Shuggs studied the sky, his eyes glassy. "Wanted ... to make a difference," he said, licking his purplish lips. "Before ... I died."

For a second, silence hung in the air.

"I'm ... dying." Shuggs groaned, attempting to roll onto his other side but failing because of the restraints restricting his movement.

Brock shook his head. "No. Don't talk that way. You lost some blood. But you'll pull through. Just like you always do. Remember that time in Chad when that group of Jihadists surrounded us, and the missile detonated under our—"

"I don't think ... I ..." Shuggs's chest heaved, "Don't have much ... time."

"Think positively—"

"That dog don't hunt. I'm a ... goner."

Brock frowned. "We've seen worse."

"Need to say something ..." Shuggs hesitated, his lips parted, and he attempted to sit upright but only succeeded in toppling to one side.

"Keep your distance from the perp!" The SWAT officer yelled.

"Why? He was my best friend."

"This man isn't your friend, Agent O'Reilly." The officer used his gun to wave Brock away from Shuggs's side. "He's one of the FBI's deadliest criminals."

Heeding the officer's commands, Brock slid away from Shuggs but kept his eyes on his face. "Hang tight."

"I'm hurt ... bad." Shuggs lifted his head. "Can see it in your ... face."

"That's not—"

"Tell ... my girls ... I loved them."

"Tell them yourself."

"Promise ... me."

"I promise. But you'll pull—"

"You're ... always ... loyal ... seeing the best in others," Shuggs said, his voice strained.

My God, did he ever know love? Ignoring the SWAT officer, Brock moved back to his spot close to Shuggs and leaned down until his face was inches away. "I lost some of my humanity a while back. I promised I'd never go there again. It's not too late for you to do the same," he whispered as he backed away.

Nodding, a lone tear streaked down Shuggs's ashen cheek.

"Step aside, agent!" The SWAT officer yelled, yanking Brock to his feet. "That's an order!"

One last time, Brock turned and stared down at Shuggs.

Shuggs's lifeless eyes were wide open, his face screwed up as if he'd seen a ghost before dying.

CHAPTER 70

D r. Harper arched her brows, scanning the small group. Six pairs of eyes watched her. Carefully draping her designer suit jacket over the back of her chair, she closed the door and rolled up her sleeves.

"You must be wondering why I have invited you here today before the briefing and debriefing we have scheduled. Especially after the exhaustive meetings and investigations we have been through for the past several months. But, before we begin, I would like to congratulate one of the members of our team before he transfers to the bureau next month." She put on her glasses and read from a paper she retrieved from her folio. "It appears that our own Agent O'Reilly has been officially nominated for the Presidential Medal of Freedom."

Oh, crap. Did I just nod off? Brock shook himself, stifling a yawn. "Come again?" he asked, taking a swig of his coffee. "I'm sorry. Fact of the matter is, I've been sleeping like garbage these days."

Pang clicked his tongue and elbowed Brock. "Probably burnout from the paparazzi," he said. "Dr. Harper was just reminding us that you're still the golden boy."

"Excuse me?" Brock stared blankly at Dr. Harper. "I didn't quite get what—"

"I apologize, Agent O'Reilly, for boring you." Dr. Harper stretched her lips into a thin smile. "Before you awoke, I was in the process of telling your colleagues about your nomination." She handed the paper to Brock and folded her arms.

Brock examined the document, and his face flushed with heat. He rubbed his eyes, studying the three men seated around an oblong conference table in a stark, windowless office outside of Virginia.

"We all deserve this."

Pang slapped Brock's back. "I agree. Besides, the White House's been handing those presidential medals out like peanuts at a circus."

Special agents Dexter and Berkley, who'd been stoic the entire time, began laughing.

Even Dr. Harper's stiffened expression relaxed into a smile.

"Yeah, that's true." Joining the group, Brock openly laughed at himself and Pang's antics. *Feels like old times. Almost.* Out of habit, he glanced to his right and froze. His vision blurred, noticing the empty chair, and he promptly forgot what he'd been laughing about. That was the seat Agent Matthew Shuggs would've taken. By his side. Looking across at the special agents, Brock flashed back to the analysts the agency had lost in the bar shooting.

Berkley put his leathery hand on Brock's shoulder and cleared his throat. "You alright, son?"

Brock blinked himself back into focus. "Yeah, I'll be fine." He looked away, resting his face in his hands, slamming the door on the flood of questions that kept him up at night. *It's been months since the analysts were killed and I witnessed Shuggs's violent death. Someone I thought was my close friend.*

Berkley sighed, straightened his tie, and exchanged looks with Dexter.

Walking to the coffee pot, Pang poured himself a cup of the steaming brew, even though he usually didn't drink coffee.

Dr. Harper twisted the wedding ring on her finger. "I suppose this is a good time to run through the summary of the final debrief." She looked at Dexter. "I believe you have our initial findings for us."

Opening a binder, Dexter leafed through the pages. "Agent Shuggs was found to have intentionally leaked highly classified information from the CIA. This includes pictures of the deceased—"

"Wait, you've got to be kidding me. Why?" Pang asked Dexter.

"To increase racial tensions both here in the US and internationally."

Cursing under his breath, Pang slammed his binder on the table.

"Agent Pang, we believe Shuggs is also responsible for orchestrating the attempts on your life while you were recovering in the hospital. This includes the incident with the poison and the orderly who was accused of cutting off your air supply."

"Didn't the orderly kill himself?" Brock asked.

"Supposedly." Dexter nodded. "However, we're in the process of re-evaluating the orderly's cause of death since Shuggs is a suspect." Dexter's face flushed. "Shuggs's motive is unclear, but it appears it's likely tied to the fact that you're—"

Pang pushed back from the table. "Married to a black woman who was inadvertently investigating TWA."

"That sounds about right." Dexter took a swig of his coffee. "Moving on to the next victim, Cynthia Shuggs. Agent Matthew Shuggs's ex-wife's death was ruled a homicide. The suspect is in custody and has provided evidence that the hit was ordered by Shuggs." He glanced at his pile of notes. "Snake was connected to Shuggs because he worked for TWA. The group needed someone who looked like Snake in order to approach Tucker Buckler, aka Uncle Buck. Snake was the third party who hired Buck's men to execute the barroom attack."

Brock frowned. "Didn't Uncle Buck send his men to eliminate Patti and Snake?"

Dexter nodded.

"Uncle Buck also terminated the siblings of the perps who'd died at the barroom shooting." Brock pointed to himself. "Then he went after me. Why?"

Dexter stared at the report. "Snake was the one who wanted to eliminate you."

"For what?" Brock asked.

"He was being paid by TWA. You were with the agency *and* friends with Patti. They wanted to eliminate ties that would've indicted them. Uncle Buck, on the other hand, was an all-or-nothing kind of fellow." Dexter looked up. "His approach was to eliminate anyone who was a threat to him and his livelihood, which is why he went after Patti and Snake."

"Can you explain that further?" Pang asked.

Dexter stroked his wisp of a beard. "He'd gotten tipped off that Patti and Snake were working undercover. Patti had been investigating his money-laundering businesses and the funds he'd channeled into a black militant operation." He motioned to his partner. "You can take it from here."

Berkley turned the page in his report. "I'd like us to revisit the report on the barroom hit. Just so we're all clear, it was orchestrated by Shuggs in his role as the leader of The White Adamites. He ordered the hit for two reasons: to further incite racial tensions and to kill the CIA analyst, Khan, who'd discovered evidence that could've blown Shuggs's cover."

"Why were other people targeted?" Pang tapped his pen on the table.

"Since Shuggs suspected Khan had discussed his findings with the other analysts, he thought it best to kill all four of them." Berkley cleared his throat. "Even before arrangements were made to meet at Rusti's, Shuggs had planned to get the analysts together to create a deadly scenario resembling an ambush. When Agent O'Reilly had invited the men to Rusti's, it had worked in Shuggs's favor to make the incident appear race-related instead of a hit. The assassins were instructed to inflict nonlethal shots on random *white* patrons."

Brock rubbed the scar above his eyebrow. "If Snake was playing the feds and TWA, why was he trying to kill us?"

"To tie up loose ends," Dr. Harper said. "By killing you *and* the Lipsetts, he would have earned a larger paycheck. Also, he wouldn't have to answer to TWA about his connections to black militants or the bureau."

"In other words, he tried to seal his loyalty and his paycheck," Brock said.

"Is there anything else you can share with us about Uncle Buck?" Pang asked.

Dr. Harper glanced at her notes. "He appeared to have been a father figure to many of his employees. The people in his community looked up to him as a hero—"

Pang pushed back from the table. "How in the world—"

"The man is impressive." Dr. Harper held up a hand. "He orchestrates free feeding programs for poor families and immigrants. His Christmas outreach is the largest in the city. He annually gives away thousands of dollars to his church, the local police department, college scholarships, and various other philanthropic efforts. His illicit dealings ran smoothly with the right political affiliations and payoffs *until* his security team unknowingly took work authorized by TWA. Like Dexter shared, they used Snake to contract Buck's company, offering a high payoff to execute various assassinations. Uncle Buck then employed his men to do the work, promising them a fifty-fifty split in compensation. His men had hopes to leave the underworld and channel the money into legitimate businesses."

"I don't get it. The perps and Uncle Buck are black. Why would they want to work for a white supremacy organization?" Pang asked.

Dr. Harper looked up from her notes. "At first, they did not know they were working for them."

Pang sniffed his coffee and set it back on the table. "Still doesn't make sense to me. They were criminals, smart enough to survive without being duped."

"Remember, Uncle Buck's people were hired through Snake, a third party," Dr. Harper said. "This is common practice because this way illegal transactions are harder to trace on both sides."

"So they believed they were just hired hitmen?" Brock rubbed his jaw. "Nothing more?"

Dexter pushed his glasses back, peering at a notepad. "Yes, these guys were products of corrosive environments. They'd been through the system, spending most of their early years in group homes, detention centers, and prisons. They were ripe targets for Uncle Buck to persuade them to be hired hitmen by offering a massive payout. He was willing to give them a piece of the pie without doing the actual hits himself."

"They also had the threat of extensive prison sentences if they got into trouble again. These men had a great incentive to do one more big job to be able to get out of the game," Berkley offered.

"This information is accurate." Dr. Harper nodded. "And as you have learned during the investigation, Patricia Pang's cover was further compromised due to the attack at the Thompson Hotel. She's under the bureau's gag order. Up until this point, we have not revealed specifics about the cases she worked as a deep-cover agent."

"Is this why Snake was meeting with Patti?" Brock asked.

"Indeed. She was working deep undercover. Snake was doing field-work for the feds as an informant posing as Patti's love interest," Dr. Harper said. "He was also working as a double agent of sorts by feeding information to TWA."

Brock turned to Pang. "Did you know Patti was involved to that extent?"

Pang sighed. "I knew enough to be worried."

"Did Buck know that Patti had been investigating him?" Brock rubbed the scar above his left eyebrow.

"Not at first. But later on, he did," Dr. Harper said. "This was because Patti's cover was compromised by Snake. Uncle Buck discovered Snake had begun extorting Patti to get her to pay him off for keeping quiet. The feds were aware of the situation and had been collecting information to build a case against Snake. Uncle Buck panicked, thinking it was just a matter of time before Snake betrayed him as well."

Brock crossed his arms. "Let me get this straight. In the beginning, Uncle Buck and his men had no idea for whom they were *really* working. After Uncle Buck uncovered the truth, he became desperate to cover his tracks. That's when he arranged for everyone affiliated with the job to be erased. All because he had an image to preserve as well as monetary, religious, and political affiliations that he didn't want to jeopardize."

Dr. Harper smiled. "Exactly."

"I still don't understand why Buck's men *and* Snake would be at the Thompson trying to kill the Lipsetts," Brock said.

"Buck's people had been hired by Snake to kill the Lipsetts." Dr. Harper used her ballpoint pen to gesture to her notes. "Snake's job was to ensure that they were eliminated. He worked for TWA as their lackey. TWA wanted the Lipsetts eliminated because of their racist ideology. However, killing Patti worked in Snake's favor because he knew she had intel gathered against him."

"That's crazy." Pang shook his head. "They were all there to kill each other like a freaking self-cleaning oven."

"When you put it that way, it sums up the truth," Brock agreed. He turned to Dr. Harper. "What's going on with Uncle Buck now? Should we be concerned about him?"

Dr. Harper shook her head. "No, he has been locked up and is cooperating with the agency."

"Since when?"

"Since he received death threats from TWA. The organization was worried he would cooperate with law enforcement," Dr. Harper said. "After that, Uncle Buck put the squeeze on his contacts to trace who had employed them to do the assassinations. When he discovered Shuggs was the shot-caller, he sang like a bird, seeking immunity and protection. He is still facing doing time. He confessed to murder while on a call with O'Reilly—"

Brock struck his binder with a balled-up fist. "I should've seen this. Figured it out." He hung his head. "I could've saved our friends. My God, I failed—"

"Listen here, O'Reilly." Pang reached over and put a hand on

Brock's shoulder. "You've got to stop this. We've been through hell and back these past few months. Patti almost lost her mom and our kids, including the baby she was carrying. I know it's been hard. Especially since you ... just lost your mom."

Dexter wiped his thick glasses with a cloth he pulled from his pocket. "We estimated that you helped save hundreds of people by your acts of heroism."

"Heck, you also spared us the embarrassment of being overrun by extremists." Berkley looked around the table. "Right?"

"Truth is, you did a bang-up job getting your hands dirty." Pang pointed to Brock. "Thanks to you, a lot more of us survived than died."

"I could've saved more people. Should've figured out what Shuggs was up to the entire time." Brock shook his head. "All the signs were there—"

"Don't do that to yourself!" Pang slapped the table. "All of us were betrayed by Shuggs. You're going to get through this, but not by playing the sick games of *blame* and *what if.* You hear me?" He stood up and pointed to Brock. "Stop beating yourself up because Shuggs only allowed us to see what he wanted us to. We were best friends with a shadow. And like all shadows, he projected only a dark illusion."

Smiling, Brock glided his fingers over the beautifully embossed letter lying in front of him.

"Pang, I appreciate those words of wisdom. Thank you," Dr. Harper said.

Pang nodded and returned to his seat.

Dr. Harper examined her wristwatch. "Now, do you know what I desire?"

"No, ma'am, but I'm sure you'll tell us," Pang said, leaning back in his chair.

CHAPTER 71

Brock took a deep breath and stood up, feeling the conference room sway before him. His heart pounded so hard against his rib cage that his pulse rang in his ears.

"You okay?" Pang asked.

"Need ... a few minutes," Brock said and opened the door.

"That is fine. I think we could all do with a break." Dr. Harper picked up her office phone. "We will take a fifteen-minute recess and then reconvene."

Suddenly, feeling cold and lost, Brock pulled his jacket tightly around him and hurried to the restroom, locking himself inside a vacant stall. *Men don't cry. Suck it up, soldier.* But no matter what he said to himself, the flow of a fountain he couldn't seem to stop unleashed.

Brock didn't know how long he stood there weeping. The complexity of what'd happened with Shuggs opened the door of his painful past and his current losses. Shuggs, a man he once thought of as a best friend, had betrayed him and was now gone. He'd been in denial, staggering through the days after Shuggs was killed. Brock held his throbbing head, reeling from two significant deaths eight weeks apart from each other. His mother's fatal heart attack forced him to face the tragedy of both casualties. He had difficulty imagining a world without a parent—his mother. Both people were now ghosts who haunted his waking and sleeping thoughts.

Staring at the blurred tiles on the bathroom floor, Brock tried to make sense of his world until he remembered something Dr. Harper had once told him. The day they'd met in the hospital chapel when they almost lost Pang. *"When living a life pleasing to God, he sees the complete picture and creates something beautiful from it. Now it is up to you to decide what matters in your story."*

Brock felt another presence that was a bright relief. It washed over him as if the sun had followed him into the stall. Warm, steady—filling him with a vibrant hope that although nothing had changed, things were better. An irrevocable promise had been etched into his heart. Trust replaced his fears.

He unlocked the door, stepped out of the stall, checked the bathroom, and found it empty. Still, the feeling persisted that someone else was there with him.

Tracing the jagged scar above his left eyebrow, a memory tugged at him. He'd had that strange sensation once before. It'd been during the loneliest time he'd ever experienced. After the arrest for his neighbor's murder, he'd been locked in solitary confinement as a juvenile. Afraid and alone, he had been visited by the same warm presence he was now experiencing. It'd been the same back then when the sun had found its way into his cell and washed over him—like a friend. It was only then that he realized he had never been by himself. He'd been able to survive the night and make it to the next morning.

Refreshed by the memory, Brock decided to get back to the meeting. Staring at his reflection while he dried his face, he again had the overwhelming sensation he'd never been alone, as if he wore a second skin shielding him from the world. He swallowed, thinking of the loyal friends and family he'd pushed far to the back of his mind. Maybe as a protective measure, but they were there. Pang, Patti, and their three boys. Mrs. Lipsett and Senator Lipsett. His father, and *even* Dr. Harper. He chuckled at that last name—she'd become like a surrogate mother to him.

***

When Brock returned to the conference room, the men busied themselves skimming through the papers Dr. Harper had distributed earlier.

Dr. Harper looked at Brock. "Perfect timing. I am ready to pick up where we left off."

"You were going to let us know what you want," Pang said.

"I want revenge."

Berkley held up a hand. "Now, Liz, you know that's not how the agency works." His frown caused his bushy white eyebrows to connect. "We have protocols and legalities regarding our approach to matters such as this."

"Not to mention, Shuggs is dead. He was orchestrating the operation," Dexter said. "Once you remove the head, the body dies."

"I would agree with you, except I think this went beyond Shuggs."

"No, Liz. Like I've told you before, the investigation rooted out all the bad apples," Berkley said.

"That's maybe what someone wants us to think."

"I'm not sure I'm following where you're going with this." Berkley threw his hands up. "We're about to wrap up this entire mess and put it behind us. Why on earth would you want to start this over again?"

"Because I want to win."

"Win what?"

"The war on hate in this country."

Berkley smirked. "You can't seriously think we can wipe away—"

"Do you truly believe Shuggs was able to pull off a massive operation like The White Adamites with the help of a handful of minions?" Dr. Harper asked, folding her arms.

"Shuggs was smart, but he wasn't that smart," Pang said, shaking his head.

Dexter shrugged and adjusted his glasses. "Our conclusions were drawn based on the evidence we found about TWA and—"

She laid her hands on the table. "What if I told you I had information that would help us see a fuller picture?"

He sat back in his chair and folded his arms. "What evidence do you have?"

"A few years ago, the agency developed a pilot program with the bureau. I was engaged with the legal aspect of the operation—"

"A program where the CIA and the FBI were working directly together?" Berkley asked, stroking his beard. "That's *very* hard to believe. They're usually rivals."

Dr. Harper relaxed her shoulders and crossed her legs. "That is correct. That's what makes this such a unique project on which they are working together."

"On what?

"A task force examining deadly homeland terrorism and their links to extremism in foreign countries." She leaned forward. "Utilizing hand-selected people no one would suspect who're adept at deep cover."

Brock raised his eyebrows. "Can you tell us who they are?"

"Anticipating your response, I invited an agent from the program to provide a briefing on their findings." Dr. Harper pressed the intercom button on the office phone. "Please send in our guest."

Dr. Harper walked to the door. "I would like to introduce you to our deep-cover agent, who will provide today's briefing." She threw the door wide open. "Please welcome Collin Gentry."

Brock sat up, recalling the name. *That's the guy Snake was impersonating.* He turned to Dexter and Berkley. They seemed as surprised as he was to see the agent who had assisted them in defeating the terrorists during the Thompson Hotel attack.

The agent's frame dwarfed Dr. Harper's five-foot-eight stature. His ebony skin appeared to glow when his face cracked open in a white smile. Gentry went around the room, shaking each person's hand and asking their names.

"Have a seat anywhere you would like, Agent Gentry," Dr. Harper said when she returned to her chair. "We are eager to hear your report."

He unbuttoned his suit jacket, exposing a wide, muscular frame, made his way to the empty chair on Brock's right, sat down, and opened his briefcase. "I know you're as knackered as I am over these endless briefings, so I shall dive right in if you don't mind." His baritone voice carried a faint British accent.

"Go for it, man," Pang said. "We're not going to mess with anyone who outdoes us bench pressing."

Gentry threw his head back and laughed so hard it generated chuckles from the group. "Good one. You're a cheeky fellow." He pointed to Pang. "I can tell we're going to get along quite well." Pulling a thick binder from his briefcase, he distributed folders to the group. "Follow along using the presentation I've prepared and try to hold questions until I've finished." He spoke like a man used to commanding authority.

"In its 2021 Annual Threat Assessment, the US Intelligence Community observed the rapid growth and deadliness of the transnational position of white supremacist movements in Europe and the United States. The accessibility of online communication and collaboration has allowed international interactions in the global white supremacist movement."

Gentry loosened his tie and wrote something down on his notepad.

"Many of you may wonder why Uncle Buck and his African American counterparts were used to do the work of a racist organization like TWA."

Brock cleared his throat. "Yeah, it doesn't seem to make sense."

"These are common tactics of white supremacists who, before the civil rights movement, brazenly murdered people without consequence," Gentry said.

"Really?" Brock asked.

"Most assuredly so. Civil rights leaders opposing their beliefs, such as Rev. George Lee, Lamar Smith, William Lewis Moore, Rev. Bruce Klunder, Jimmie Lee Jackson, Rev. James Reeb, Herbert Lee, Medgar Evers, Dr. Martin Luther King, and countless others, were murdered by law enforcement, state legislators, and self-proclaimed white supremacists. Since the civil rights movement, where perpetrators risk facing consequences for acting out on their racist beliefs, they hire perpetrators of color. This is based on the modern-day belief in Accelerationism—"

"Never heard of that term before," Pang said. He turned to his colleagues. "Have you?"

Dr. Harper nodded. "It is the idea that white supremacists should accelerate chaos and civil disorder to polarize people by ruining political order."

"That's correct," Gentry agreed. "Ultimately, their goal is to incite a race war they anticipate winning. Which is why they have a proclivity to stockpile weaponry, using every opportunity to pit different ethnic groups against each other."

He examined his notepad. "Skip past the bureaucratic rubbish to 'Operation: Task Force Aries' on page 91." He looked around the room until everyone located the page. Using his pen as a guide, he ran down the length of the document. "Our findings revealed that a third of violent white supremacist extremist groups since 2011 were instigated by foreigners in European countries. Most conspicuously, the Christchurch massacre in New Zealand in 2020 streamed in real-time on Facebook for seventeen minutes, motivated by the manifesto of Anders Breivik, who'd murdered seventy-seven soft targets—innocent unarmed civilians, including women, children, and the elderly—in Oslo, Norway."

Gentry put down his pen and rubbed his clean-shaven head. "We've been gutted by the fact that there's a direct path for foreigners to expedite extremist ideology in America." He gestured to the group. "Perhaps you've observed this in your travels, but the white supremacist movement has been having a go at the States. It's evident."

"We did see evidence of increased neo-Nazism when we were in Europe a few years ago," Pang said.

"Yes. In fact, the director of a neo-Nazi group named The Base and the creator of *The Daily Stormer* ran their operation from Russia, promoting white supremacy in the United States," Gentry said. "We also have data indicating American white supremacists are receiving tactical training in the Ukraine. Currently, the FBI is investigating foreign financing assistance in orchestrating the Thompson Hotel attack and the Capitol insurrection."

Gentry shut his binder and removed a linen kerchief from his breast pocket. "Here's where you and I come in," he said, dabbing his glistening forehead. "Our team has been handpicked for a special assignment I shall be commanding. This unit is a hybrid called Task Force Aries. It'll consist of elite personnel from the CIA, the FBI, and special forces from the military. As a task force, we'll spearhead the effort to combat challenges faced during an unprecedented time in history."

"This is massive." Standing, Gentry pushed his chair aside and took a deep breath. "I'm assured that with a commitment to recruitment for your professional skills, we might not win the war against hate during our lifetime, but we'll put up a darn good fight."

He bent over with his hands splayed on the table. "So, my friends, what do you say?"

"Listening to you, I believe we have already put up a good fight in the war on hate," Dr. Harper nodded to Brock, "but that is only one-fifth of the story."

"Yeah. Sounds like you want us to join you in making America what it *could* be," Brock said with a smile.

Pointing to Brock, Gentry returned the smile. "That is *exactly* what I'm saying."

ABOUT THE AUTHOR

Author, speaker, and editor–Katherine Hutchinson-Hayes, Ed.D., is a freelance writer/content editor. She works for Iron Stream Media as a book coach, editor, and sensitivity reader for Sensitivity Between the Lines. She's a review board member and contributor to Inkspirations (an online magazine for Christian writers), and her writing has been published in Guideposts. Her work in art/writing is distinguished by awards, including the New York Mayor's Contribution to the Arts, Outstanding Resident Artist of Arizona, and the Foundations Awards at the Blue Ridge Mountains Christian Writer's Conference (2016, 2019, 2021, 2022). She was a finalist in the Genesis Contest ACFW (American Christian Fiction Writers/Romantic Suspense 2022). She was a finalist for the Claymore Award 2022 (Thriller Division) for the best-unpublished manuscript. She is a member of Word Weavers International and serves as an online chapter president and mentor. She belongs to FWA (Florida Writers Association), ACFW (American Christian Fiction Writers), CWoC (Crime Writers of Color), AWSA (Advanced Writers and Speakers Association), and AASA (American Association of School Administrators). She serves on the board of 540 Writers Community and Submersion 14 and is an art instructor and virtual exhibition specialist for the nonprofit organization Light for the Future. Katherine is the host of the podcast Murder, Mystery & Mayhem Laced with Morality. She has authored a Christian Bible study for women and is currently working on the sequel and prequel to her first general market thriller novel, *A Fifth of the Story*. She lives in Florida with three of her four daughters, her grandson, her husband, and two fur babies.